BATTLING BOY

BATTLING BOY

PAUL POPE

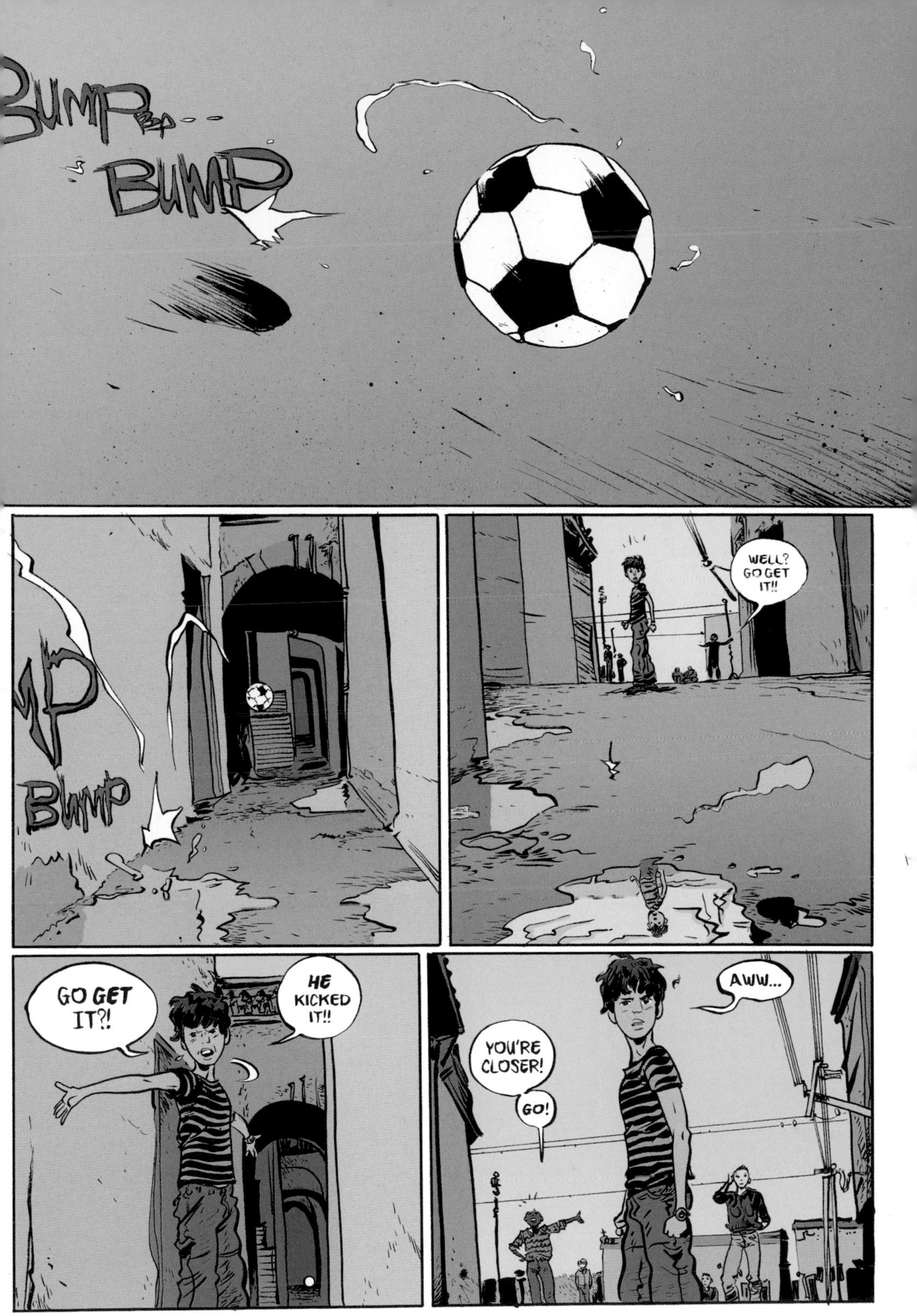
BUMP BP...
BUMP
BUMP
BLUMP
WELL? GO GET IT!!
GO GET IT?!
HE KICKED IT!!
AWW...
YOU'RE CLOSER!
GO!

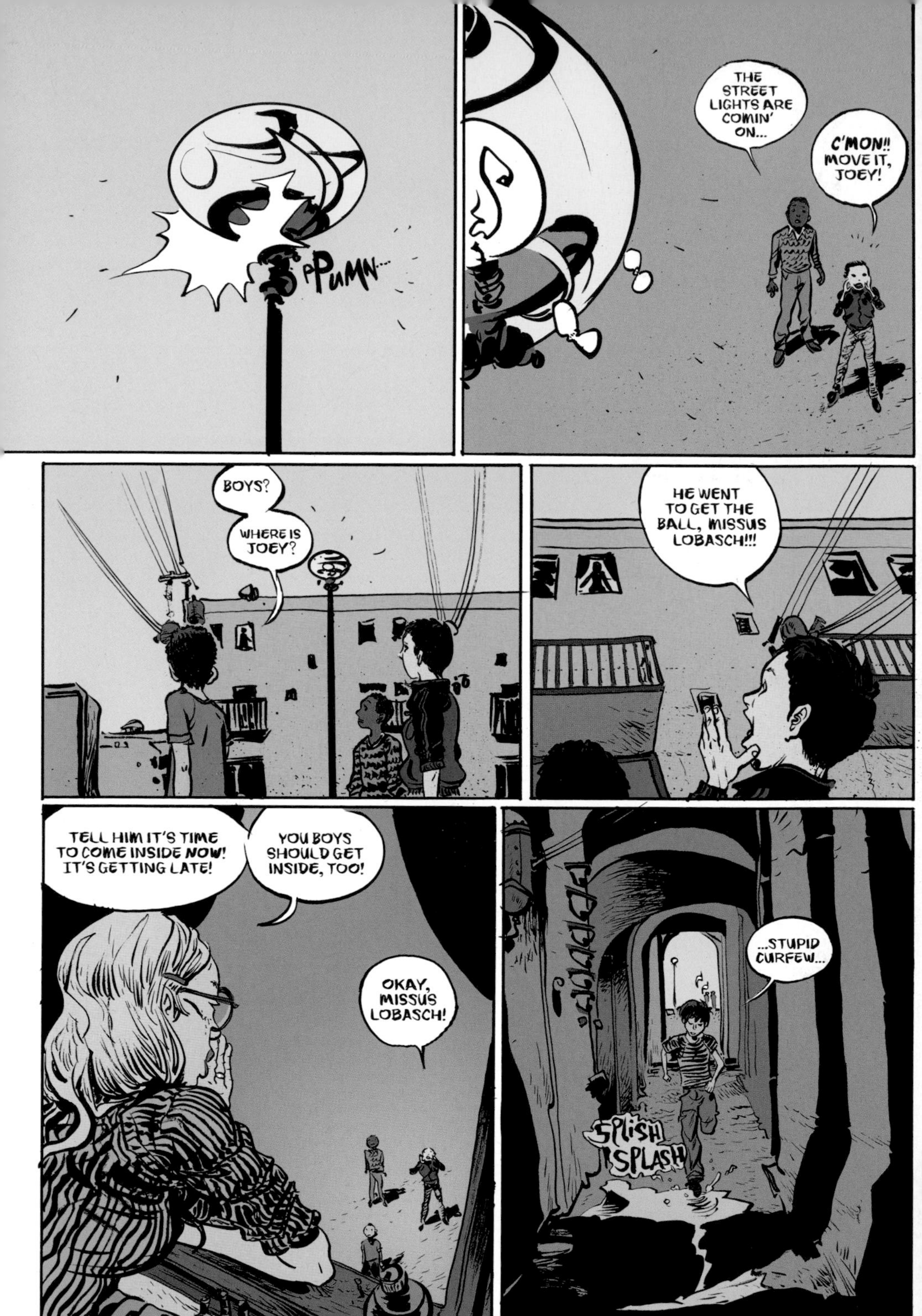
PPUMN...
THE STREET LIGHTS ARE COMIN' ON...
C'MON!! MOVE IT, JOEY!
BOYS?
WHERE IS JOEY?
HE WENT TO GET THE BALL, MISSUS LOBASCH!!!
TELL HIM IT'S TIME TO COME INSIDE NOW! IT'S GETTING LATE!
YOU BOYS SHOULD GET INSIDE, TOO!
OKAY, MISSUS LOBASCH!
...STUPID CURFEW...
SPLISH SPLASH

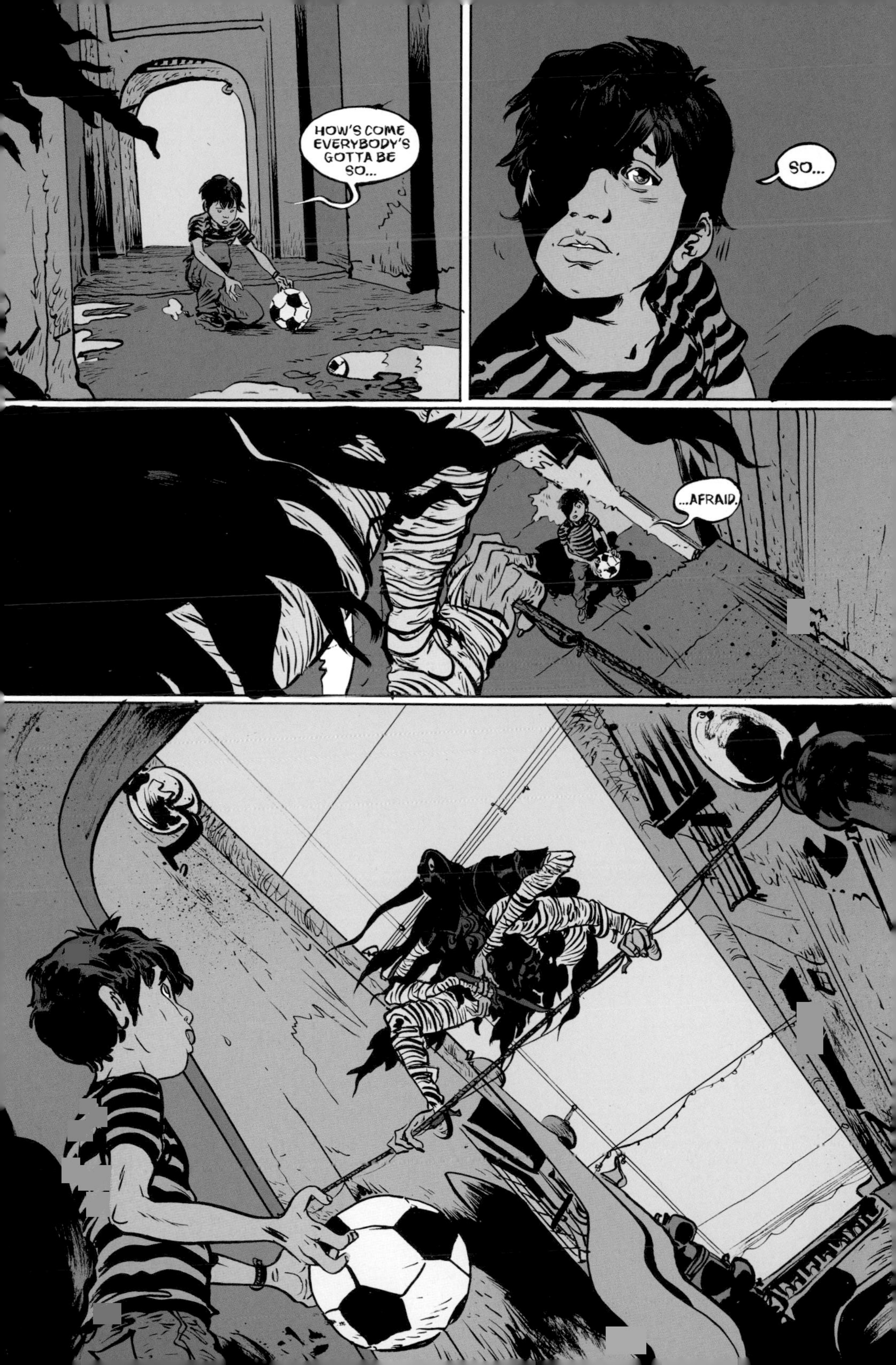
HOW'S COME EVERYBODY'S GOTTA BE SO...
SO...
...AFRAID.

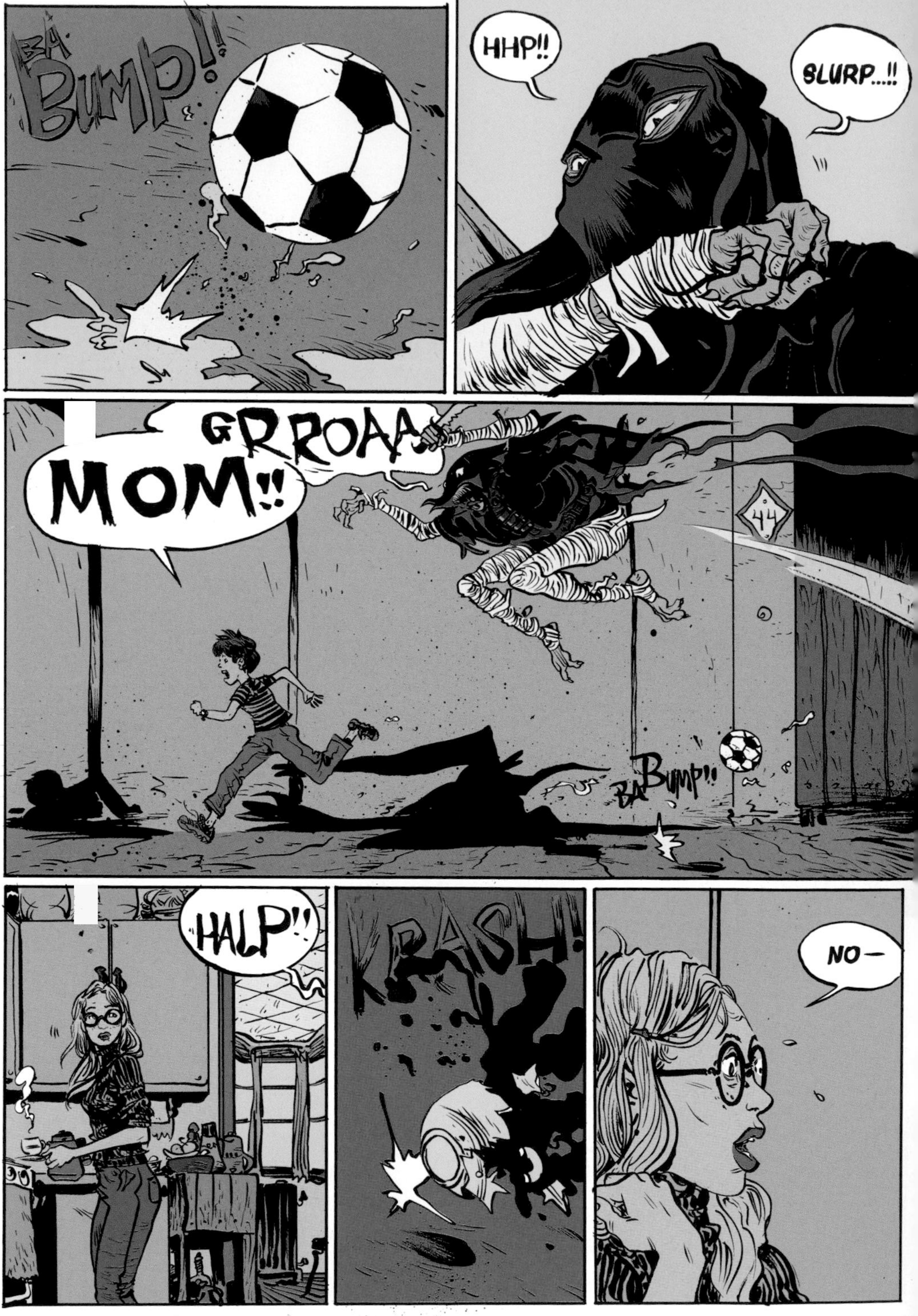
BA-BUMP!!
HHP!!
SLURP...!!
GRROAA
MOM!!
44
BA BUMP!!
HALP!!
KRASH!
NO—

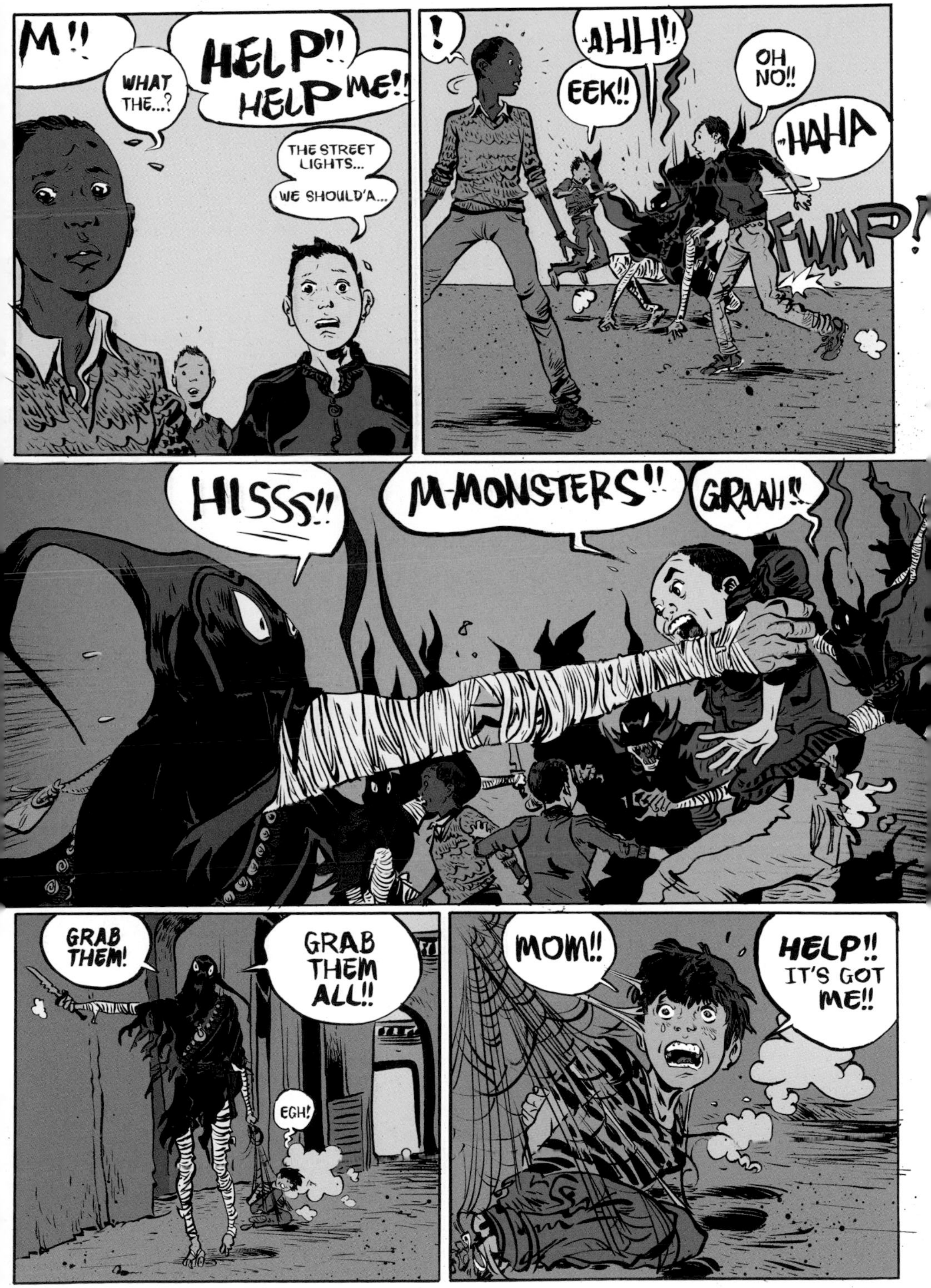
M!!
WHAT THE...?
HELP!! HELP ME!!
THE STREET LIGHTS...
WE SHOULD'A...
!
AHH!!
EEK!!
OH NO!!
HAHA
FWAP!
HISSS!!
M-MONSTERS!!
GRAAH!!
GRAB THEM!
GRAB THEM ALL!!
EGH!
MOM!!
HELP!! IT'S GOT ME!!

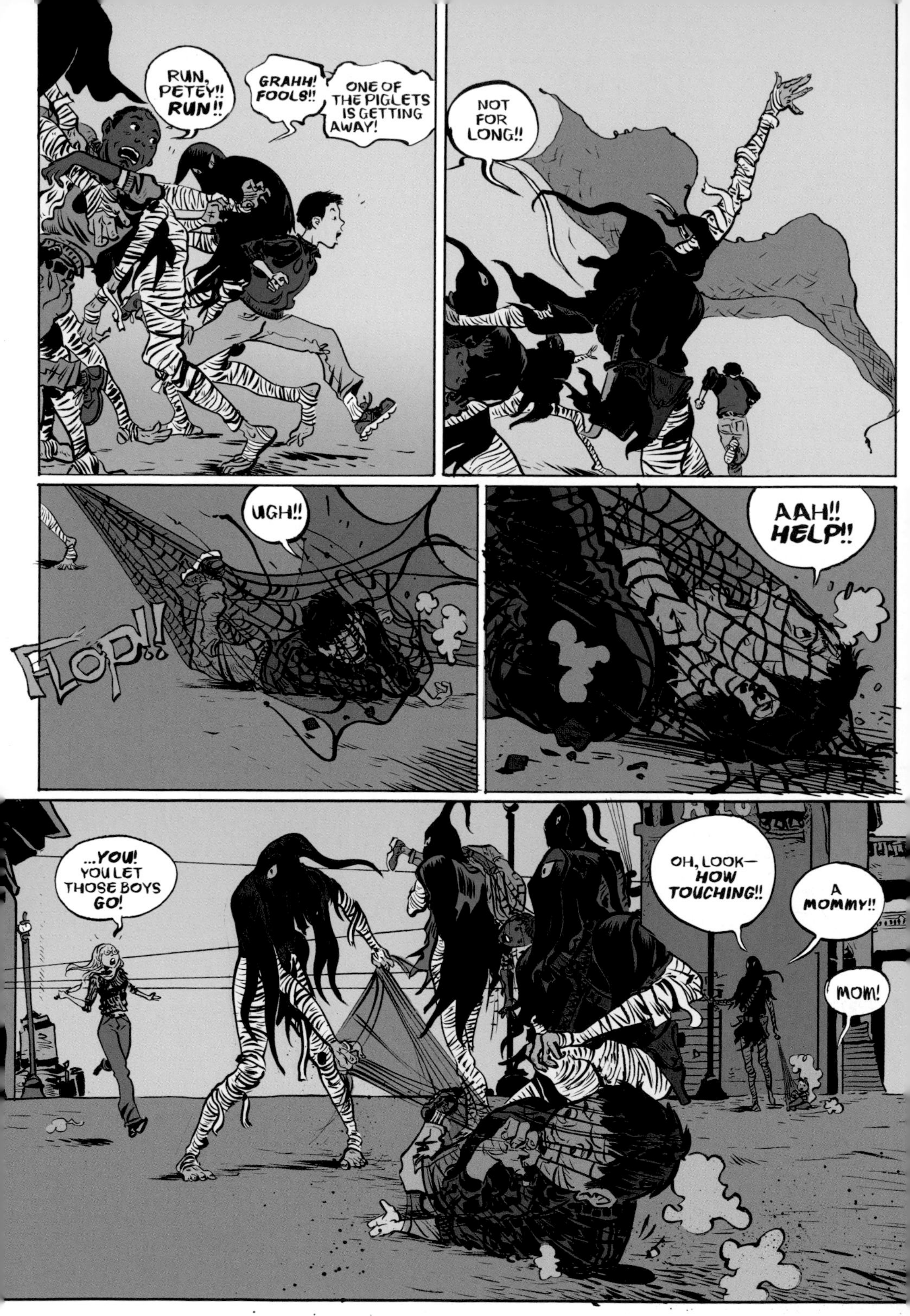
RUN, PETEY!! RUN!!
GRAHH! FOOLS!!
ONE OF THE PIGLETS IS GETTING AWAY!
NOT FOR LONG!!
UGH!!
FLOP!!
AAH!! HELP!!
...YOU! YOU LET THOSE BOYS GO!
OH, LOOK— HOW TOUCHING!!
A MOMMY!!
MOM!

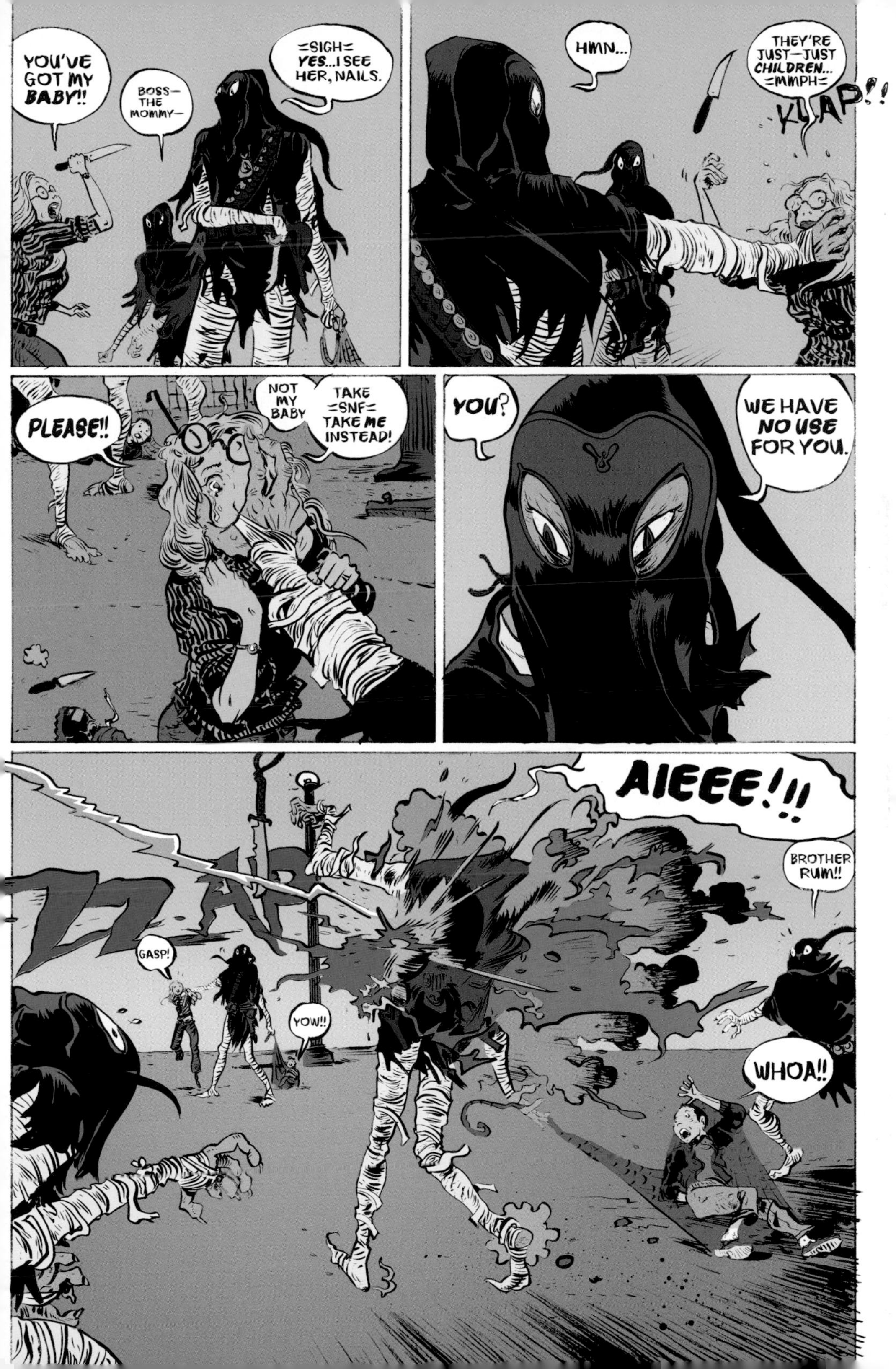
YOU'VE GOT MY BABY!!
BOSS—THE MOMMY—
=SIGH= YES...I SEE HER, NAILS.
HMN...
THEY'RE JUST—JUST CHILDREN... =MMPH=
KLAP!!
PLEASE!!
NOT MY BABY
TAKE =SNF= TAKE ME INSTEAD!
YOU?
WE HAVE NO USE FOR YOU.
AIEEE!!!
BROTHER RUM!!
GASP!
YOW!!
WHOA!!

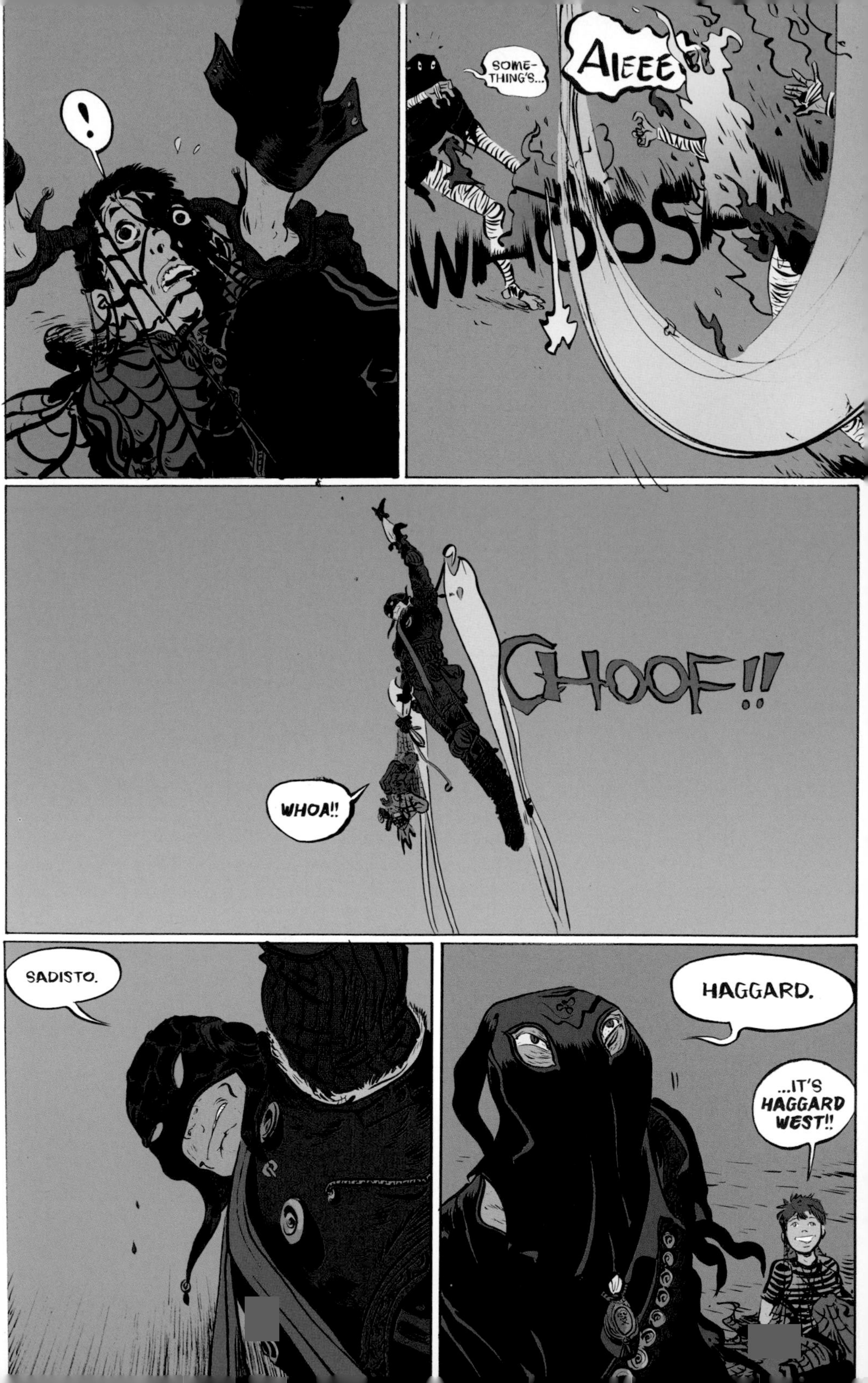
!
SOME-THING'S...
AIEEE
WHOOSH
CHOOF!!
WHOA!!
SADISTO.
HAGGARD.
...IT'S HAGGARD WEST!!

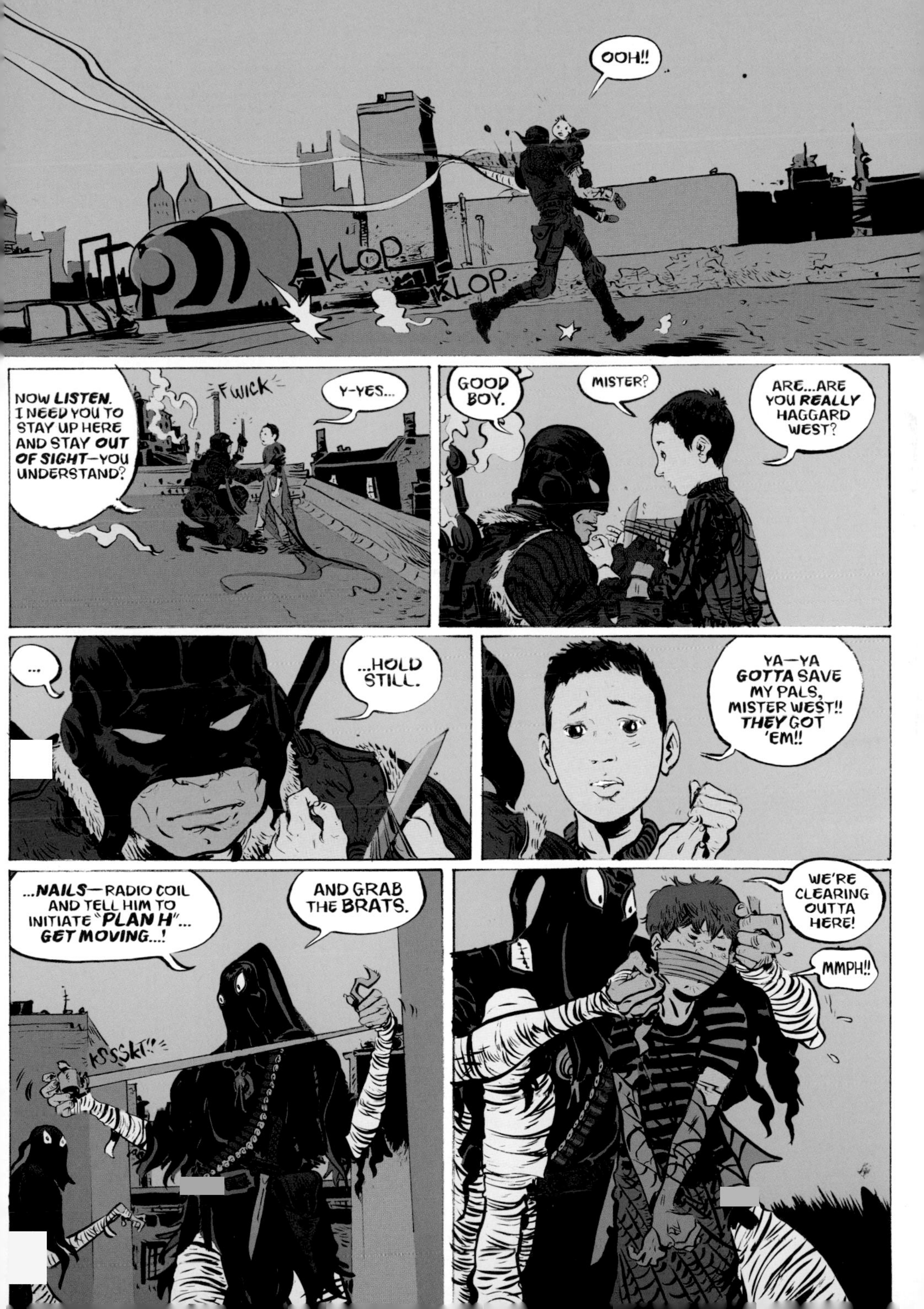
OOH!!
KLOP
KLOP
NOW LISTEN. I NEED YOU TO STAY UP HERE AND STAY OUT OF SIGHT—YOU UNDERSTAND?
FWICK
Y-YES...
GOOD BOY.
MISTER?
ARE...ARE YOU REALLY HAGGARD WEST?
...
...HOLD STILL.
YA—YA GOTTA SAVE MY PALS, MISTER WEST!! THEY GOT 'EM!!
...NAILS— RADIO COIL AND TELL HIM TO INITIATE "PLAN H"... GET MOVING...!
AND GRAB THE BRATS.
KSSSKT!!
WE'RE CLEARING OUTTA HERE!
MMPH!!

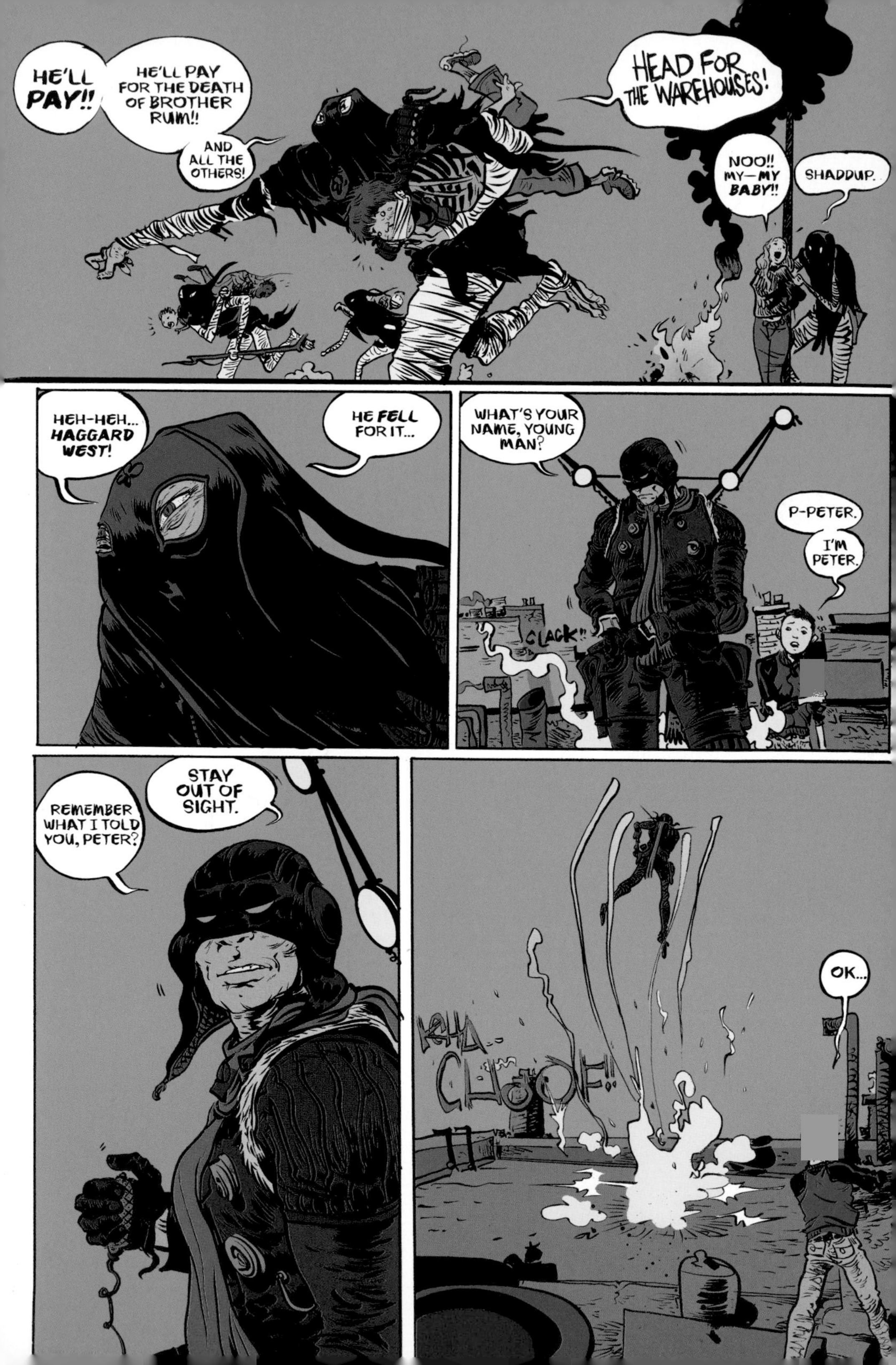
HE'LL PAY!!
HE'LL PAY FOR THE DEATH OF BROTHER RUM!!
AND ALL THE OTHERS!
HEAD FOR THE WAREHOUSES!
NOO!! MY—MY BABY!!
SHADDUP.
HEH-HEH... HAGGARD WEST!
HE FELL FOR IT...
WHAT'S YOUR NAME, YOUNG MAN?
P-PETER.
I'M PETER.
CLACK!!
REMEMBER WHAT I TOLD YOU, PETER?
STAY OUT OF SIGHT.
KCHA CHOOF!!
OK...

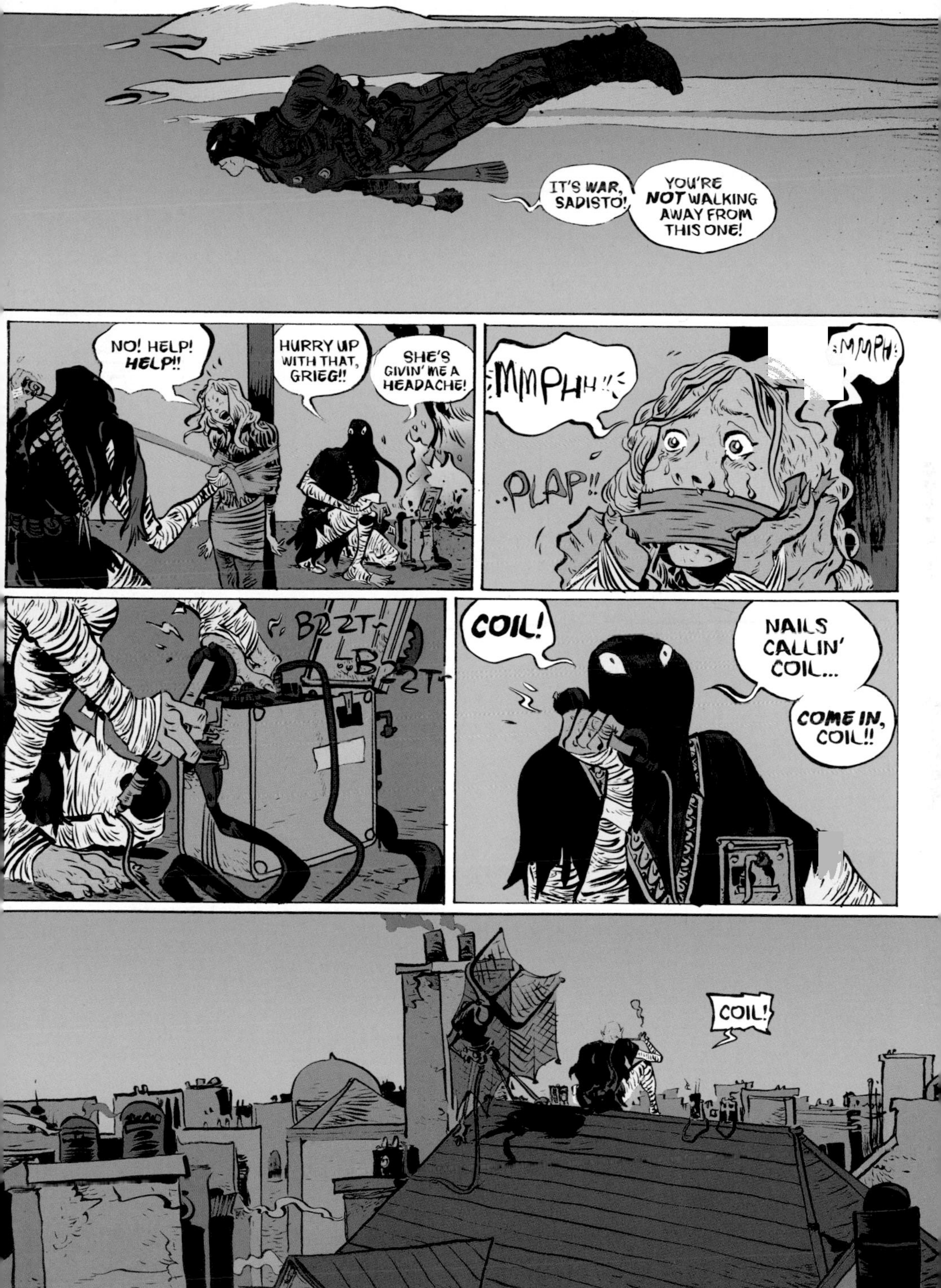
IT'S WAR, SADISTO!
YOU'RE NOT WALKING AWAY FROM THIS ONE!
NO! HELP! HELP!!
HURRY UP WITH THAT, GRIEG!!
SHE'S GIVIN' ME A HEADACHE!
MMPHH!!
PLAP!!
MMPH!
BZZT
BZZT
COIL!
NAILS CALLIN' COIL...
COME IN, COIL!!
COIL!

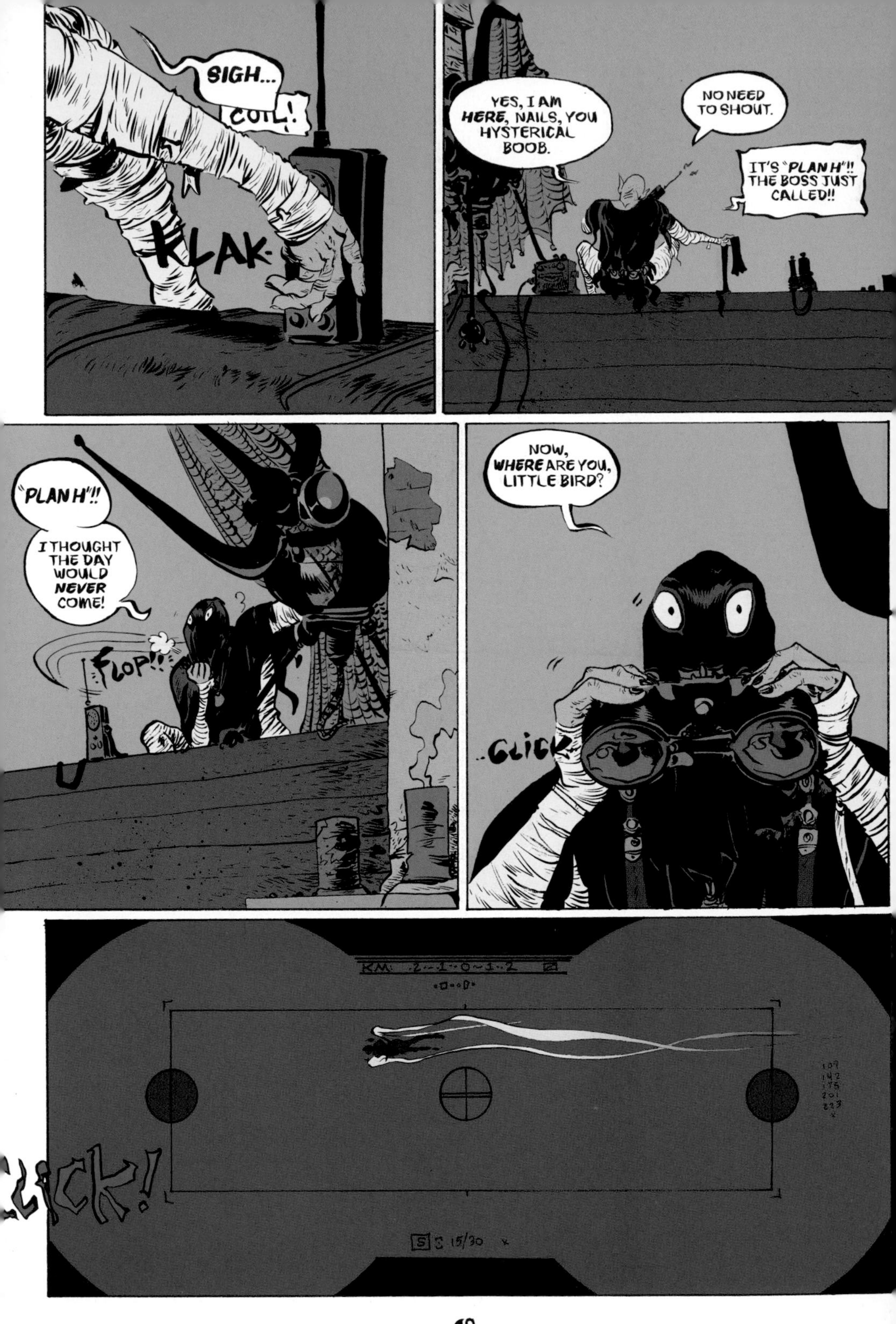
SIGH...
COIL!
KLAK
YES, I AM HERE, NAILS, YOU HYSTERICAL BOOB.
NO NEED TO SHOUT.
IT'S "PLAN H"!! THE BOSS JUST CALLED!!
"PLAN H"!!
I THOUGHT THE DAY WOULD NEVER COME!
FLOP!!
NOW, WHERE ARE YOU, LITTLE BIRD?
..CLICK
KM. 2 1 0 1 2
S 15/30
CLICK!

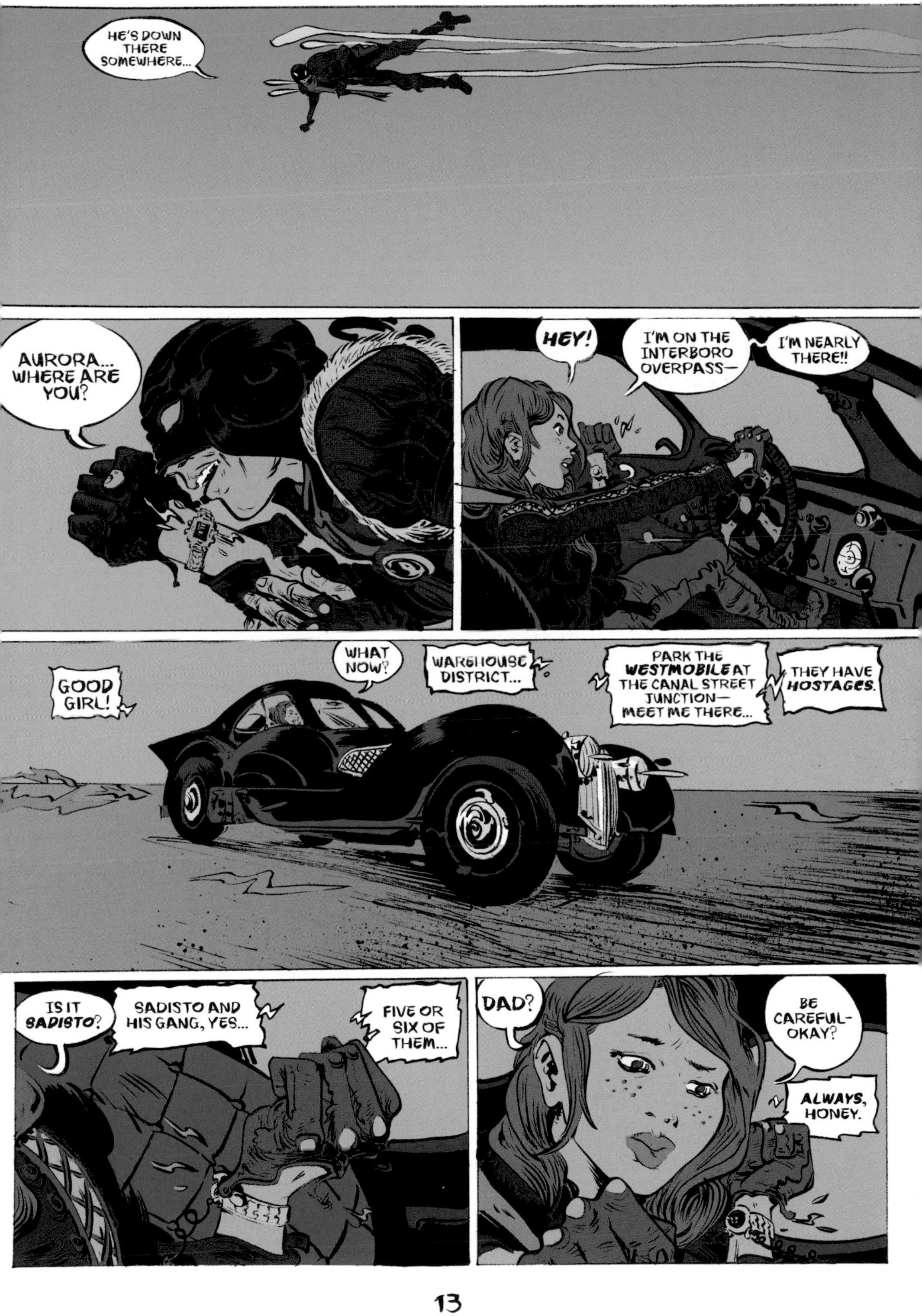
HE'S DOWN THERE SOMEWHERE...
AURORA... WHERE ARE YOU?
HEY!
I'M ON THE INTERBORO OVERPASS—
I'M NEARLY THERE!!
GOOD GIRL!
WHAT NOW?
WAREHOUSE DISTRICT...
PARK THE WESTMOBILE AT THE CANAL STREET JUNCTION— MEET ME THERE...
THEY HAVE HOSTAGES.
IS IT SADISTO?
SADISTO AND HIS GANG, YES...
FIVE OR SIX OF THEM...
DAD?
BE CAREFUL- OKAY?
ALWAYS, HONEY.

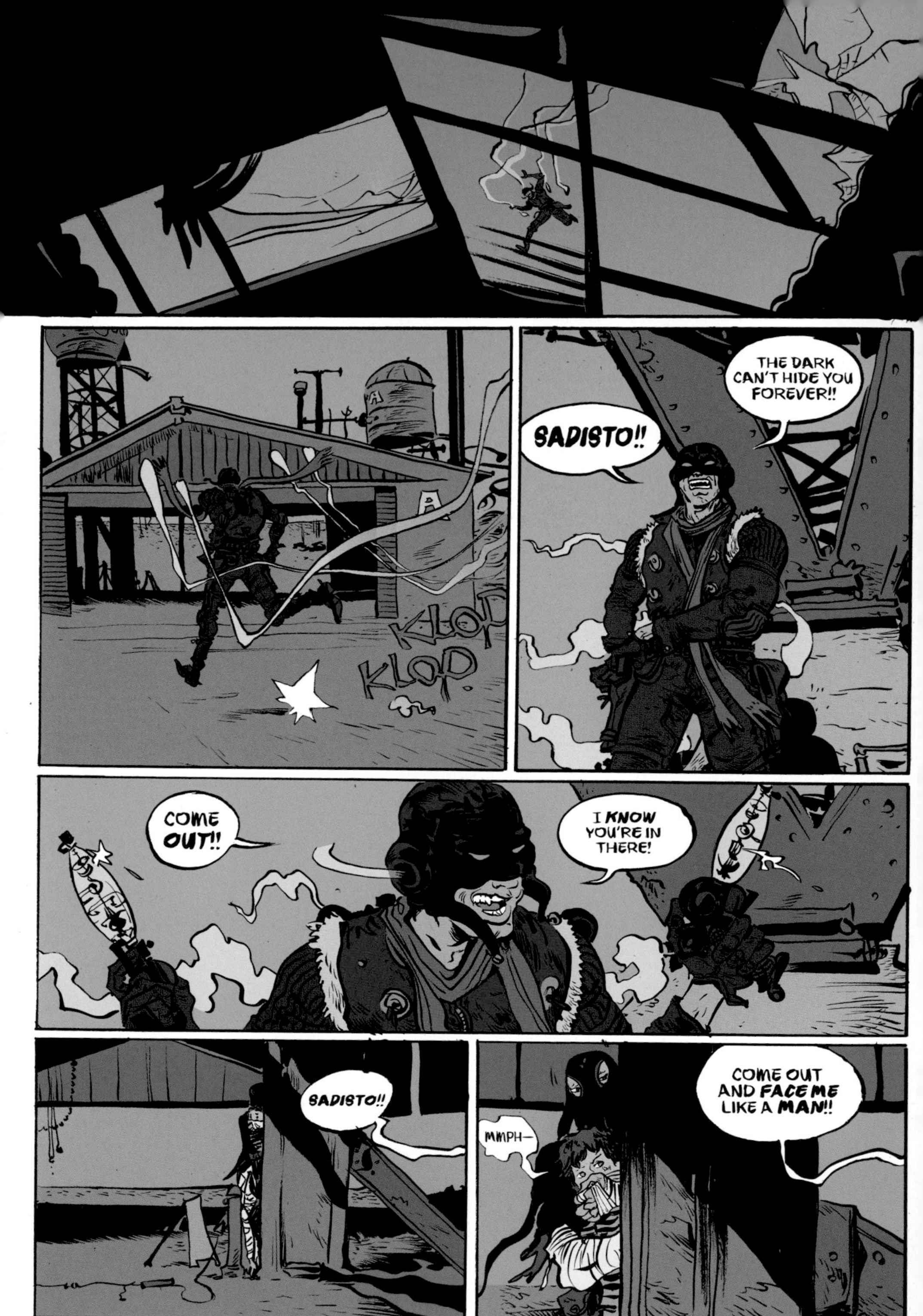
KLOP
KLOP
SADISTO!!
THE DARK CAN'T HIDE YOU FOREVER!!
COME OUT!!
I KNOW YOU'RE IN THERE!
SADISTO!!
MMPH—
COME OUT AND FACE ME LIKE A MAN!!

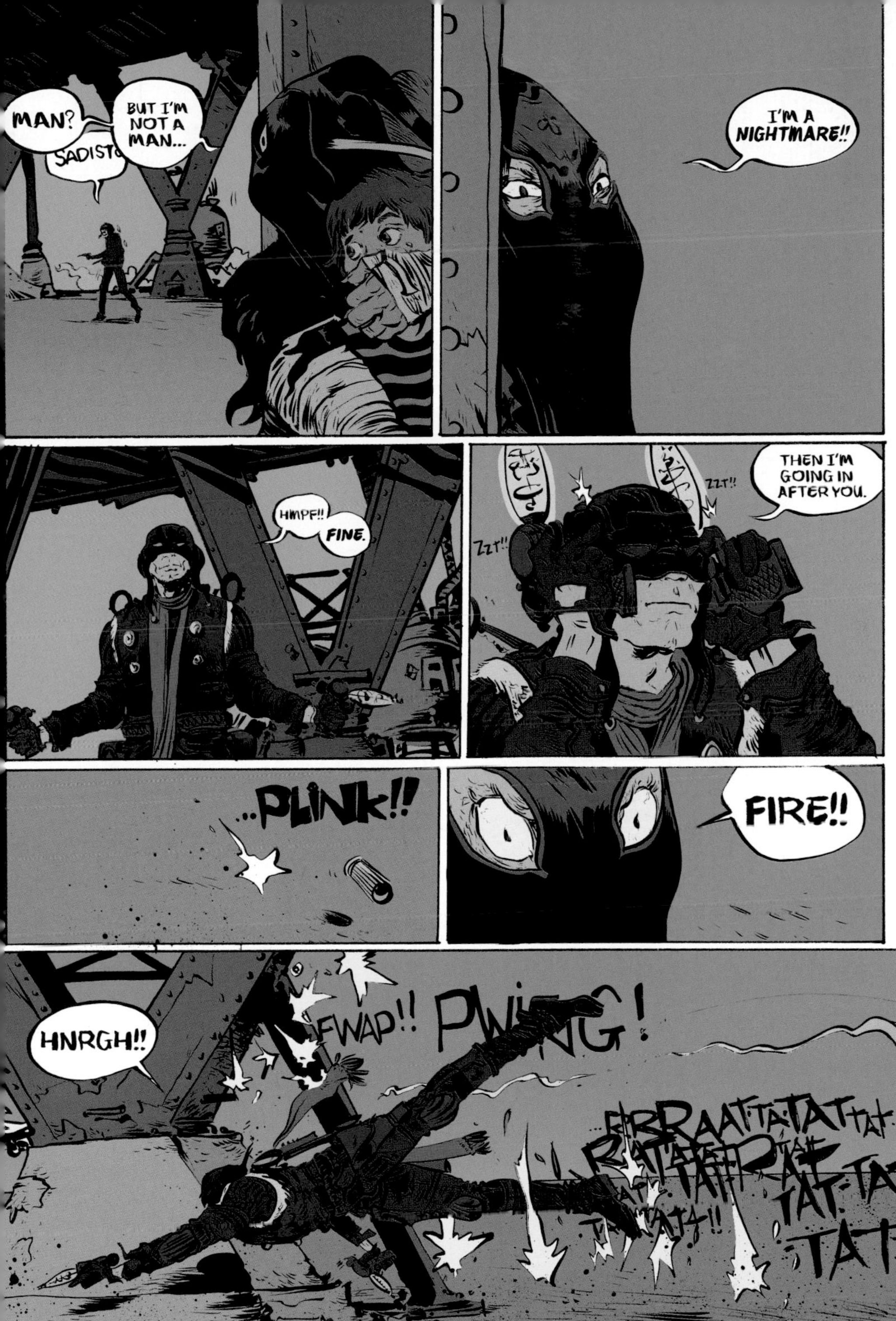
MAN?
SADIST
BUT I'M NOT A MAN...
I'M A NIGHTMARE!!
HMPF!! FINE.
ZZT!!
ZZT!!
THEN I'M GOING IN AFTER YOU.
...PLINK!!
FIRE!!
HNRGH!!
FWAP!!
PWING!

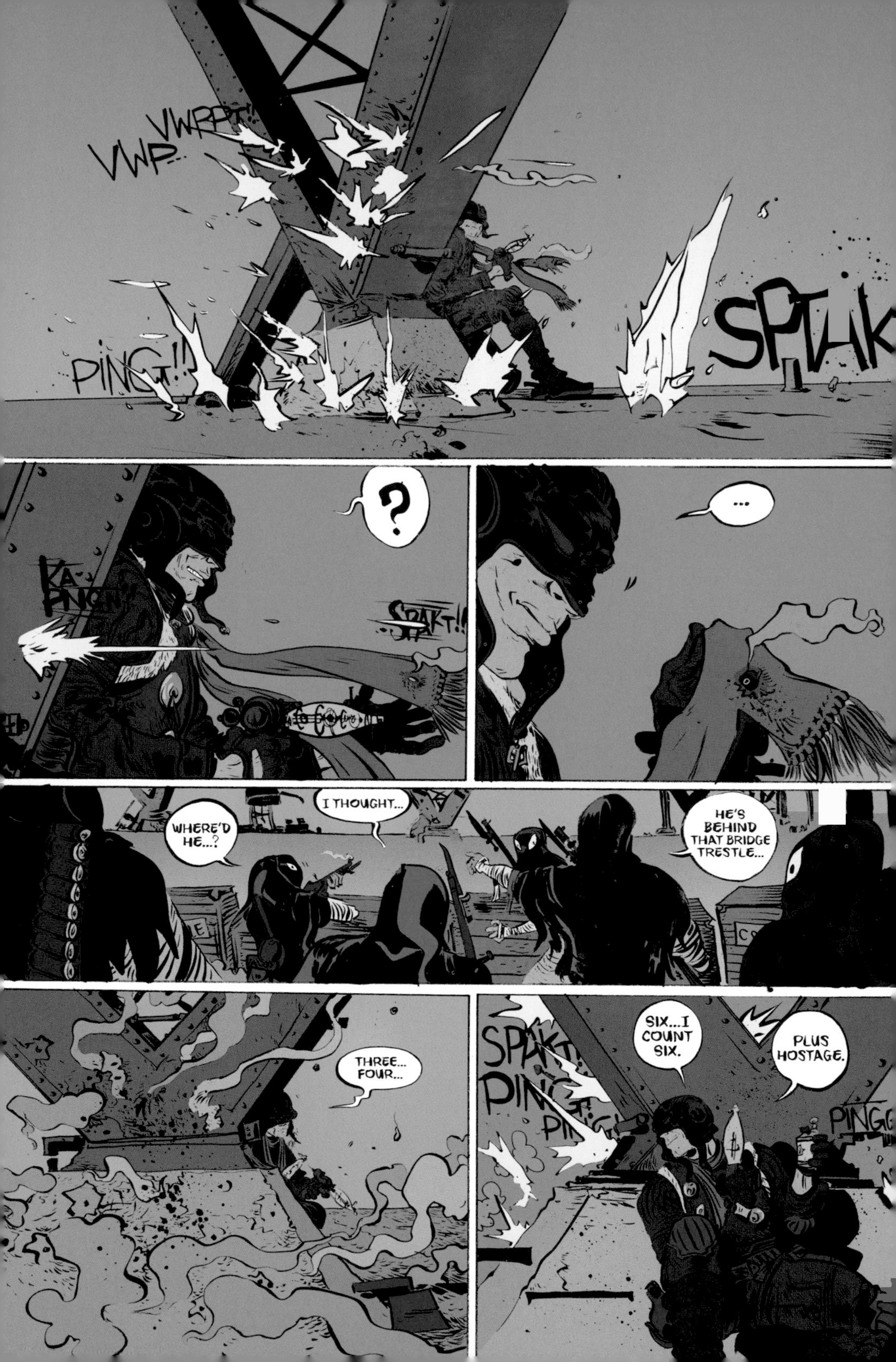
VWRPPT
VWP
PING!!
SPTAK
KA PINGN
?
SPAKT!!
...
WHERE'D HE...?
I THOUGHT...
HE'S BEHIND THAT BRIDGE TRESTLE...
THREE... FOUR...
SIX...I COUNT SIX.
PLUS HOSTAGE.
PING
PING

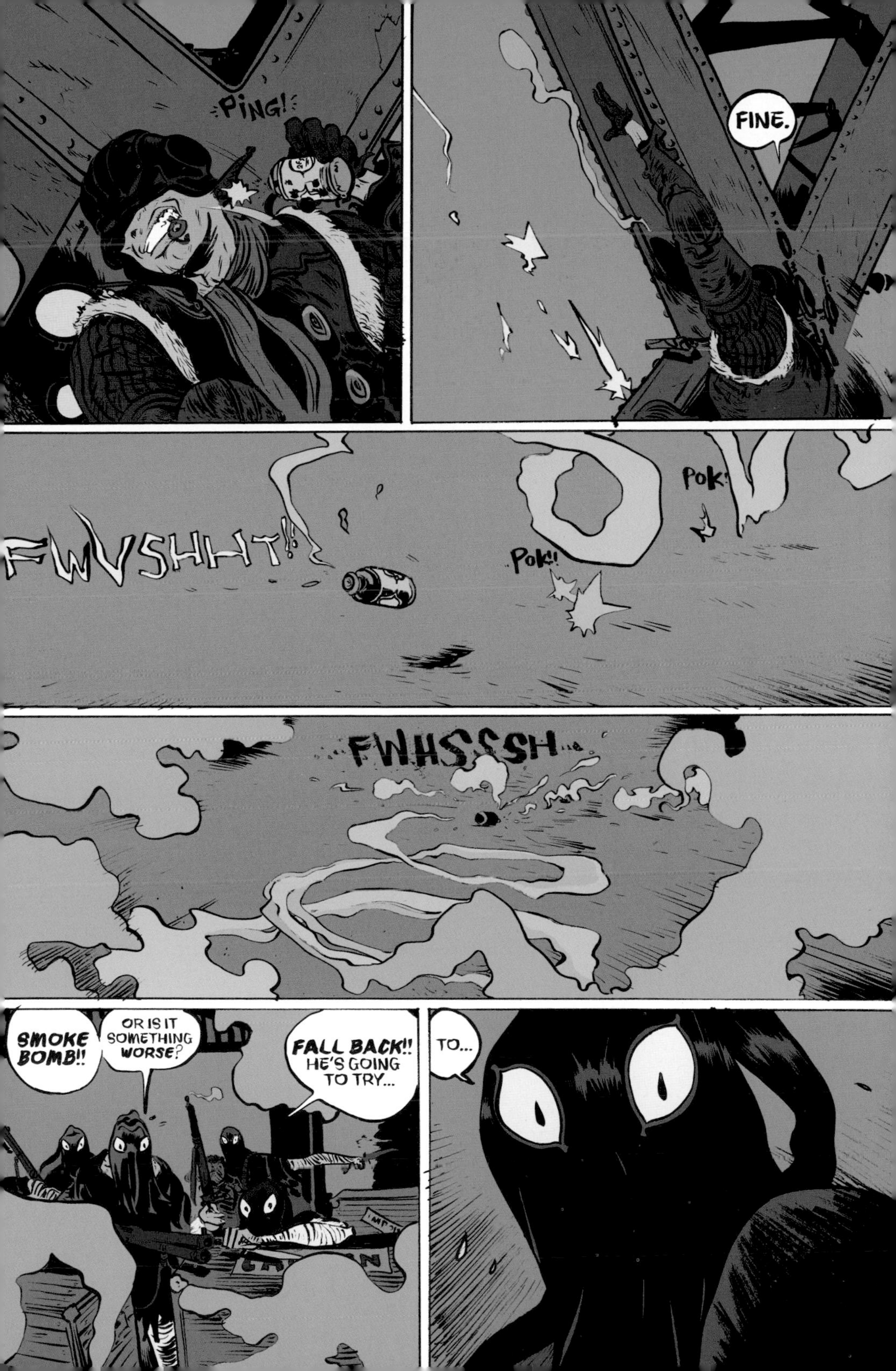
PING!
FINE.
FWVSHHT!!
POK!
POK!!
FWHSSSH
SMOKE BOMB!!
OR IS IT SOMETHING WORSE?
FALL BACK!! HE'S GOING TO TRY...
TO...

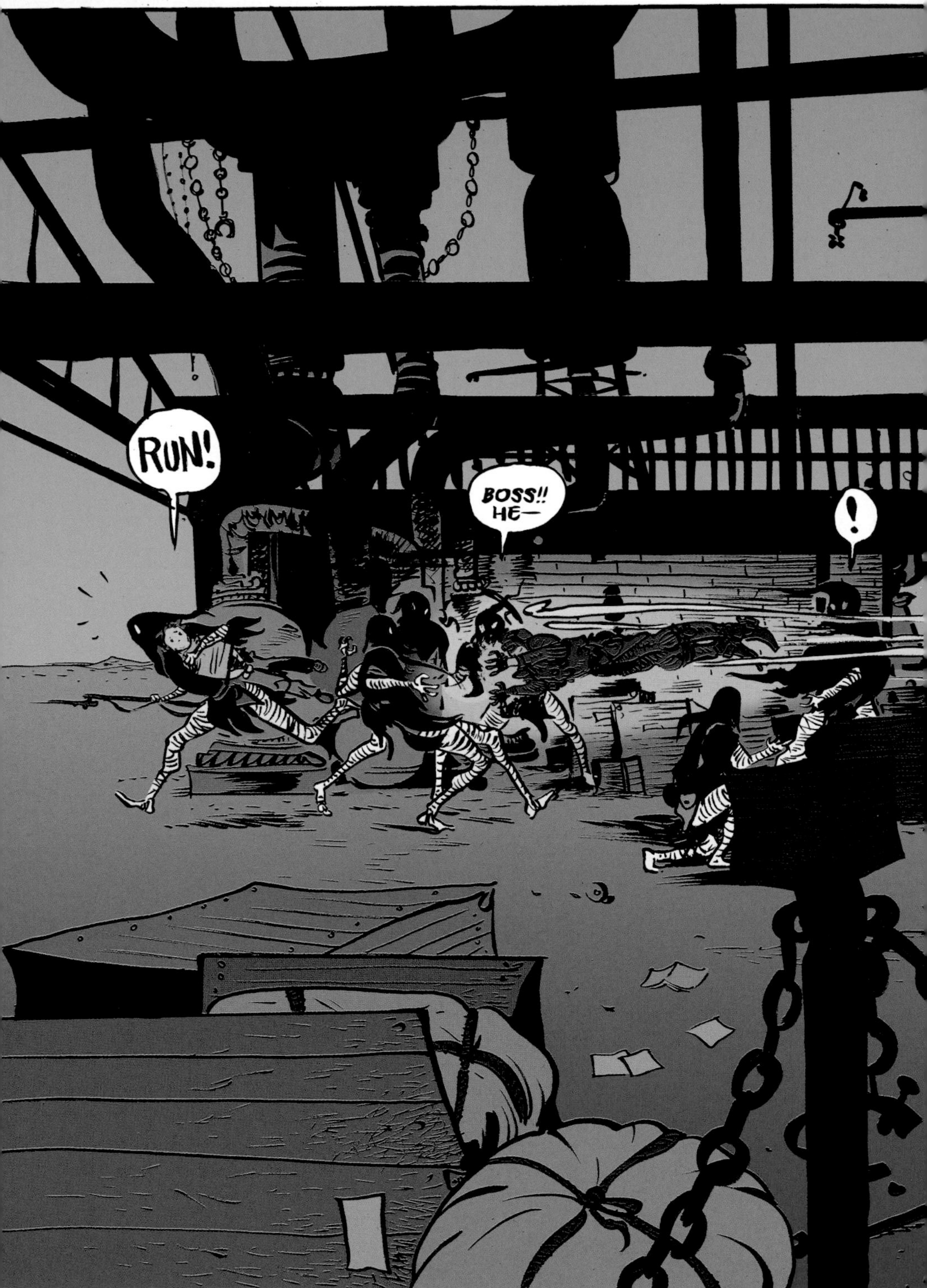
RUN!
BOSS!! HE—
!

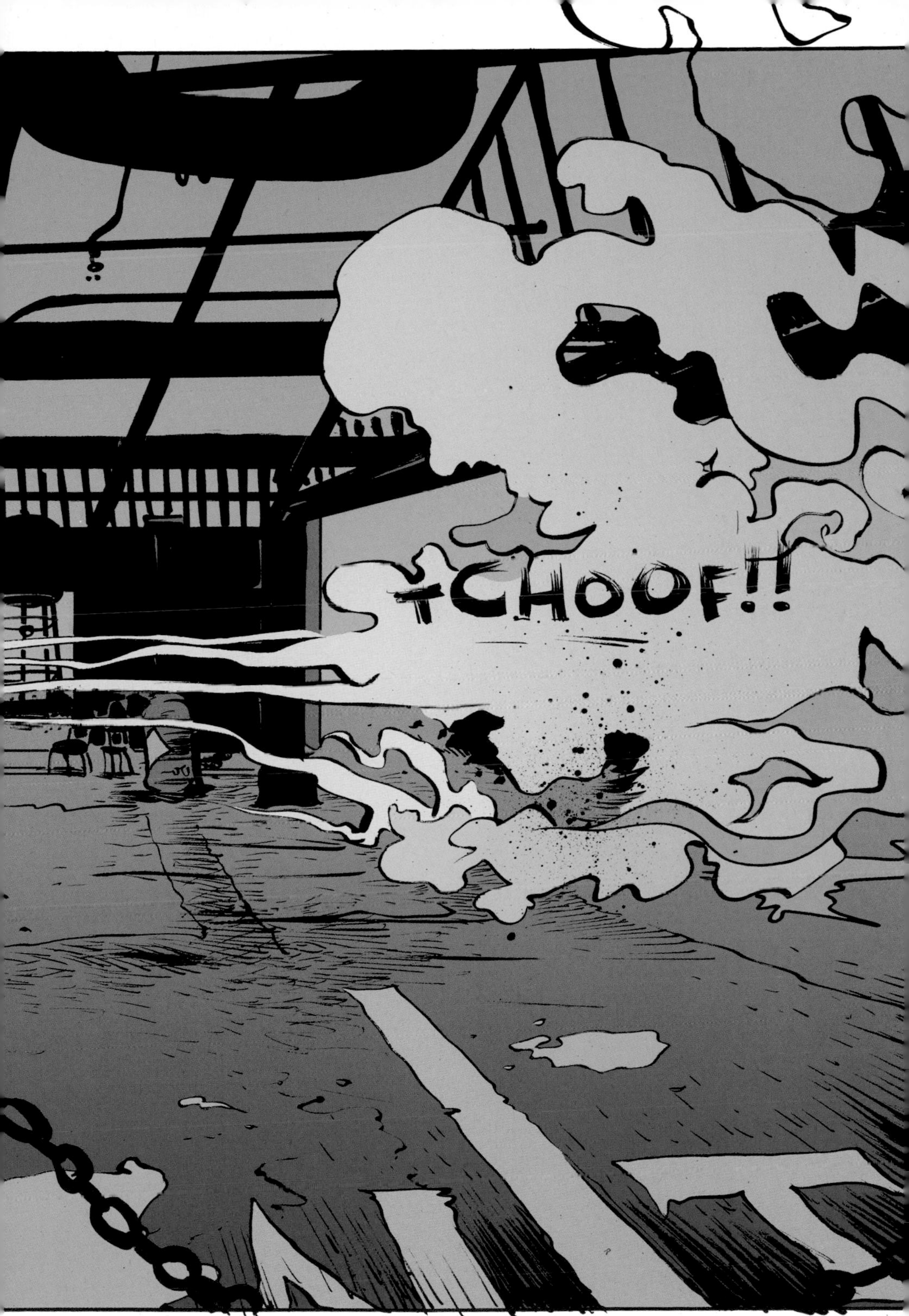
TCHOOF!!

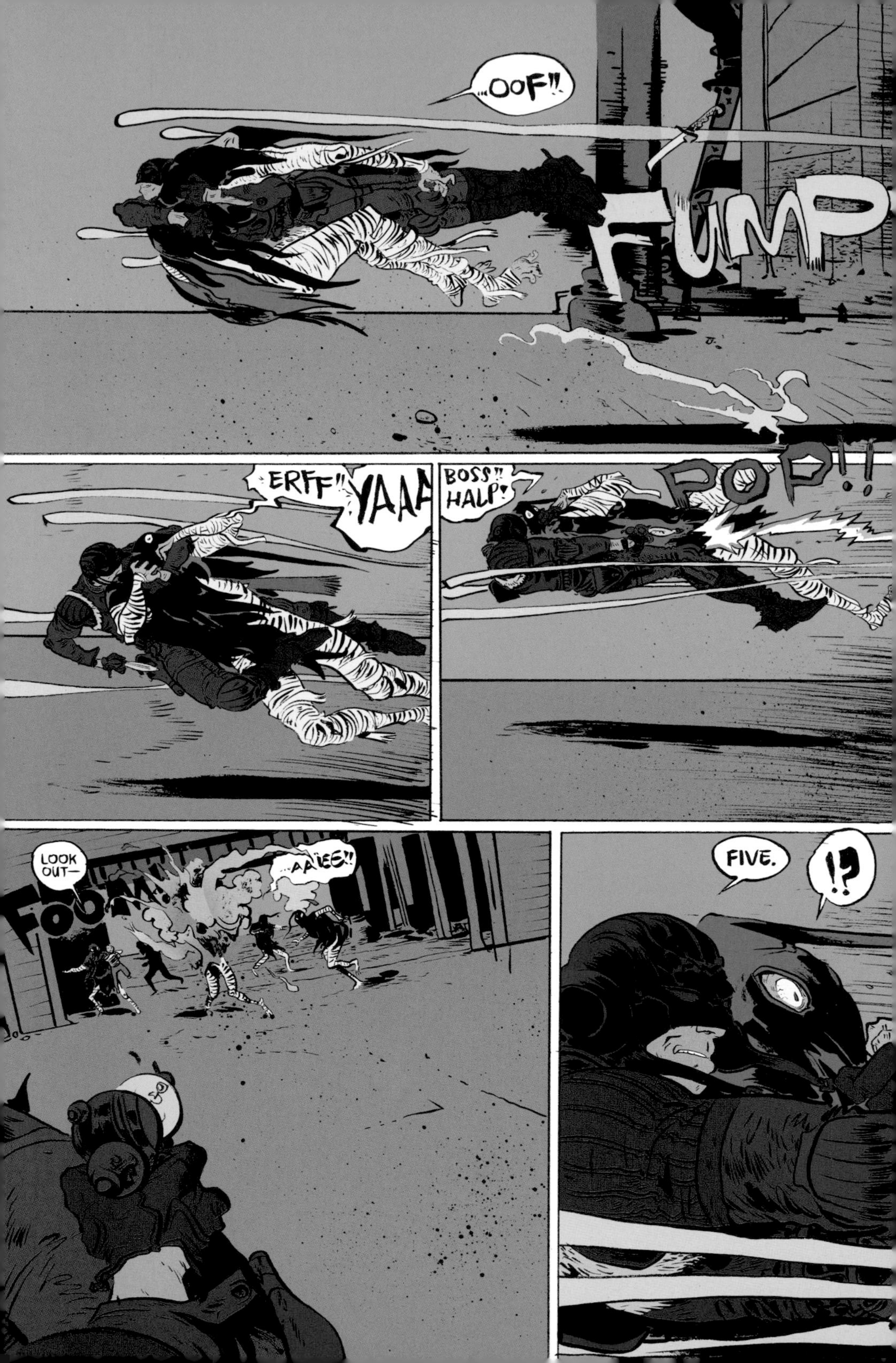
...OOF!!
FUMP
ERFF!!
YAAA
BOSS!! HALP!
POP!!
LOOK OUT—
FOOM
...AAEE!!
FIVE.
!?

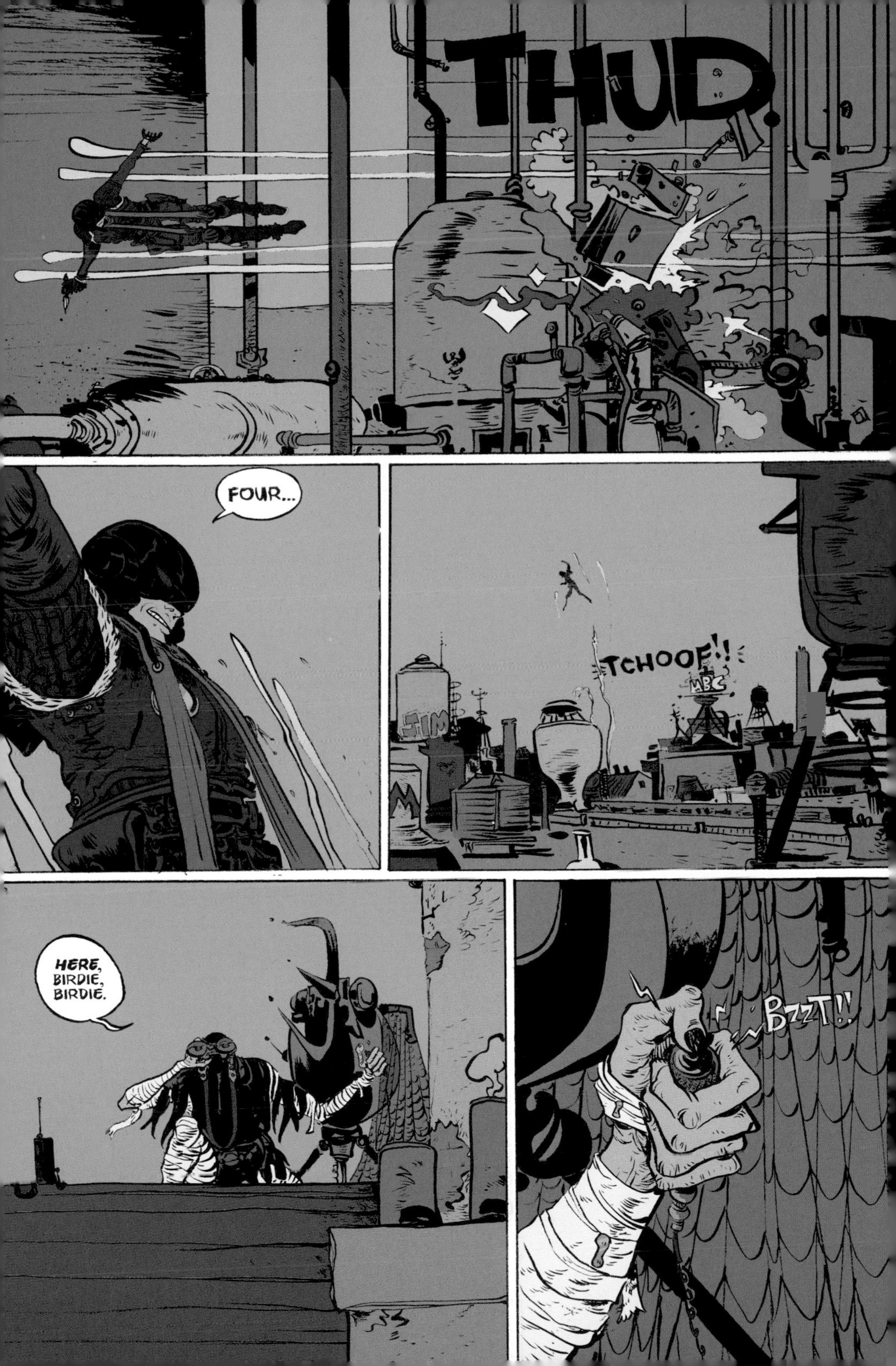
THUD
FOUR...
TCHOOF!!
JIM
HERE, BIRDIE, BIRDIE.
BzzT!!

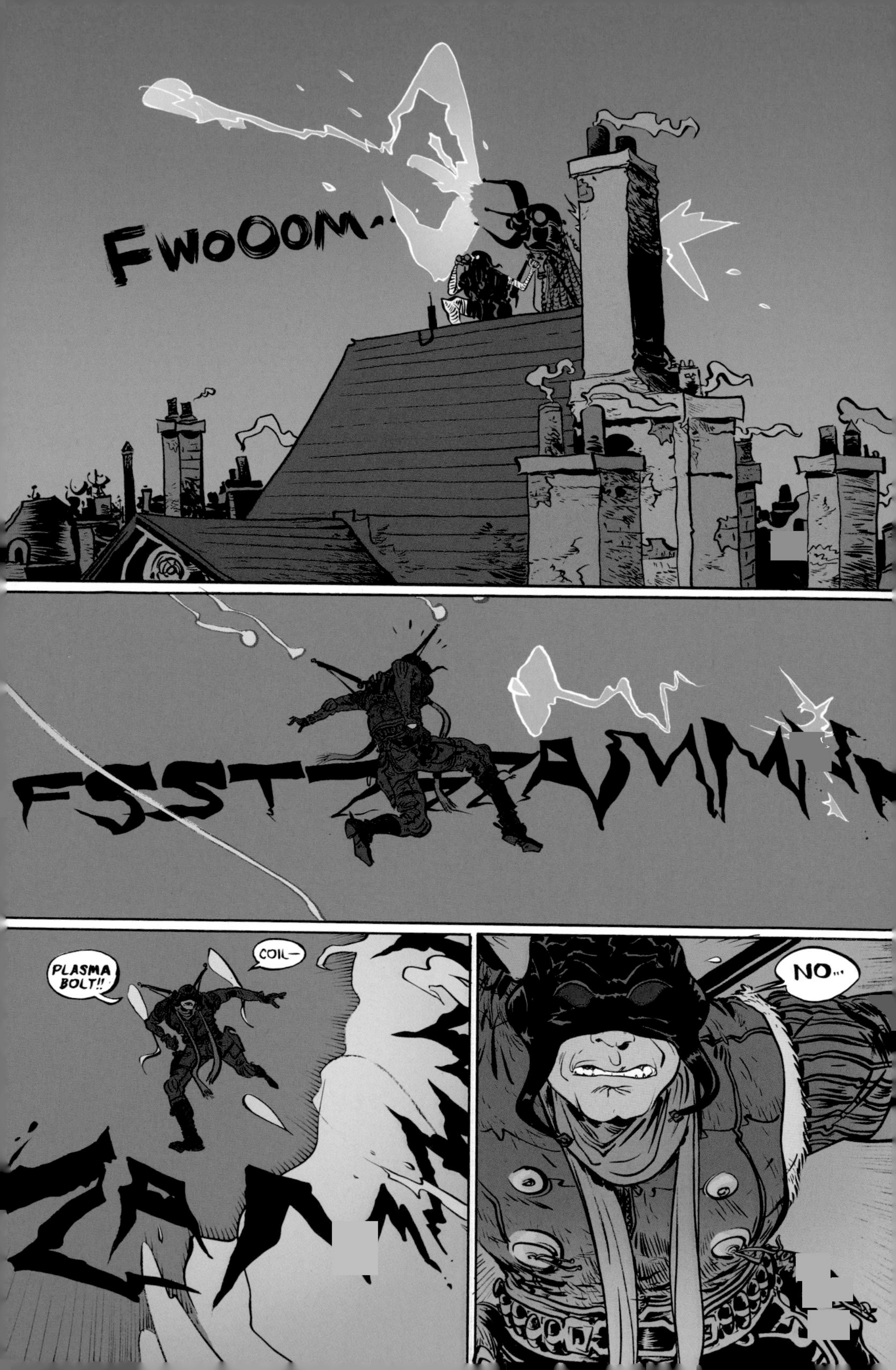
FWOOOM..
FSST—
PLASMA BOLT!!
COIL—
NO...

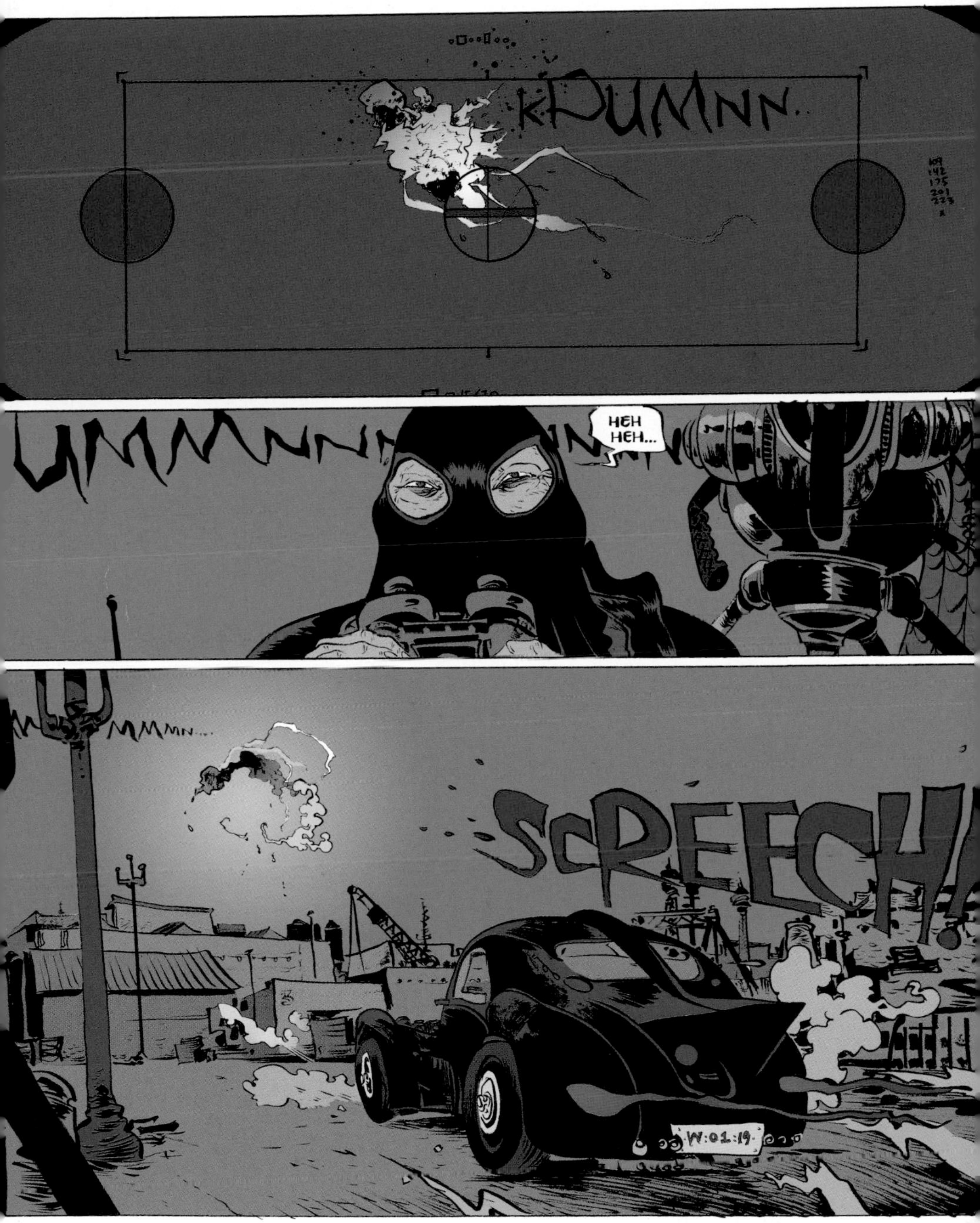
KRUMNN.
UMMNNN
HEH HEH...
MMMN...
SCREECH!
W:01:19

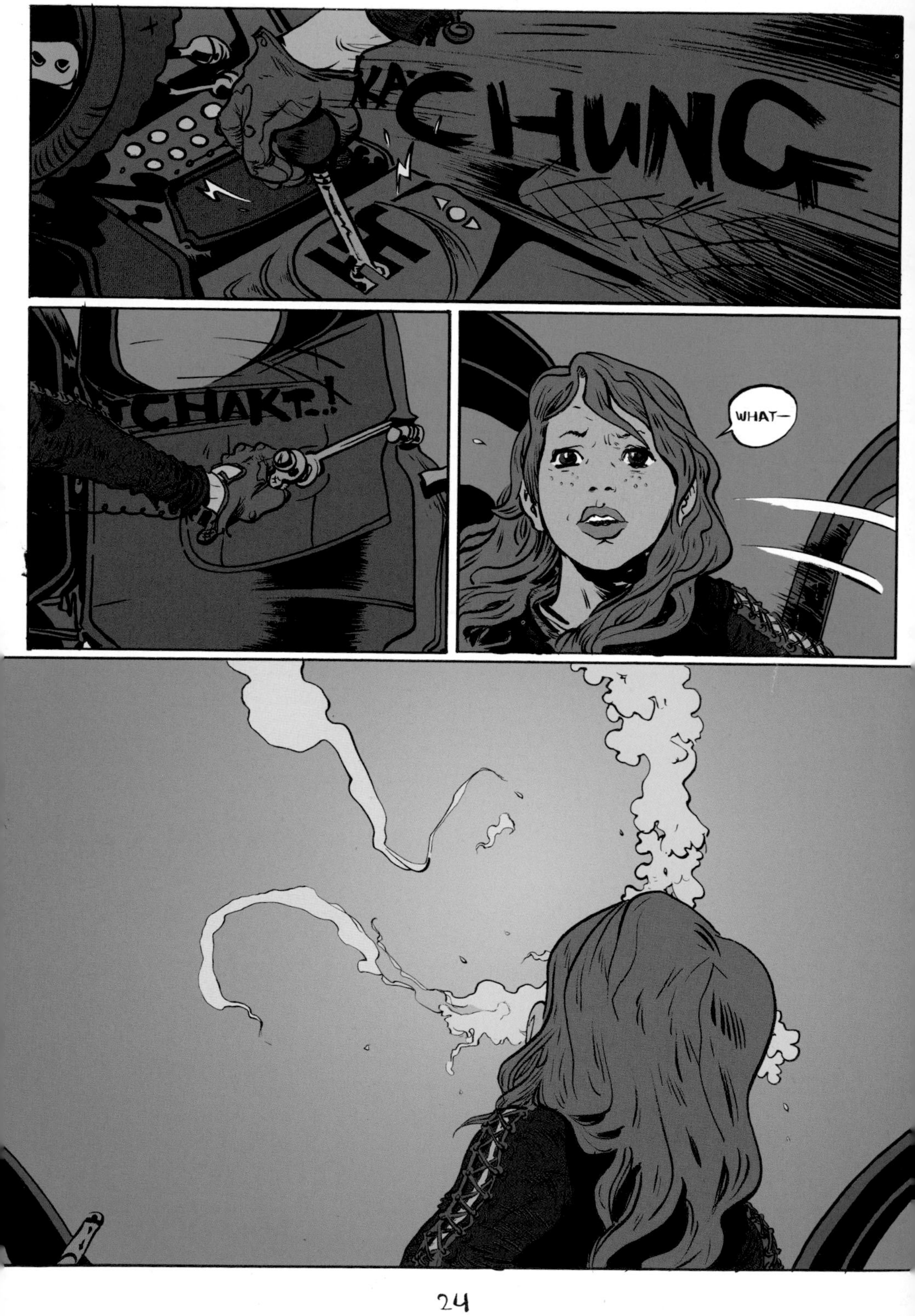
KA'CHUNG
TCHAKT..!
WHAT—

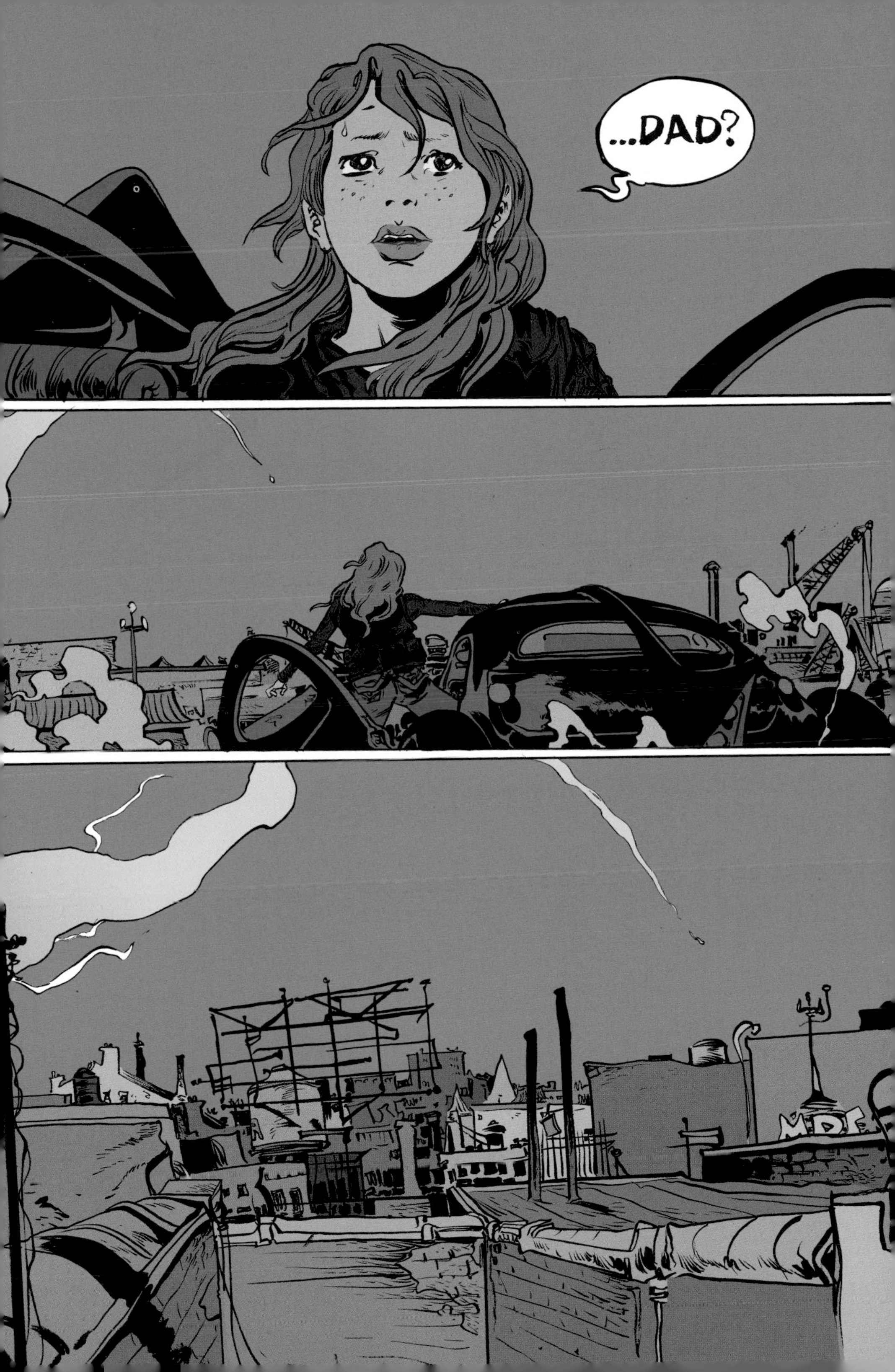
...DAD?

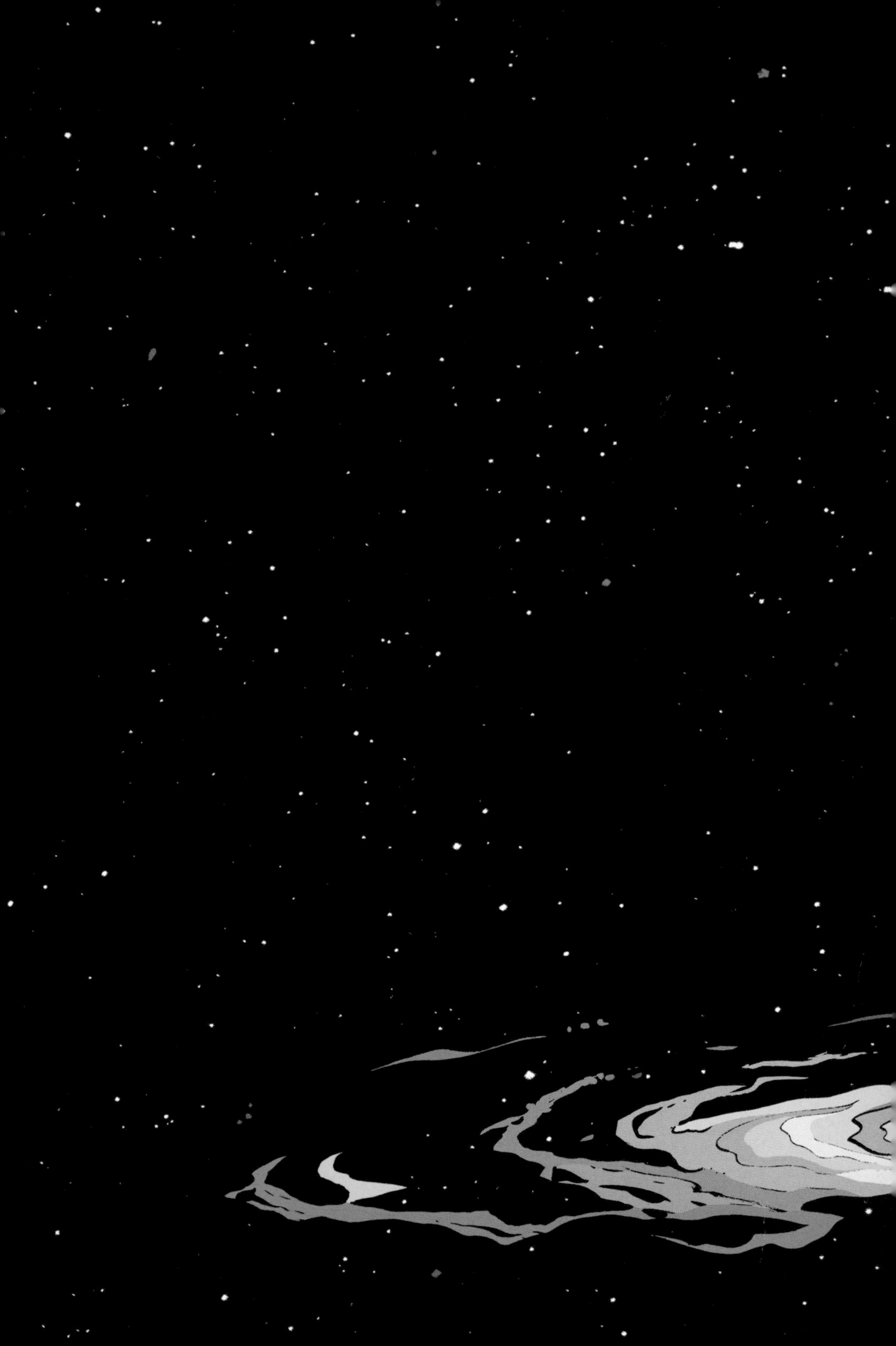

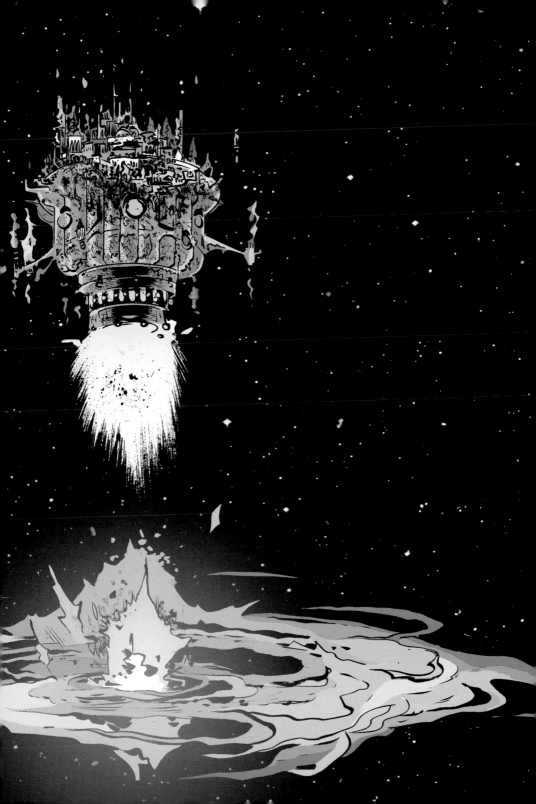

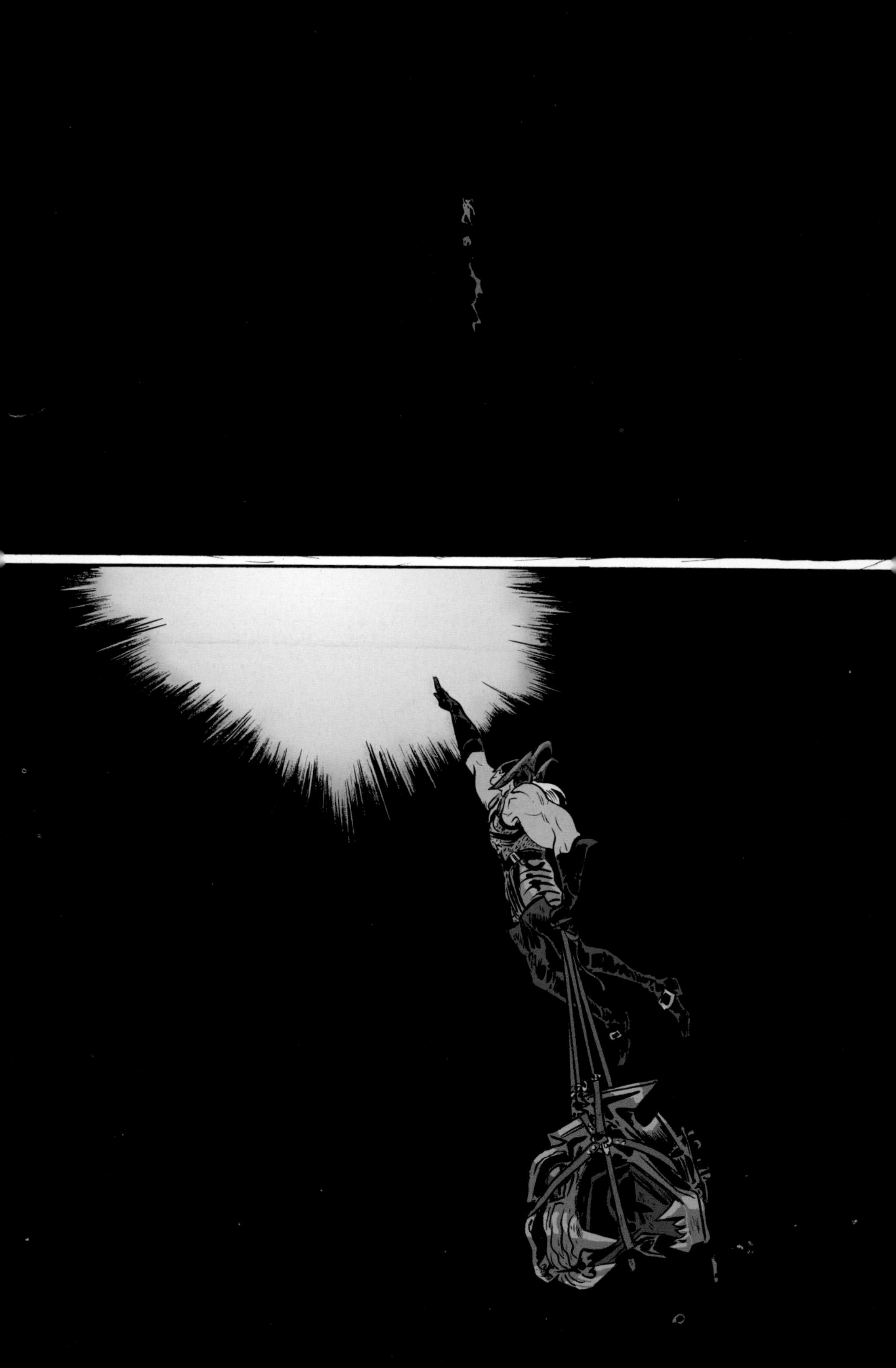

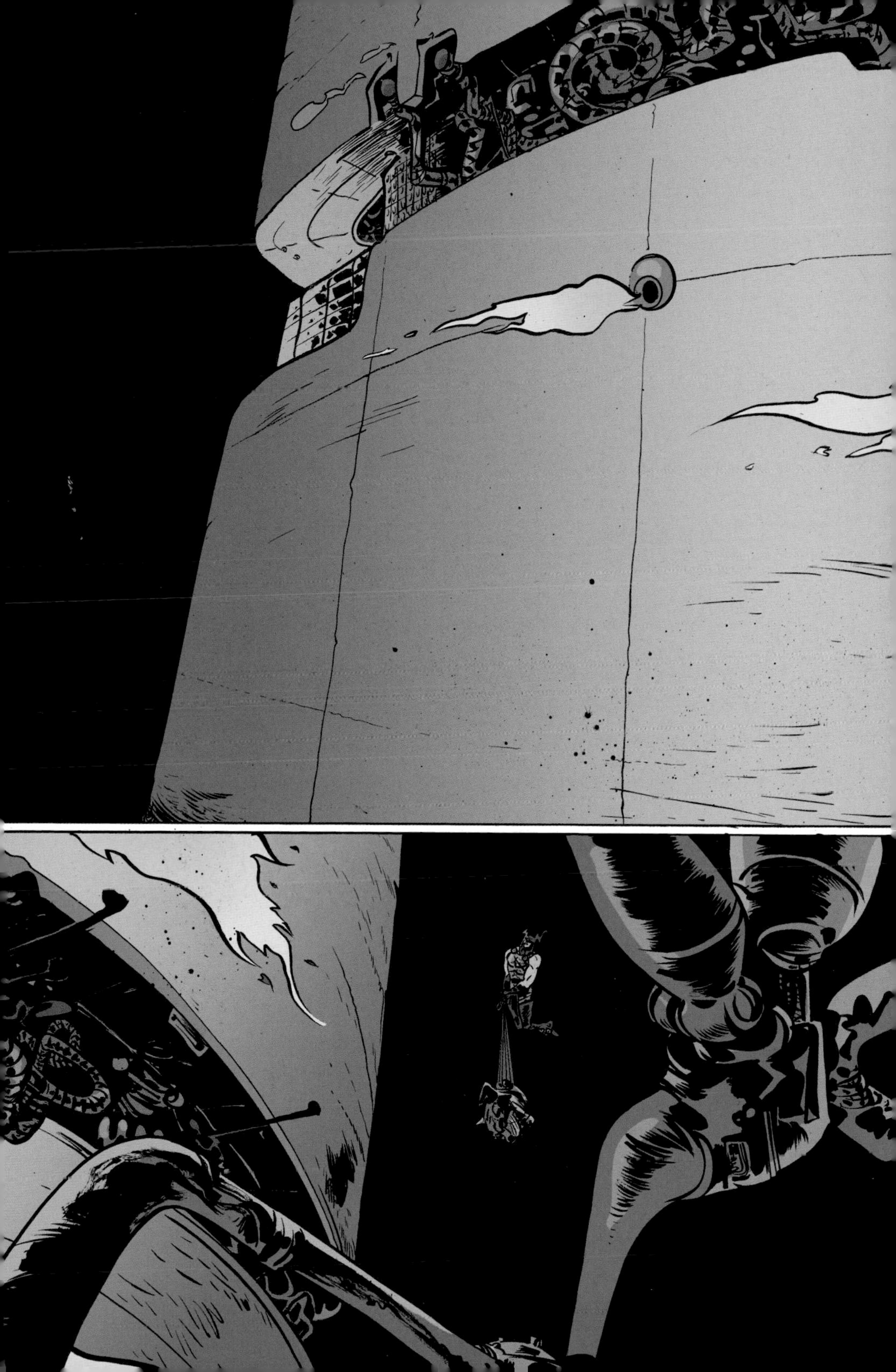

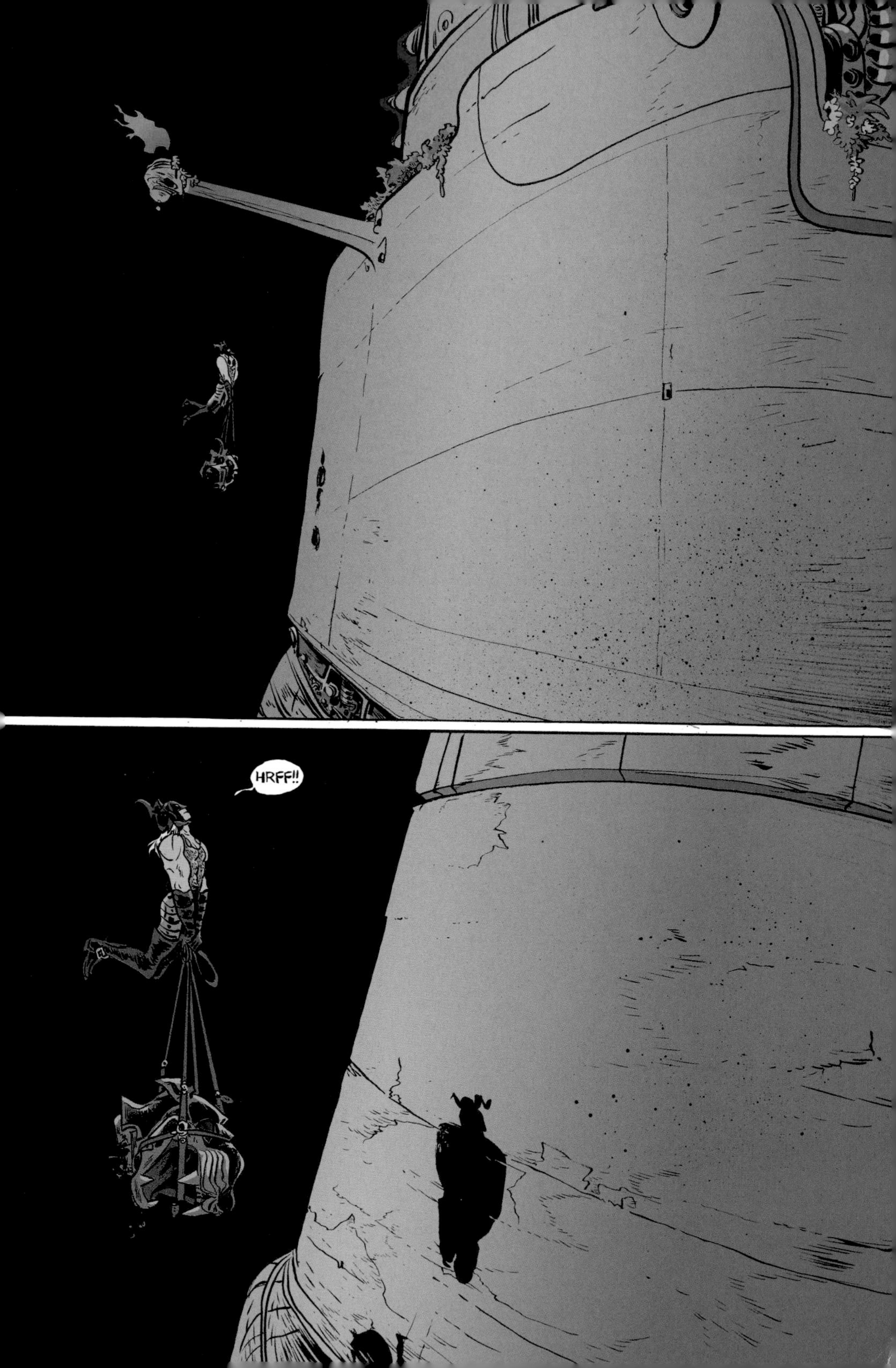
HRFF!!

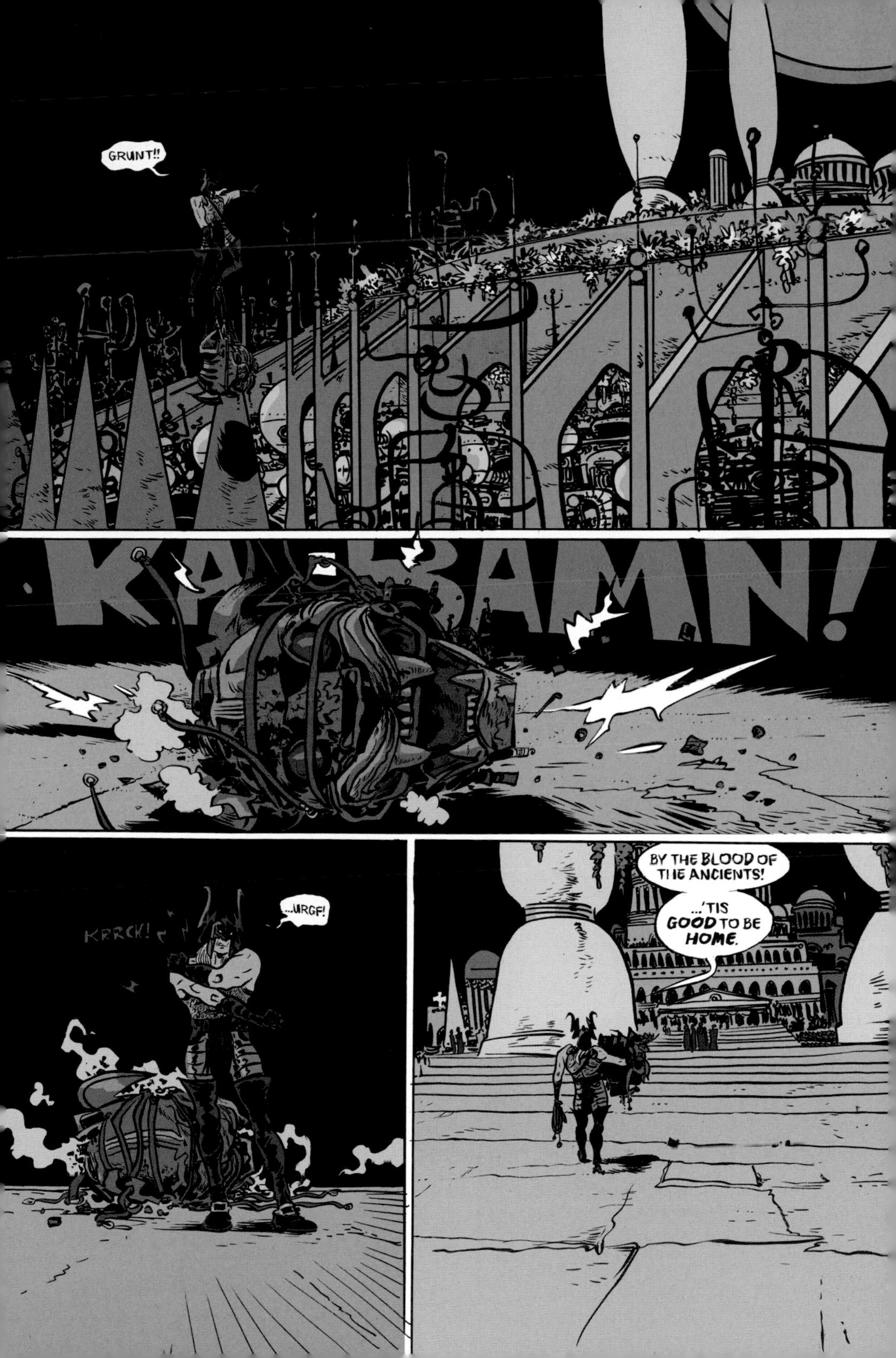
GRUNT!!
BAMN!
KRRCK!
...URGF!
BY THE BLOOD OF THE ANCIENTS!
...'TIS GOOD TO BE HOME.

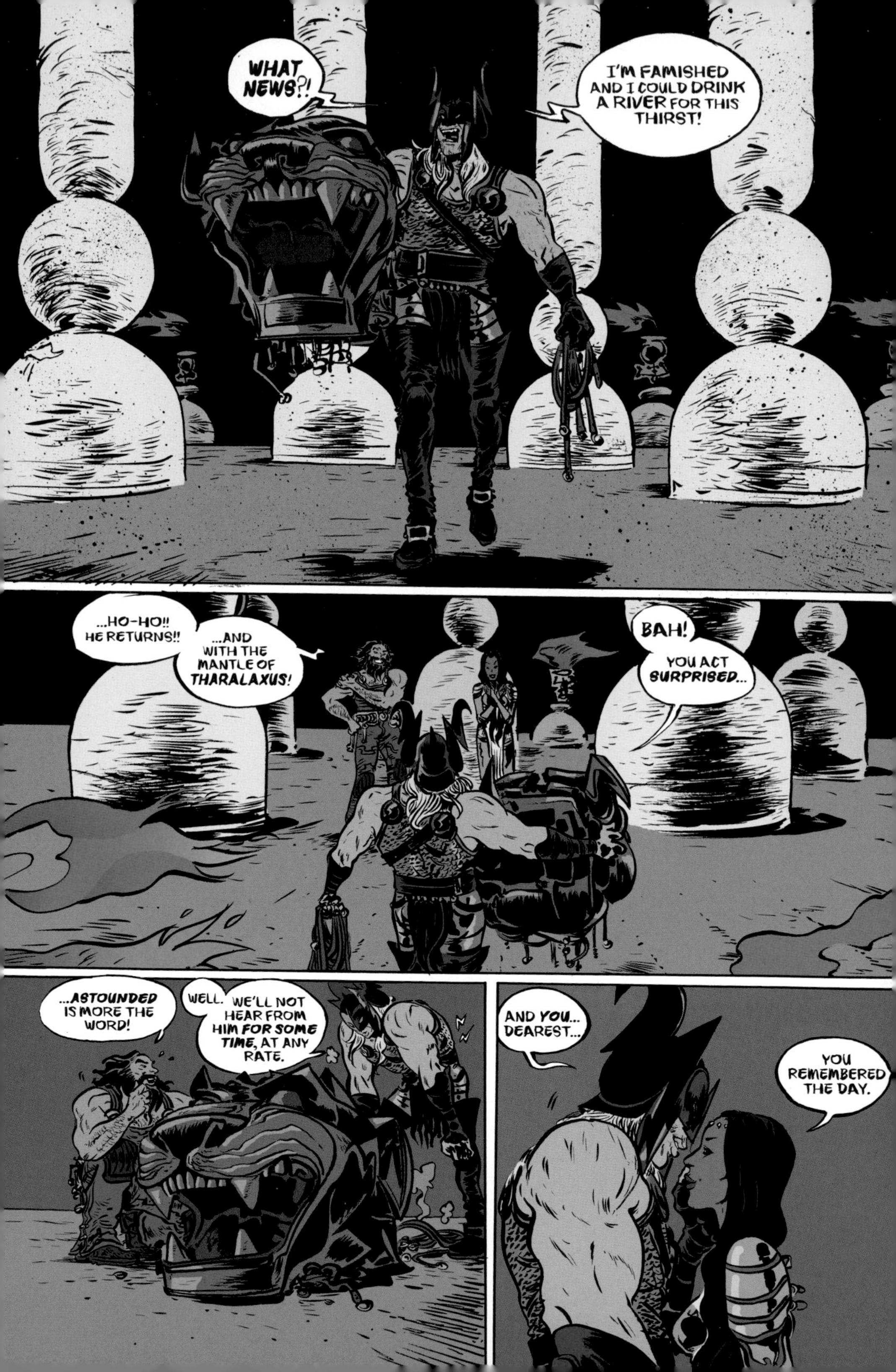
WHAT NEWS?!
I'M FAMISHED AND I COULD DRINK A RIVER FOR THIS THIRST!
...HO-HO!! HE RETURNS!!
...AND WITH THE MANTLE OF THARALAXUS!
BAH!
YOU ACT SURPRISED...
...ASTOUNDED IS MORE THE WORD!
WELL.
WE'LL NOT HEAR FROM HIM FOR SOME TIME, AT ANY RATE.
AND YOU... DEAREST...
YOU REMEMBERED THE DAY.

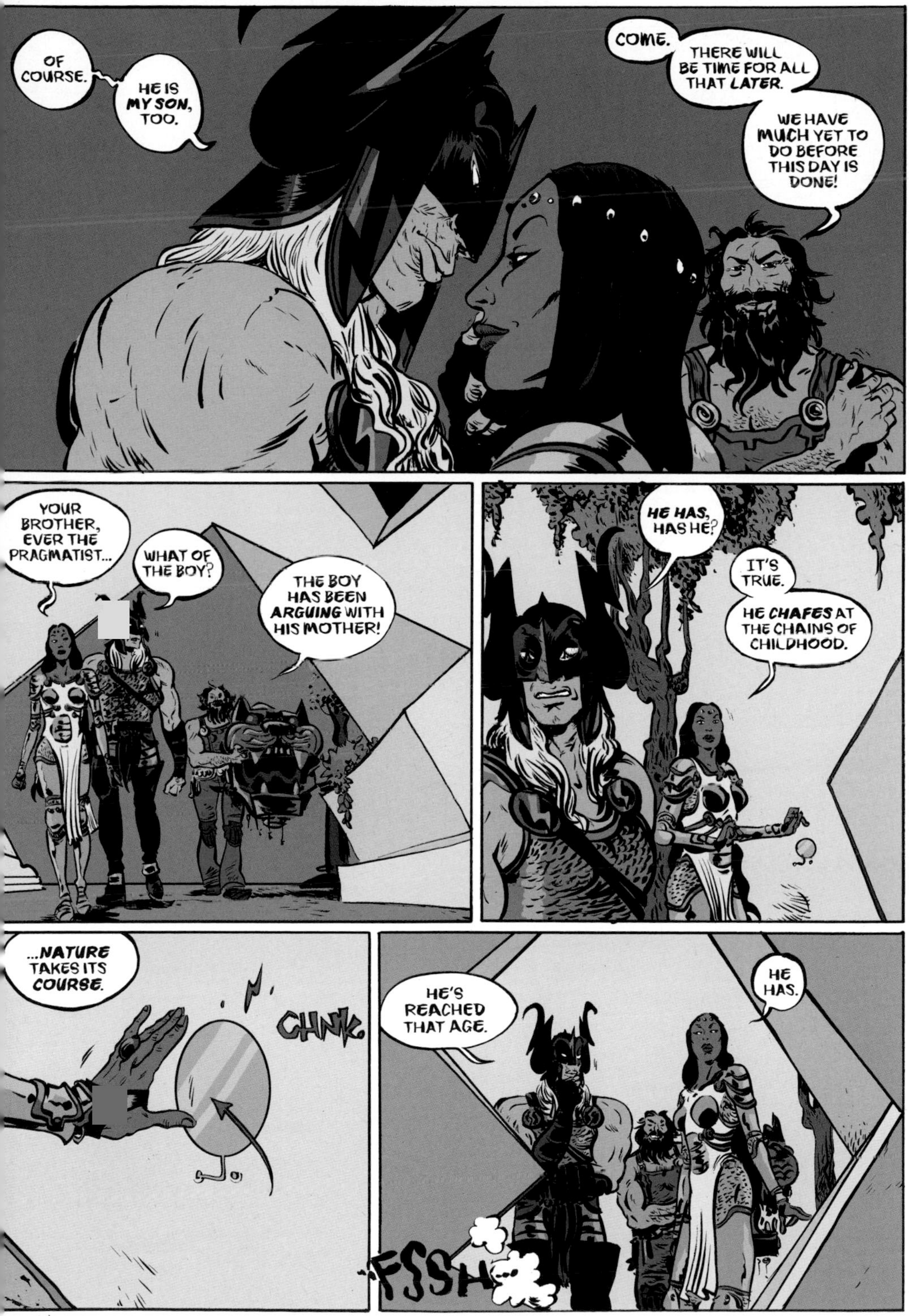
OF COURSE.
HE IS MY SON, TOO.
COME.
THERE WILL BE TIME FOR ALL THAT LATER.
WE HAVE MUCH YET TO DO BEFORE THIS DAY IS DONE!
YOUR BROTHER, EVER THE PRAGMATIST...
WHAT OF THE BOY?
THE BOY HAS BEEN ARGUING WITH HIS MOTHER!
HE HAS, HAS HE?
IT'S TRUE.
HE CHAFES AT THE CHAINS OF CHILDHOOD.
...NATURE TAKES ITS COURSE.
CHNK.
HE'S REACHED THAT AGE.
HE HAS.
FSSH

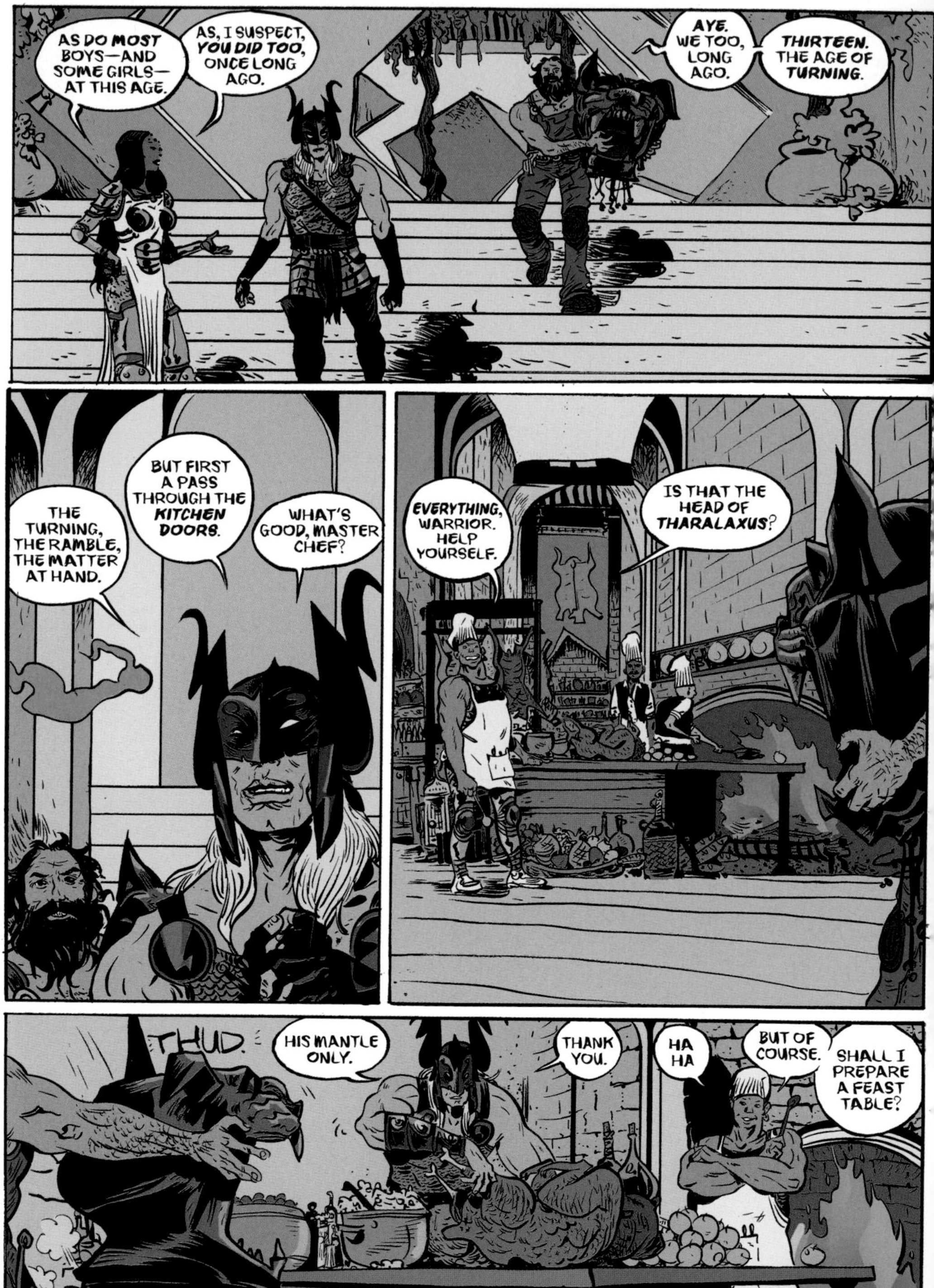
AS DO MOST BOYS—AND SOME GIRLS—AT THIS AGE.
AS, I SUSPECT, YOU DID TOO, ONCE LONG AGO.
AYE. WE TOO, LONG AGO.
THIRTEEN. THE AGE OF TURNING.
THE TURNING, THE RAMBLE, THE MATTER AT HAND.
BUT FIRST A PASS THROUGH THE KITCHEN DOORS.
WHAT'S GOOD, MASTER CHEF?
EVERYTHING, WARRIOR. HELP YOURSELF.
IS THAT THE HEAD OF THARALAXUS?
THUD.
HIS MANTLE ONLY.
THANK YOU.
HA HA
BUT OF COURSE.
SHALL I PREPARE A FEAST TABLE?

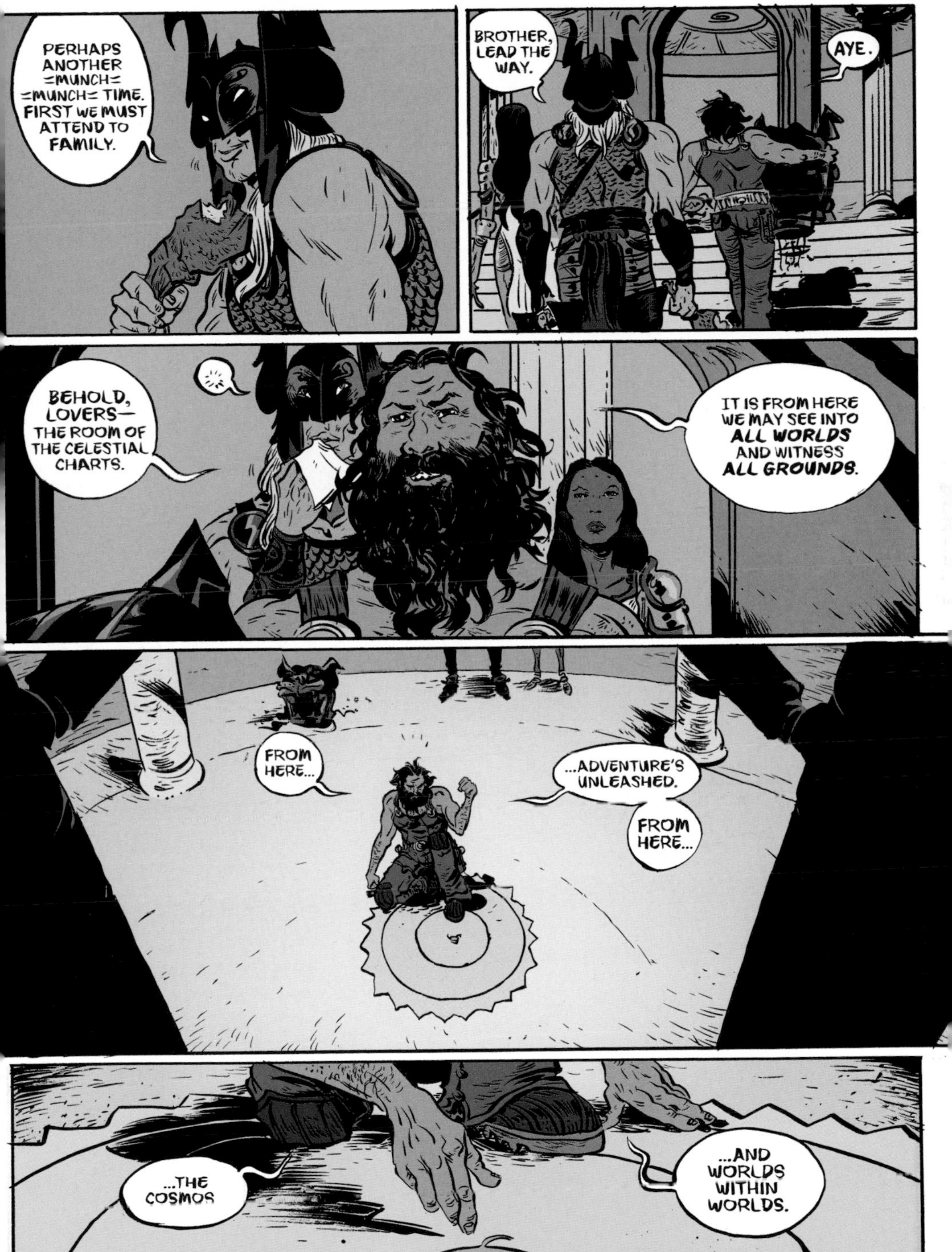
PERHAPS ANOTHER =MUNCH= =MUNCH= TIME. FIRST WE MUST ATTEND TO FAMILY.
BROTHER, LEAD THE WAY.
AYE.
BEHOLD, LOVERS— THE ROOM OF THE CELESTIAL CHARTS.
IT IS FROM HERE WE MAY SEE INTO ALL WORLDS AND WITNESS ALL GROUNDS.
FROM HERE...
...ADVENTURE'S UNLEASHED.
FROM HERE...
...THE COSMOS
...AND WORLDS WITHIN WORLDS.

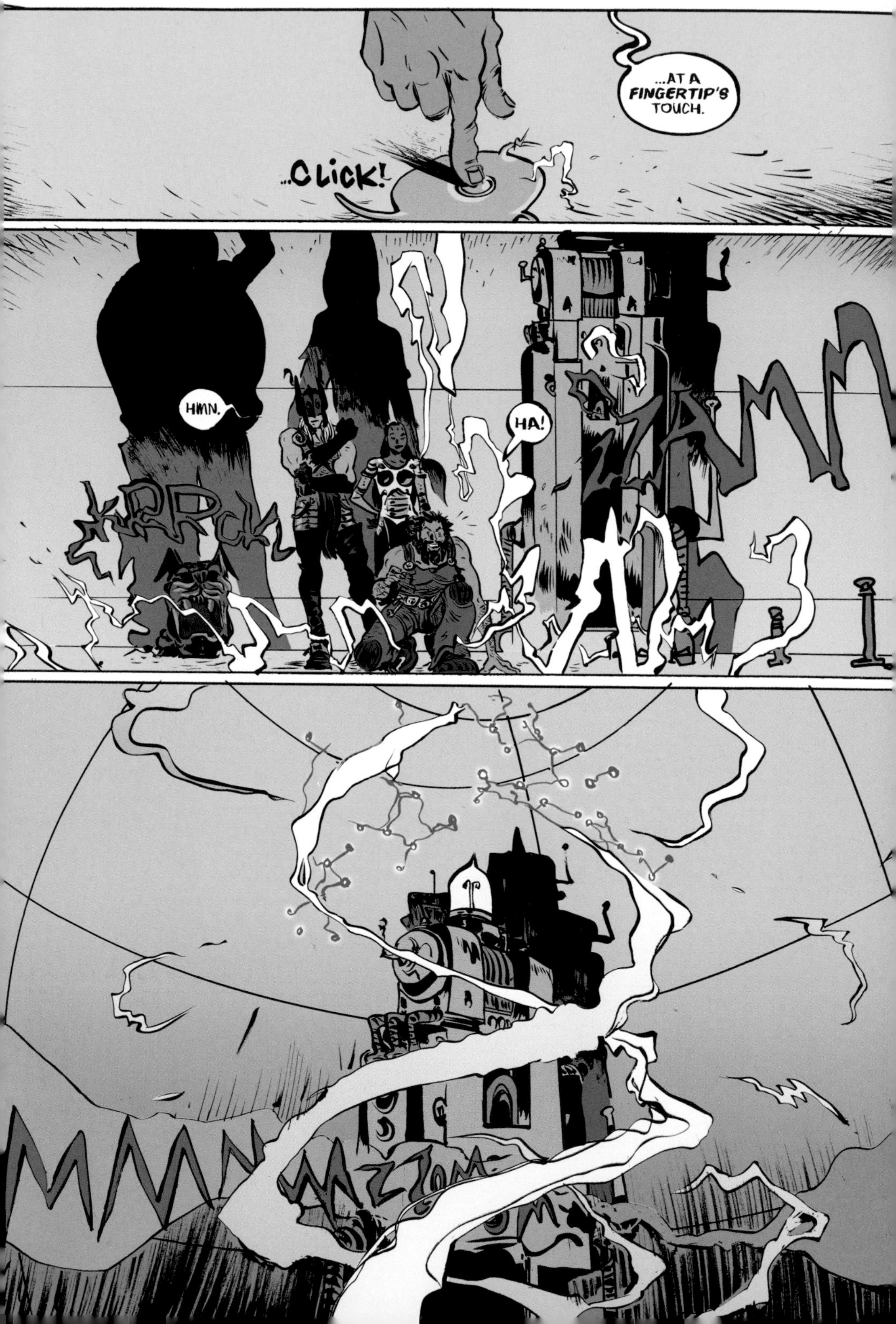
...AT A FINGERTIP'S TOUCH.
...CLICK!
HMN.
HA!

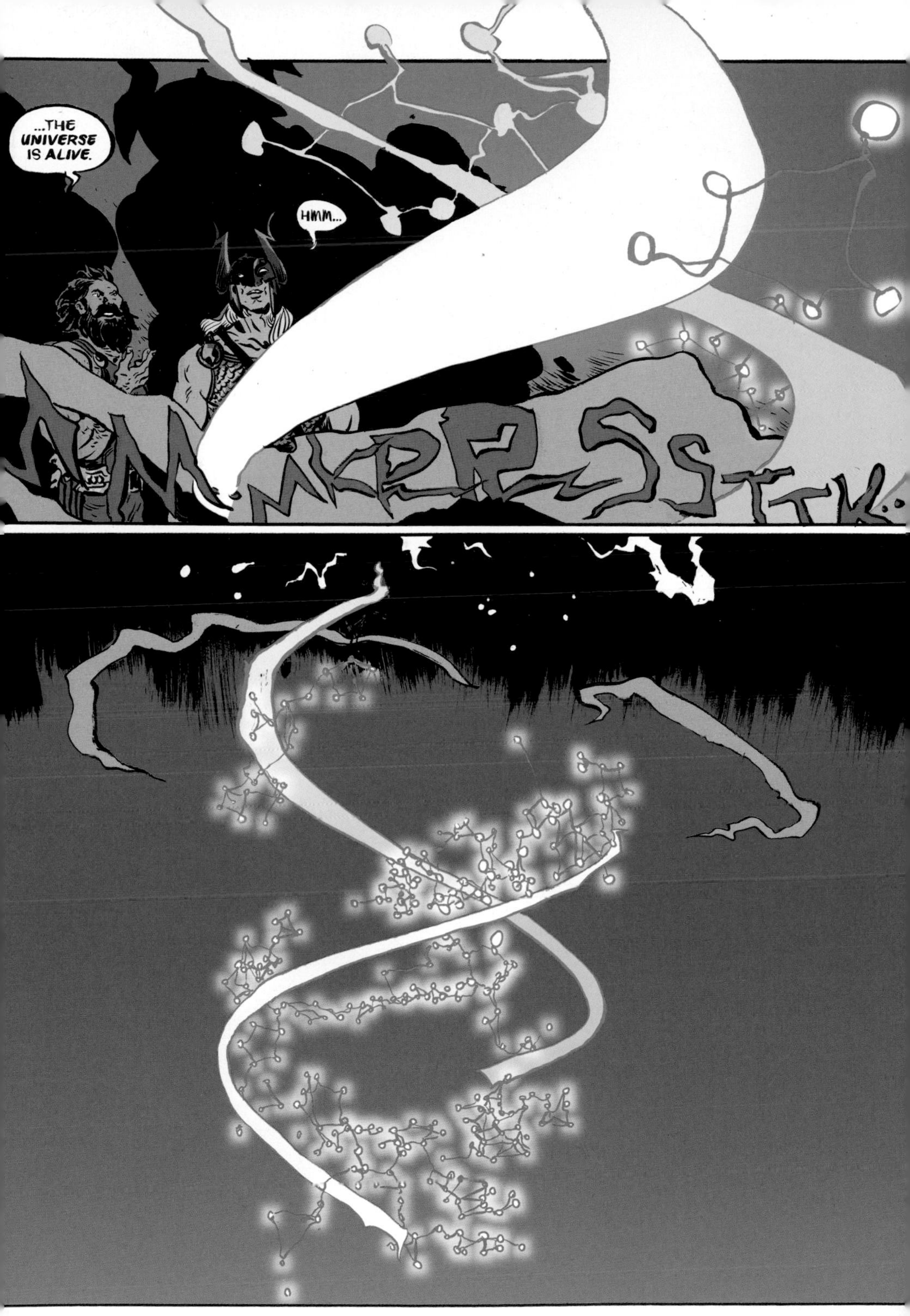
...THE UNIVERSE IS ALIVE.
HMM...
MMKRRSSTTK

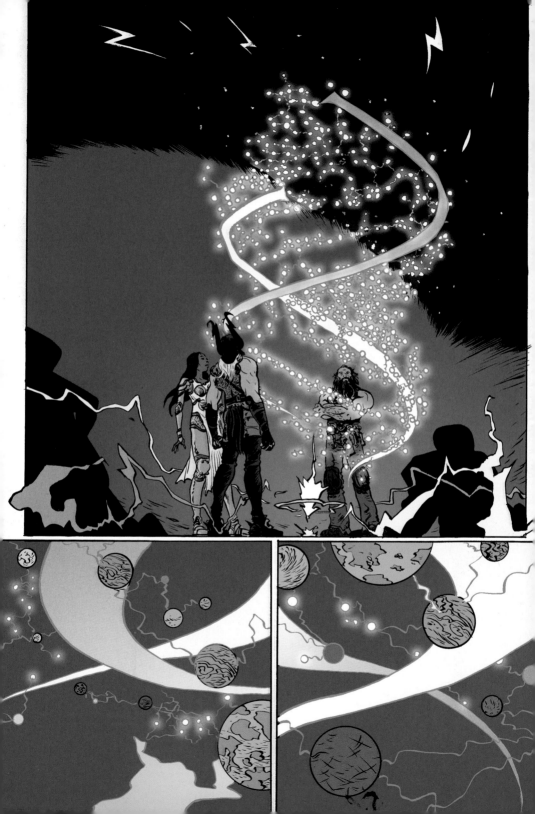

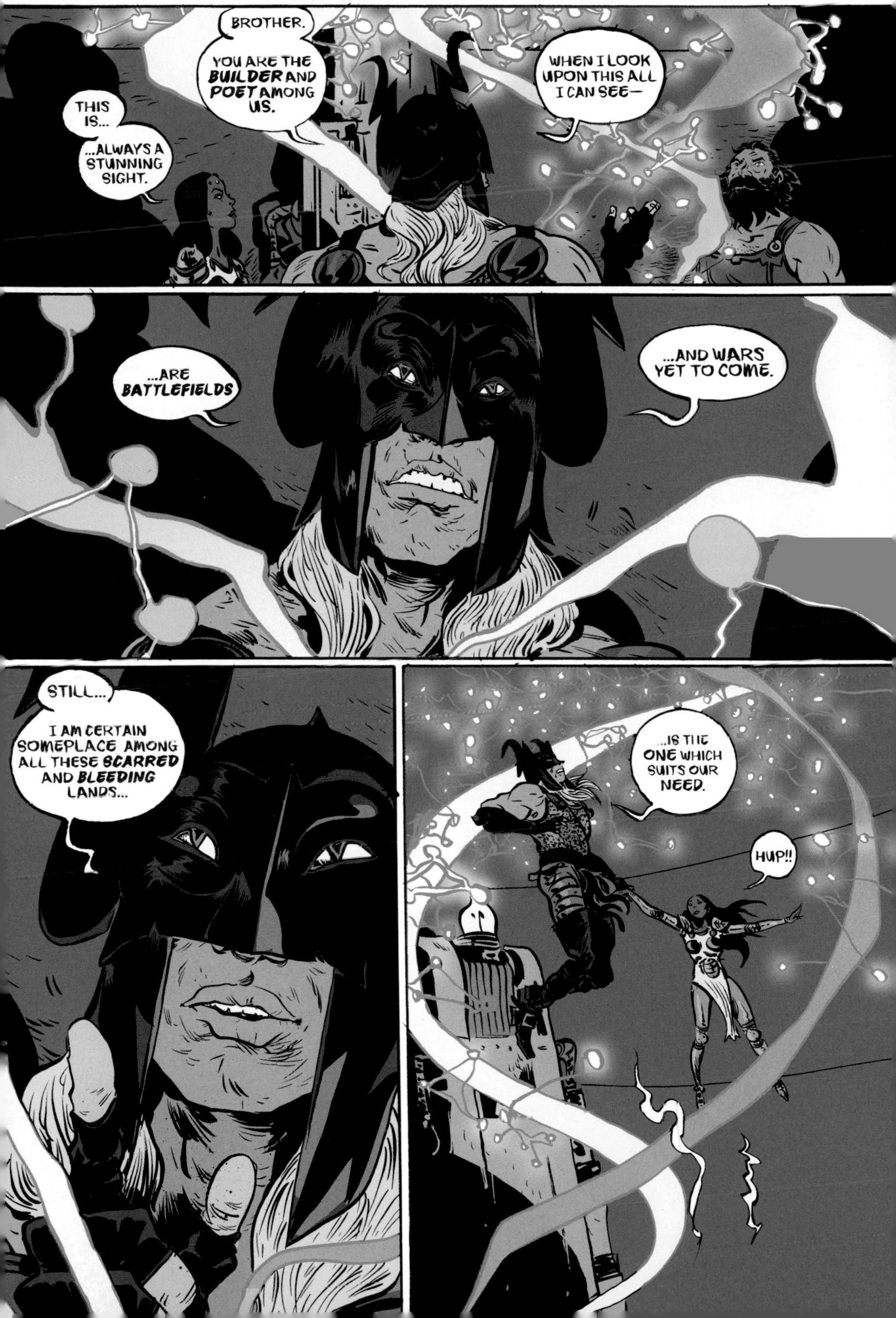
THIS IS... ...ALWAYS A STUNNING SIGHT.
BROTHER.
YOU ARE THE BUILDER AND POET AMONG US.
WHEN I LOOK UPON THIS ALL I CAN SEE—
...ARE BATTLEFIELDS
...AND WARS YET TO COME.
STILL...
I AM CERTAIN SOMEPLACE AMONG ALL THESE SCARRED AND BLEEDING LANDS...
...IS THE ONE WHICH SUITS OUR NEED.
HUP!!

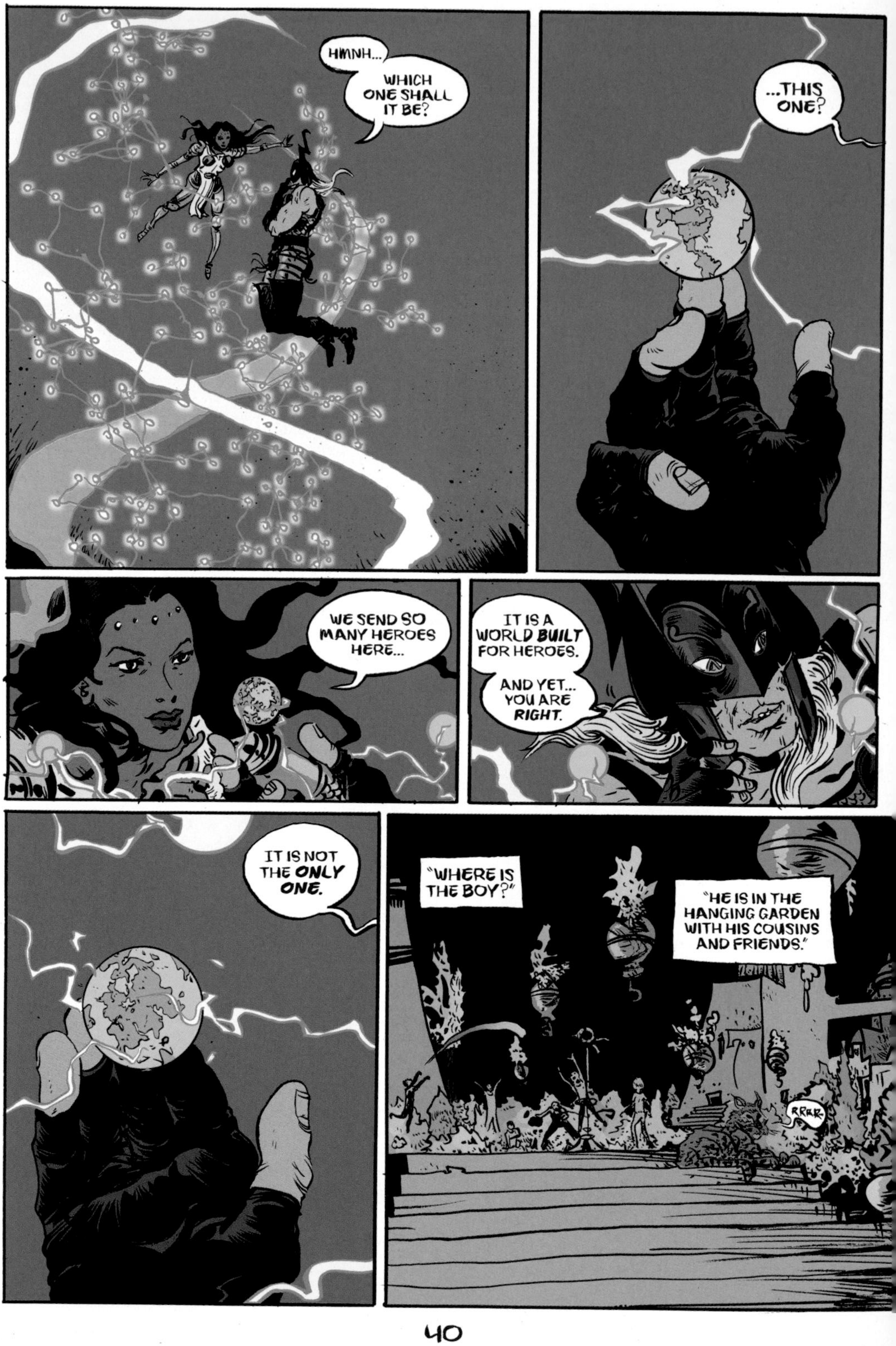
HMNH...
WHICH ONE SHALL IT BE?
...THIS ONE?
WE SEND SO MANY HEROES HERE...
IT IS A WORLD **BUILT** FOR HEROES.
AND YET... YOU ARE **RIGHT**.
IT IS NOT THE **ONLY ONE**.
"WHERE IS THE BOY?"
"HE IS IN THE HANGING GARDEN WITH HIS COUSINS AND FRIENDS."
RRRR-

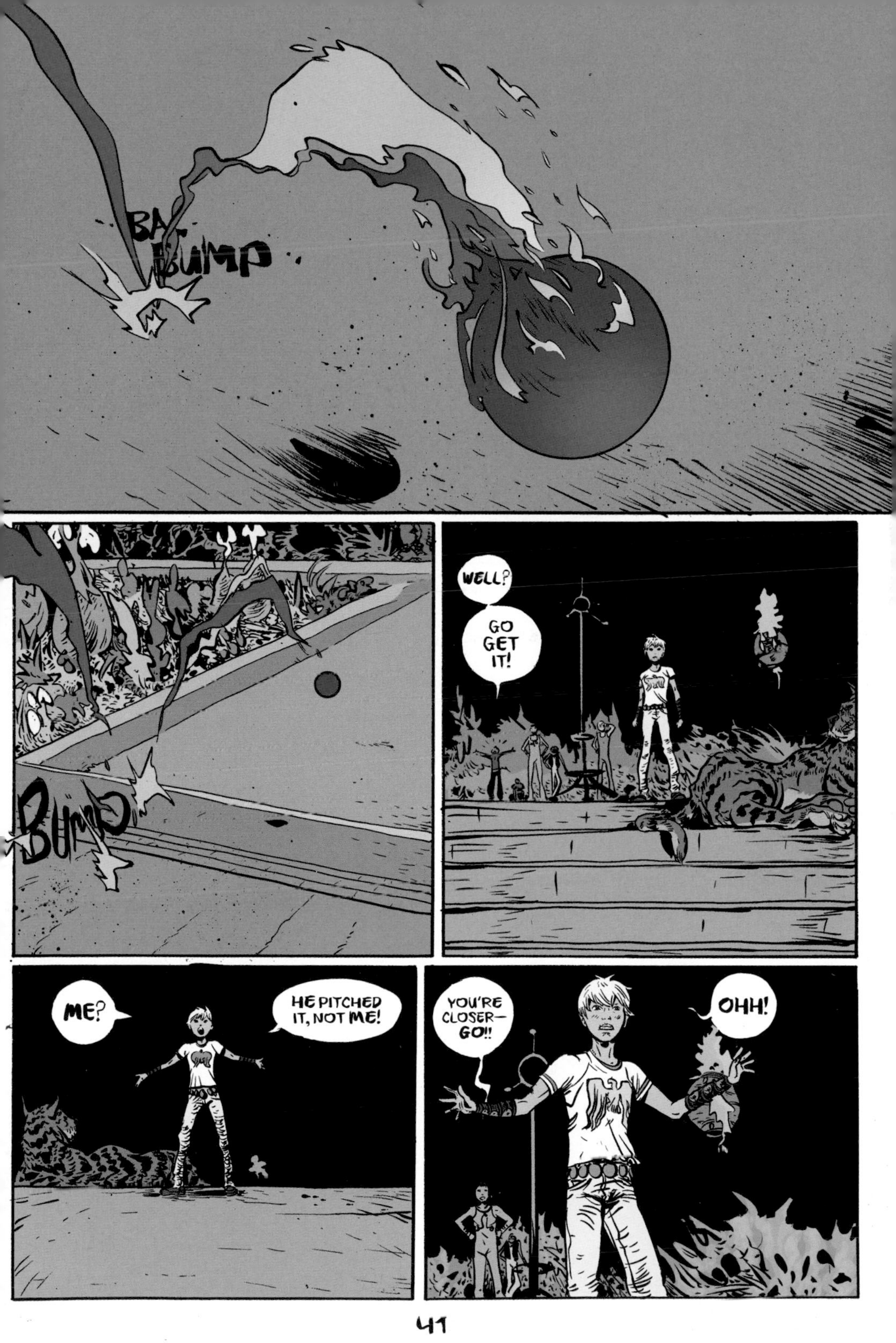
BA-BUMP
BUMP
WELL?
GO GET IT!
ME?
HE PITCHED IT, NOT ME!
YOU'RE CLOSER— GO!!
OHH!

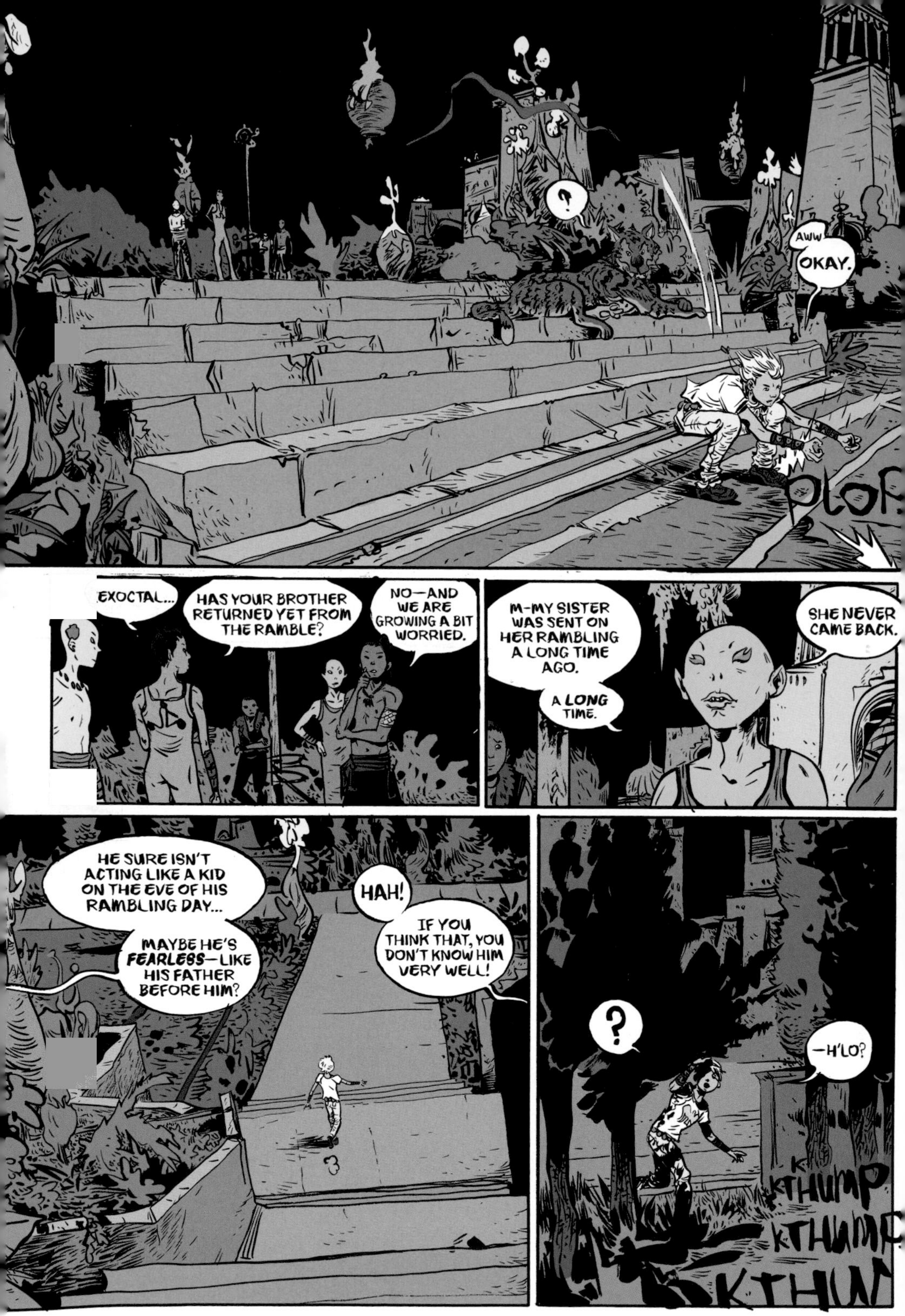
?
AWW
OKAY.
PLOP
EXOCTAL...
HAS YOUR BROTHER RETURNED YET FROM THE RAMBLE?
NO—AND WE ARE GROWING A BIT WORRIED.
M-MY SISTER WAS SENT ON HER RAMBLING A LONG TIME AGO.
A **LONG** TIME.
SHE NEVER CAME BACK.
HE SURE ISN'T ACTING LIKE A KID ON THE EVE OF HIS RAMBLING DAY...
MAYBE HE'S ***FEARLESS***—LIKE HIS FATHER BEFORE HIM?
HAH!
IF YOU THINK THAT, YOU DON'T KNOW HIM VERY WELL!
?
—H'LO?
KTHUMP
KTHUMP
KTHUM

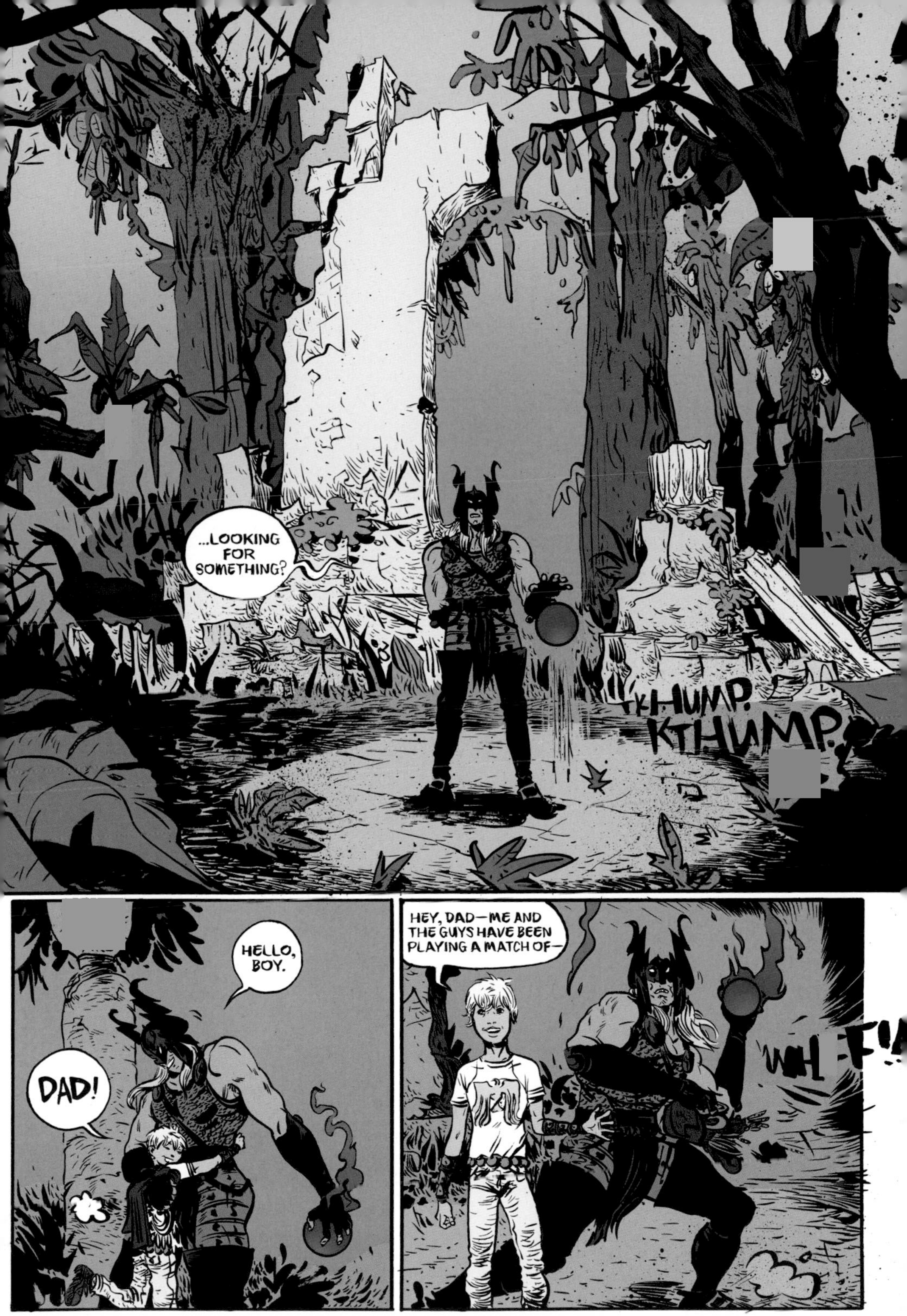
...LOOKING FOR SOMETHING?
KHUMP.
KTHUMP.
HELLO, BOY.
DAD!
HEY, DAD—ME AND THE GUYS HAVE BEEN PLAYING A MATCH OF—

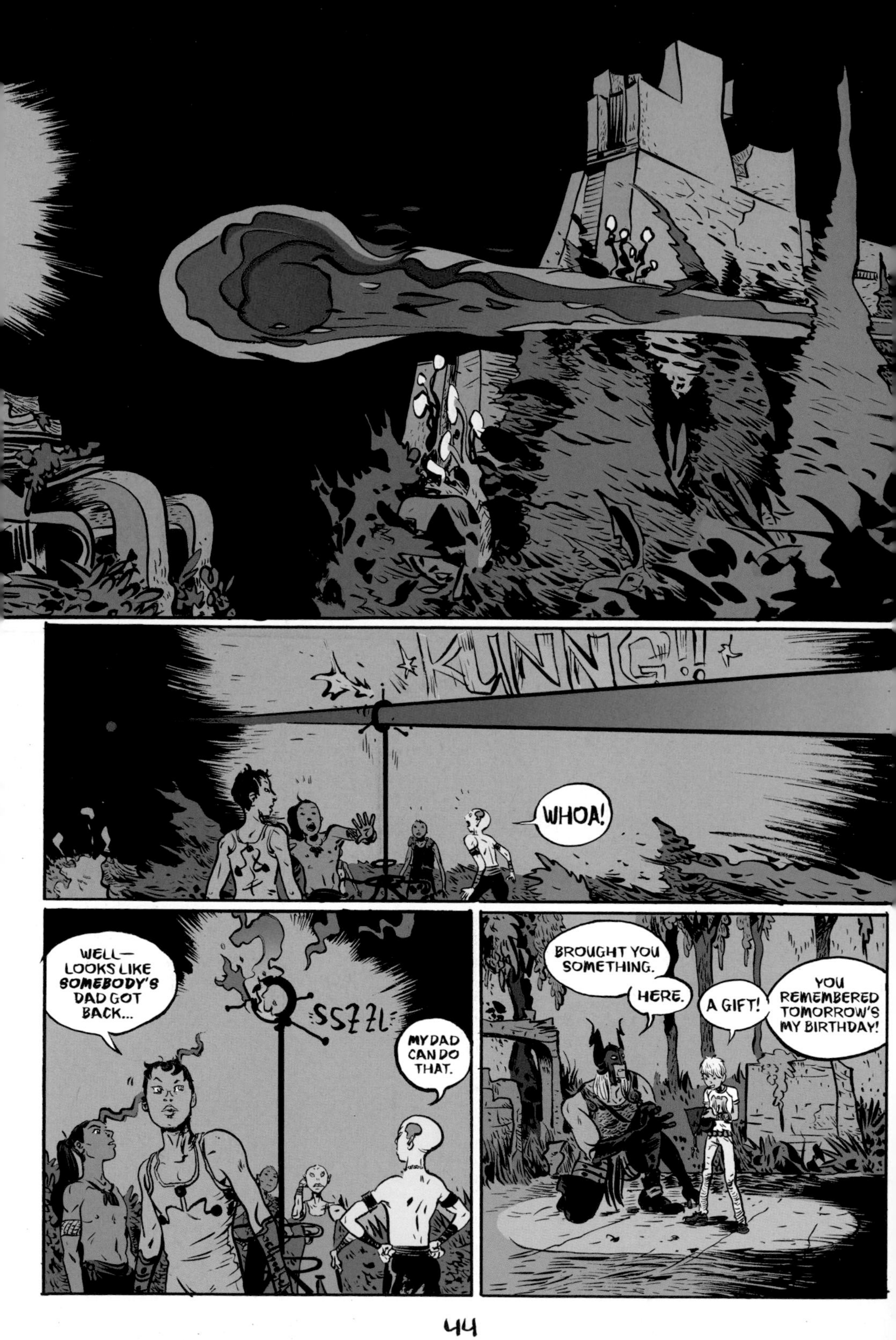
KUNNG!!
WHOA!
WELL— LOOKS LIKE SOMEBODY'S DAD GOT BACK...
SSZZL
MY DAD CAN DO THAT.
BROUGHT YOU SOMETHING.
HERE.
A GIFT!
YOU REMEMBERED TOMORROW'S MY BIRTHDAY!

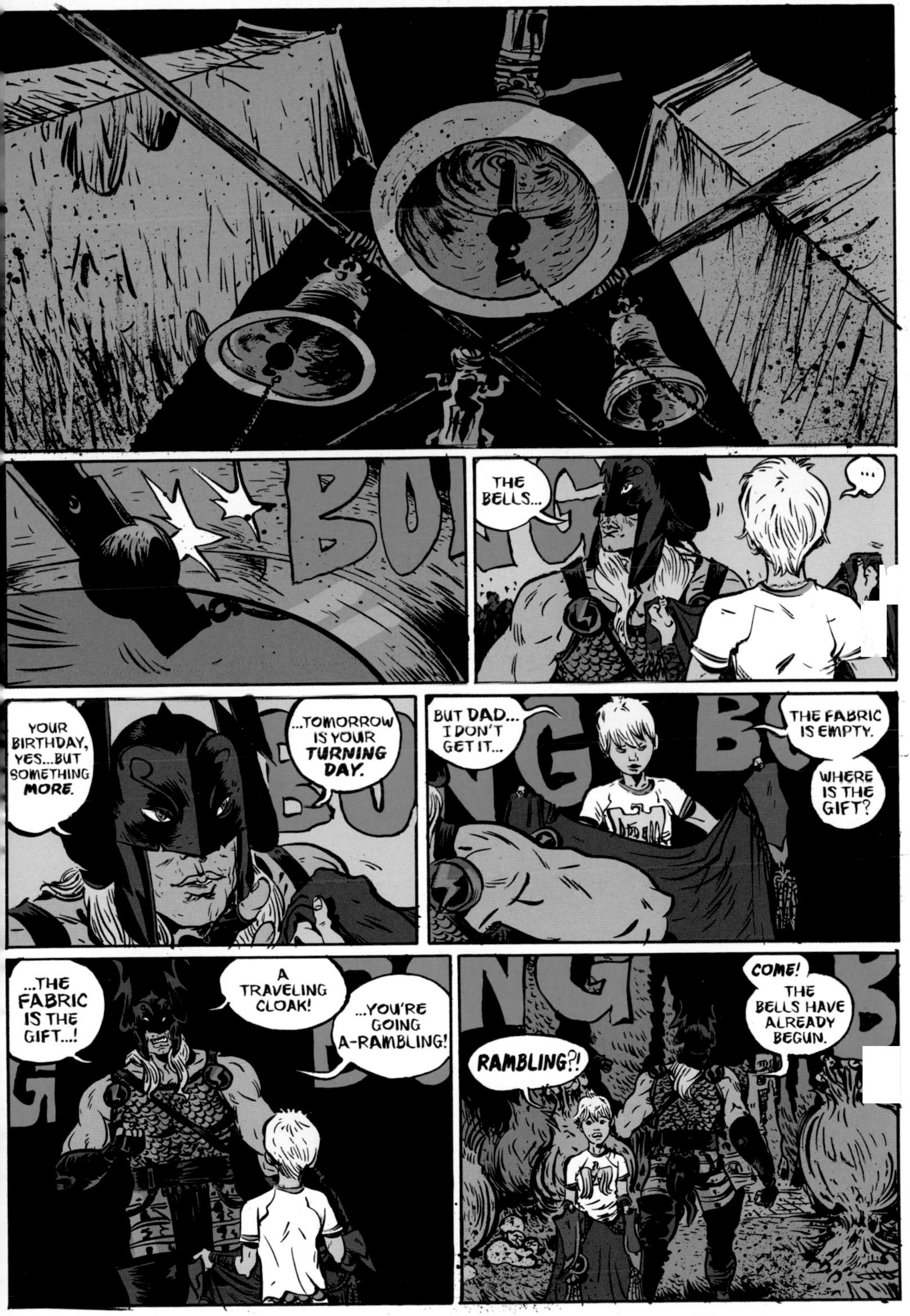

BONG
THE BELLS...
...
YOUR BIRTHDAY, YES...BUT SOMETHING MORE.
...TOMORROW IS YOUR TURNING DAY.
BUT DAD... I DON'T GET IT...
THE FABRIC IS EMPTY.
WHERE IS THE GIFT?
...THE FABRIC IS THE GIFT...!
A TRAVELING CLOAK!
...YOU'RE GOING A-RAMBLING!
RAMBLING?!
COME!
THE BELLS HAVE ALREADY BEGUN.

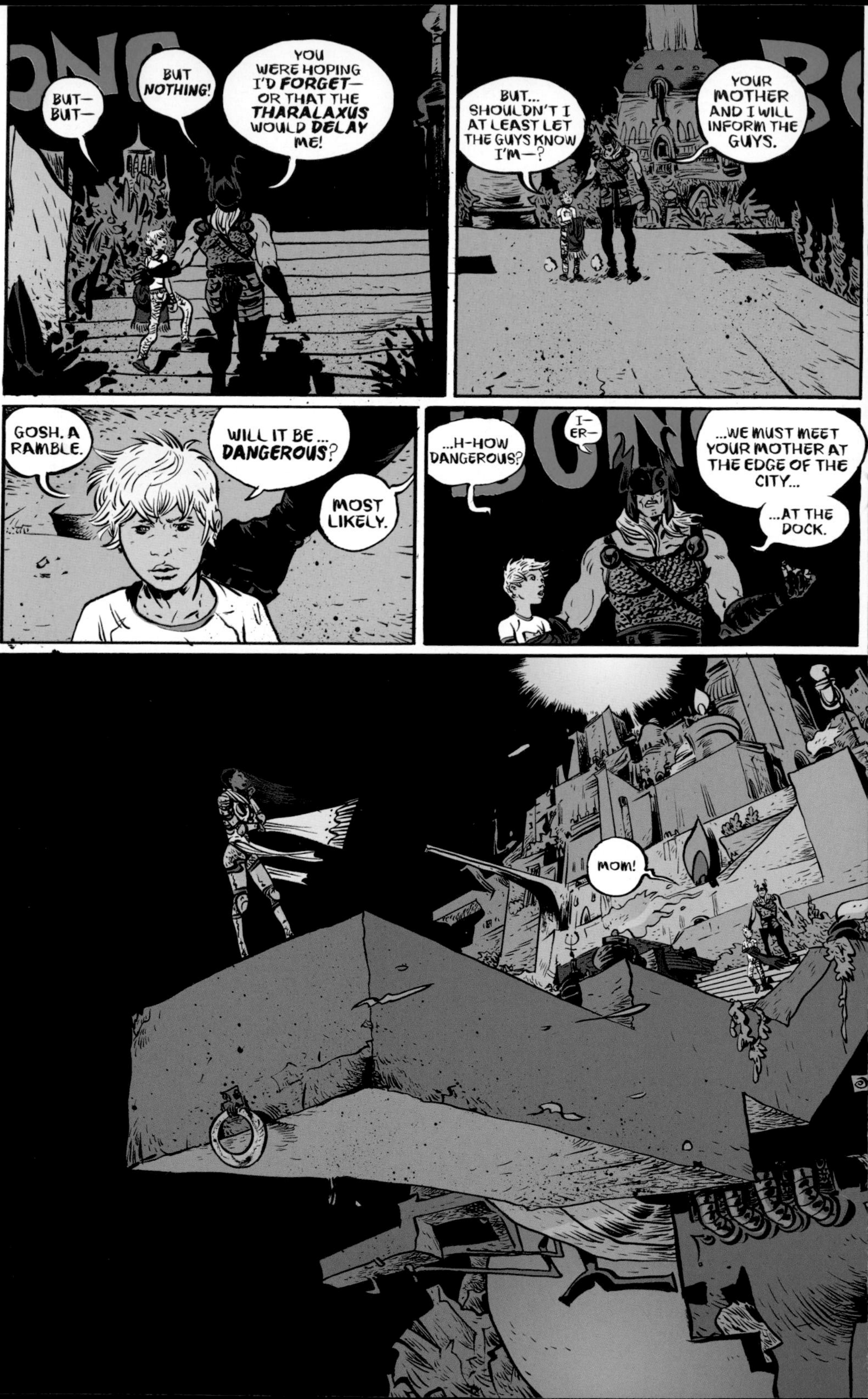
BONG
BUT—
BUT—
BUT NOTHING!
YOU WERE HOPING I'D FORGET— OR THAT THE THARALAXUS WOULD DELAY ME!
BUT... SHOULDN'T I AT LEAST LET THE GUYS KNOW I'M—?
YOUR MOTHER AND I WILL INFORM THE GUYS.
GOSH. A RAMBLE.
WILL IT BE ... DANGEROUS?
MOST LIKELY.
...H-HOW DANGEROUS?
I—
ER—
...WE MUST MEET YOUR MOTHER AT THE EDGE OF THE CITY...
...AT THE DOCK.
MOM!

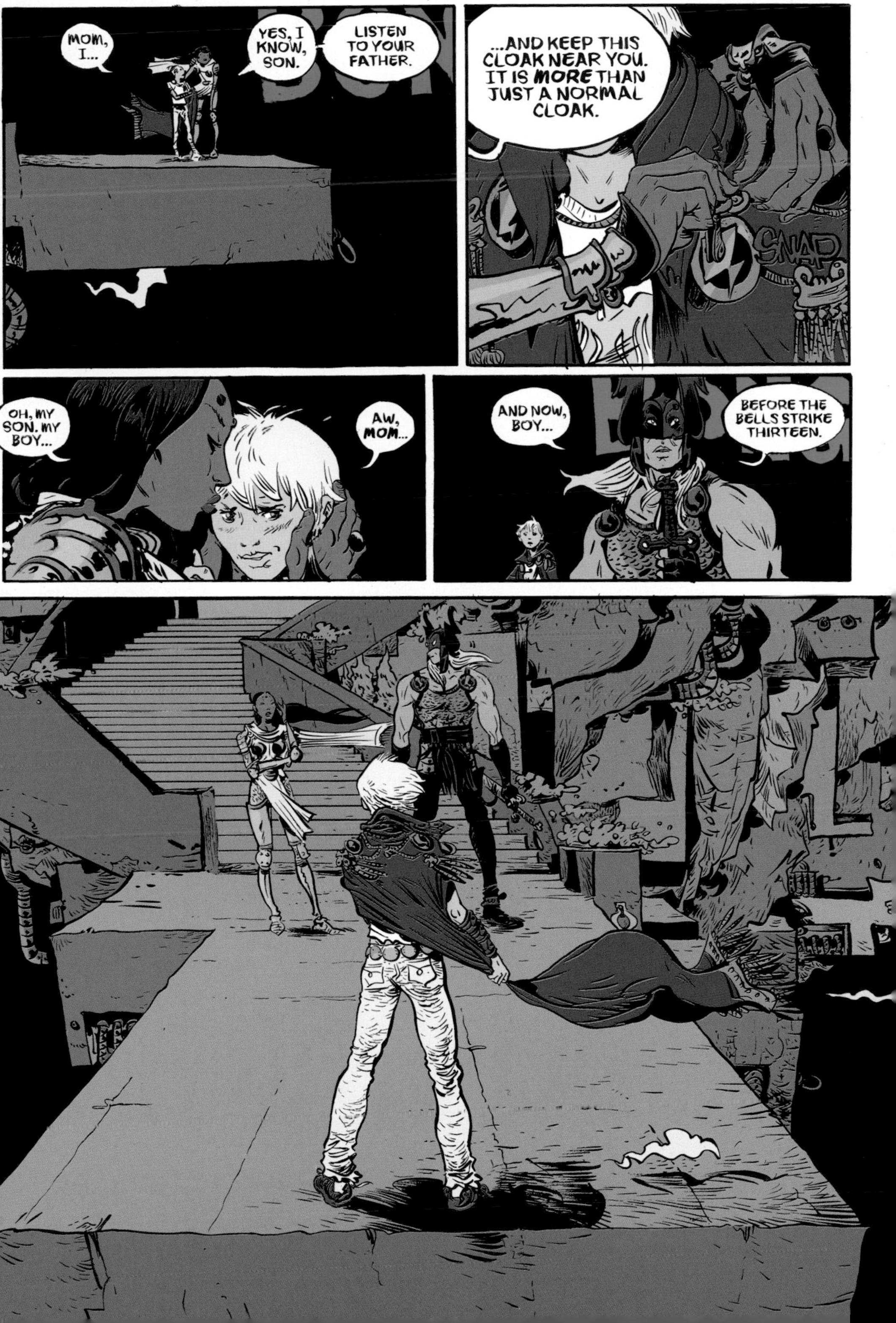
MOM, I...
YES, I KNOW, SON.
LISTEN TO YOUR FATHER.
...AND KEEP THIS CLOAK NEAR YOU. IT IS MORE THAN JUST A NORMAL CLOAK.
SNAP
OH, MY SON. MY BOY...
AW, MOM...
AND NOW, BOY...
BEFORE THE BELLS STRIKE THIRTEEN.

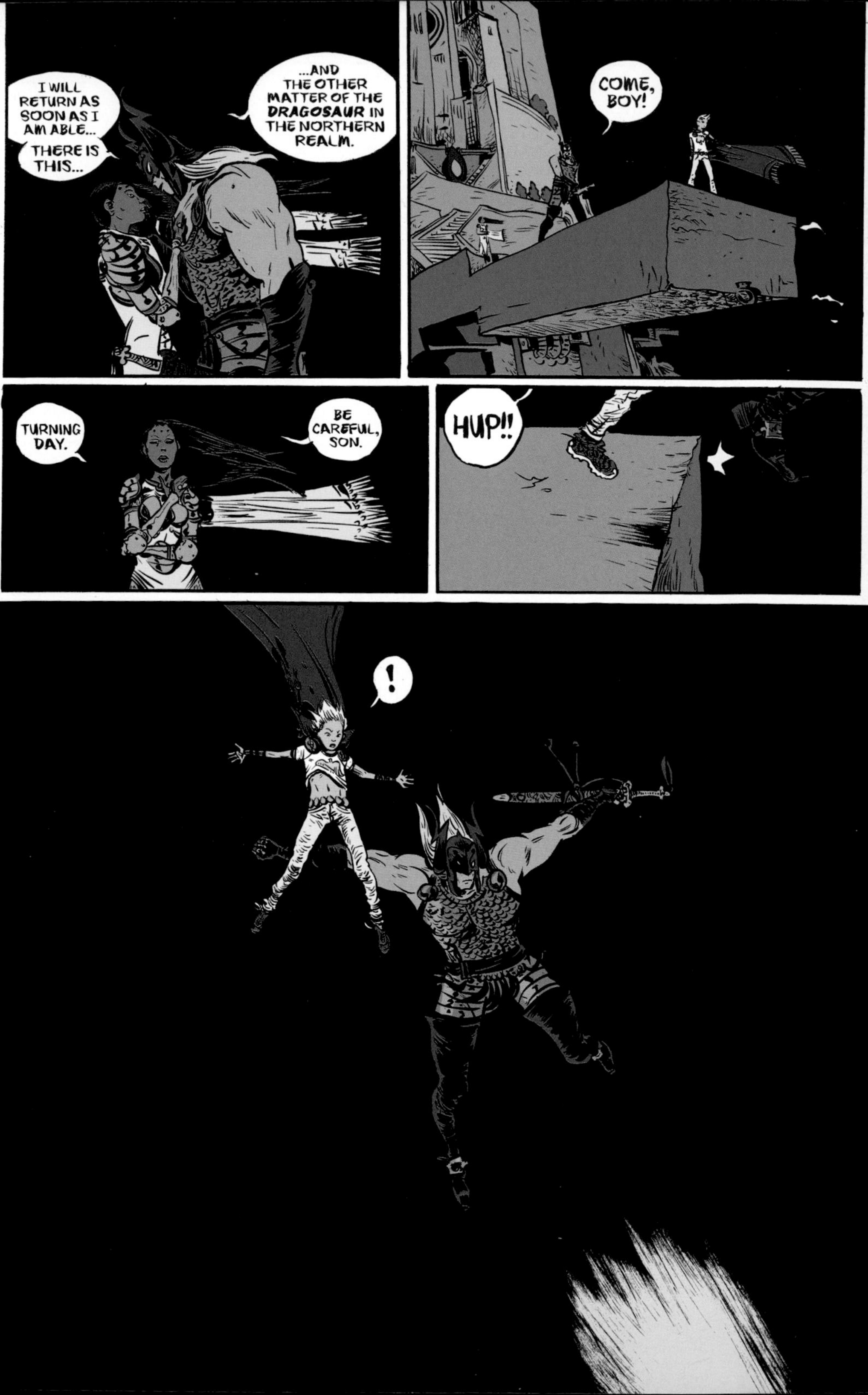
I WILL RETURN AS SOON AS I AM ABLE...
THERE IS THIS...
...AND THE OTHER MATTER OF THE DRAGOSAUR IN THE NORTHERN REALM.
COME, BOY!
TURNING DAY.
BE CAREFUL, SON.
HUP!!
!

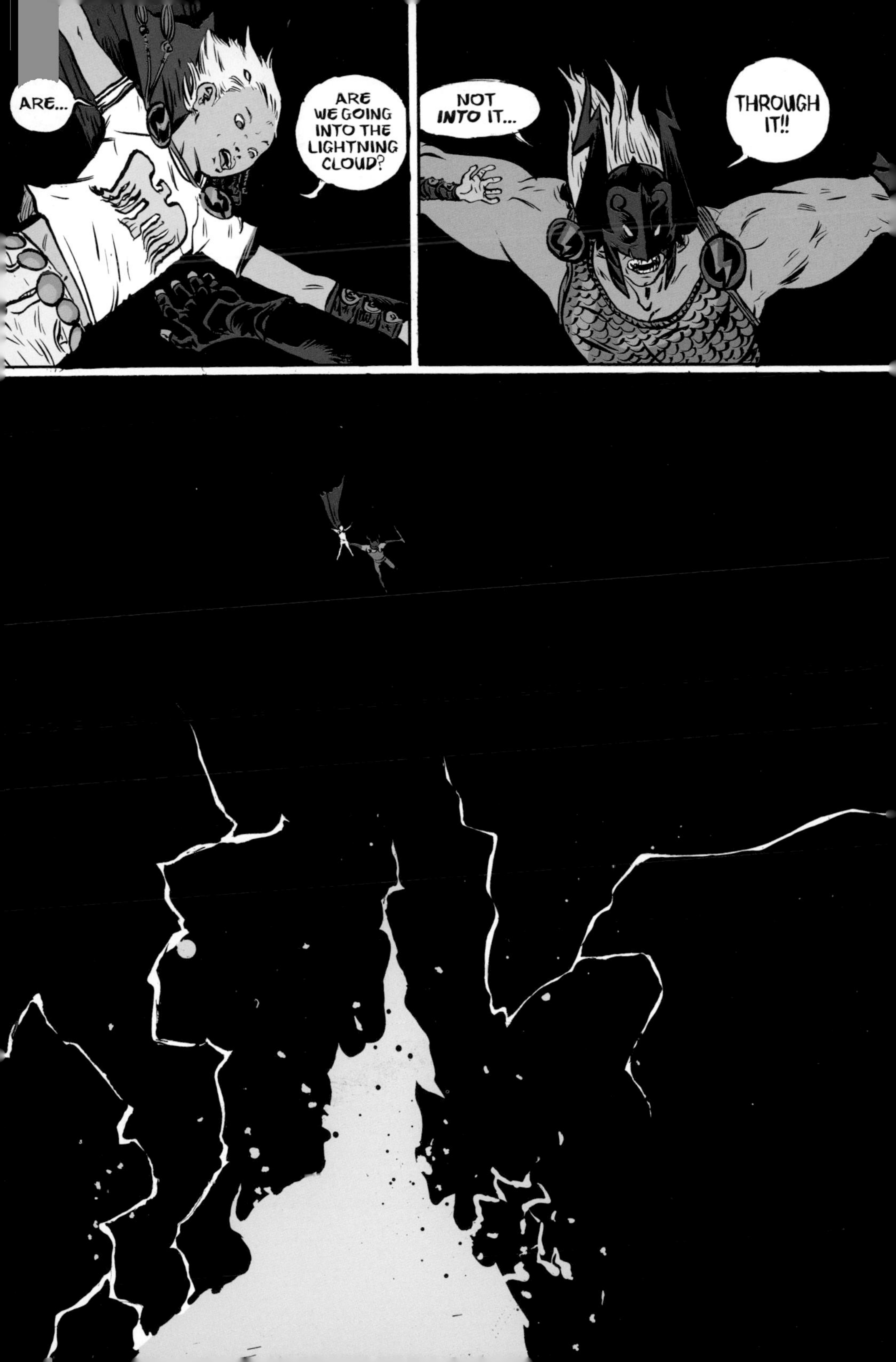
ARE...
ARE WE GOING INTO THE LIGHTNING CLOUD?
NOT INTO IT...
THROUGH IT!!

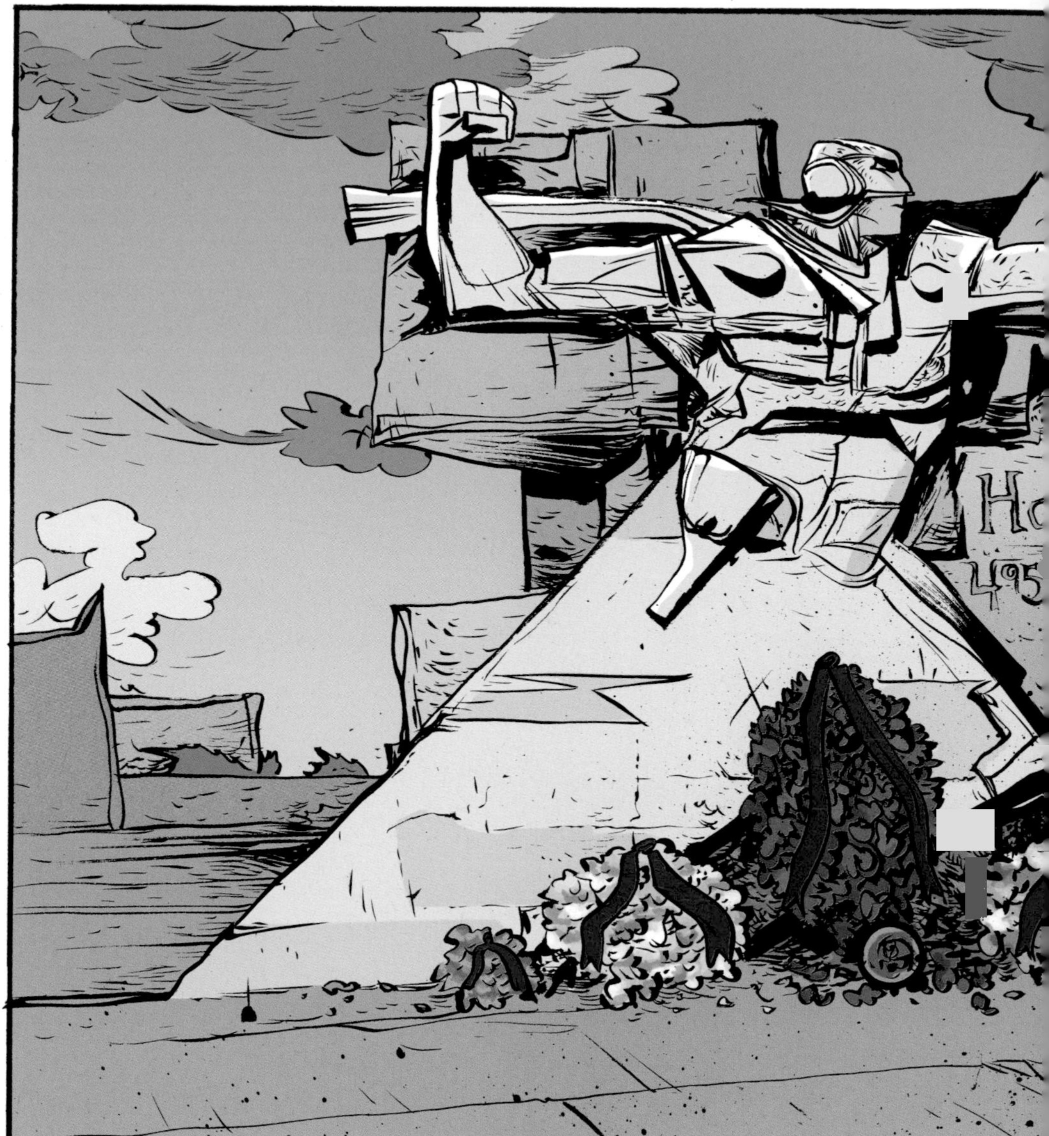

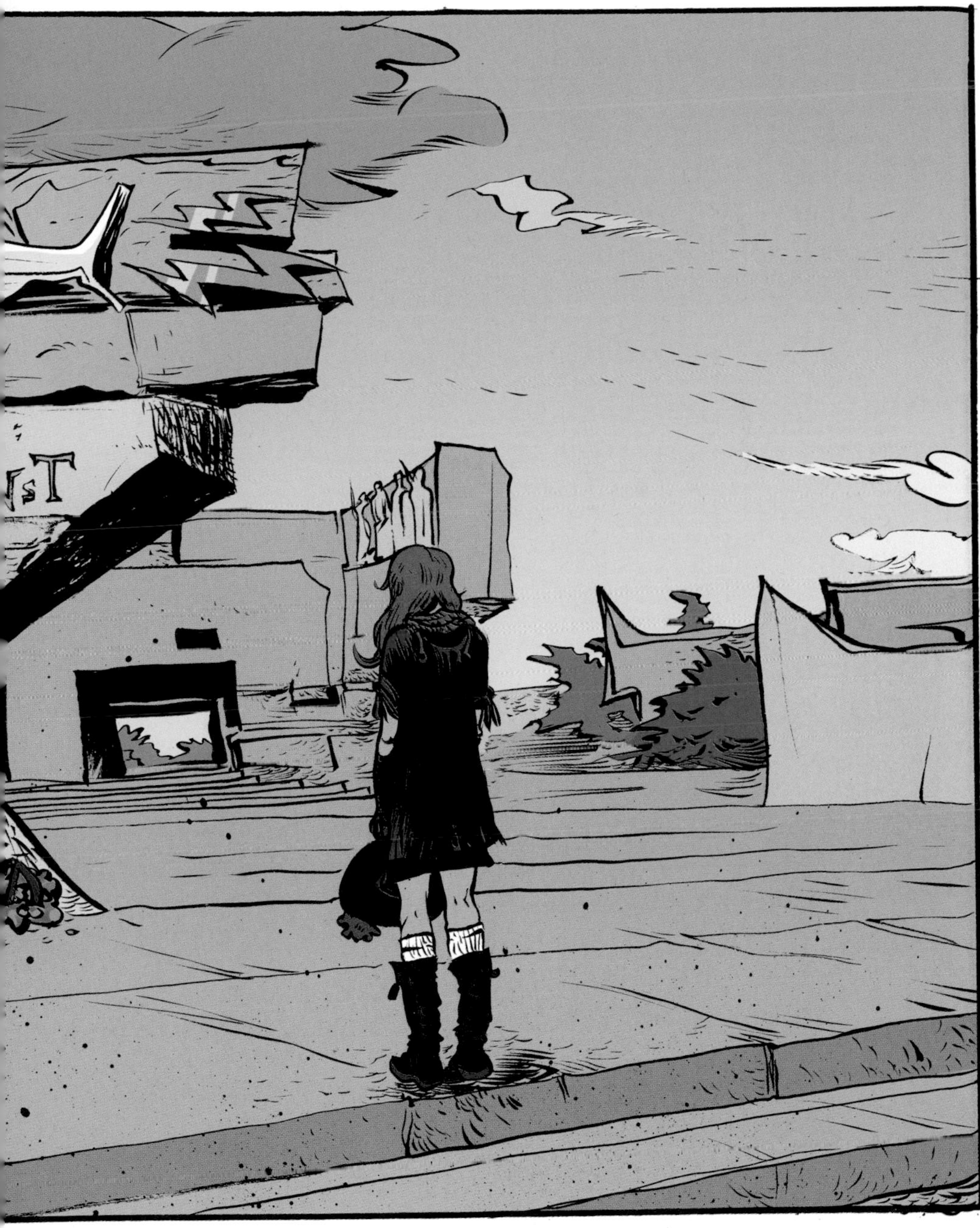

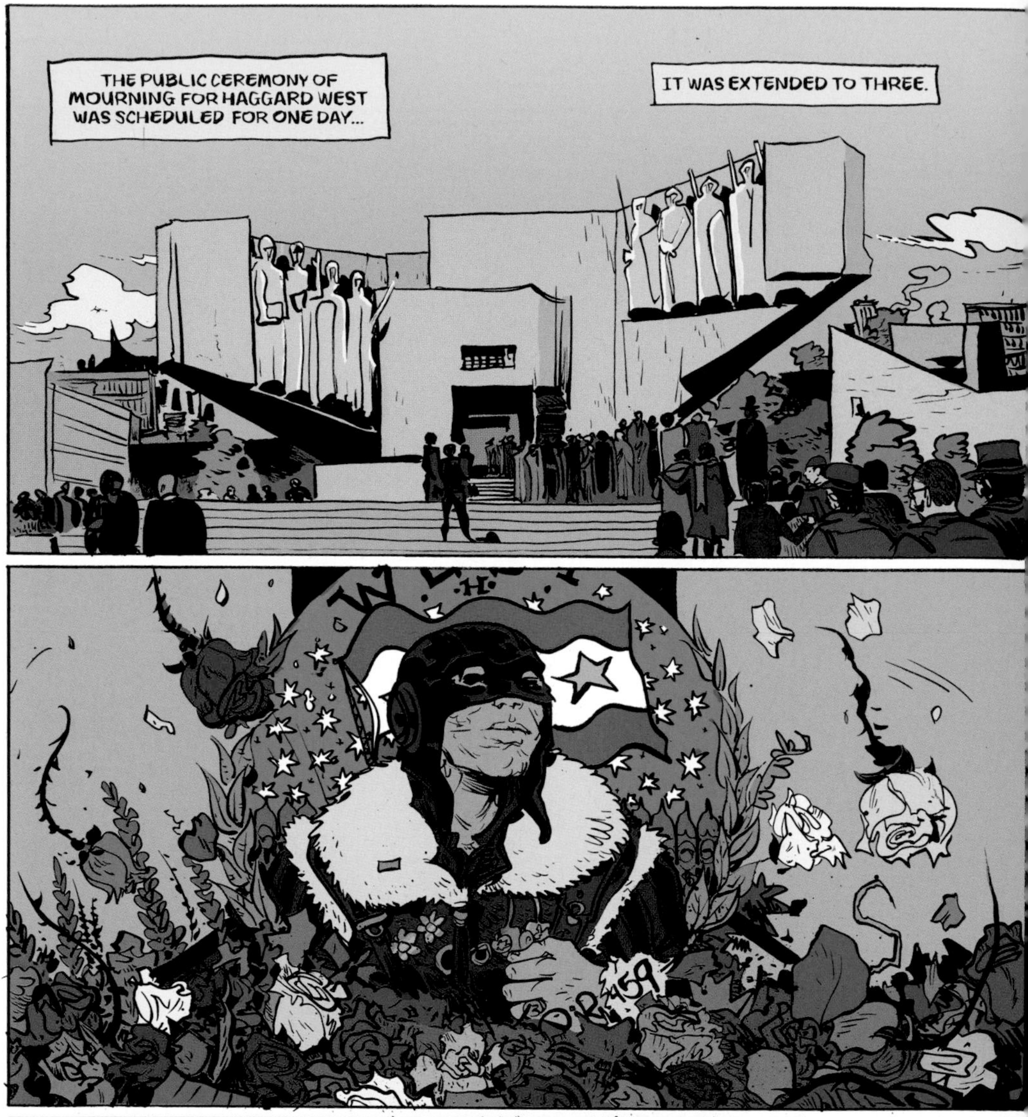
THE PUBLIC CEREMONY OF MOURNING FOR HAGGARD WEST WAS SCHEDULED FOR ONE DAY...
IT WAS EXTENDED TO THREE.
THE PRIVATE FUNERAL FOLLOWED.
A SOMBER AFFAIR, BY NECESSITY CLOSED-CASKET...AND IT RAINED.

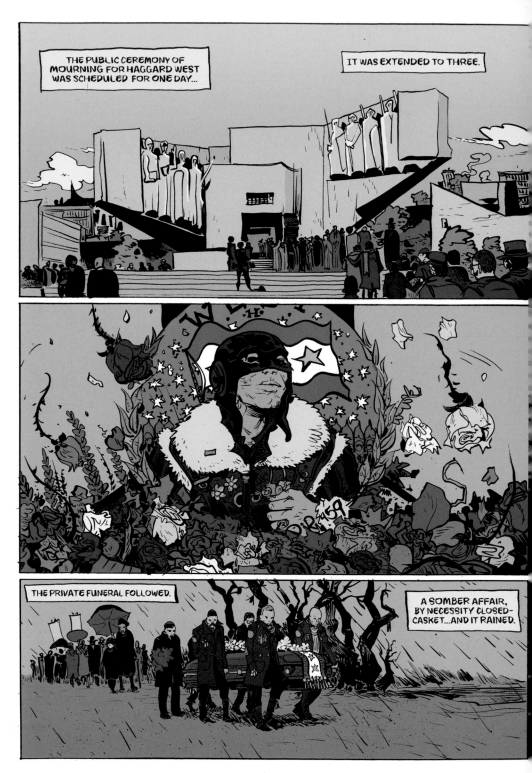

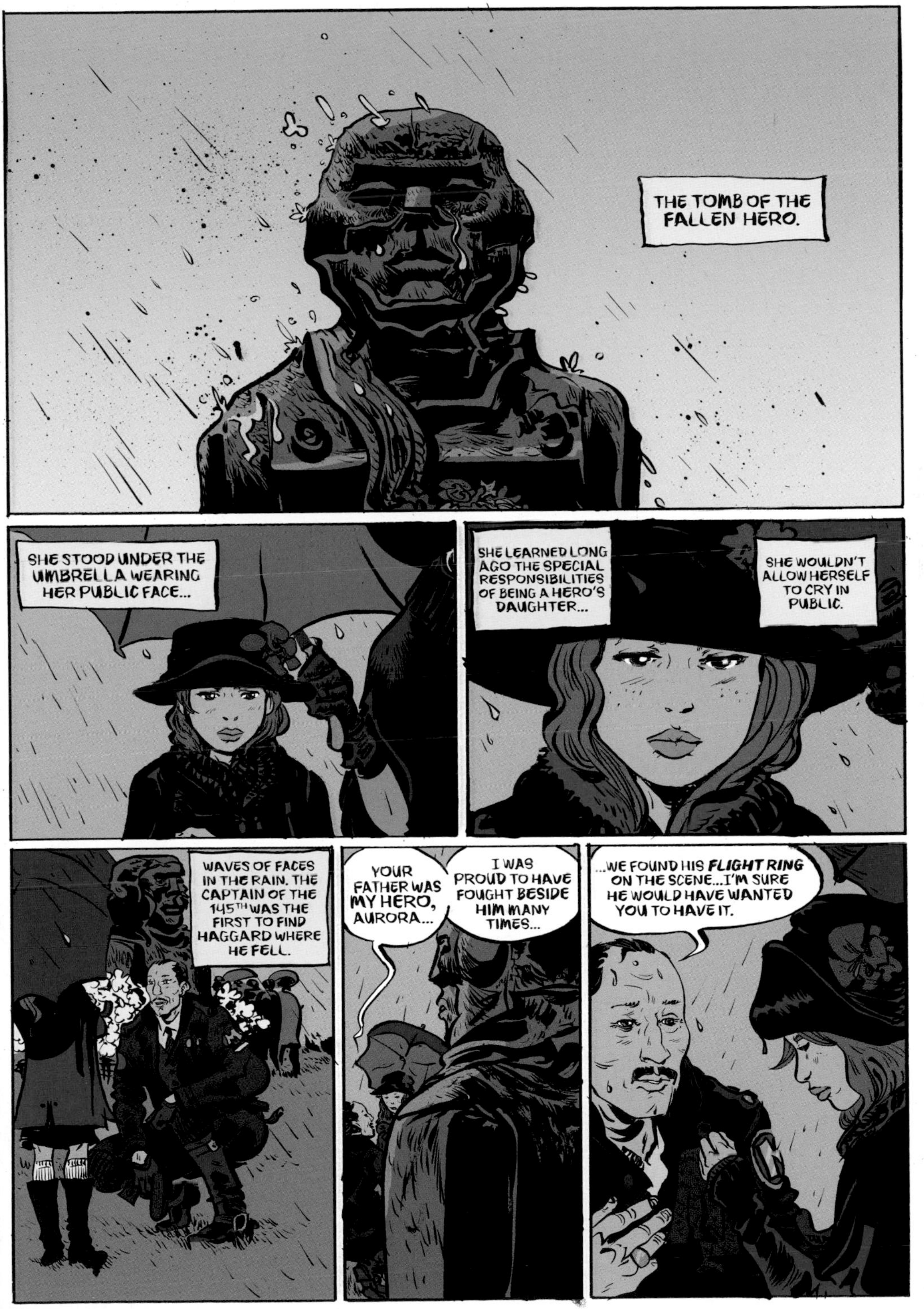
THE TOMB OF THE FALLEN HERO.
SHE STOOD UNDER THE UMBRELLA WEARING HER PUBLIC FACE...
SHE LEARNED LONG AGO THE SPECIAL RESPONSIBILITIES OF BEING A HERO'S DAUGHTER...
SHE WOULDN'T ALLOW HERSELF TO CRY IN PUBLIC.
WAVES OF FACES IN THE RAIN. THE CAPTAIN OF THE 145TH WAS THE FIRST TO FIND HAGGARD WHERE HE FELL.
YOUR FATHER WAS MY HERO, AURORA...
I WAS PROUD TO HAVE FOUGHT BESIDE HIM MANY TIMES...
...WE FOUND HIS FLIGHT RING ON THE SCENE...I'M SURE HE WOULD HAVE WANTED YOU TO HAVE IT.

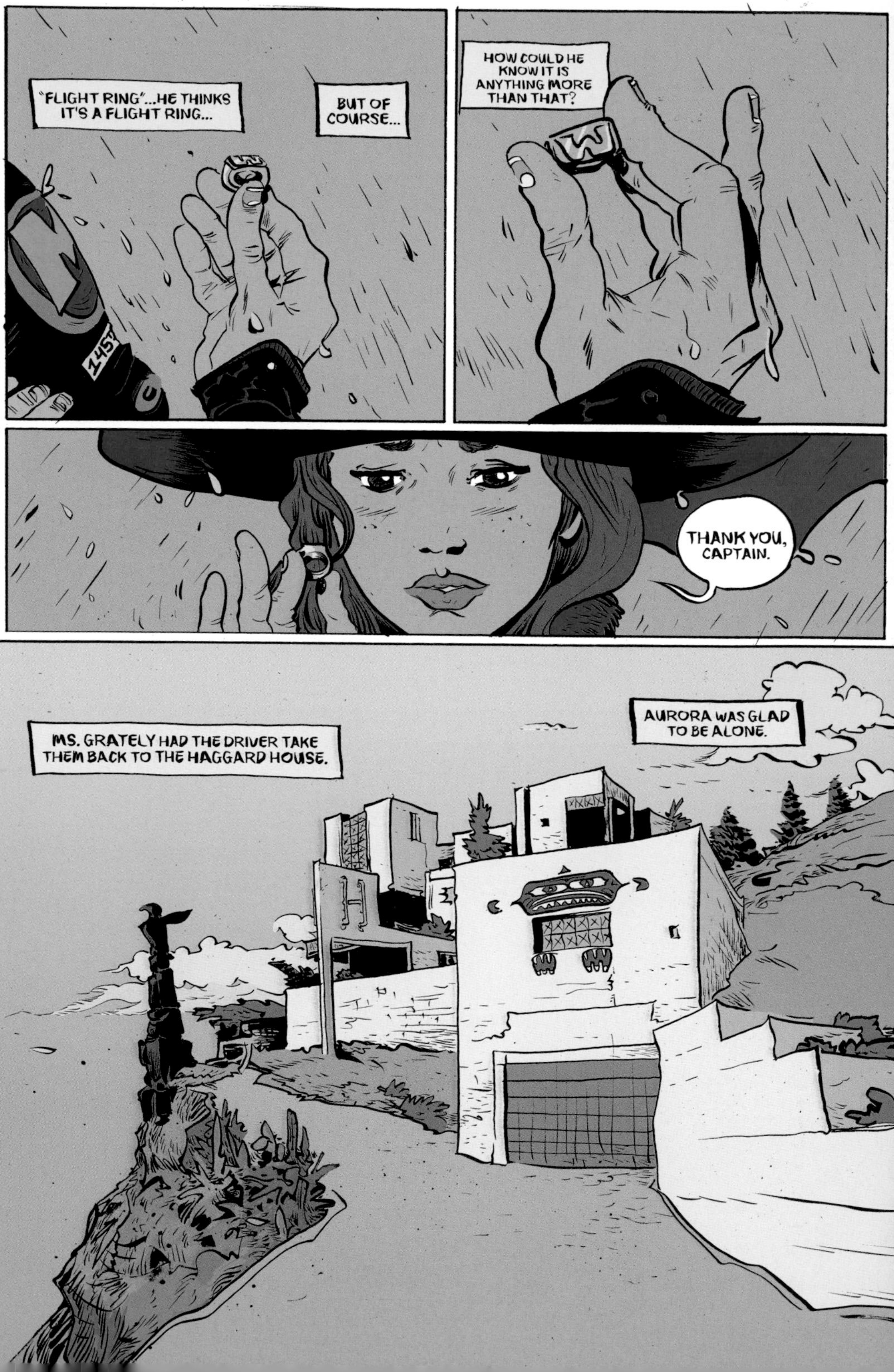
"FLIGHT RING"...HE THINKS IT'S A FLIGHT RING...
BUT OF COURSE...
HOW COULD HE KNOW IT IS ANYTHING MORE THAN THAT?
THANK YOU, CAPTAIN.
MS. GRATELY HAD THE DRIVER TAKE THEM BACK TO THE HAGGARD HOUSE.
AURORA WAS GLAD TO BE ALONE.

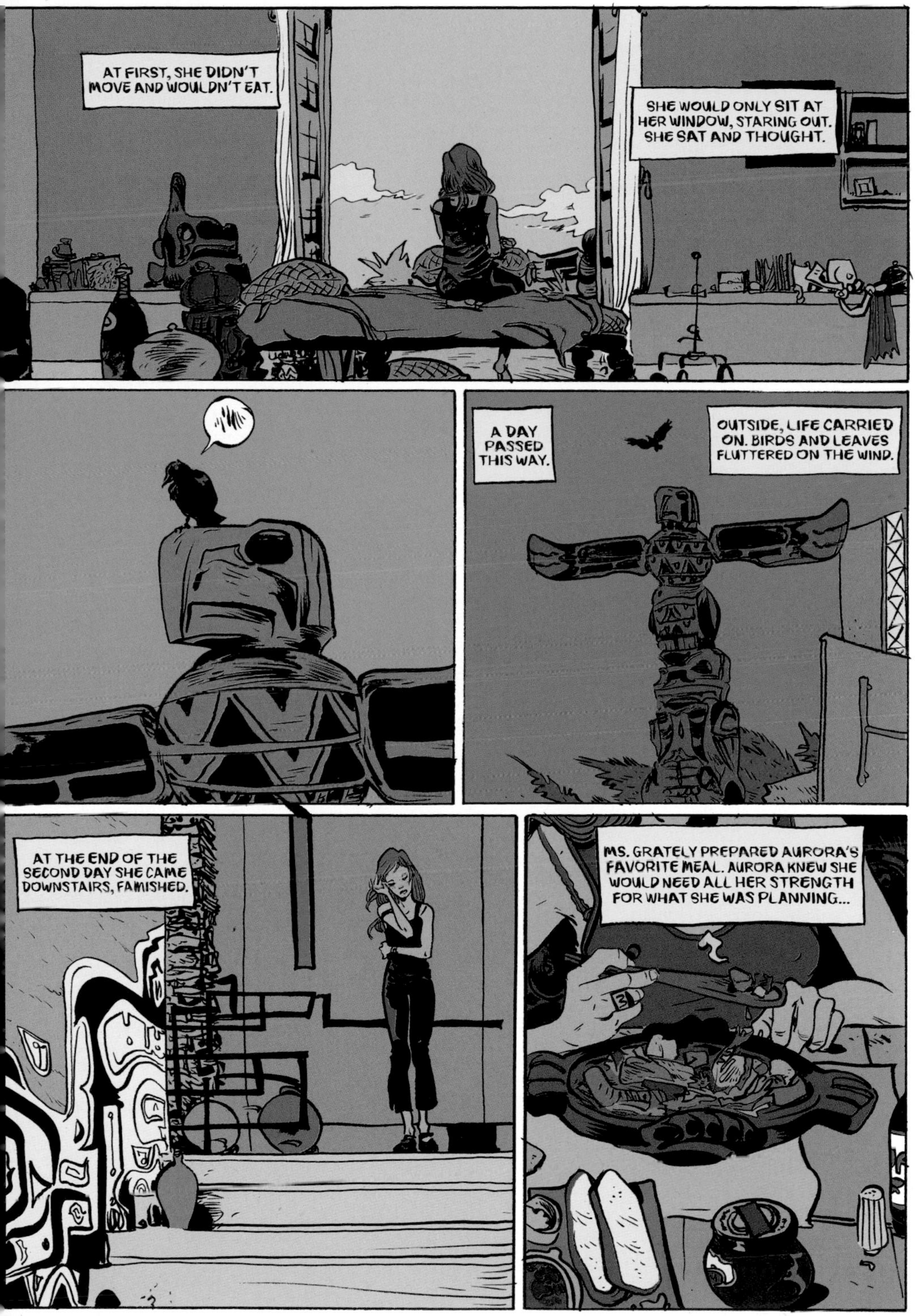
AT FIRST, SHE DIDN'T MOVE AND WOULDN'T EAT.
SHE WOULD ONLY SIT AT HER WINDOW, STARING OUT. SHE SAT AND THOUGHT.
A DAY PASSED THIS WAY.
OUTSIDE, LIFE CARRIED ON. BIRDS AND LEAVES FLUTTERED ON THE WIND.
AT THE END OF THE SECOND DAY SHE CAME DOWNSTAIRS, FAMISHED.
MS. GRATELY PREPARED AURORA'S FAVORITE MEAL. AURORA KNEW SHE WOULD NEED ALL HER STRENGTH FOR WHAT SHE WAS PLANNING...

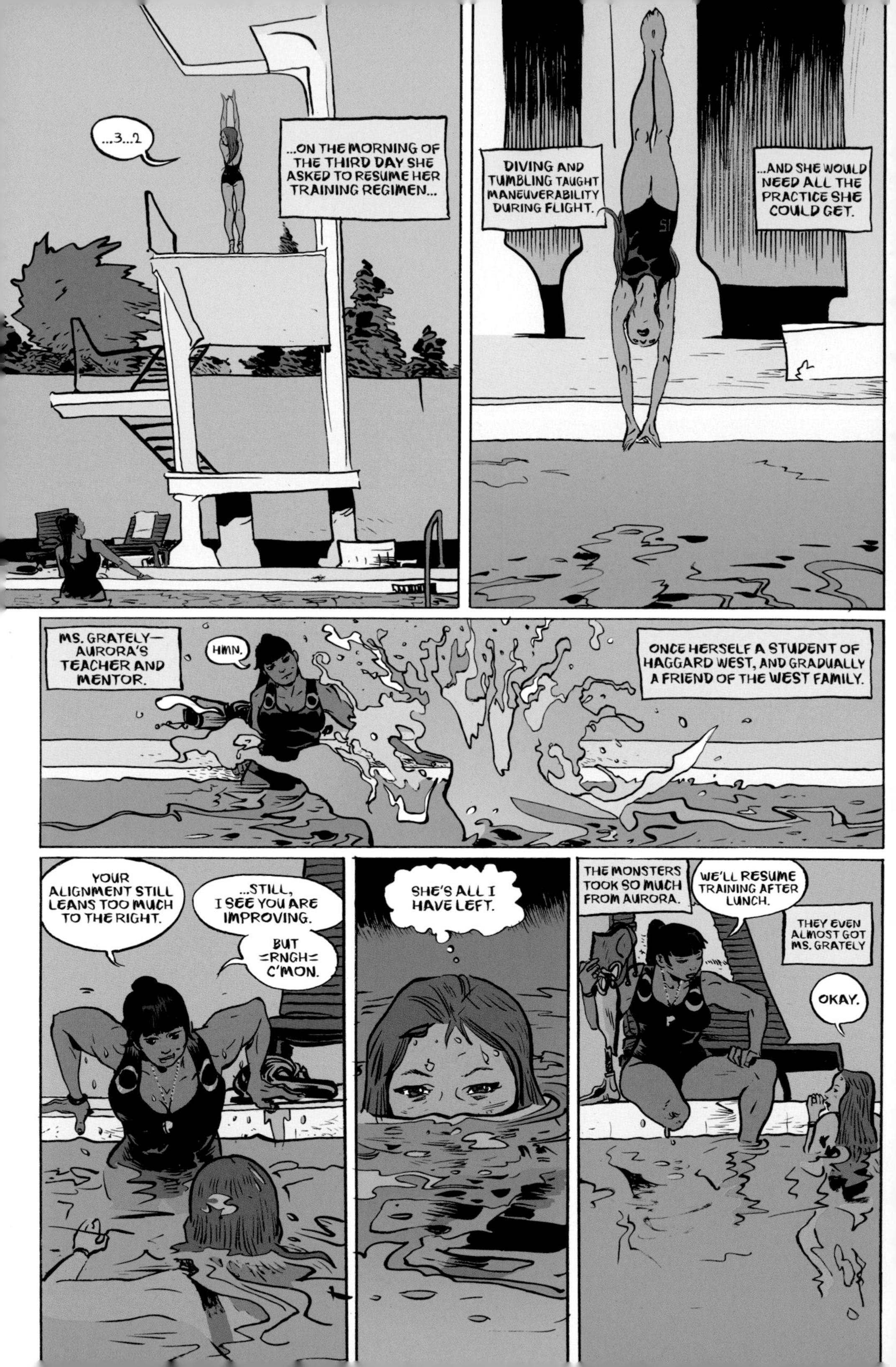
...3...2
...ON THE MORNING OF THE THIRD DAY SHE ASKED TO RESUME HER TRAINING REGIMEN...
DIVING AND TUMBLING TAUGHT MANEUVERABILITY DURING FLIGHT.
...AND SHE WOULD NEED ALL THE PRACTICE SHE COULD GET.
MS. GRATELY— AURORA'S TEACHER AND MENTOR.
HMN.
ONCE HERSELF A STUDENT OF HAGGARD WEST, AND GRADUALLY A FRIEND OF THE WEST FAMILY.
YOUR ALIGNMENT STILL LEANS TOO MUCH TO THE RIGHT.
...STILL, I SEE YOU ARE IMPROVING.
BUT =RNGH= C'MON.
SHE'S ALL I HAVE LEFT.
THE MONSTERS TOOK SO MUCH FROM AURORA.
WE'LL RESUME TRAINING AFTER LUNCH.
THEY EVEN ALMOST GOT MS. GRATELY
OKAY.

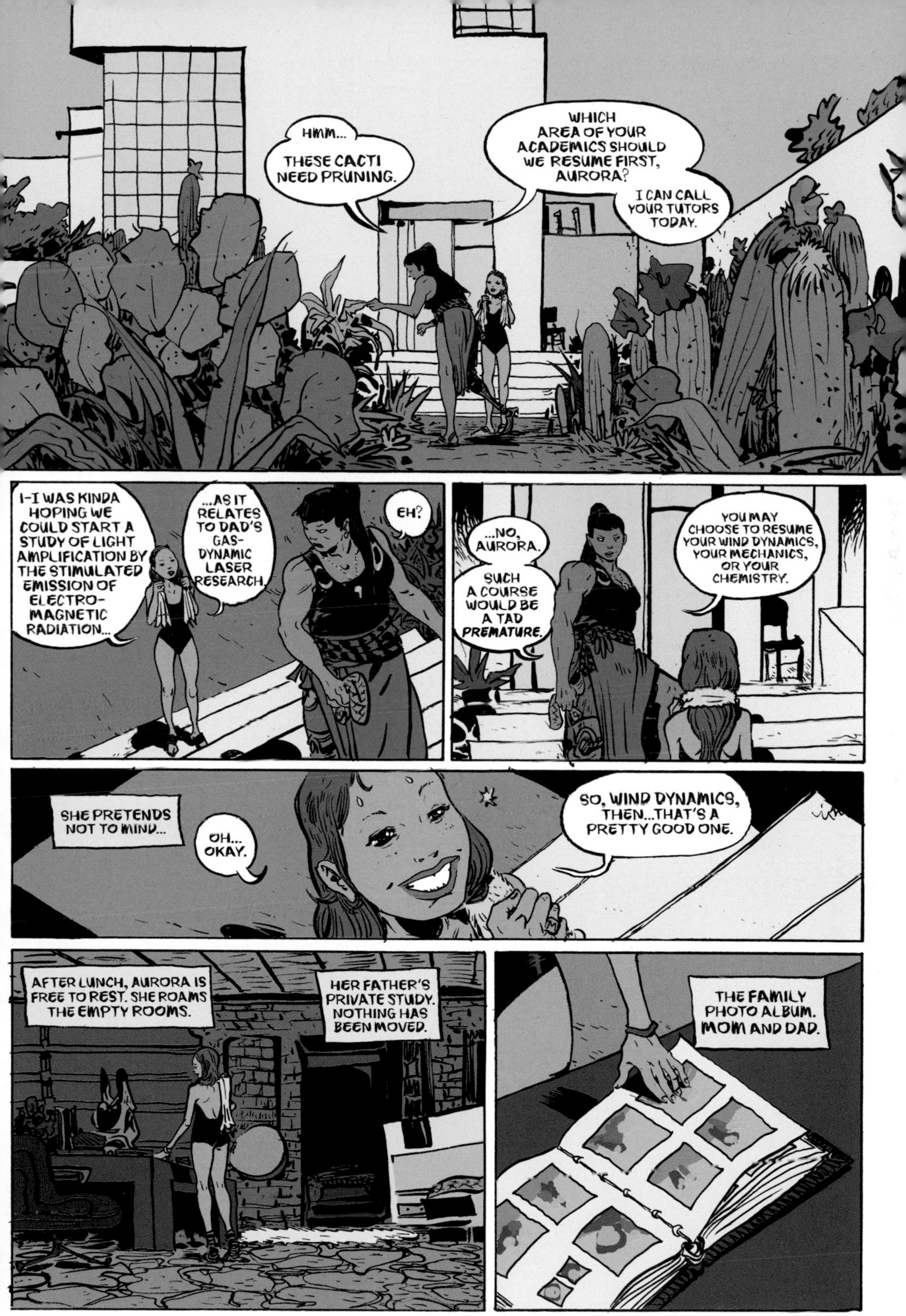
HMM...
THESE CACTI NEED PRUNING.
WHICH AREA OF YOUR ACADEMICS SHOULD WE RESUME FIRST, AURORA?
I CAN CALL YOUR TUTORS TODAY.
I-I WAS KINDA HOPING WE COULD START A STUDY OF LIGHT AMPLIFICATION BY THE STIMULATED EMISSION OF ELECTRO-MAGNETIC RADIATION...
...AS IT RELATES TO DAD'S GAS-DYNAMIC LASER RESEARCH.
EH?
...NO, AURORA.
SUCH A COURSE WOULD BE A TAD PREMATURE.
YOU MAY CHOOSE TO RESUME YOUR WIND DYNAMICS, YOUR MECHANICS, OR YOUR CHEMISTRY.
SHE PRETENDS NOT TO MIND...
OH... OKAY.
SO, WIND DYNAMICS, THEN...THAT'S A PRETTY GOOD ONE.
AFTER LUNCH, AURORA IS FREE TO REST. SHE ROAMS THE EMPTY ROOMS.
HER FATHER'S PRIVATE STUDY. NOTHING HAS BEEN MOVED.
THE FAMILY PHOTO ALBUM. MOM AND DAD.

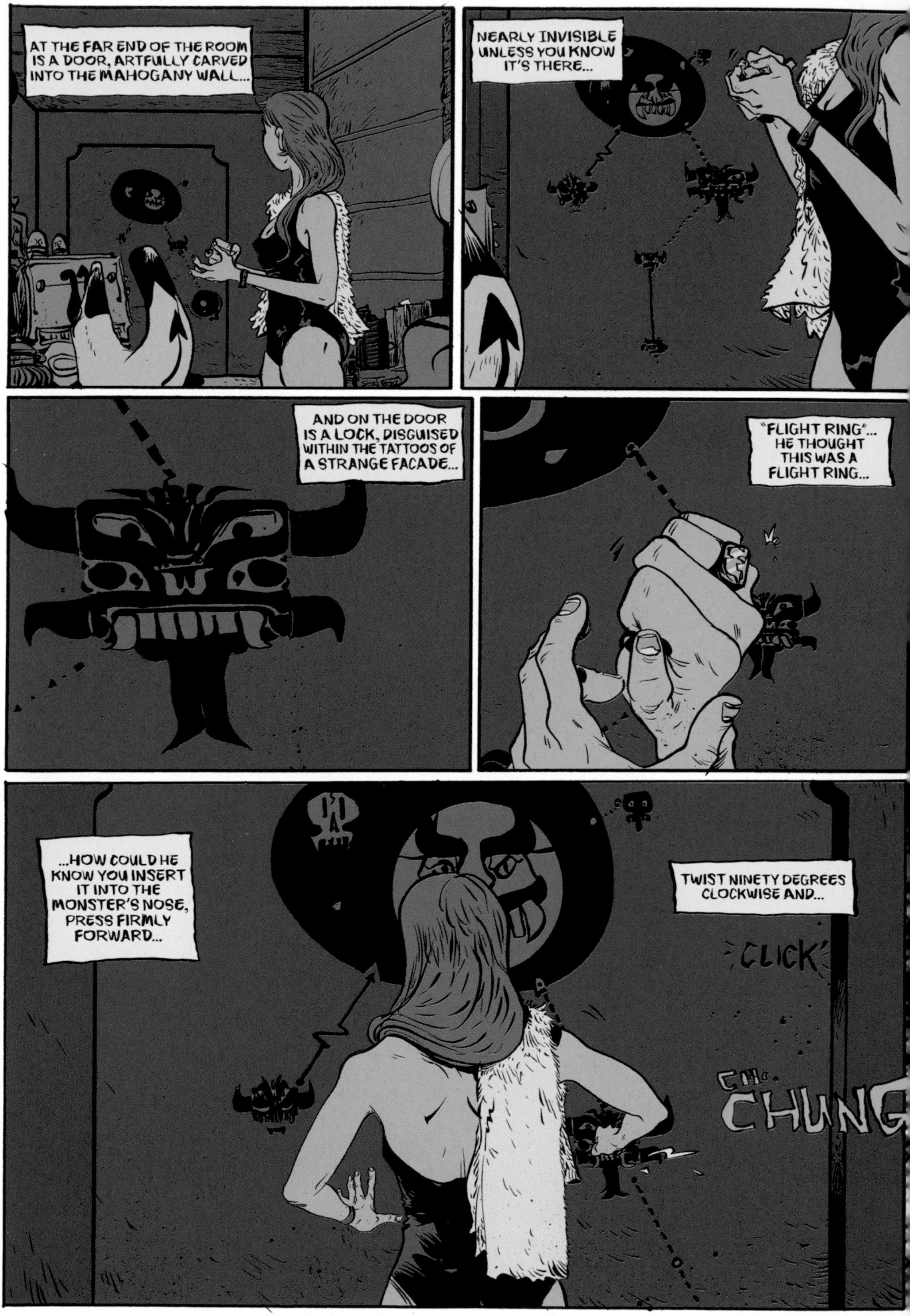
AT THE FAR END OF THE ROOM IS A DOOR, ARTFULLY CARVED INTO THE MAHOGANY WALL...
NEARLY INVISIBLE UNLESS YOU KNOW IT'S THERE...
AND ON THE DOOR IS A LOCK, DISGUISED WITHIN THE TATTOOS OF A STRANGE FACADE...
"FLIGHT RING"... HE THOUGHT THIS WAS A FLIGHT RING...
...HOW COULD HE KNOW YOU INSERT IT INTO THE MONSTER'S NOSE, PRESS FIRMLY FORWARD...
TWIST NINETY DEGREES CLOCKWISE AND...
CLICK
CH. CHUNG

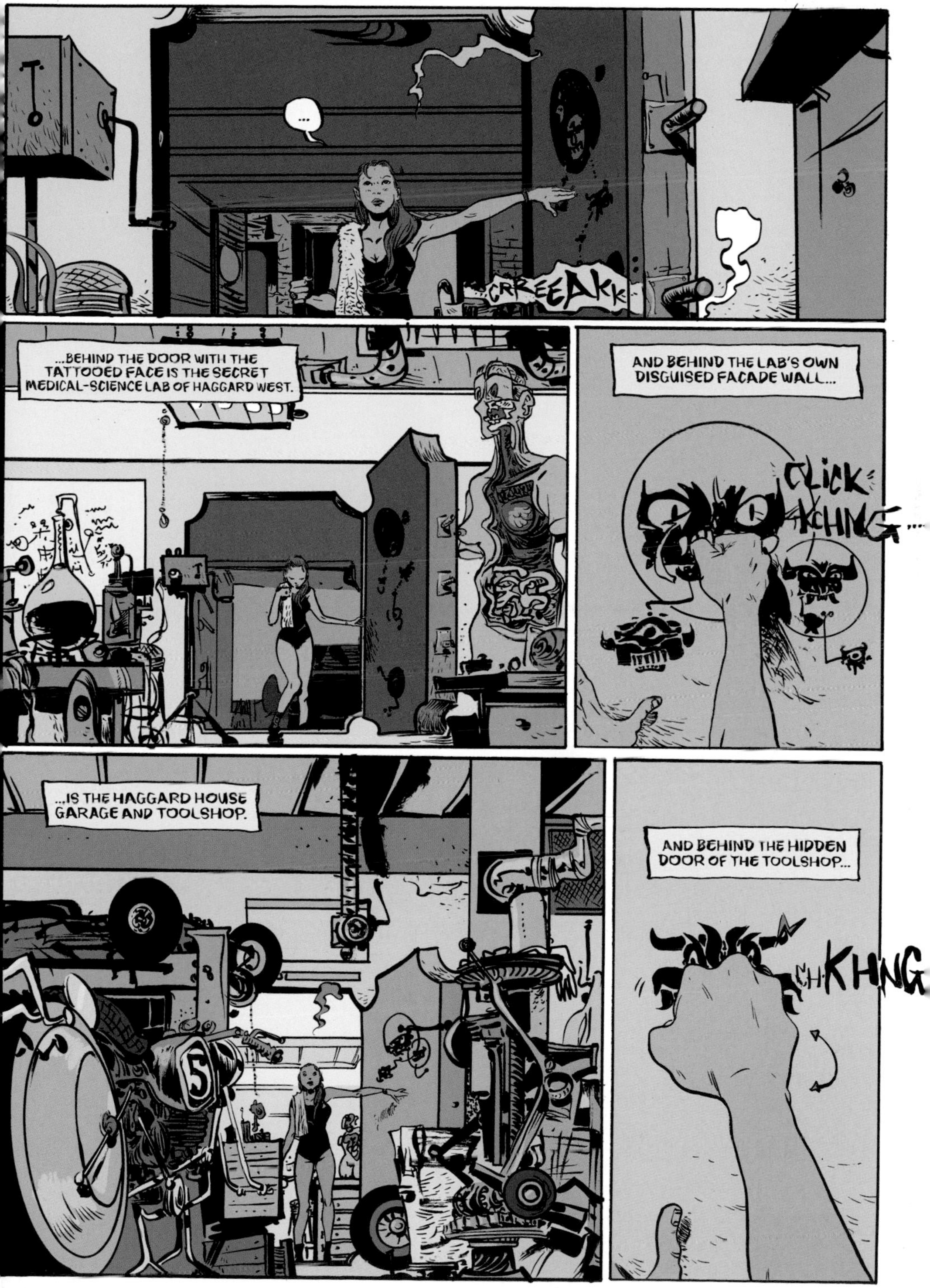
...
CRREEAKK
...BEHIND THE DOOR WITH THE TATTOOED FACE IS THE SECRET MEDICAL-SCIENCE LAB OF HAGGARD WEST.
AND BEHIND THE LAB'S OWN DISGUISED FACADE WALL...
CLICK
KCHNG...
...IS THE HAGGARD HOUSE GARAGE AND TOOLSHOP.
AND BEHIND THE HIDDEN DOOR OF THE TOOLSHOP...
CHKHNG

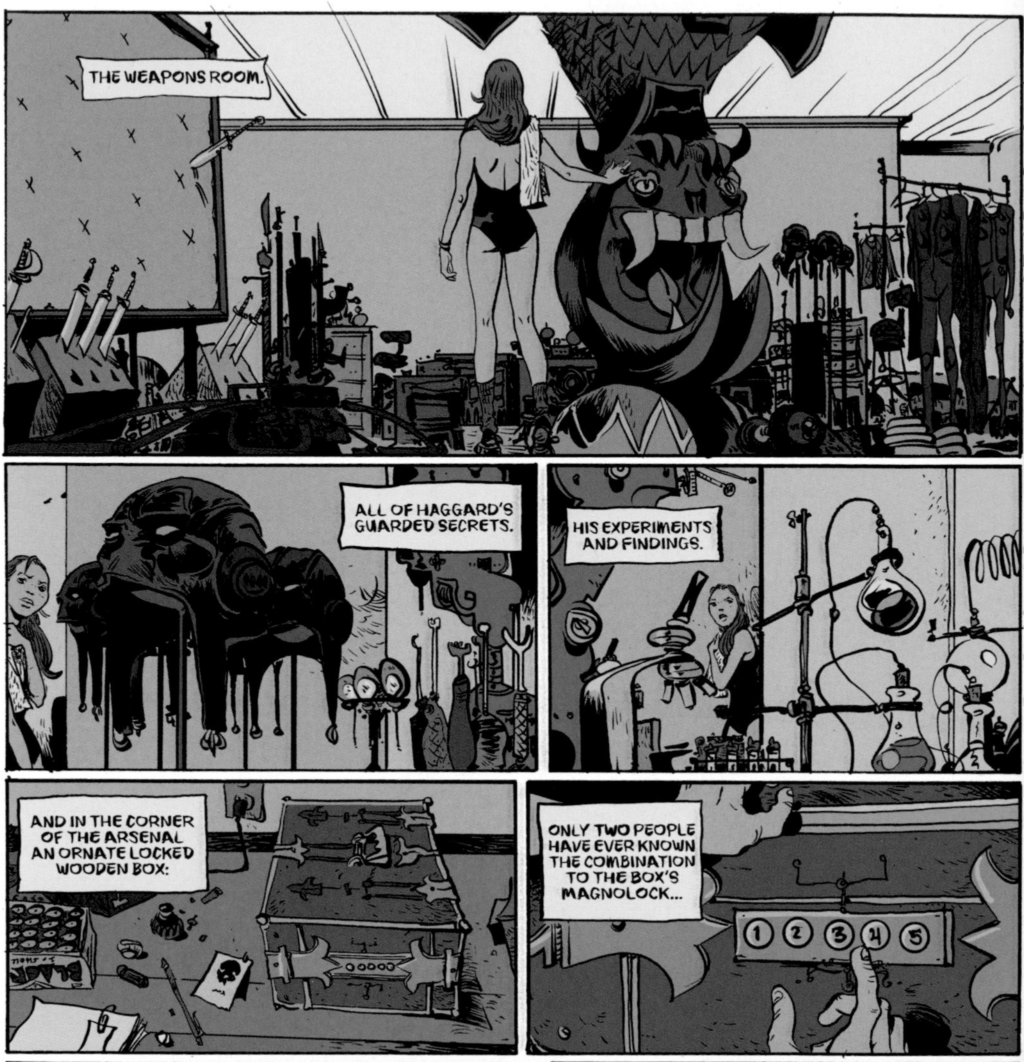
THE WEAPONS ROOM.
ALL OF HAGGARD'S GUARDED SECRETS.
HIS EXPERIMENTS AND FINDINGS.
AND IN THE CORNER OF THE ARSENAL AN ORNATE LOCKED WOODEN BOX:
ONLY **TWO** PEOPLE HAVE EVER KNOWN THE COMBINATION TO THE BOX'S MAGNOLOCK...
1 2 3 4 5
BLEEP
BLOOP
BLP
...NOW, IT'S ONLY ***ONE***.
TCHKT!!
KACHACHT
1 2 3 4 5

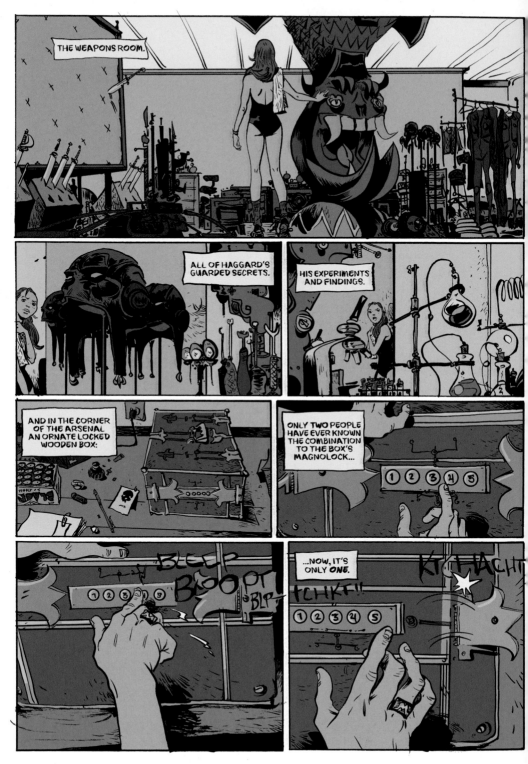

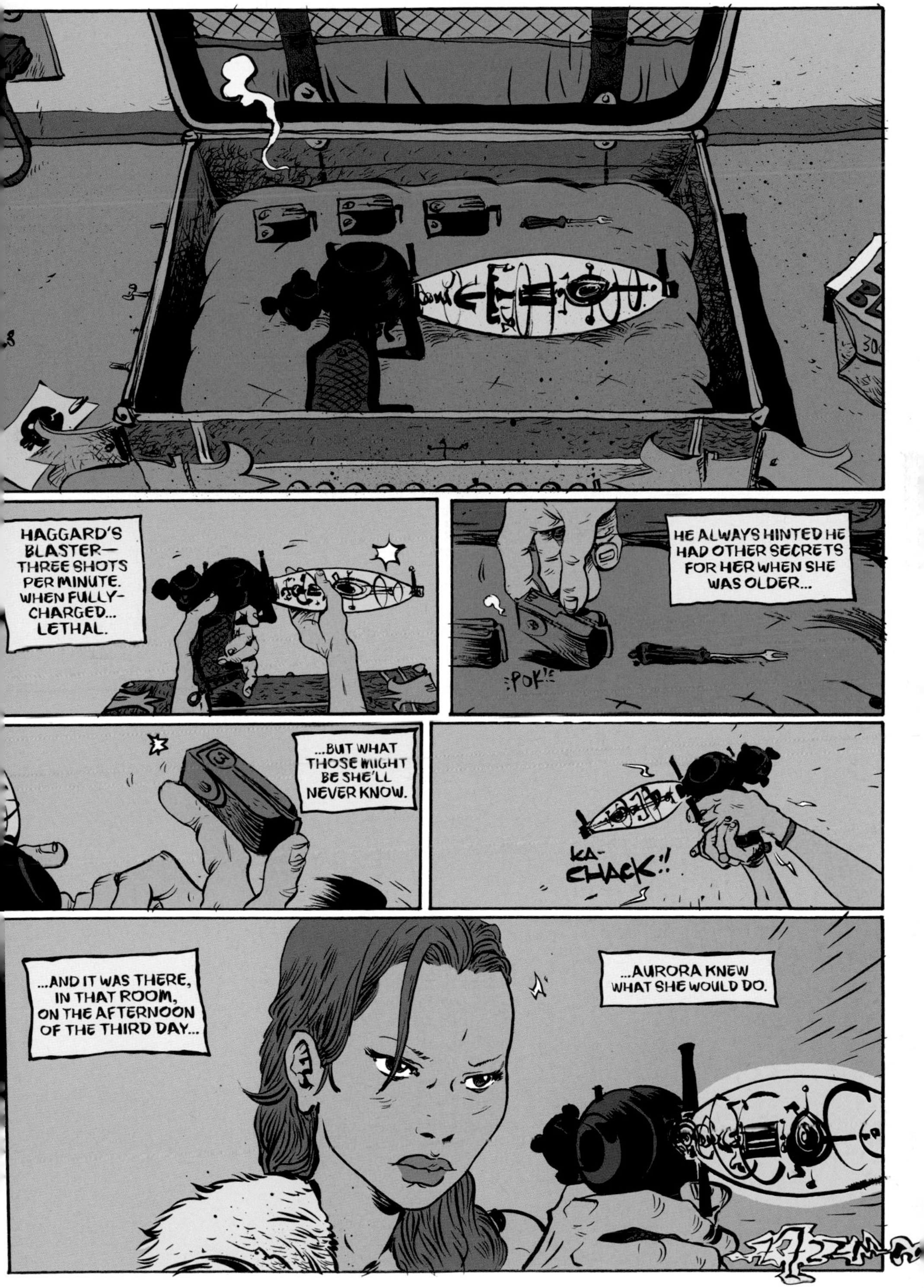
HAGGARD'S BLASTER— THREE SHOTS PER MINUTE. WHEN FULLY-CHARGED... LETHAL.
HE ALWAYS HINTED HE HAD OTHER SECRETS FOR HER WHEN SHE WAS OLDER...
POK!
...BUT WHAT THOSE MIGHT BE SHE'LL NEVER KNOW.
KA-CHACK!!
...AND IT WAS THERE, IN THAT ROOM, ON THE AFTERNOON OF THE THIRD DAY...
...AURORA KNEW WHAT SHE WOULD DO.

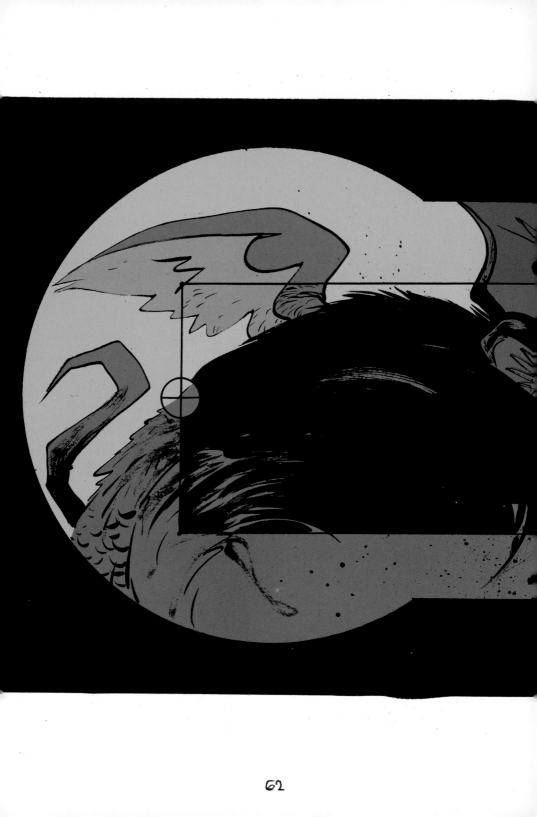

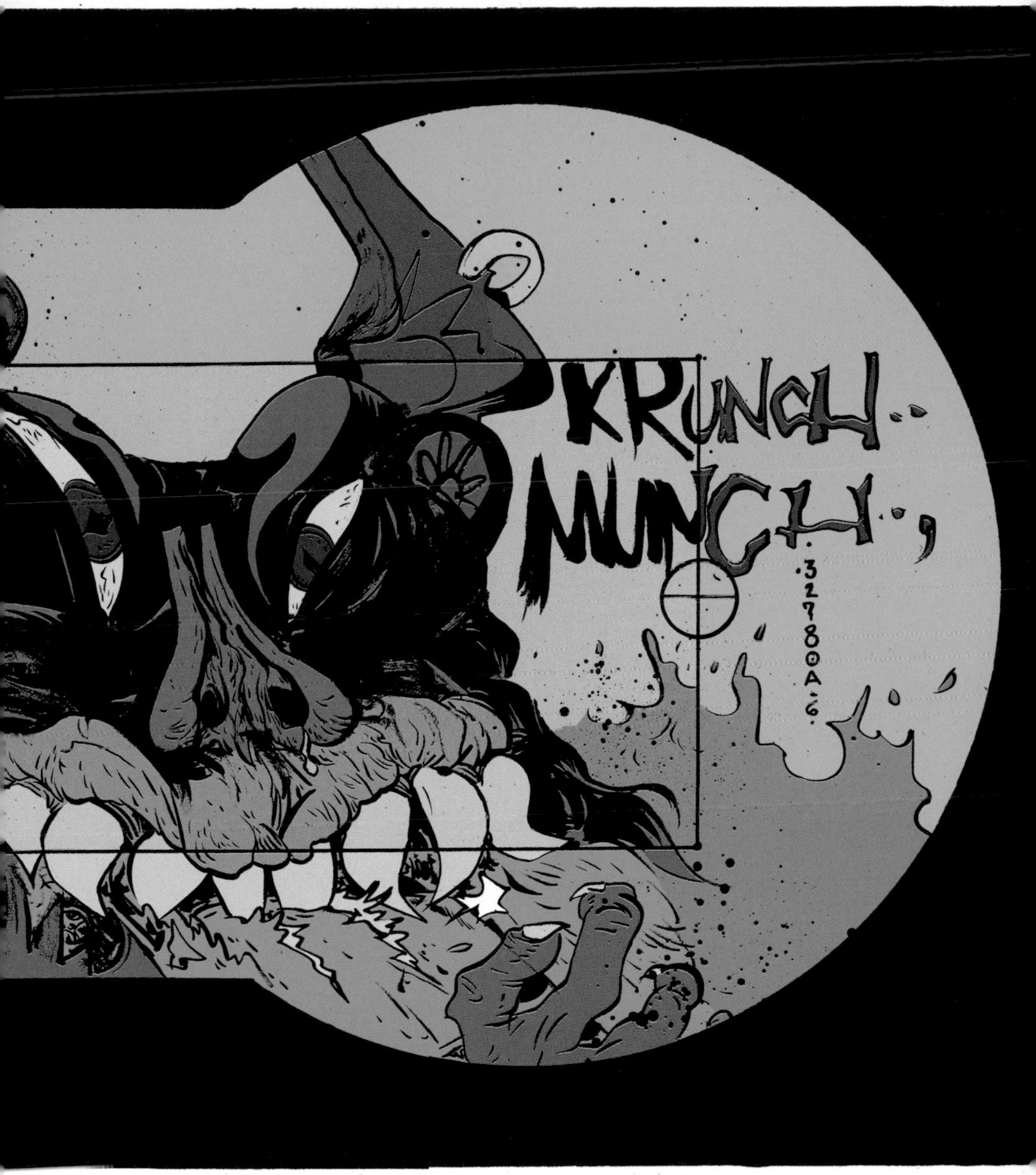
KRUNCH..
MUNCH..,
.3.2.7.8.0.A.6.

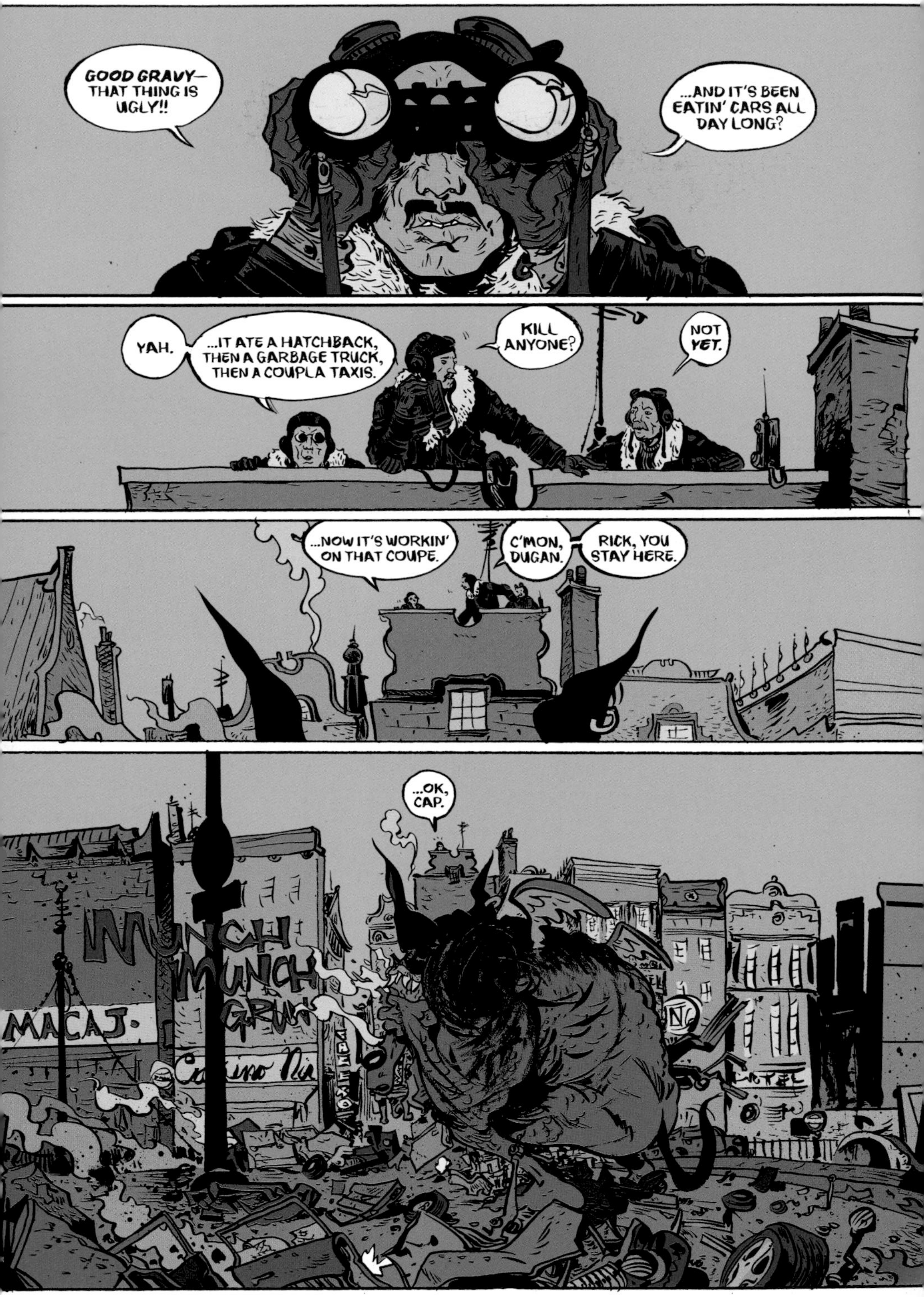
GOOD GRAVY—THAT THING IS UGLY!!
...AND IT'S BEEN EATIN' CARS ALL DAY LONG?
YAH.
...IT ATE A HATCHBACK, THEN A GARBAGE TRUCK, THEN A COUPLA TAXIS.
KILL ANYONE?
NOT YET.
...NOW IT'S WORKIN' ON THAT COUPE.
C'MON, DUGAN.
RICK, YOU STAY HERE.
...OK, CAP.
MUNCH
MUNCH

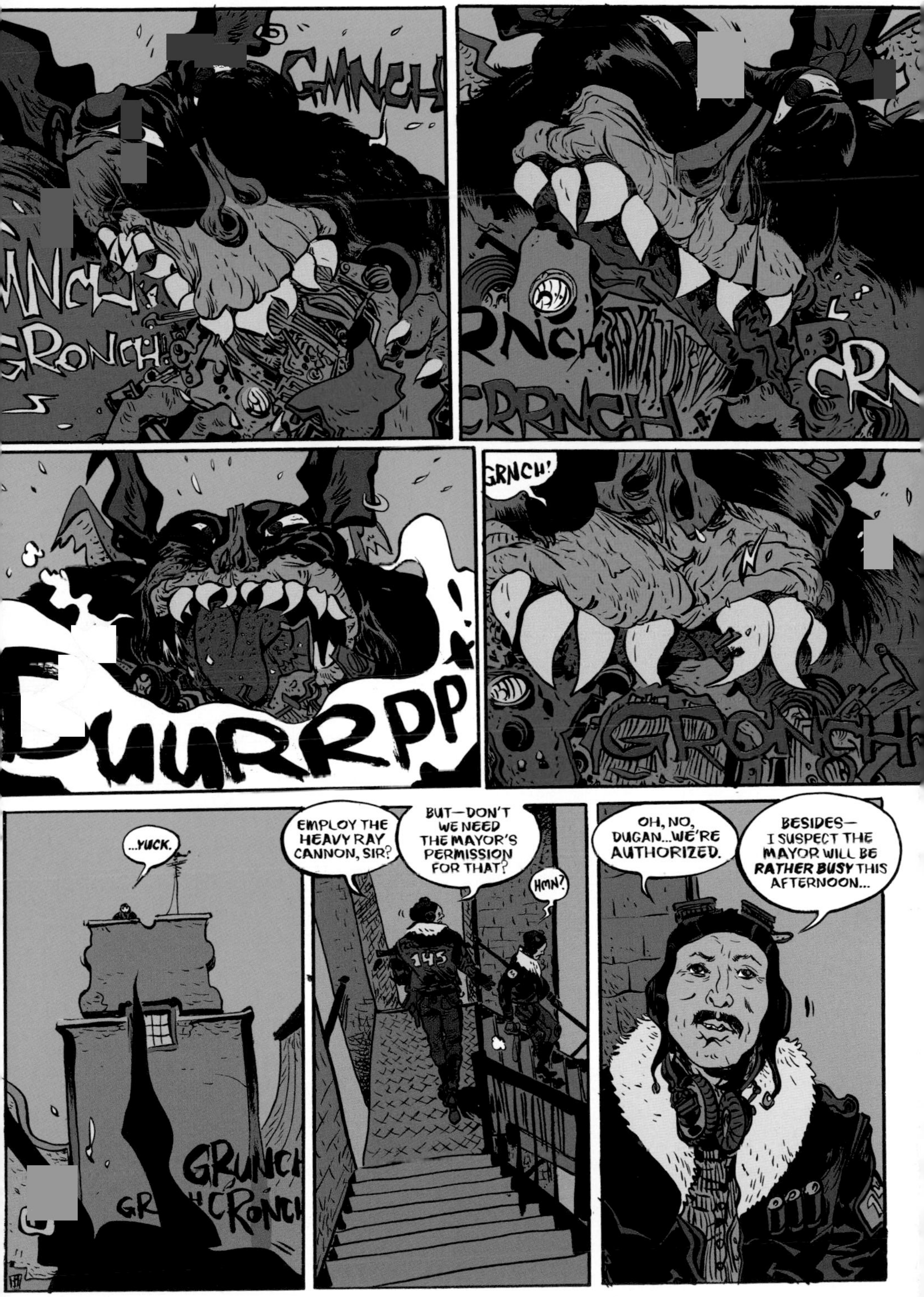
GRNCH
GRONCH!
RNCH
CRRNCH
UURRPP
GRNCH!
GRONCH
...YUCK.
GRUNCH
CRONCH
EMPLOY THE HEAVY RAY CANNON, SIR?
BUT—DON'T WE NEED THE MAYOR'S PERMISSION FOR THAT?
HMN?
OH, NO, DUGAN...WE'RE AUTHORIZED.
BESIDES— I SUSPECT THE MAYOR WILL BE RATHER BUSY THIS AFTERNOON...

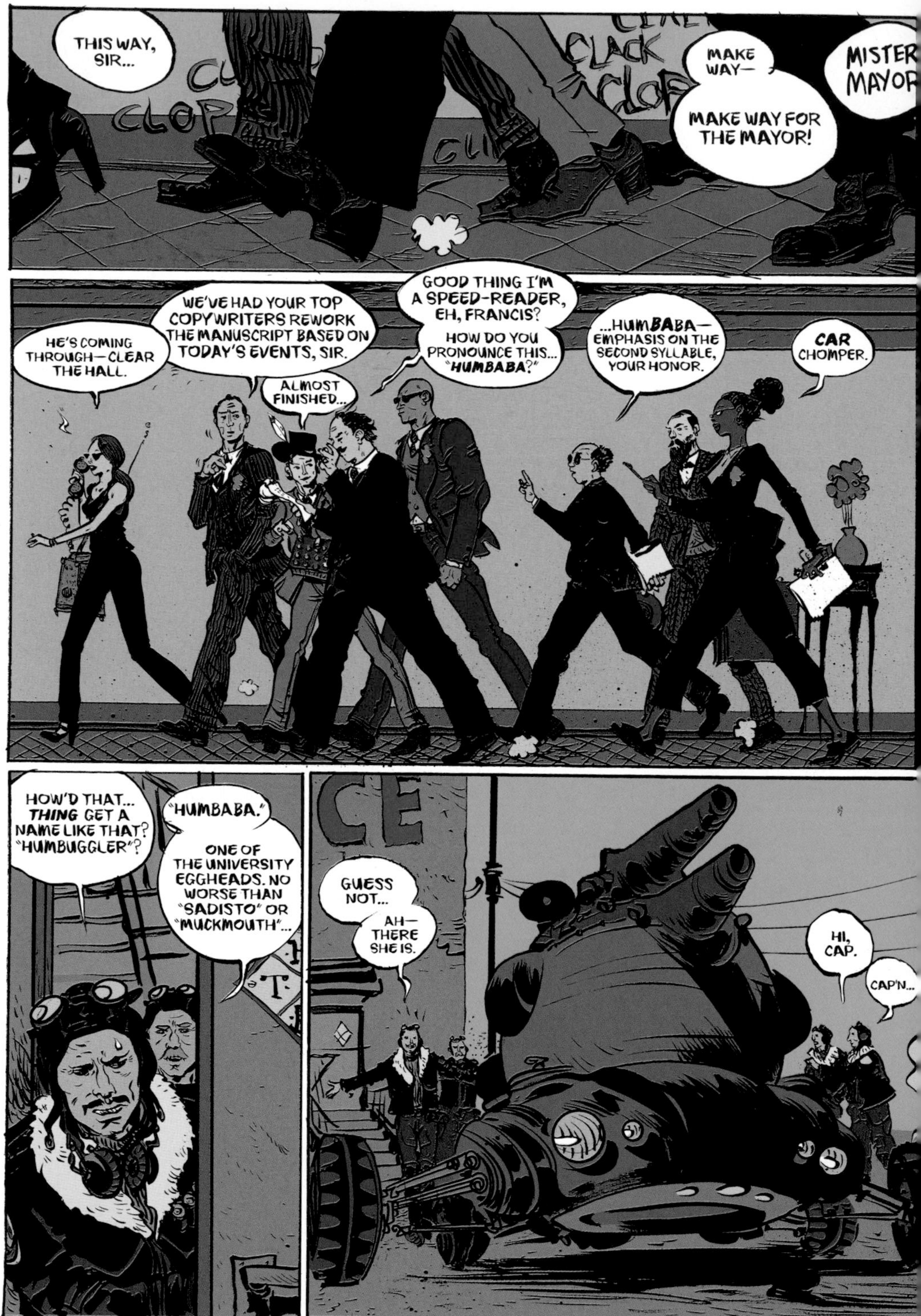
THIS WAY, SIR...
CLI
CLOP
CLACK
CLOP
CLI
MAKE WAY—
MAKE WAY FOR THE MAYOR!
MISTER MAYOR
HE'S COMING THROUGH—CLEAR THE HALL.
WE'VE HAD YOUR TOP COPYWRITERS REWORK THE MANUSCRIPT BASED ON TODAY'S EVENTS, SIR.
ALMOST FINISHED...
GOOD THING I'M A SPEED-READER, EH, FRANCIS?
HOW DO YOU PRONOUNCE THIS... "HUMBABA?"
...HUMBABA—EMPHASIS ON THE SECOND SYLLABLE, YOUR HONOR.
CAR CHOMPER.
HOW'D THAT... THING GET A NAME LIKE THAT? "HUMBUGGLER"?
"HUMBABA."
ONE OF THE UNIVERSITY EGGHEADS. NO WORSE THAN "SADISTO" OR "MUCKMOUTH"...
GUESS NOT...
AH—THERE SHE IS.
HI, CAP.
CAP'N...

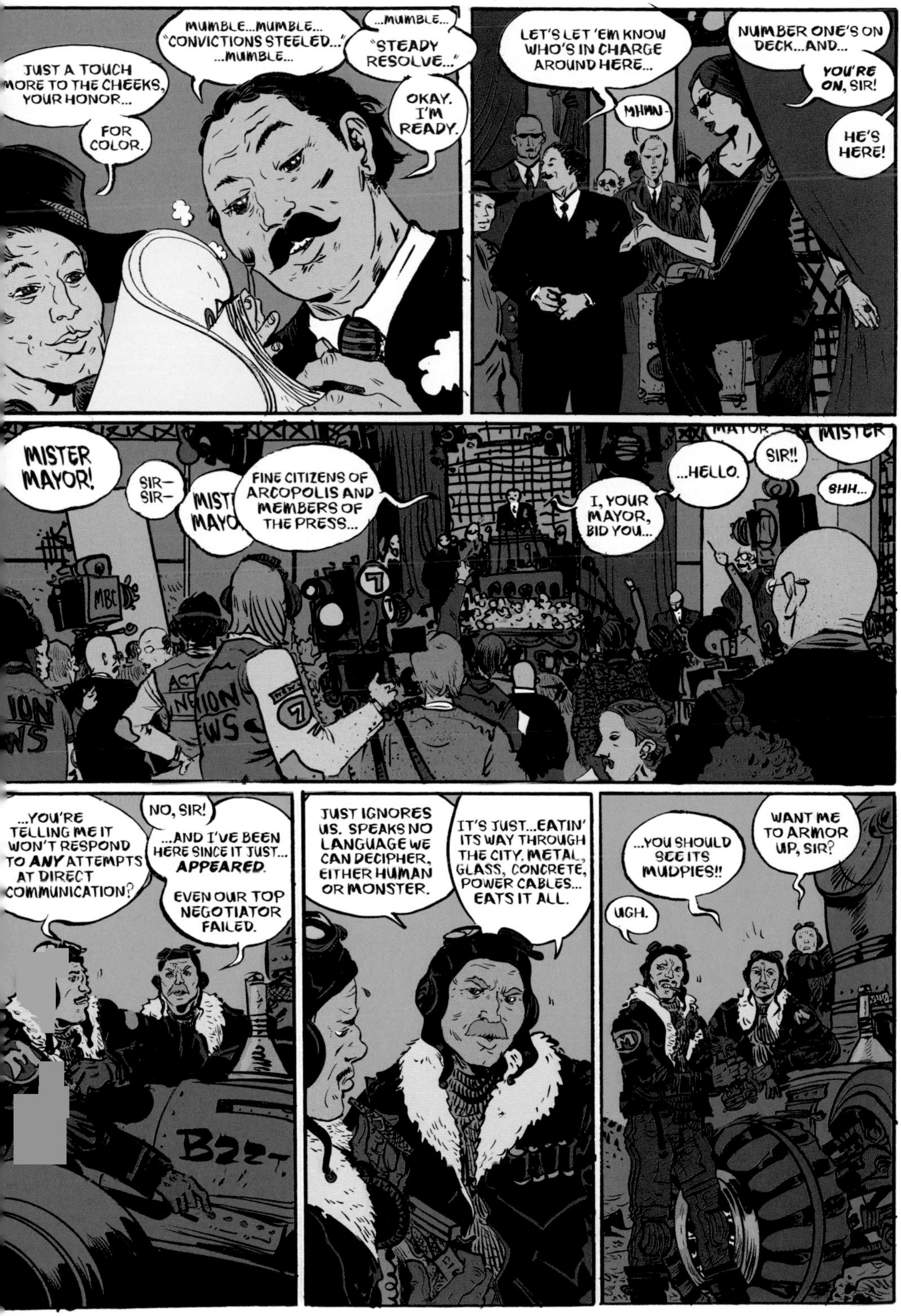
JUST A TOUCH MORE TO THE CHEEKS, YOUR HONOR...
FOR COLOR.
MUMBLE...MUMBLE... "CONVICTIONS STEELED..." ...MUMBLE...
...MUMBLE...
"STEADY RESOLVE..."
OKAY. I'M READY.
LET'S LET 'EM KNOW WHO'S IN CHARGE AROUND HERE...
MHMN-
NUMBER ONE'S ON DECK...AND...
YOU'RE ON, SIR!
HE'S HERE!
MISTER MAYOR!
SIR— SIR—
MIST MAYO
FINE CITIZENS OF ARCOPOLIS AND MEMBERS OF THE PRESS...
I, YOUR MAYOR, BID YOU...
...HELLO.
MAYOR
SIR!!
MISTER
SHH...
MBC
7
...YOU'RE TELLING ME IT WON'T RESPOND TO ANY ATTEMPTS AT DIRECT COMMUNICATION?
NO, SIR!
...AND I'VE BEEN HERE SINCE IT JUST... APPEARED.
EVEN OUR TOP NEGOTIATOR FAILED.
BZZT
JUST IGNORES US. SPEAKS NO LANGUAGE WE CAN DECIPHER, EITHER HUMAN OR MONSTER.
IT'S JUST...EATIN' ITS WAY THROUGH THE CITY. METAL, GLASS, CONCRETE, POWER CABLES... EATS IT ALL.
...YOU SHOULD SEE ITS MUDPIES!!
UGH.
WANT ME TO ARMOR UP, SIR?

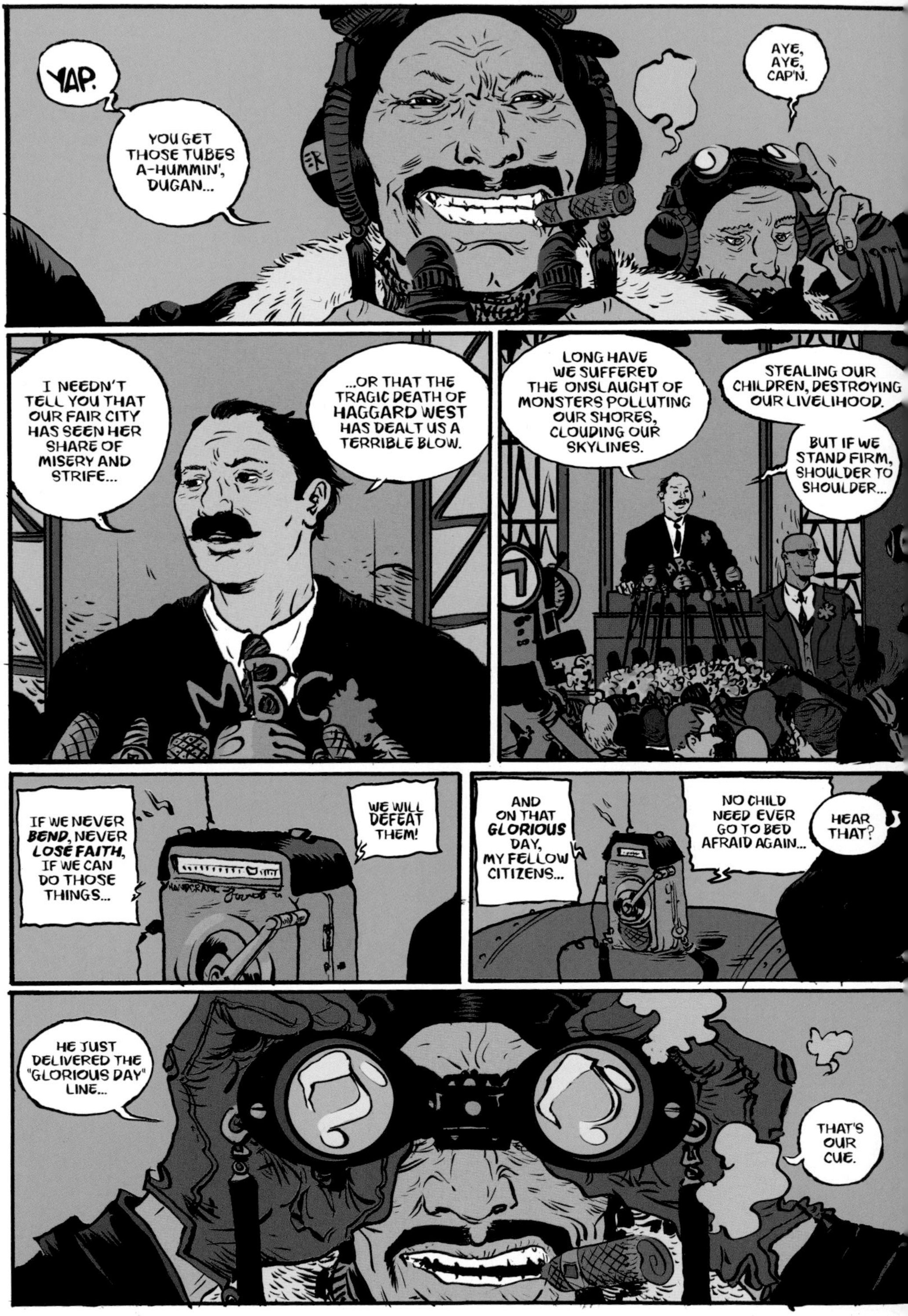
YAP.
YOU GET THOSE TUBES A-HUMMIN', DUGAN...
AYE, AYE, CAP'N.
I NEEDN'T TELL YOU THAT OUR FAIR CITY HAS SEEN HER SHARE OF MISERY AND STRIFE...
...OR THAT THE TRAGIC DEATH OF HAGGARD WEST HAS DEALT US A TERRIBLE BLOW.
LONG HAVE WE SUFFERED THE ONSLAUGHT OF MONSTERS POLLUTING OUR SHORES, CLOUDING OUR SKYLINES.
STEALING OUR CHILDREN, DESTROYING OUR LIVELIHOOD.
BUT IF WE STAND FIRM, SHOULDER TO SHOULDER...
IF WE NEVER BEND, NEVER LOSE FAITH, IF WE CAN DO THOSE THINGS...
WE WILL DEFEAT THEM!
AND ON THAT GLORIOUS DAY, MY FELLOW CITIZENS...
NO CHILD NEED EVER GO TO BED AFRAID AGAIN...
HEAR THAT?
HE JUST DELIVERED THE "GLORIOUS DAY" LINE...
THAT'S OUR CUE.

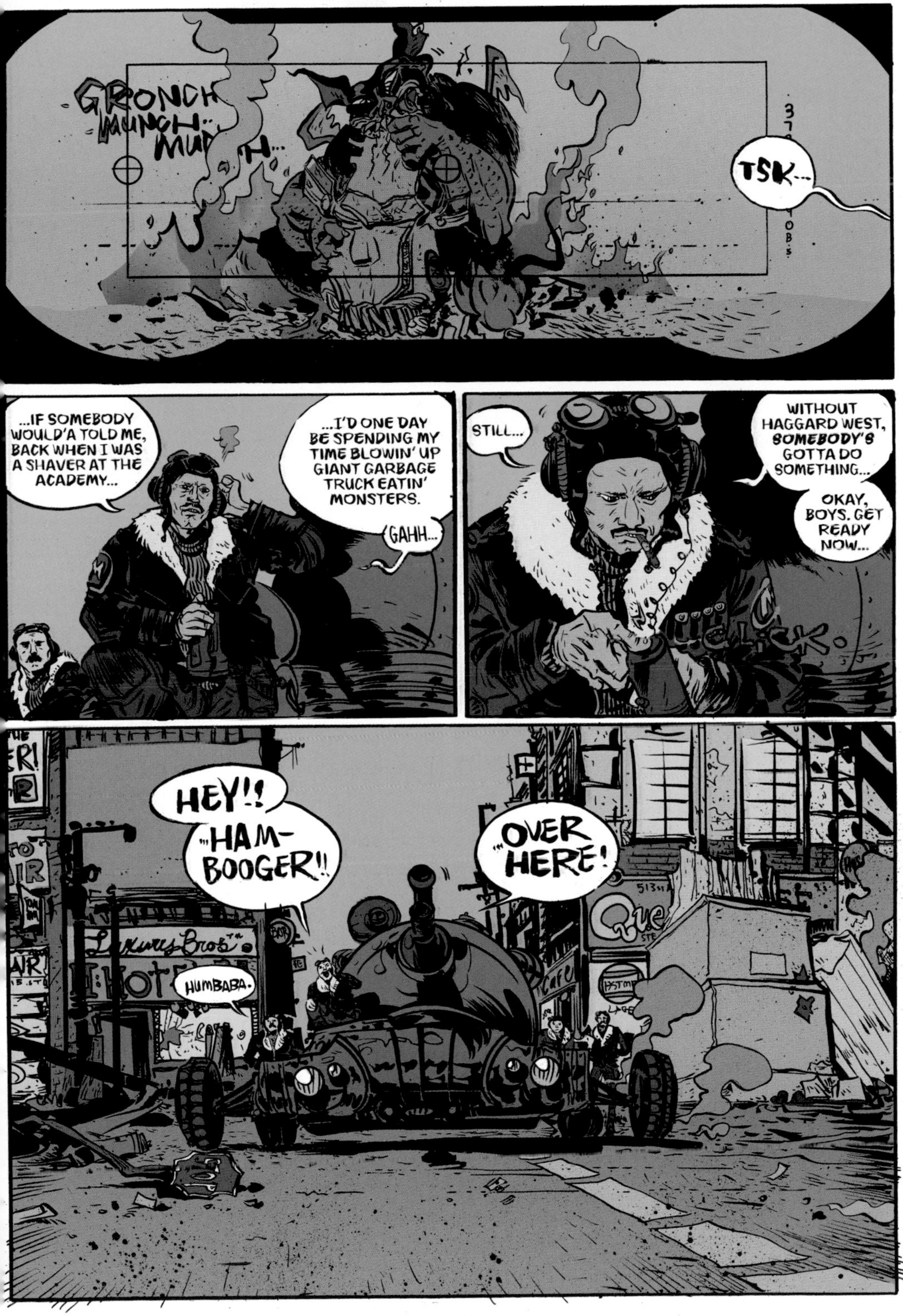
GRONCH MUNCH... MUNCH...
TSK...
...IF SOMEBODY WOULD'A TOLD ME, BACK WHEN I WAS A SHAVER AT THE ACADEMY...
...I'D ONE DAY BE SPENDING MY TIME BLOWIN' UP GIANT GARBAGE TRUCK EATIN' MONSTERS.
GAHH...
STILL...
WITHOUT HAGGARD WEST, SOMEBODY'S GOTTA DO SOMETHING...
OKAY, BOYS. GET READY NOW...
CLICK
HEY!! HAM-BOOGER!!
OVER HERE!
HUMBABA.

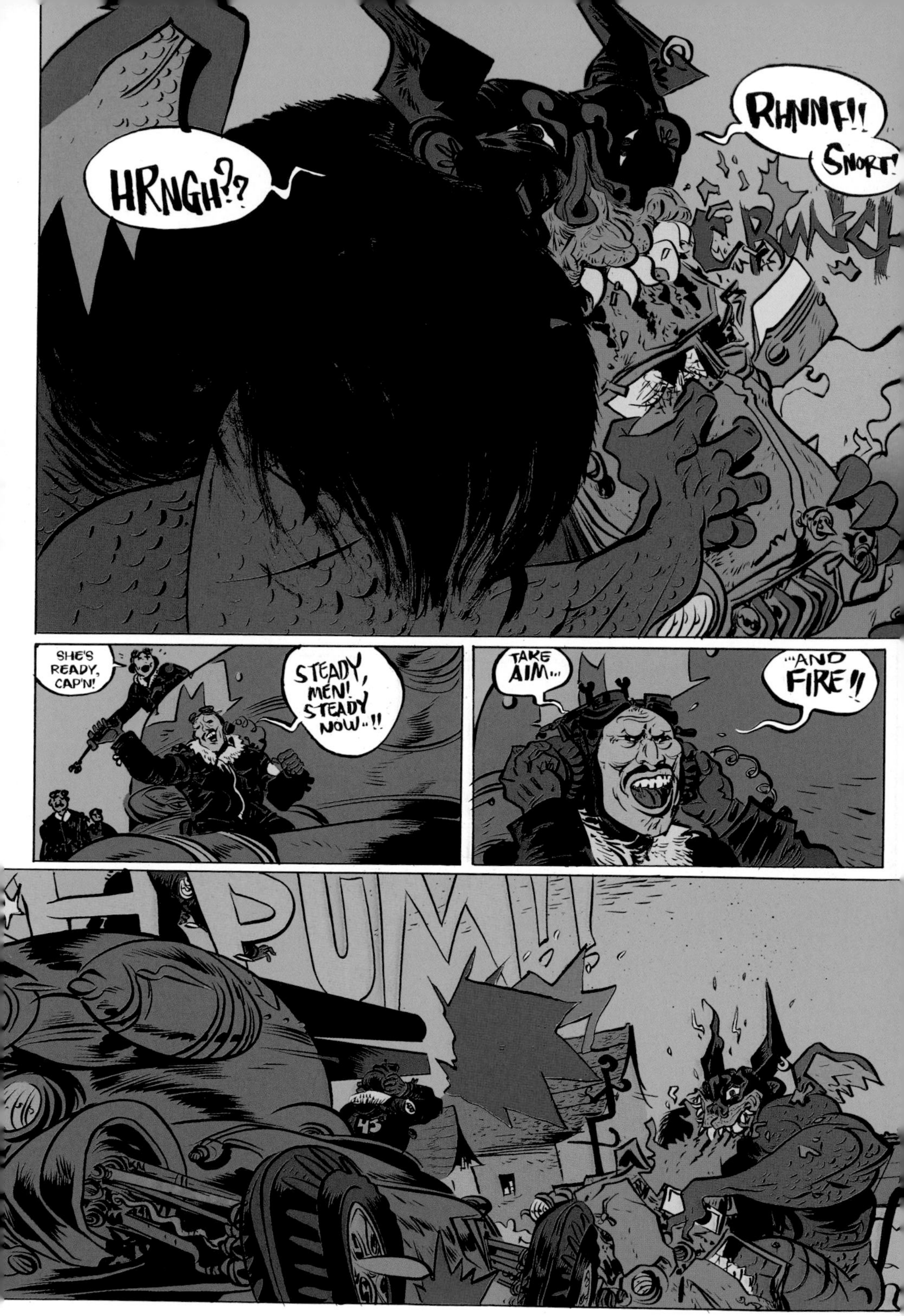
HRNGH?!?
RHNNF!!
SNORT!
CRUNCH
SHE'S READY, CAP'N!
STEADY, MEN! STEADY NOW..!!
TAKE AIM...
...AND FIRE!!
PUM!!

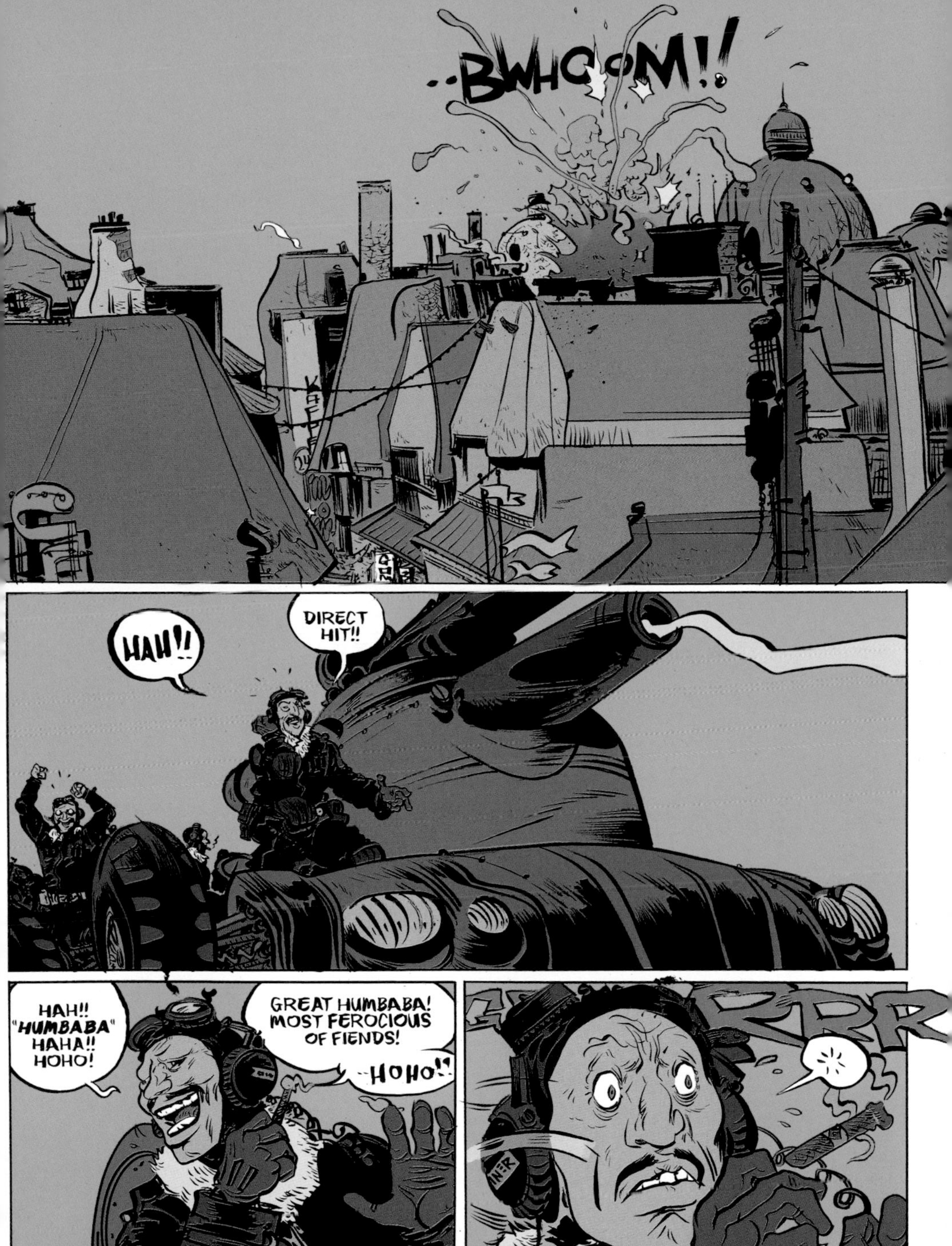
BWHOOM!!
HAH!!
DIRECT HIT!!
HAH!! "HUMBABA" HAHA!! HOHO!
GREAT HUMBABA! MOST FEROCIOUS OF FIENDS!
HOHO!!

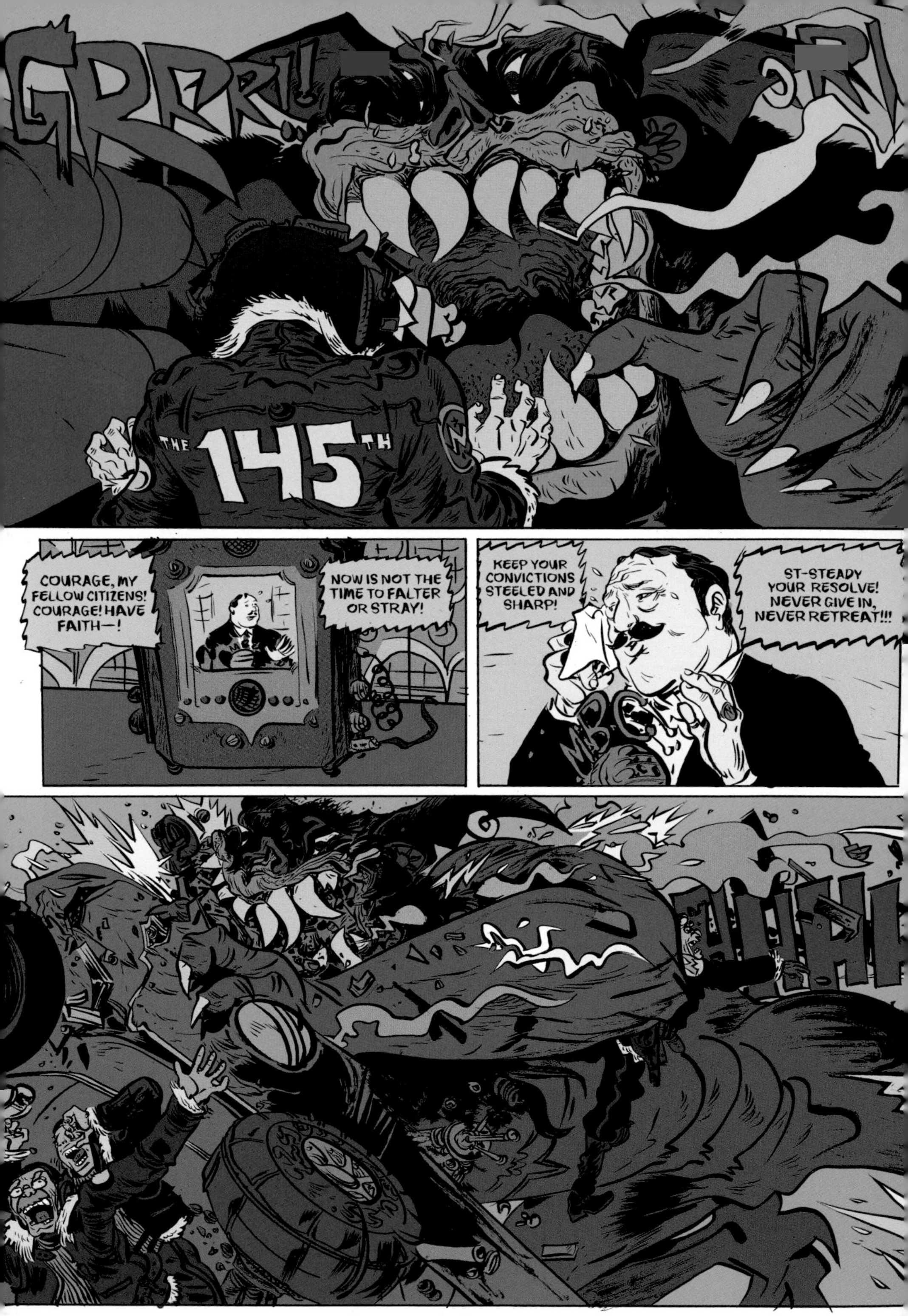
GRRR!
RR!
THE 145TH
COURAGE, MY FELLOW CITIZENS! COURAGE! HAVE FAITH—!
NOW IS NOT THE TIME TO FALTER OR STRAY!
KEEP YOUR CONVICTIONS STEELED AND SHARP!
ST-STEADY YOUR RESOLVE! NEVER GIVE IN, NEVER RETREAT!!!

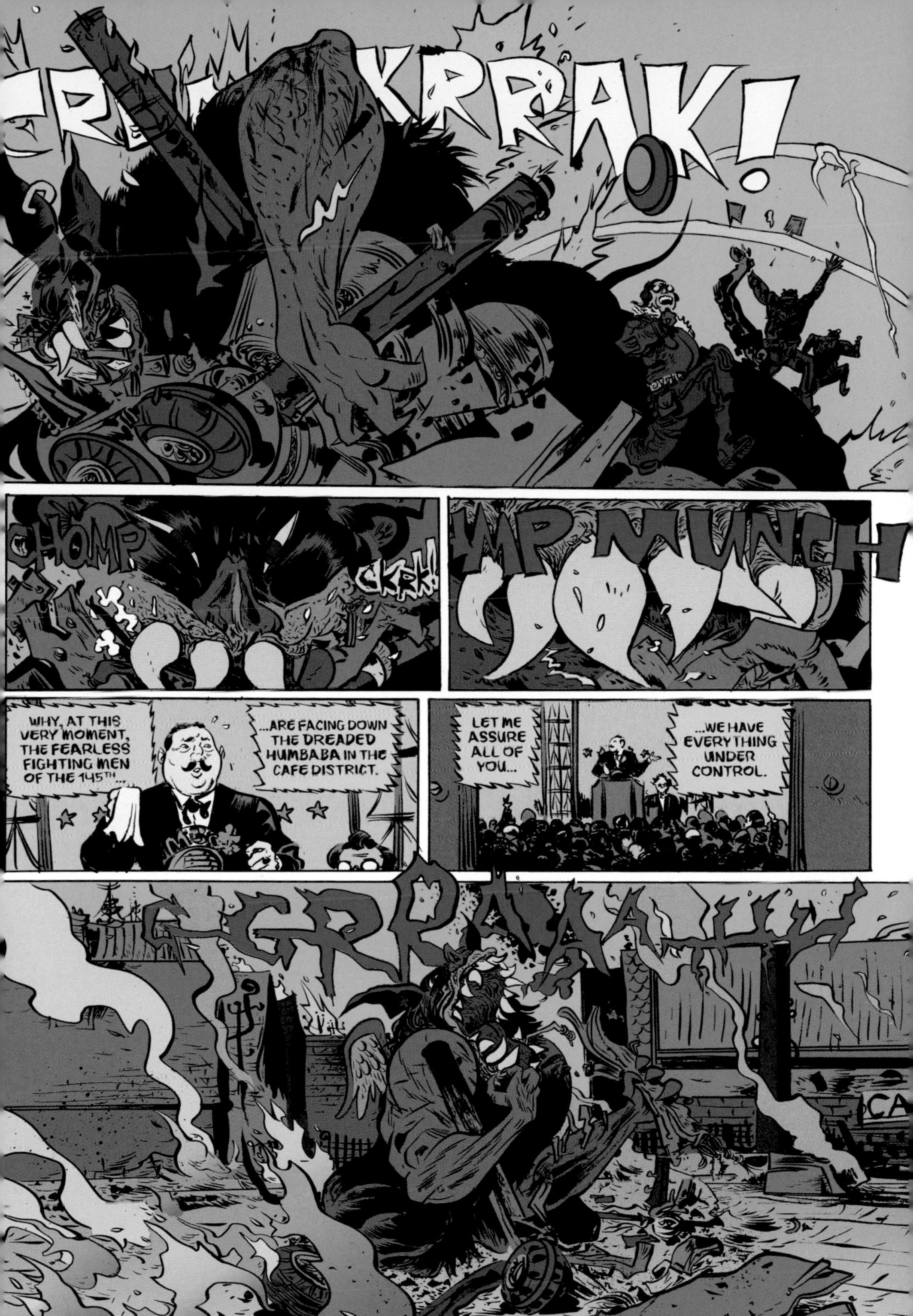
KRRAK!
CHOMP
CKRK!
MP MUNCH
WHY, AT THIS VERY MOMENT, THE FEARLESS FIGHTING MEN OF THE 145TH...
...ARE FACING DOWN THE DREADED HUMBABA IN THE CAFE DISTRICT.
LET ME ASSURE ALL OF YOU...
...WE HAVE EVERYTHING UNDER CONTROL.
GRRAAAHH
CA

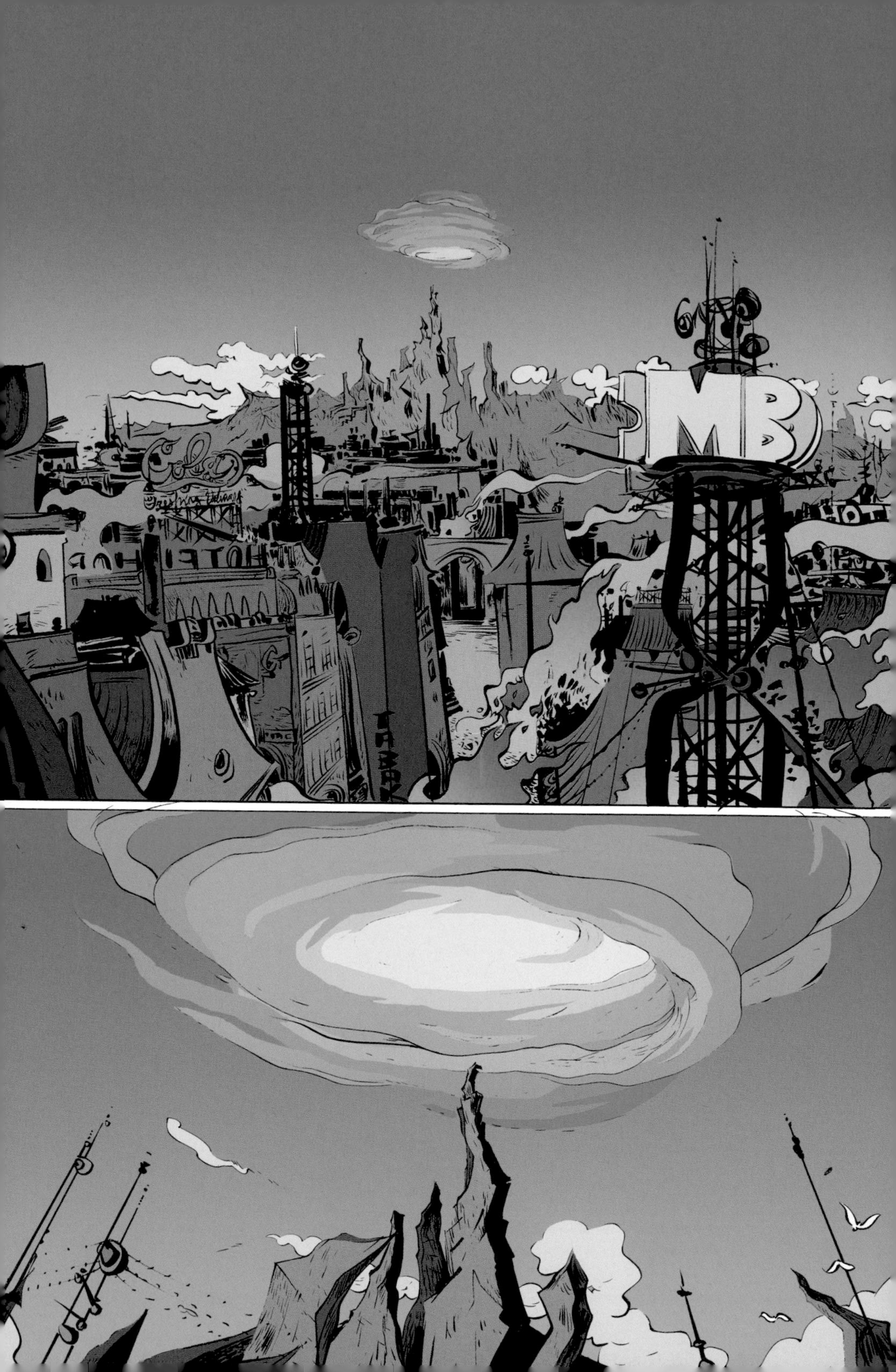
MB

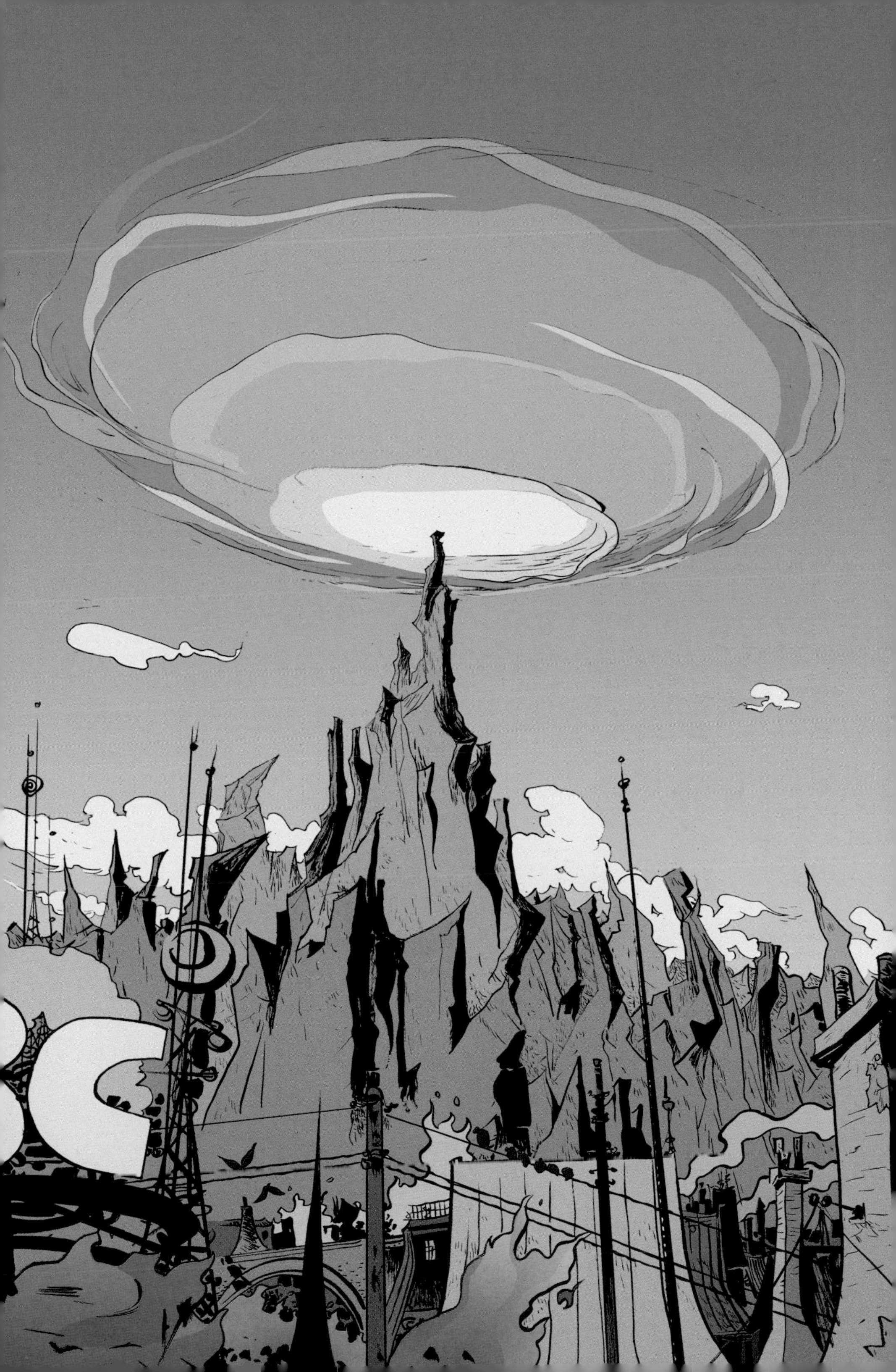

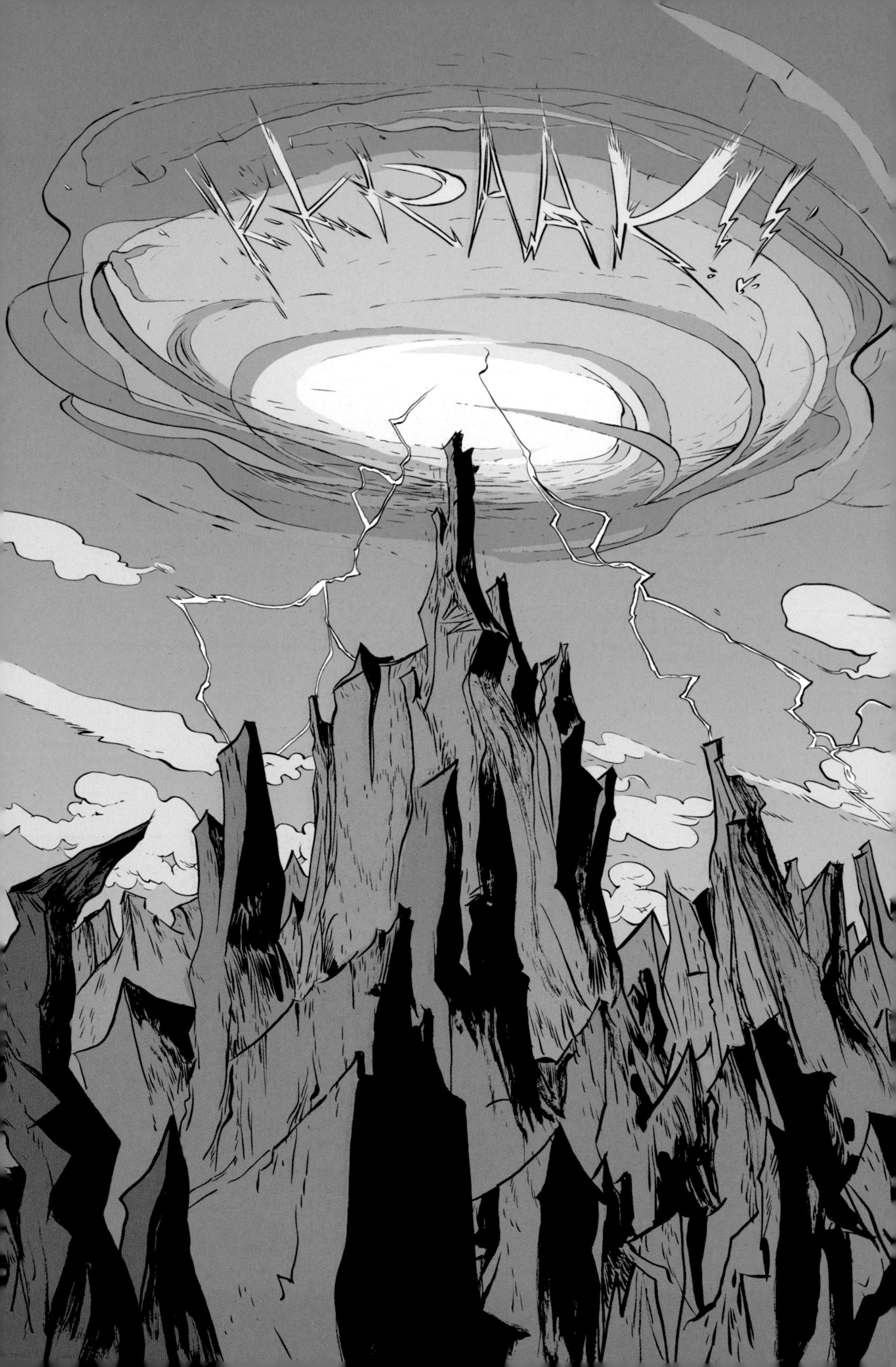
KKRAAK!!

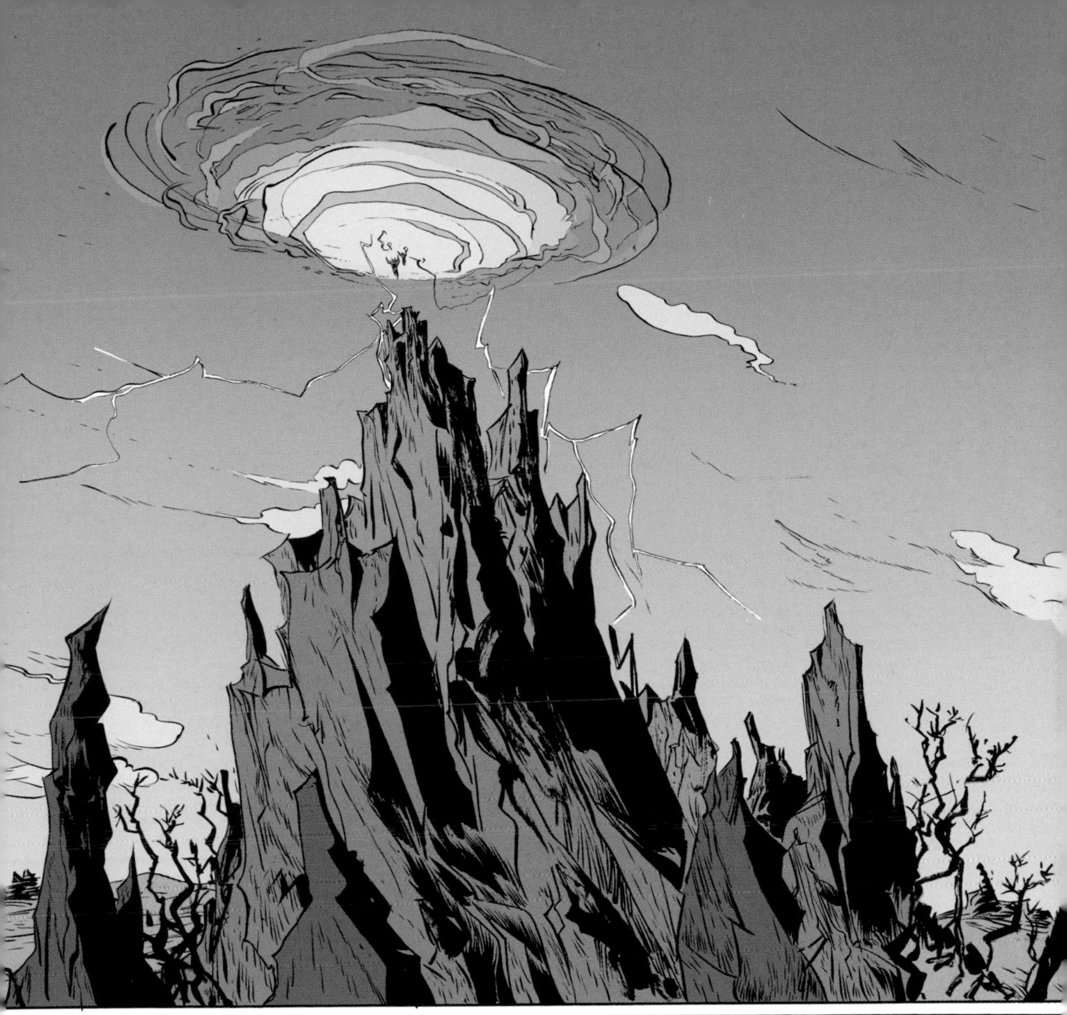

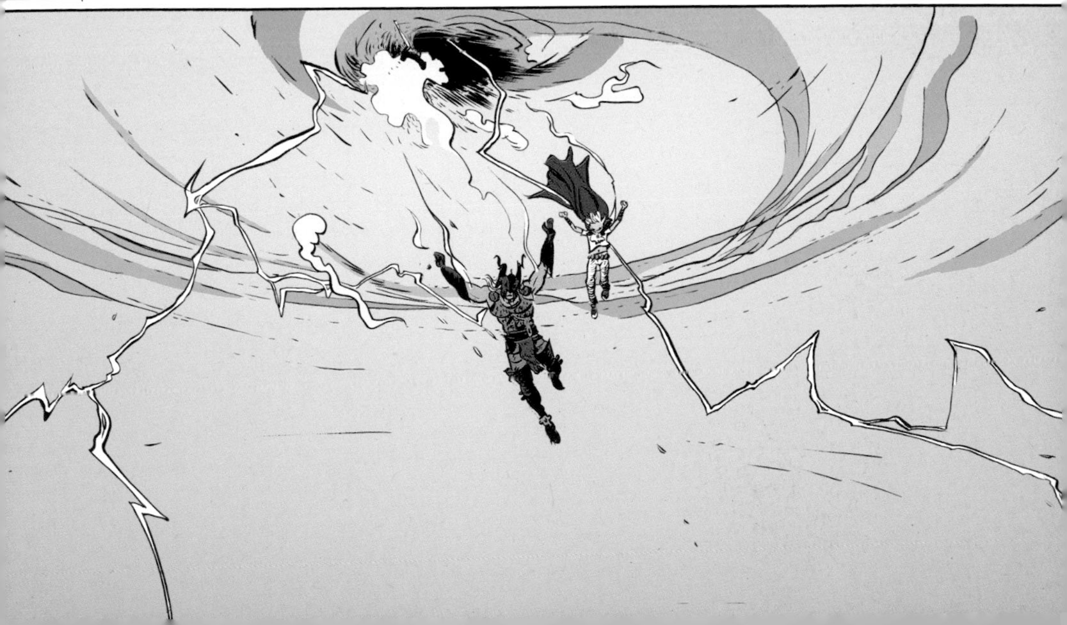

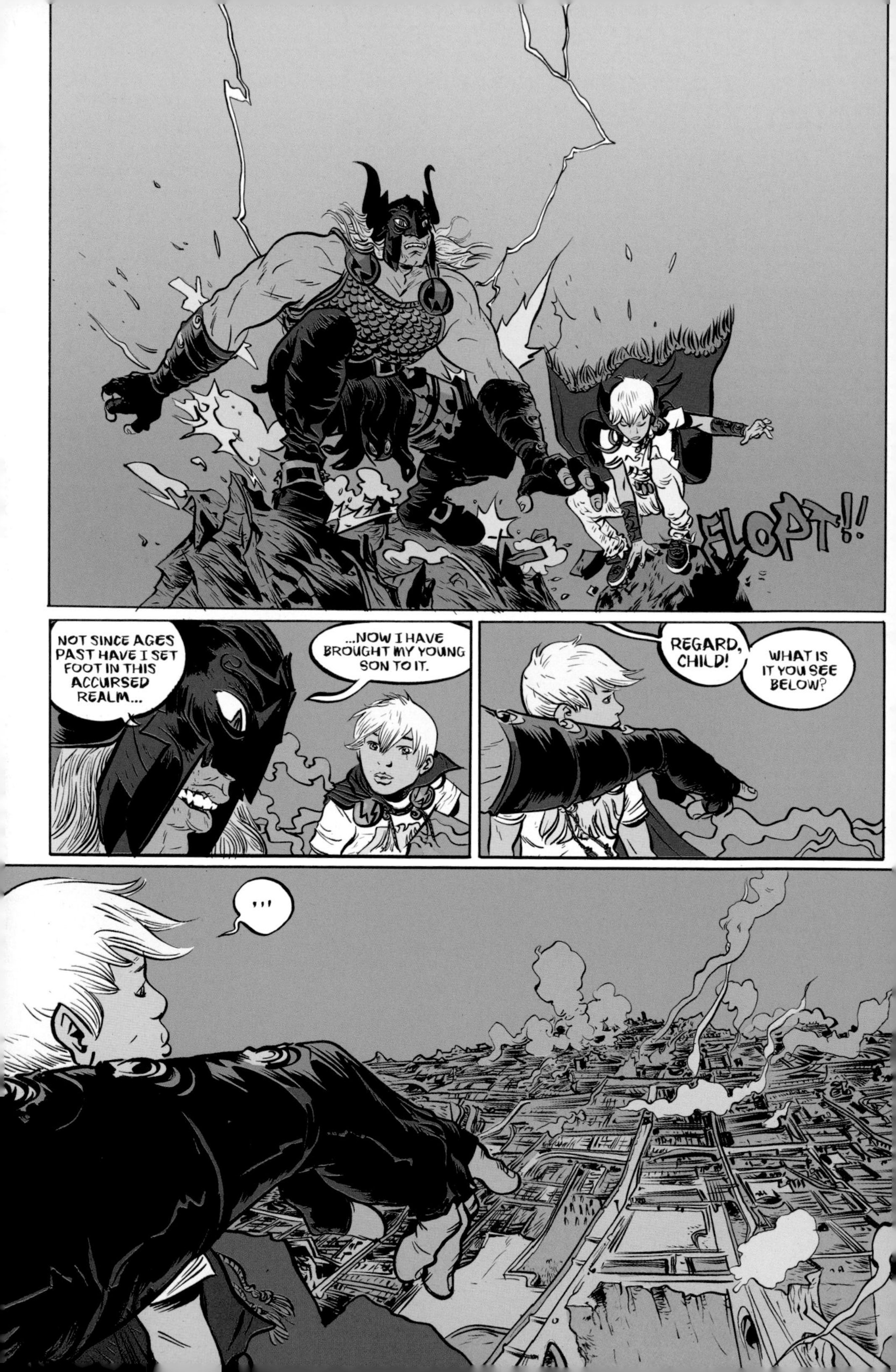
FLOPT!!
NOT SINCE AGES PAST HAVE I SET FOOT IN THIS ACCURSED REALM...
...NOW I HAVE BROUGHT MY YOUNG SON TO IT.
REGARD, CHILD!
WHAT IS IT YOU SEE BELOW?
...

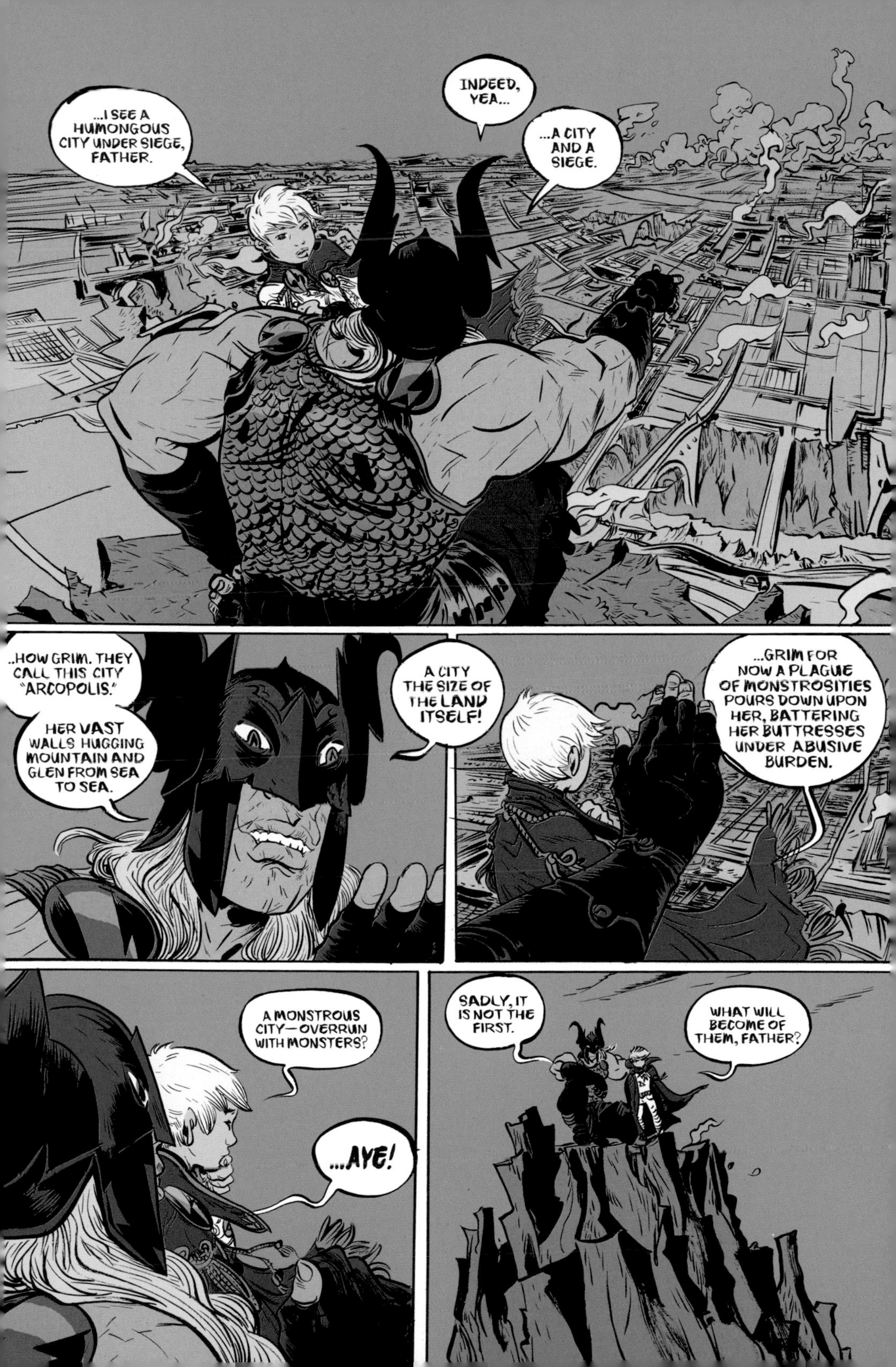
...I SEE A HUMONGOUS CITY UNDER SIEGE, FATHER.
INDEED, YEA...
...A CITY AND A SIEGE.
..HOW GRIM. THEY CALL THIS CITY "ARCOPOLIS."
HER VAST WALLS HUGGING MOUNTAIN AND GLEN FROM SEA TO SEA.
A CITY THE SIZE OF THE LAND ITSELF!
...GRIM FOR NOW A PLAGUE OF MONSTROSITIES POURS DOWN UPON HER, BATTERING HER BUTTRESSES UNDER ABUSIVE BURDEN.
A MONSTROUS CITY—OVERRUN WITH MONSTERS?
...AYE!
SADLY, IT IS NOT THE FIRST.
WHAT WILL BECOME OF THEM, FATHER?

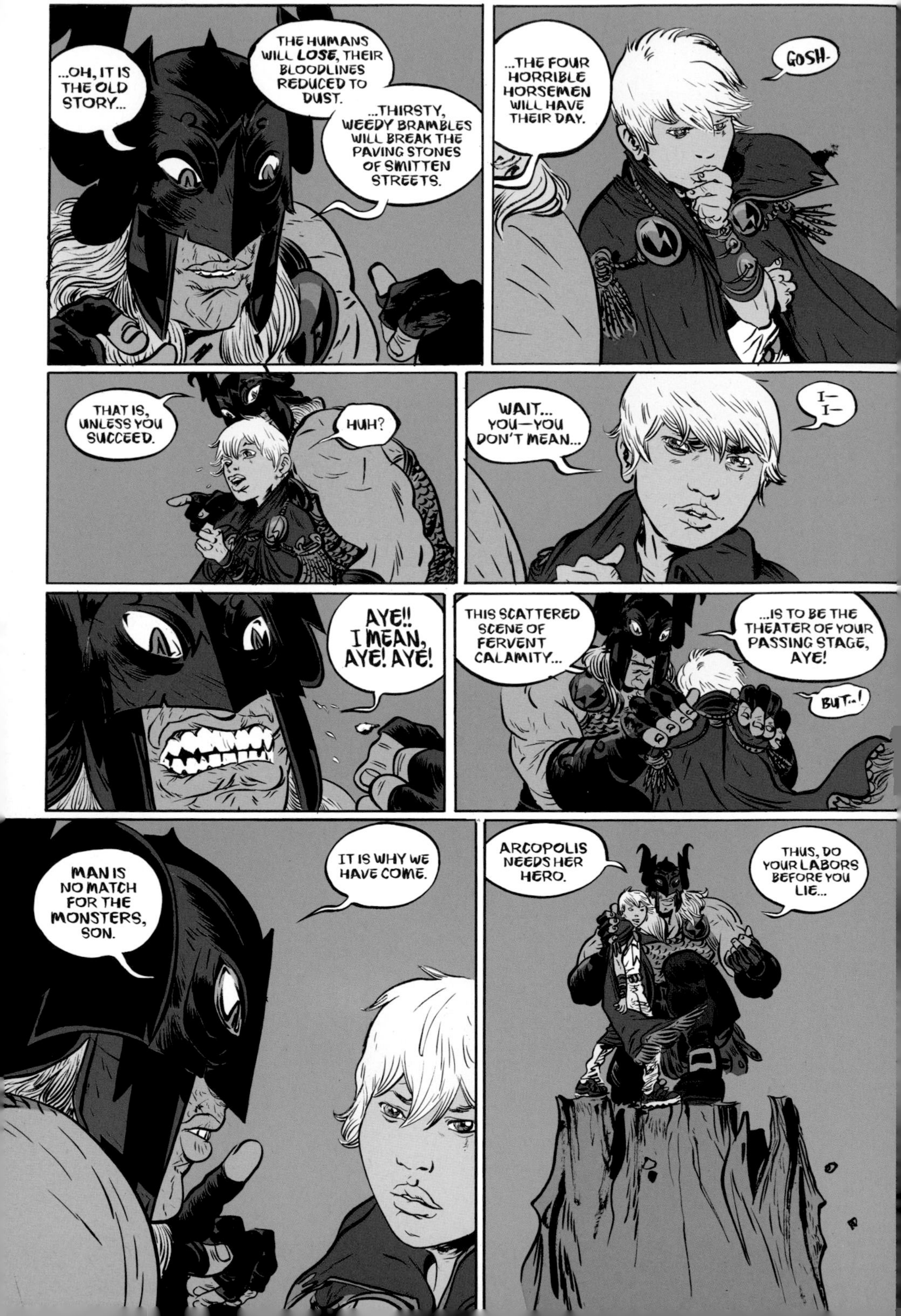
...OH, IT IS THE OLD STORY...
THE HUMANS WILL LOSE, THEIR BLOODLINES REDUCED TO DUST.
...THIRSTY, WEEDY BRAMBLES WILL BREAK THE PAVING STONES OF SMITTEN STREETS.
...THE FOUR HORRIBLE HORSEMEN WILL HAVE THEIR DAY.
GOSH.
THAT IS, UNLESS YOU SUCCEED.
HUH?
WAIT... YOU—YOU DON'T MEAN...
I— I—
AYE!! I MEAN, AYE! AYE!
THIS SCATTERED SCENE OF FERVENT CALAMITY...
...IS TO BE THE THEATER OF YOUR PASSING STAGE, AYE!
BUT..!
MAN IS NO MATCH FOR THE MONSTERS, SON.
IT IS WHY WE HAVE COME.
ARCOPOLIS NEEDS HER HERO.
THUS, DO YOUR LABORS BEFORE YOU LIE...

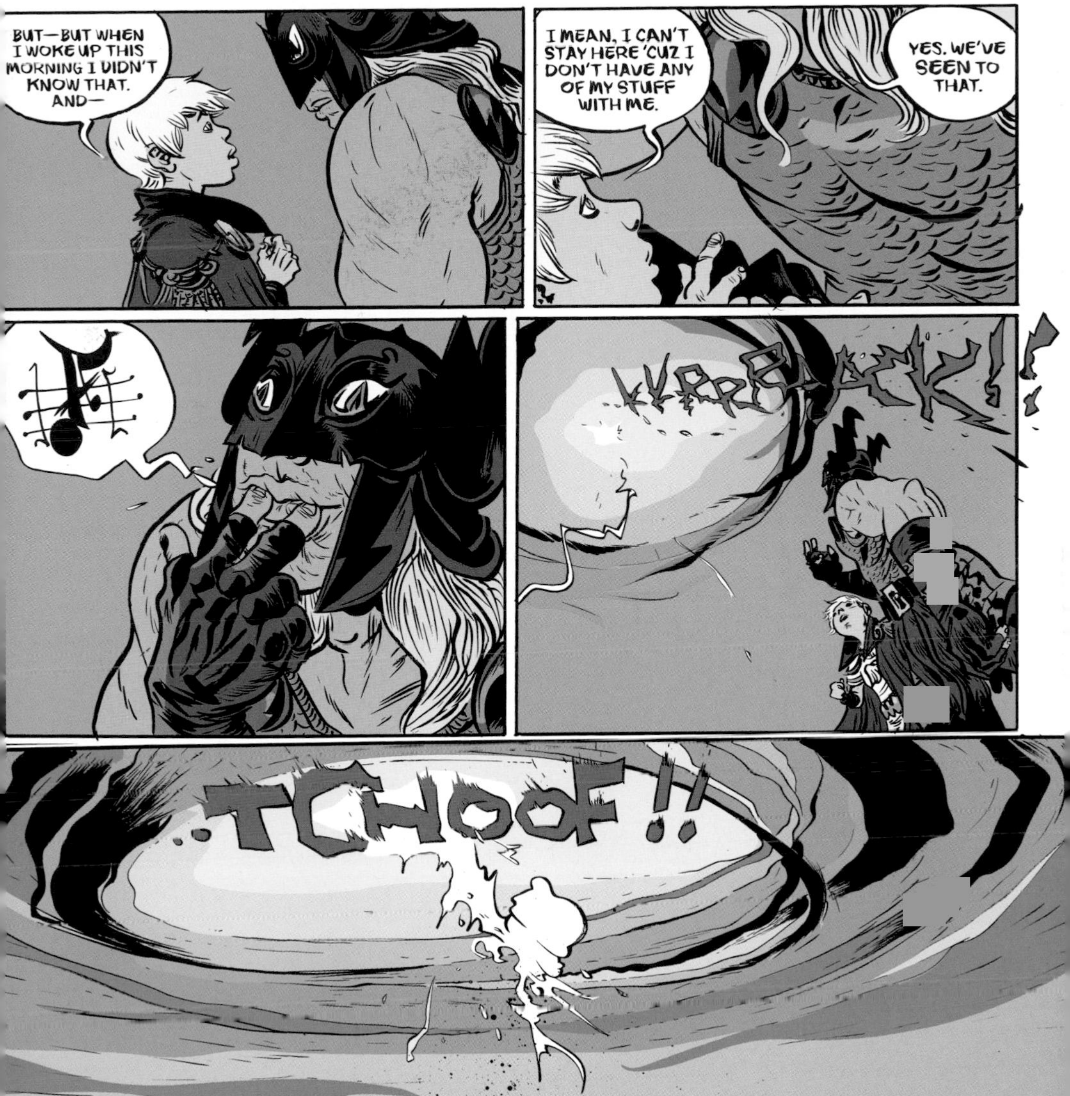

BUT—BUT WHEN I WOKE UP THIS MORNING I DIDN'T KNOW THAT. AND—
I MEAN, I CAN'T STAY HERE 'CUZ I DON'T HAVE ANY OF MY STUFF WITH ME.
YES. WE'VE SEEN TO THAT.
TCHOOF!!

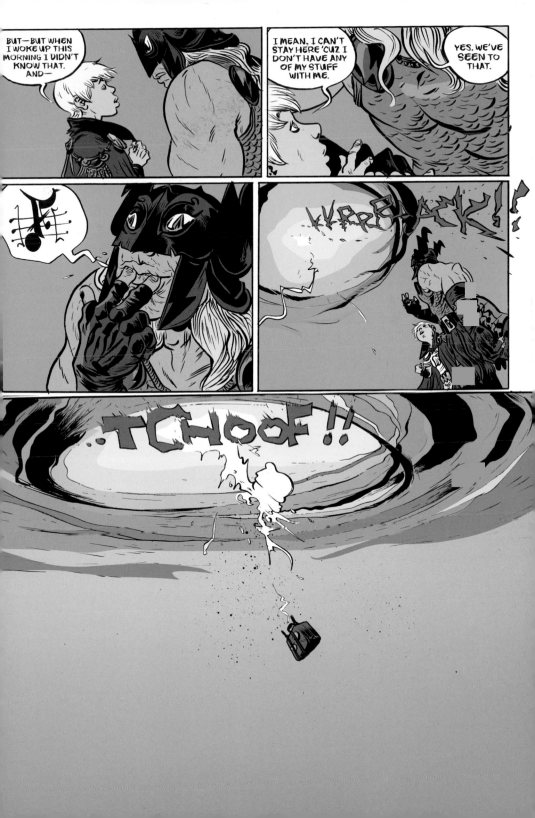

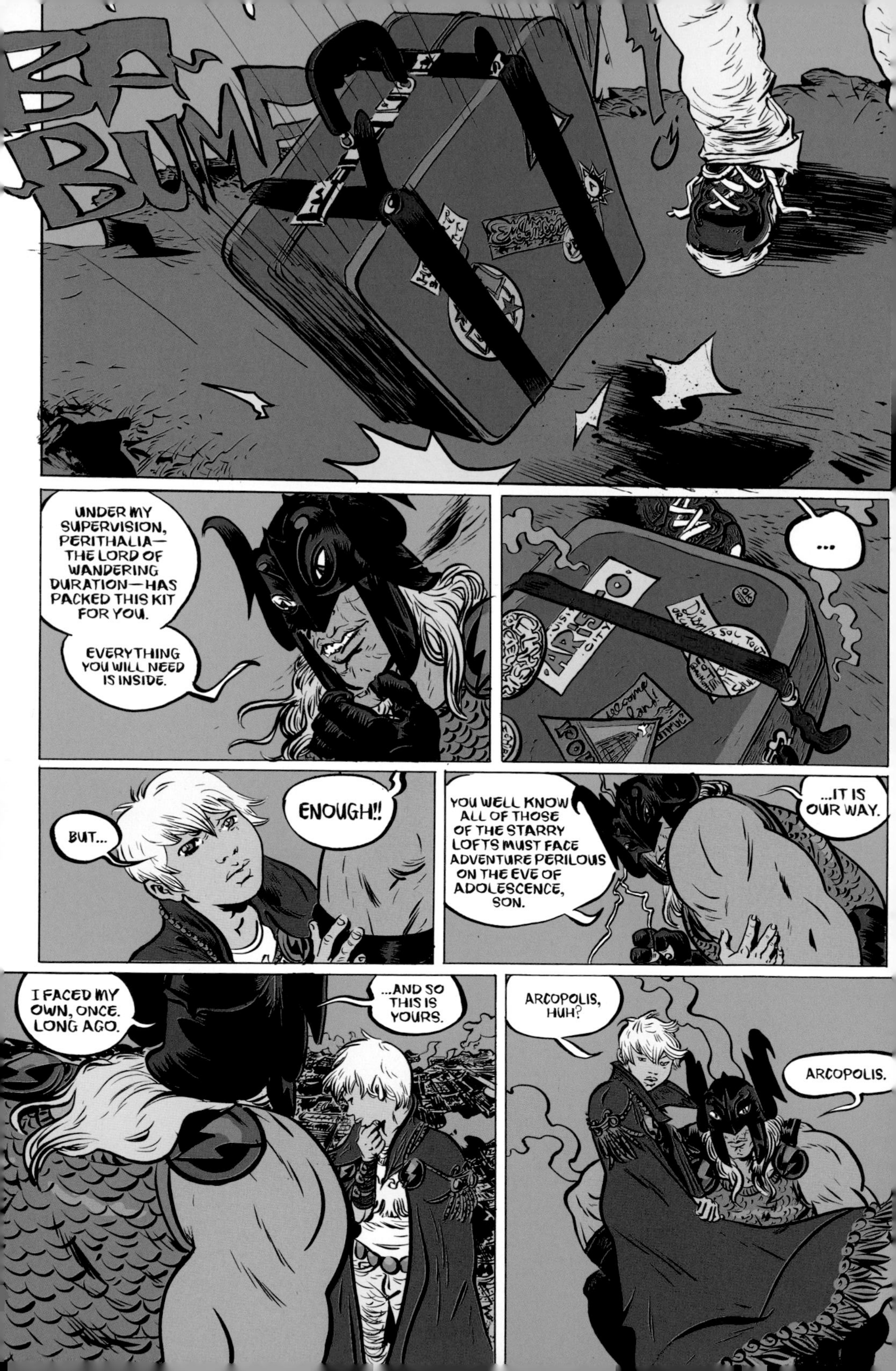
BA-BUMF!
UNDER MY SUPERVISION, PERITHALIA—THE LORD OF WANDERING DURATION—HAS PACKED THIS KIT FOR YOU.
EVERYTHING YOU WILL NEED IS INSIDE.
...
BUT...
ENOUGH!!
YOU WELL KNOW ALL OF THOSE OF THE STARRY LOFTS MUST FACE ADVENTURE PERILOUS ON THE EVE OF ADOLESCENCE, SON.
...IT IS OUR WAY.
I FACED MY OWN, ONCE. LONG AGO.
...AND SO THIS IS YOURS.
ARCOPOLIS, HUH?
ARCOPOLIS.

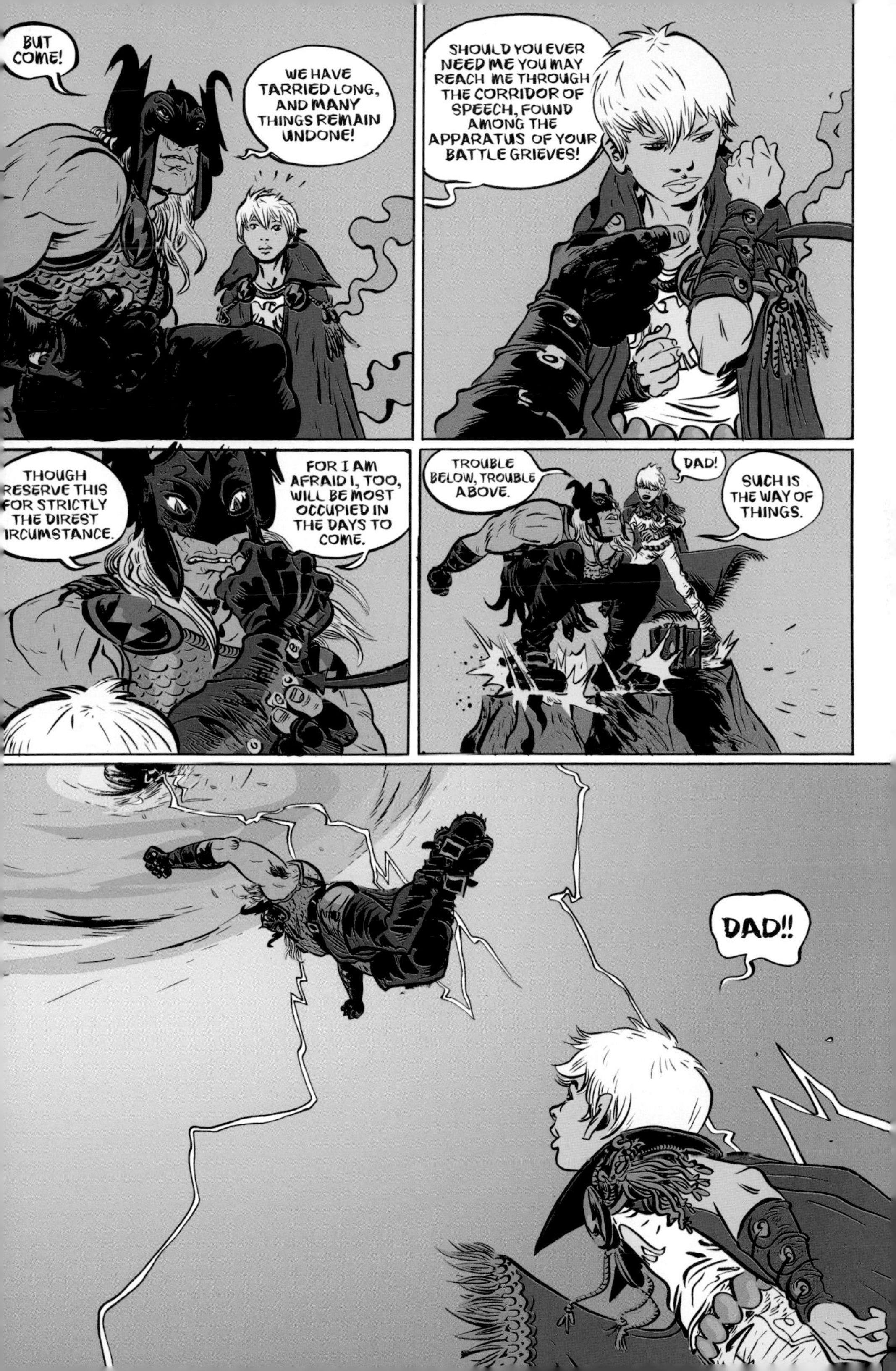
BUT COME!
WE HAVE TARRIED LONG, AND MANY THINGS REMAIN UNDONE!
SHOULD YOU EVER NEED ME YOU MAY REACH ME THROUGH THE CORRIDOR OF SPEECH, FOUND AMONG THE APPARATUS OF YOUR BATTLE GRIEVES!
THOUGH RESERVE THIS FOR STRICTLY THE DIREST IRCUMSTANCE.
FOR I AM AFRAID I, TOO, WILL BE MOST OCCUPIED IN THE DAYS TO COME.
TROUBLE BELOW, TROUBLE ABOVE.
DAD!
SUCH IS THE WAY OF THINGS.
DAD!!

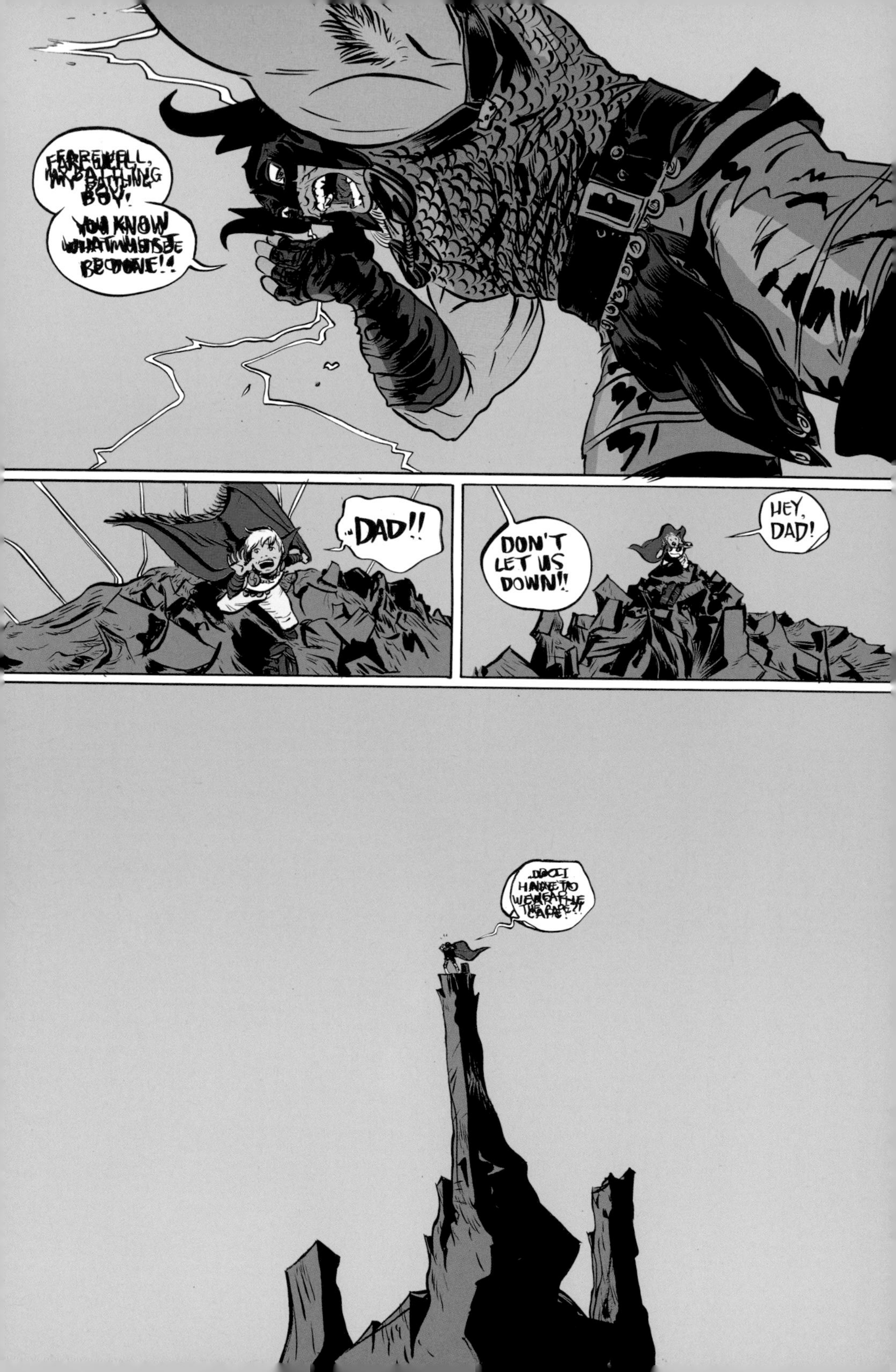
FAREWELL, MY BATTLING BOY!
YOU KNOW WHAT MUST BE DONE!!
...DAD!!
HEY, DAD!
DON'T LET US DOWN!!
...DO I HAVE TO WEAR THE CAPE?!

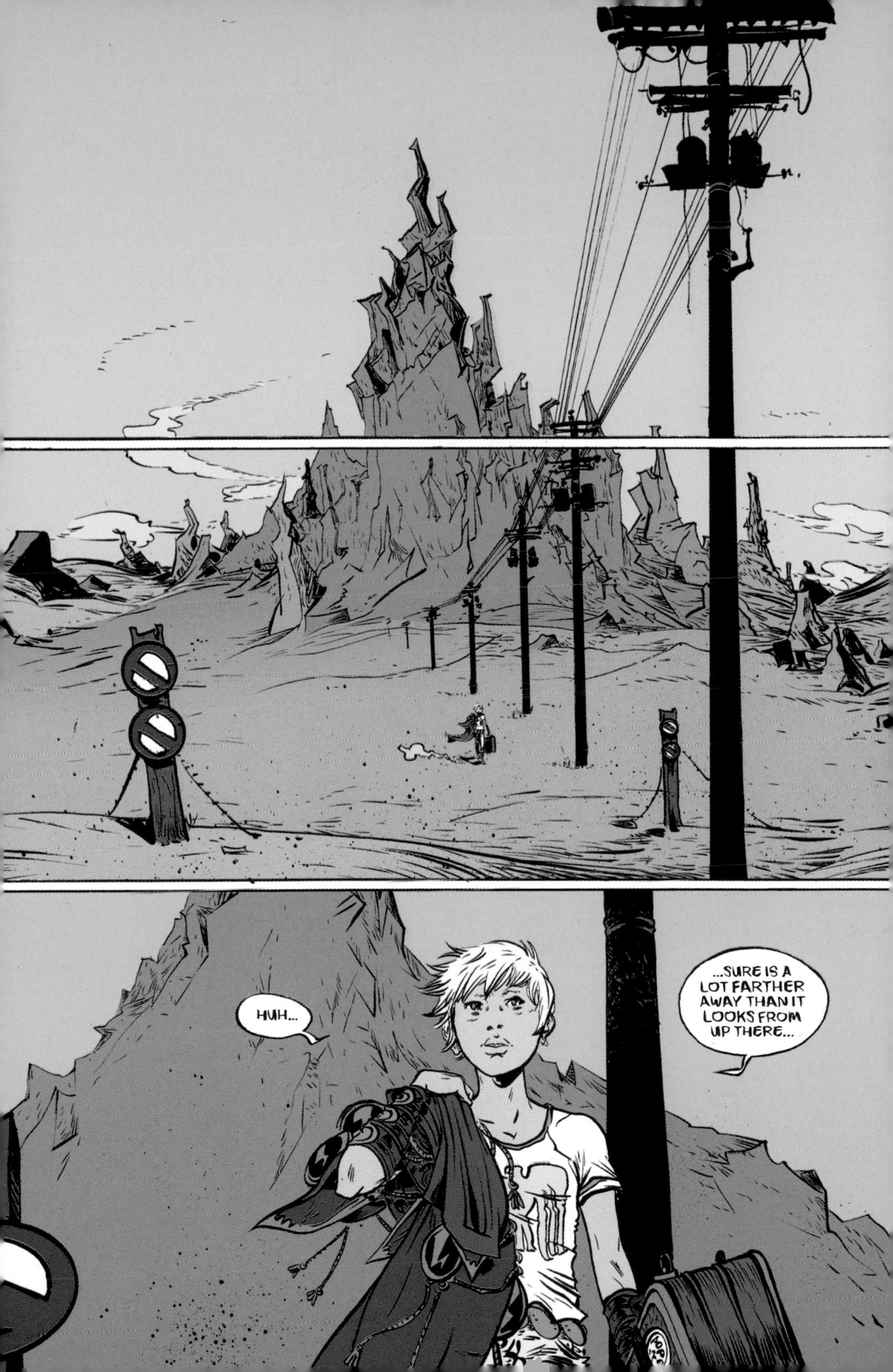
HUH...
...SURE IS A LOT FARTHER AWAY THAN IT LOOKS FROM UP THERE...

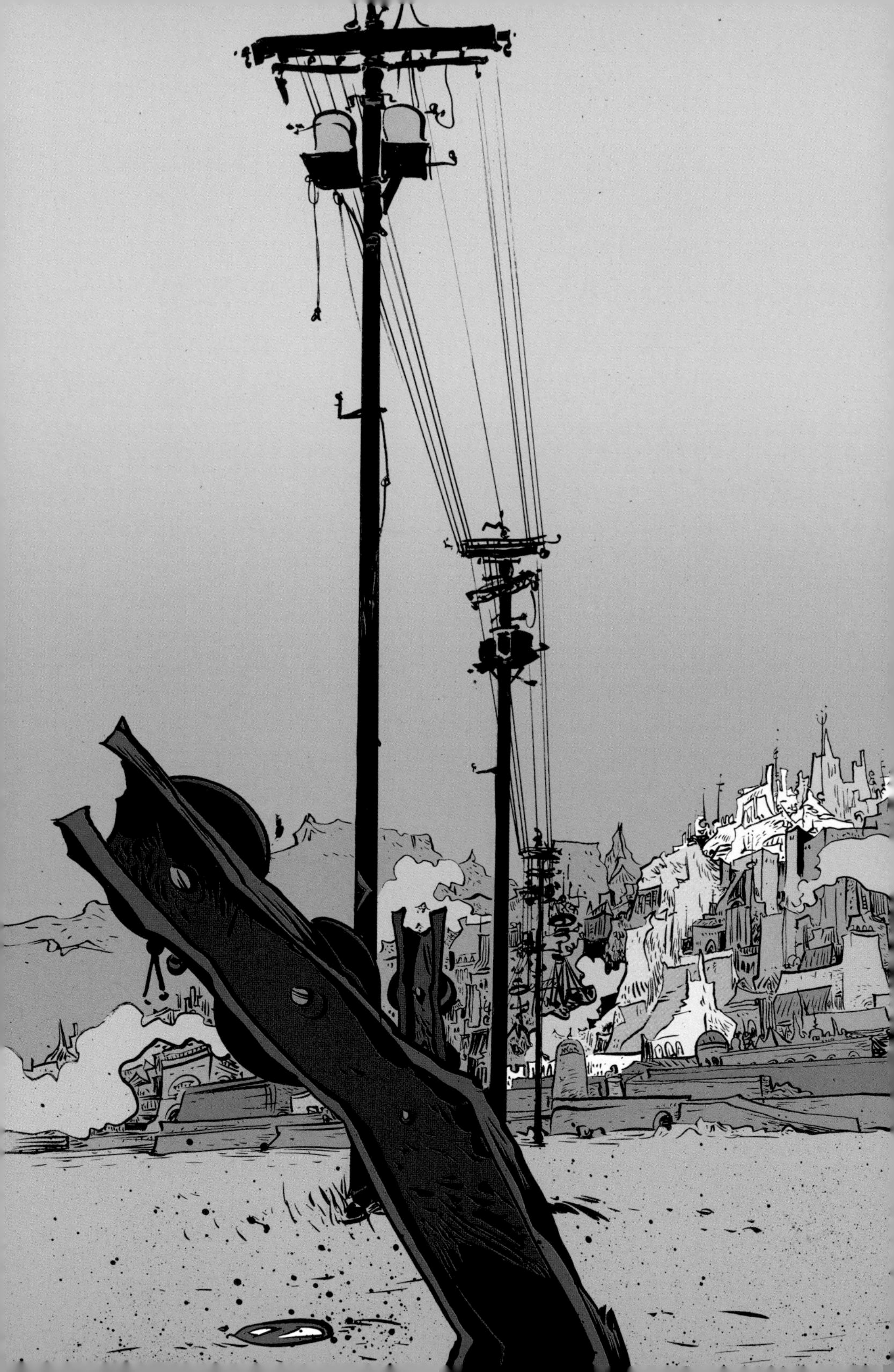

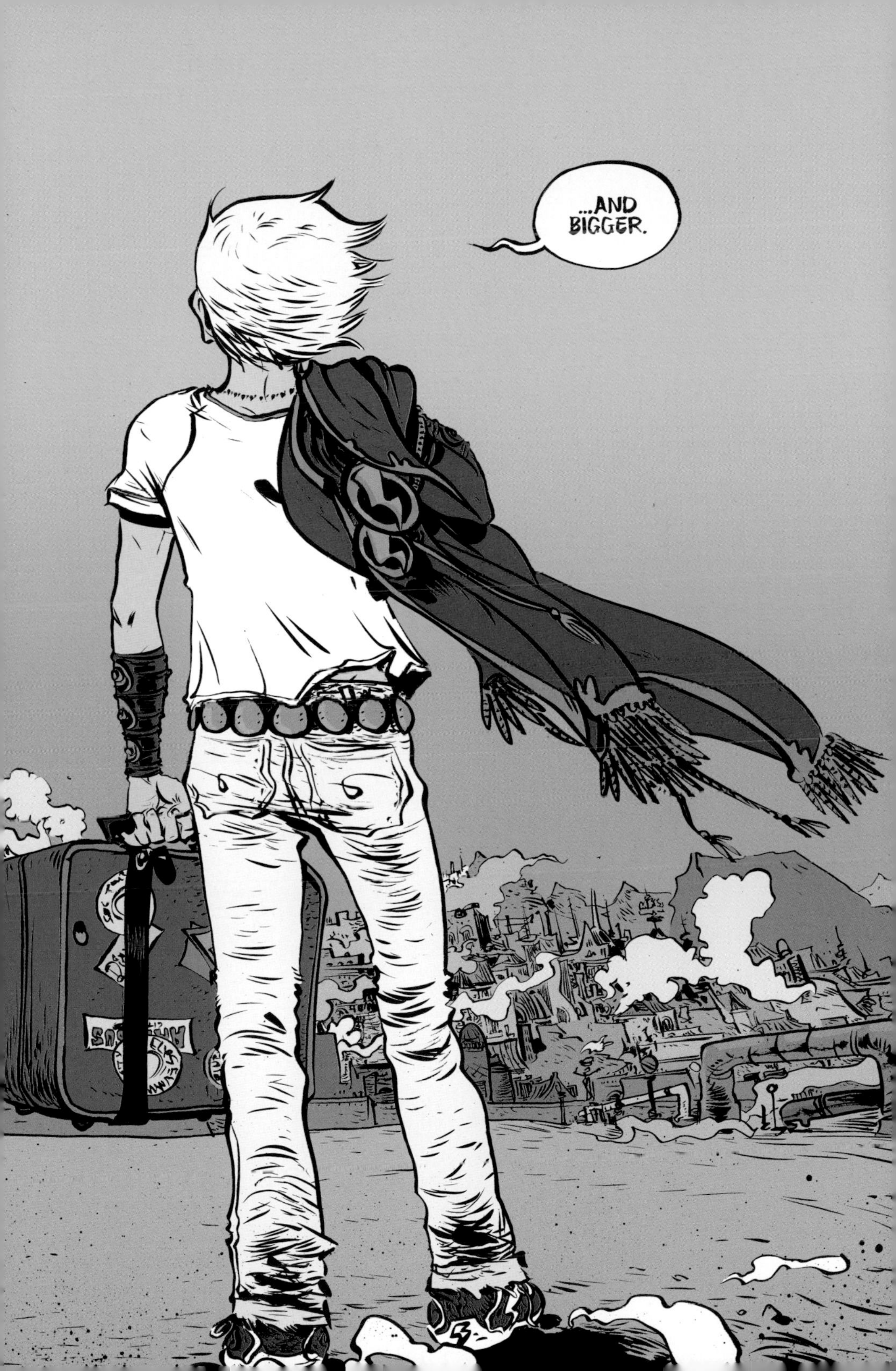
...AND BIGGER.

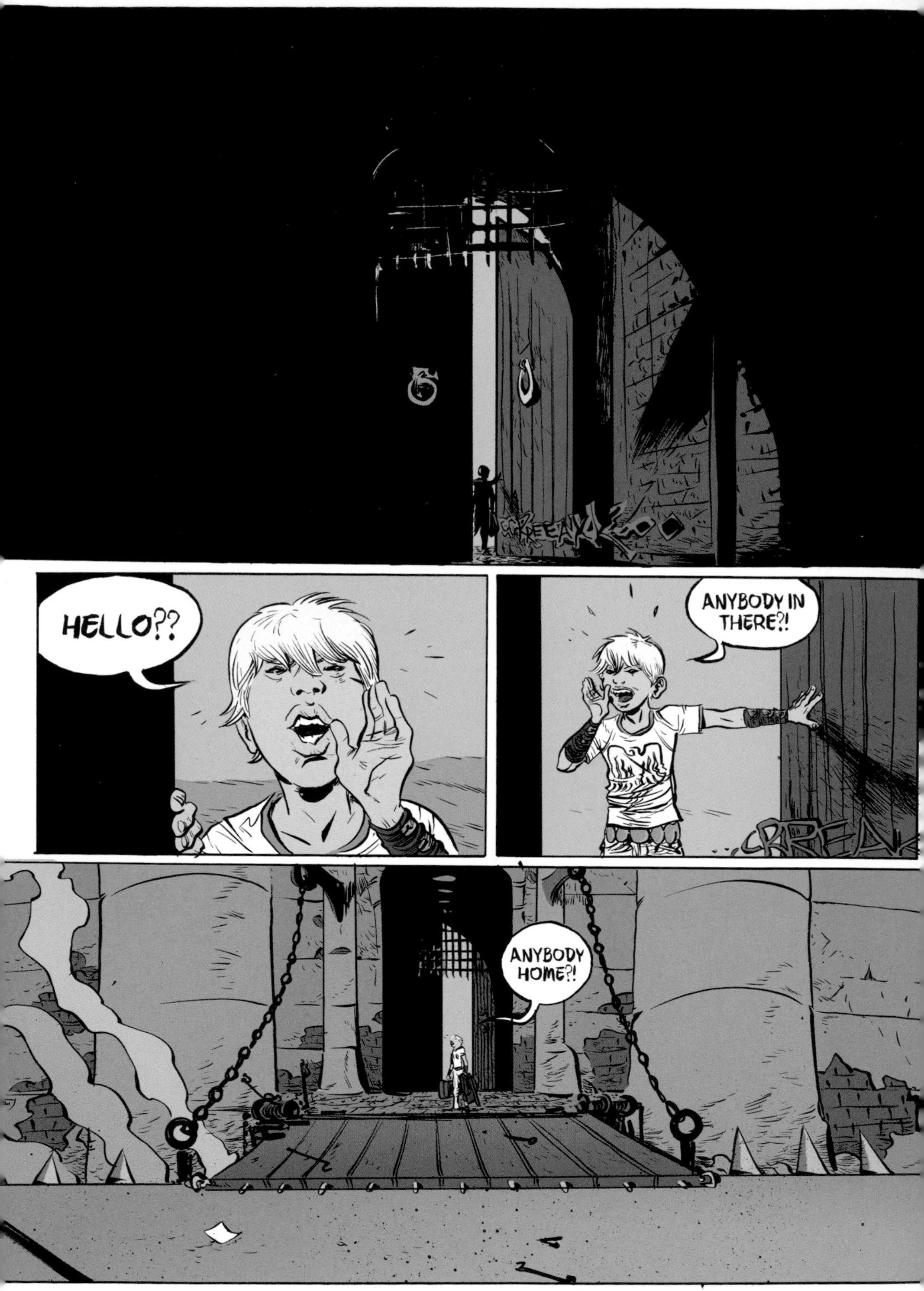
CRREEAAK
HELLO??
ANYBODY IN THERE?!
CRREAK
ANYBODY HOME?!

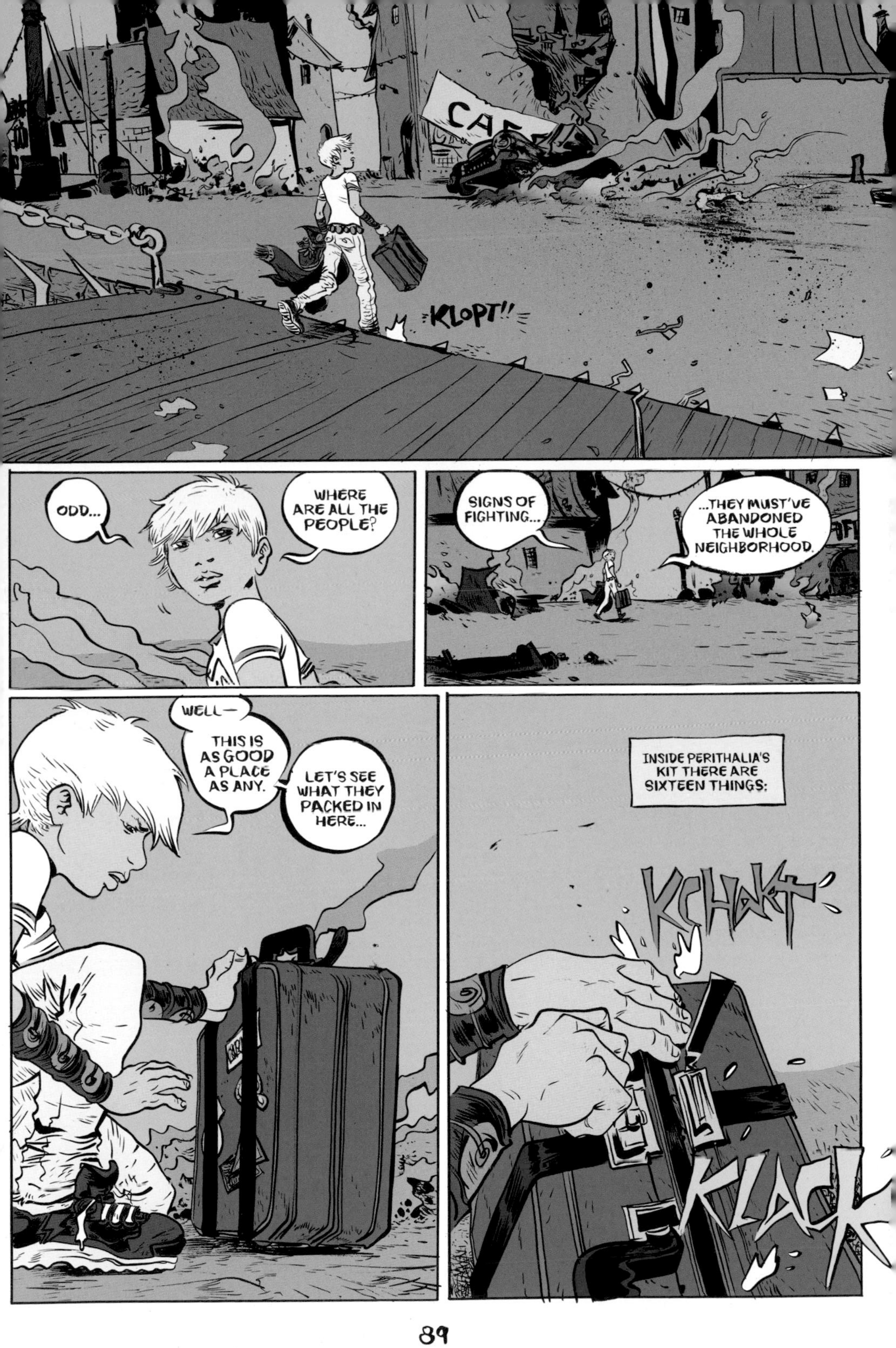
KLOPT!!
ODD...
WHERE ARE ALL THE PEOPLE?
SIGNS OF FIGHTING...
...THEY MUST'VE ABANDONED THE WHOLE NEIGHBORHOOD.
WELL—
THIS IS AS GOOD A PLACE AS ANY.
LET'S SEE WHAT THEY PACKED IN HERE...
INSIDE PERITHALIA'S KIT THERE ARE SIXTEEN THINGS:
KCHAKT
KLACK

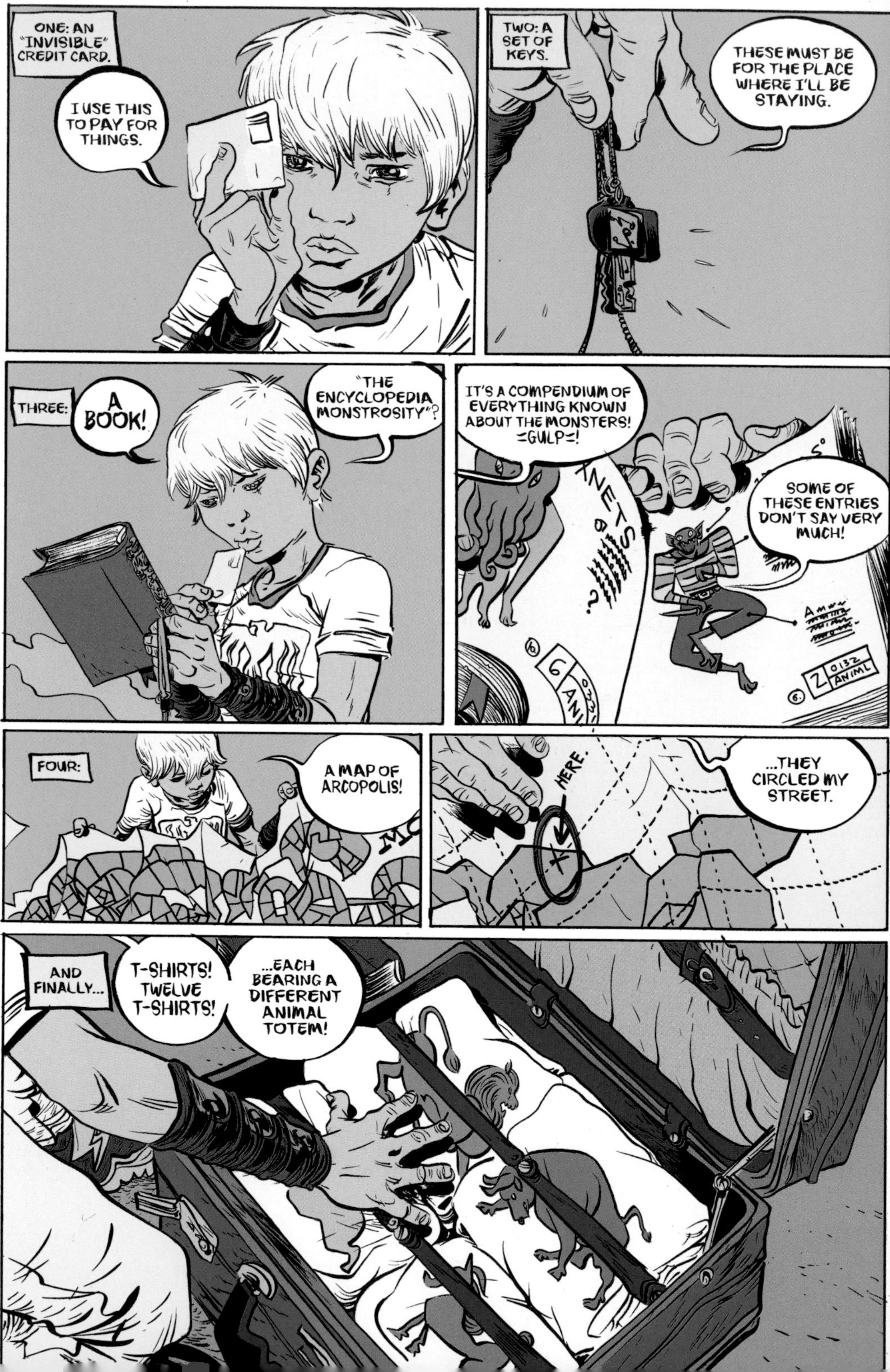
ONE: AN "INVISIBLE" CREDIT CARD.
I USE THIS TO PAY FOR THINGS.
TWO: A SET OF KEYS.
THESE MUST BE FOR THE PLACE WHERE I'LL BE STAYING.
THREE:
A BOOK!
"THE ENCYCLOPEDIA MONSTROSITY"?
IT'S A COMPENDIUM OF EVERYTHING KNOWN ABOUT THE MONSTERS! =GULP=!
SOME OF THESE ENTRIES DON'T SAY VERY MUCH!
FOUR:
A MAP OF ARCOPOLIS!
HERE.
...THEY CIRCLED MY STREET.
AND FINALLY...
T-SHIRTS! TWELVE T-SHIRTS!
...EACH BEARING A DIFFERENT ANIMAL TOTEM!

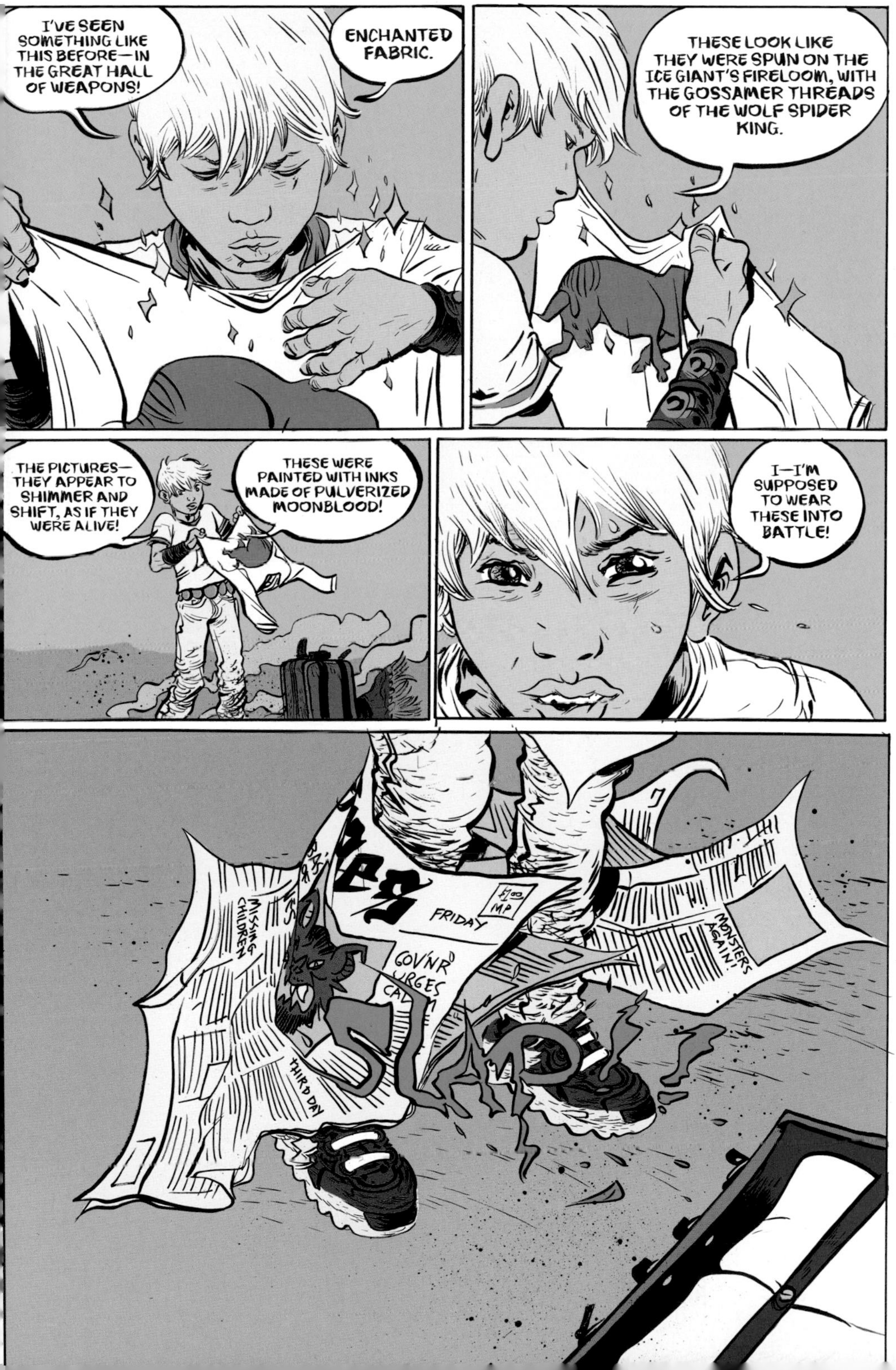
I'VE SEEN SOMETHING LIKE THIS BEFORE—IN THE GREAT HALL OF WEAPONS!
ENCHANTED FABRIC.
THESE LOOK LIKE THEY WERE SPUN ON THE ICE GIANT'S FIRELOOM, WITH THE GOSSAMER THREADS OF THE WOLF SPIDER KING.
THE PICTURES—THEY APPEAR TO SHIMMER AND SHIFT, AS IF THEY WERE ALIVE!
THESE WERE PAINTED WITH INKS MADE OF PULVERIZED MOONBLOOD!
I—I'M SUPPOSED TO WEAR THESE INTO BATTLE!
MISSING CHILDREN
FRIDAY
GOV'NR URGES CALM
MONSTERS AGAIN!
THIRD DAY

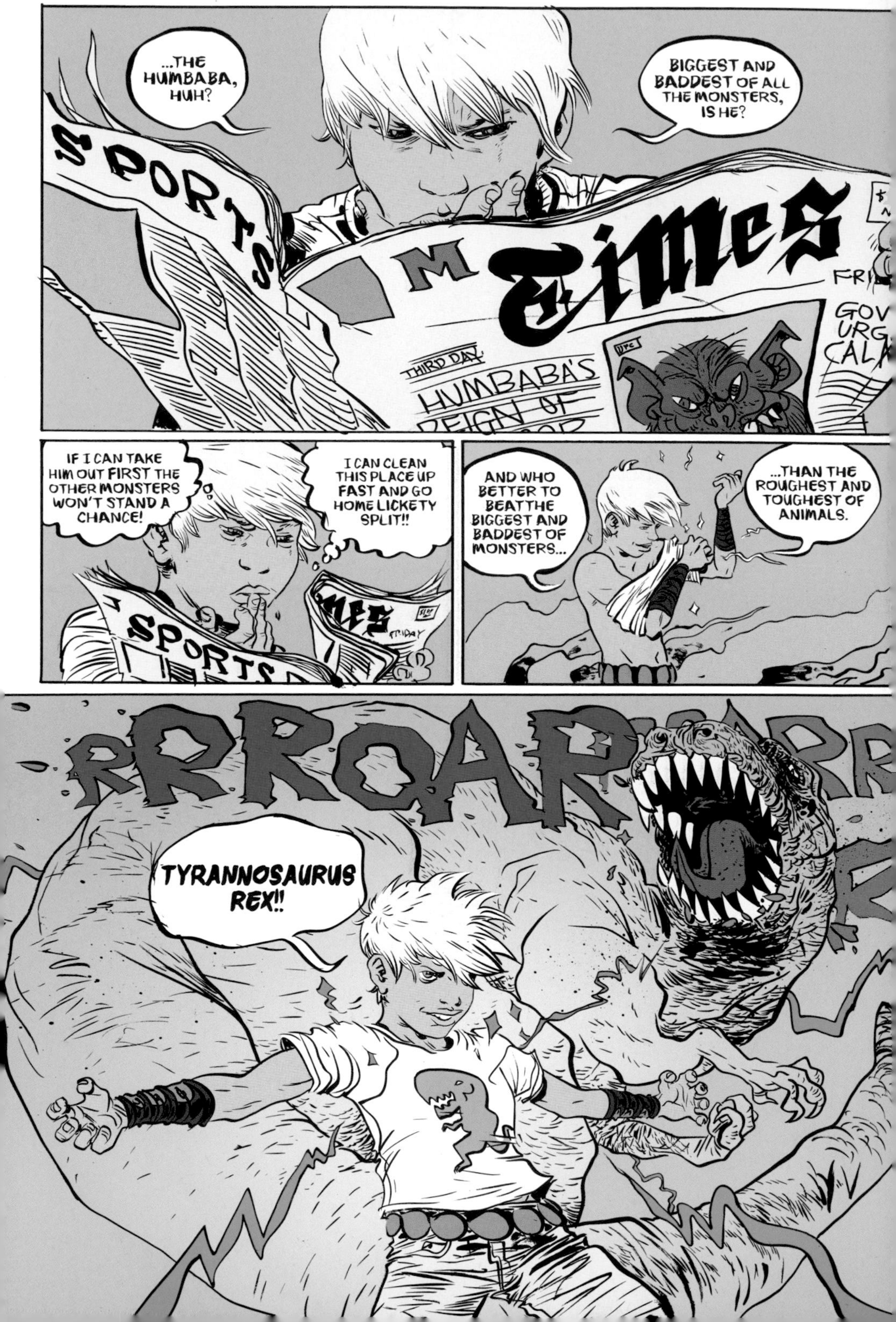

...THE HUMBABA, HUH?
BIGGEST AND BADDEST OF ALL THE MONSTERS, IS HE?
SPORTS
Times
THIRD DAY
HUMBABA'S
IF I CAN TAKE HIM OUT FIRST THE OTHER MONSTERS WON'T STAND A CHANCE!
I CAN CLEAN THIS PLACE UP FAST AND GO HOME LICKETY SPLIT!!
AND WHO BETTER TO BEAT THE BIGGEST AND BADDEST OF MONSTERS...
...THAN THE ROUGHEST AND TOUGHEST OF ANIMALS.
RRROAR
TYRANNOSAURUS REX!!

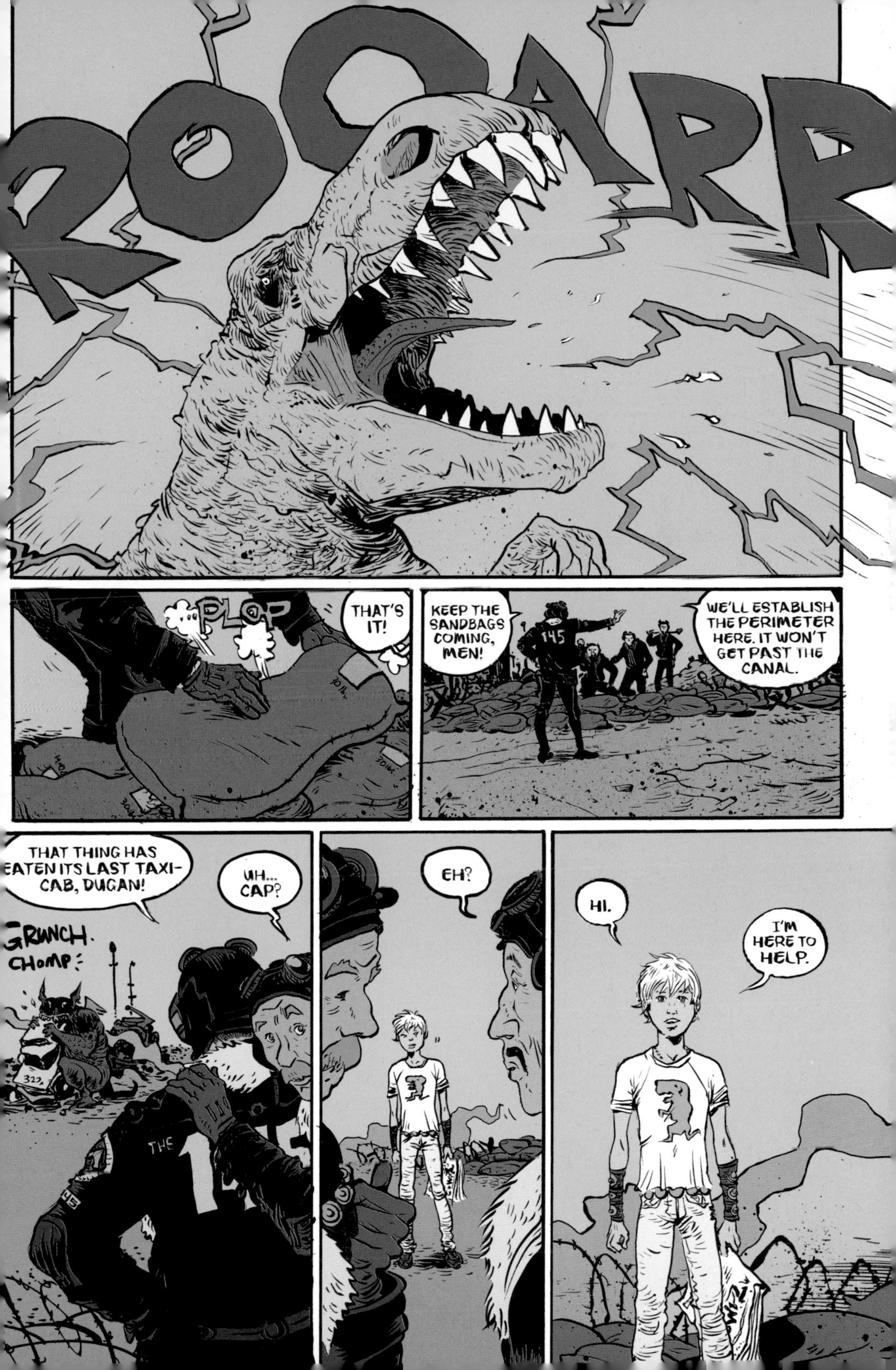
ROOARR
PLOP
THAT'S IT!
KEEP THE SANDBAGS COMING, MEN!
WE'LL ESTABLISH THE PERIMETER HERE. IT WON'T GET PAST THE CANAL.
THAT THING HAS EATEN ITS LAST TAXI-CAB, DUGAN!
UH... CAP?
GRUNCH.
CHOMP
EH?
HI.
I'M HERE TO HELP.

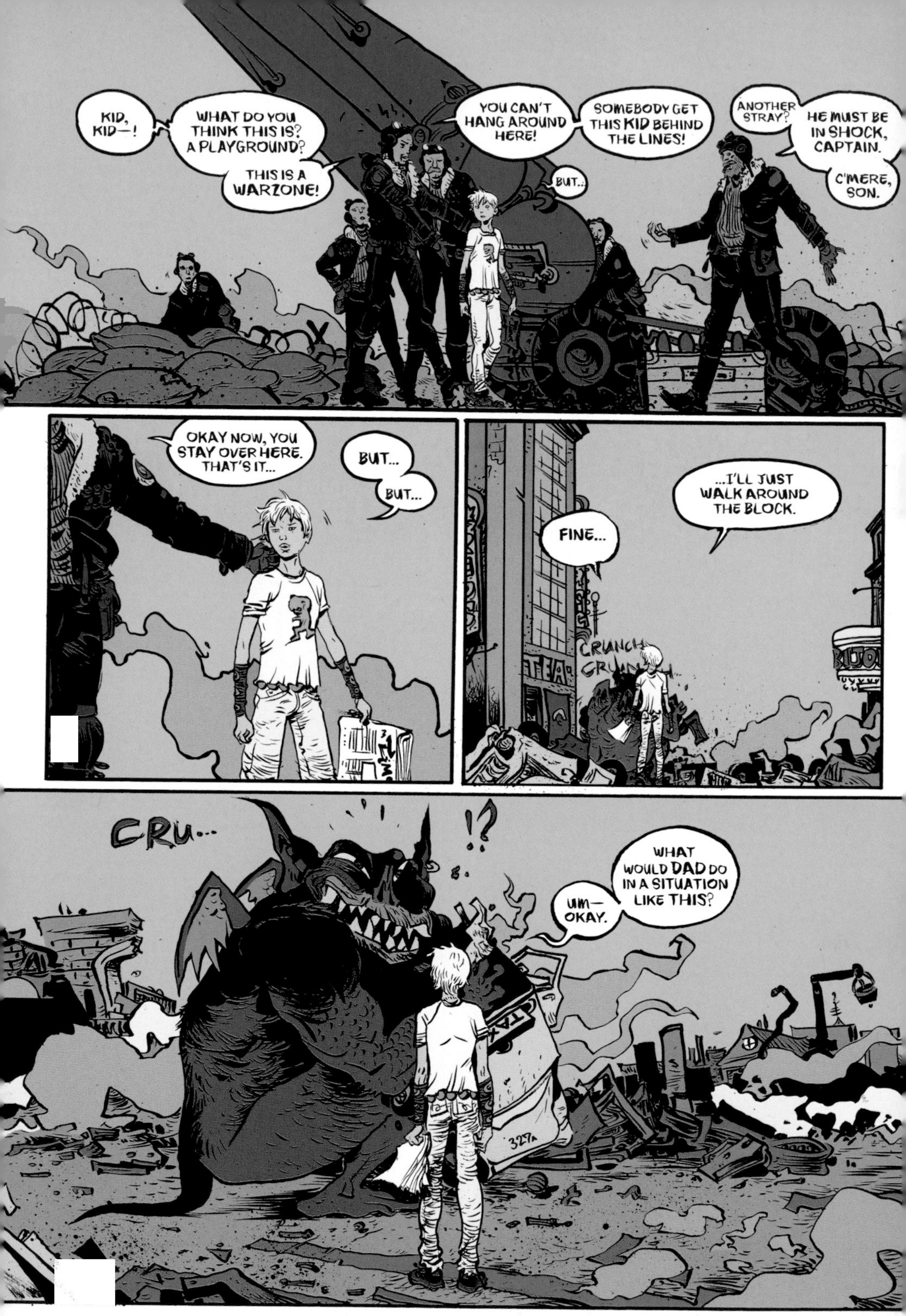
KID, KID—!
WHAT DO YOU THINK THIS IS? A PLAYGROUND?
THIS IS A WARZONE!
YOU CAN'T HANG AROUND HERE!
SOMEBODY GET THIS KID BEHIND THE LINES!
BUT...
ANOTHER STRAY?
HE MUST BE IN SHOCK, CAPTAIN.
C'MERE, SON.
OKAY NOW, YOU STAY OVER HERE. THAT'S IT...
BUT...
BUT...
...I'LL JUST WALK AROUND THE BLOCK.
FINE...
CRUNCH
CRU...
!?
WHAT WOULD DAD DO IN A SITUATION LIKE THIS?
UM—OKAY.

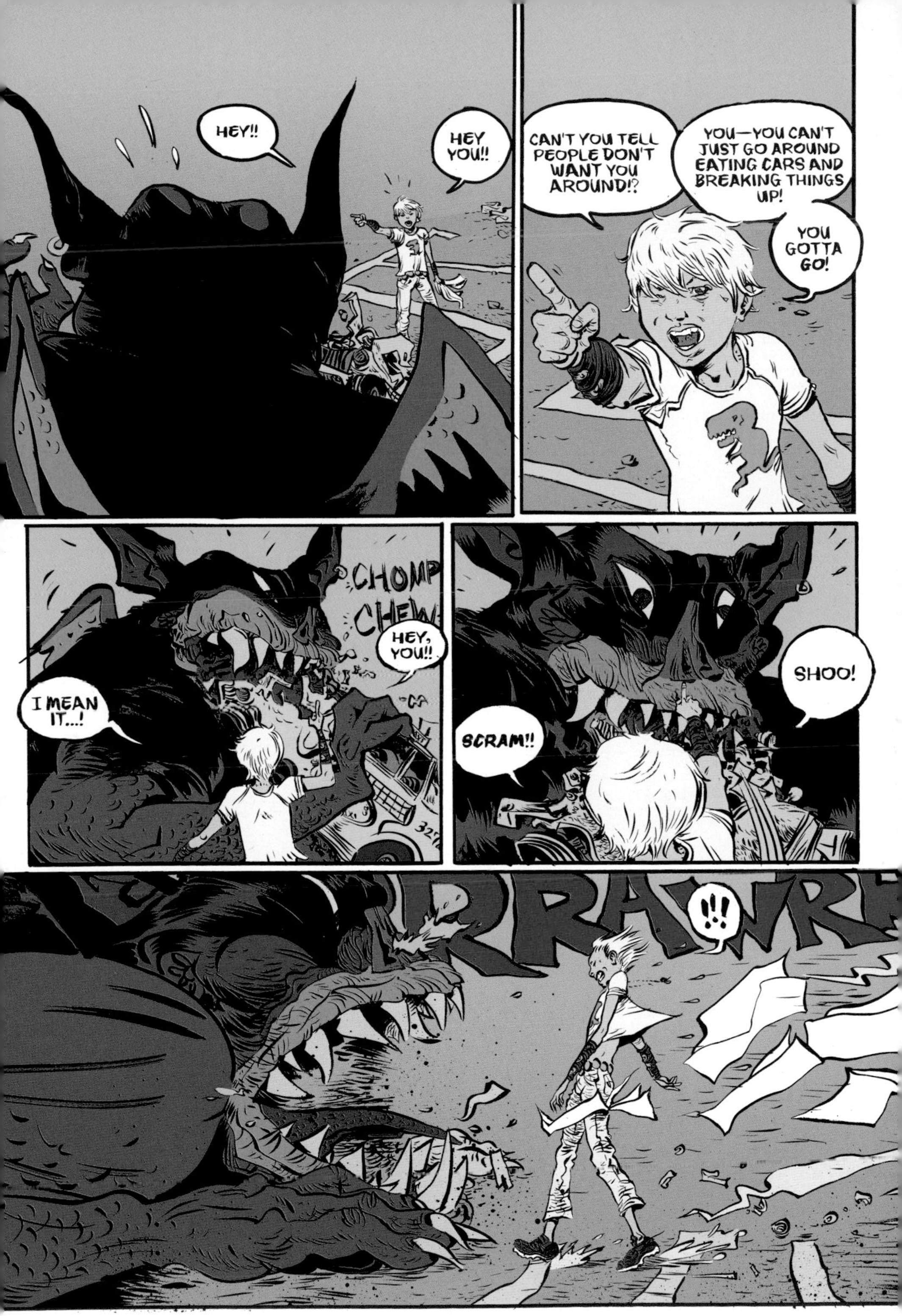

HEY!!
HEY YOU!!
CAN'T YOU TELL PEOPLE DON'T WANT YOU AROUND!?
YOU—YOU CAN'T JUST GO AROUND EATING CARS AND BREAKING THINGS UP!
YOU GOTTA GO!
CHOMP
CHEW
HEY, YOU!!
I MEAN IT...!
SHOO!
SCRAM!!
RAWR
!!!

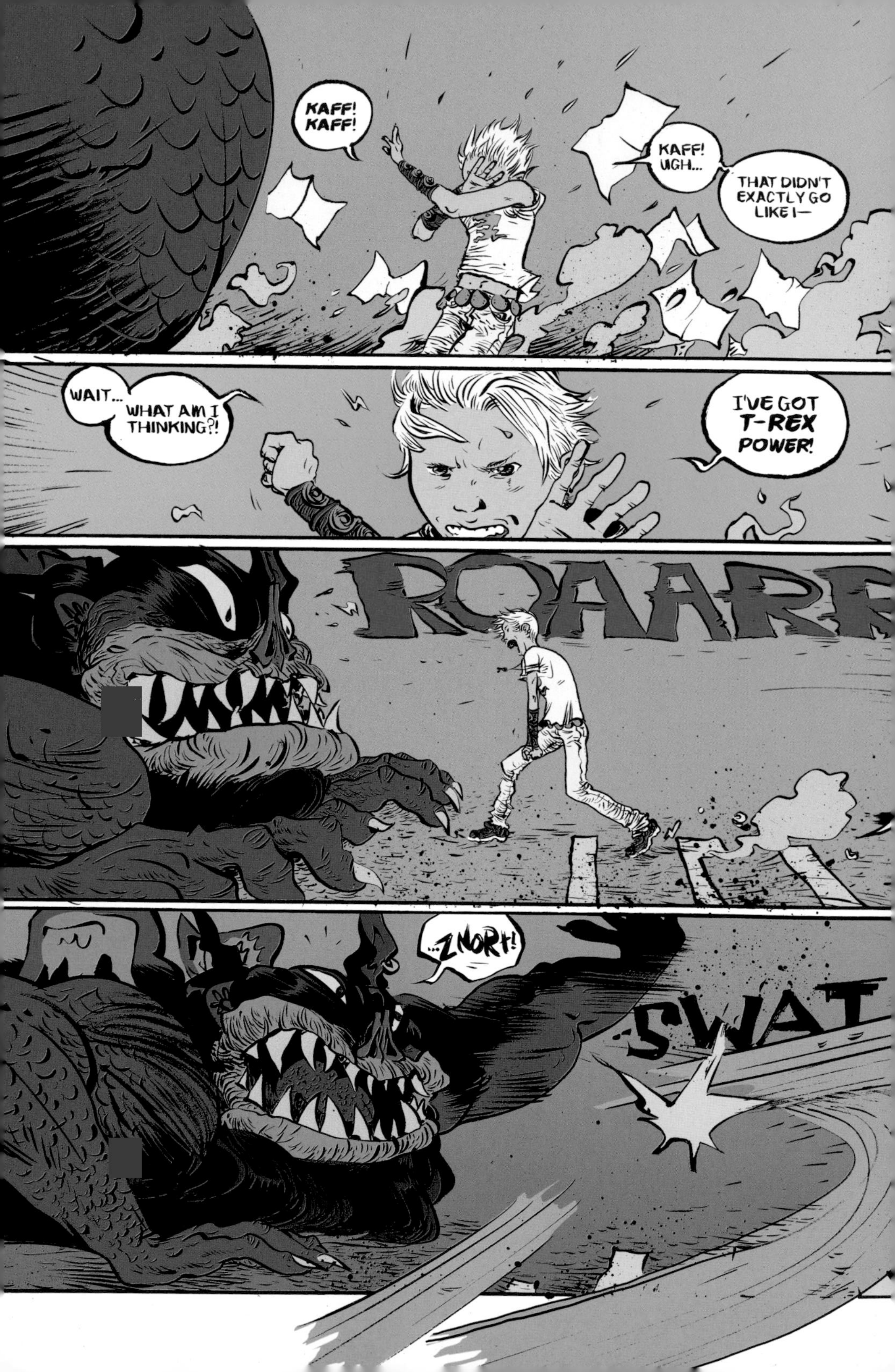
KAFF! KAFF!
KAFF! UGH...
THAT DIDN'T EXACTLY GO LIKE I—
WAIT... WHAT AM I THINKING?!
I'VE GOT **T-REX** POWER!
ROAARR
...ZNORT!
SWAT

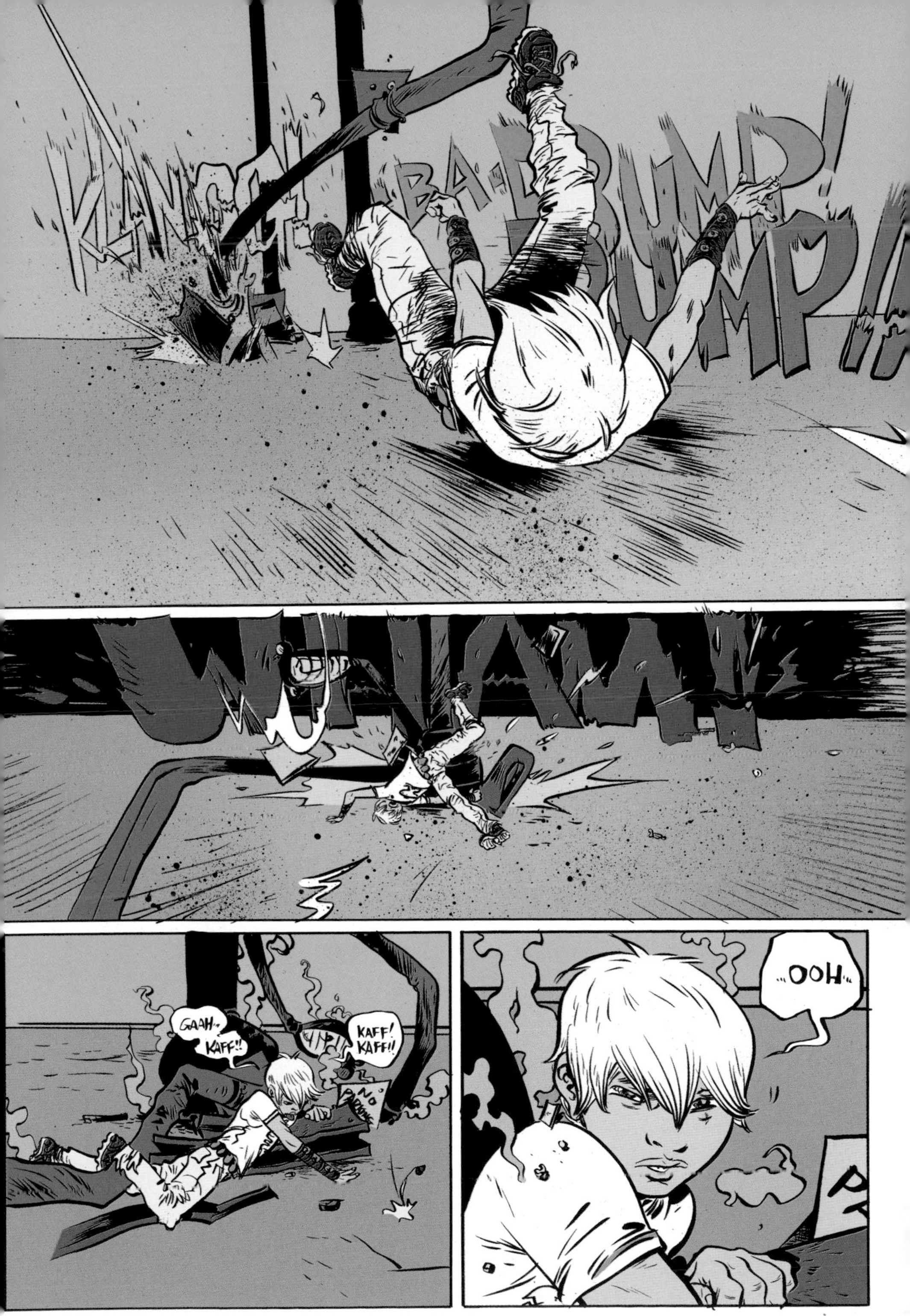
BA-BUMP!
BUMP!!
WHAM!
GAAH.. KAFF!!
KAFF! KAFF!!
..OOH..

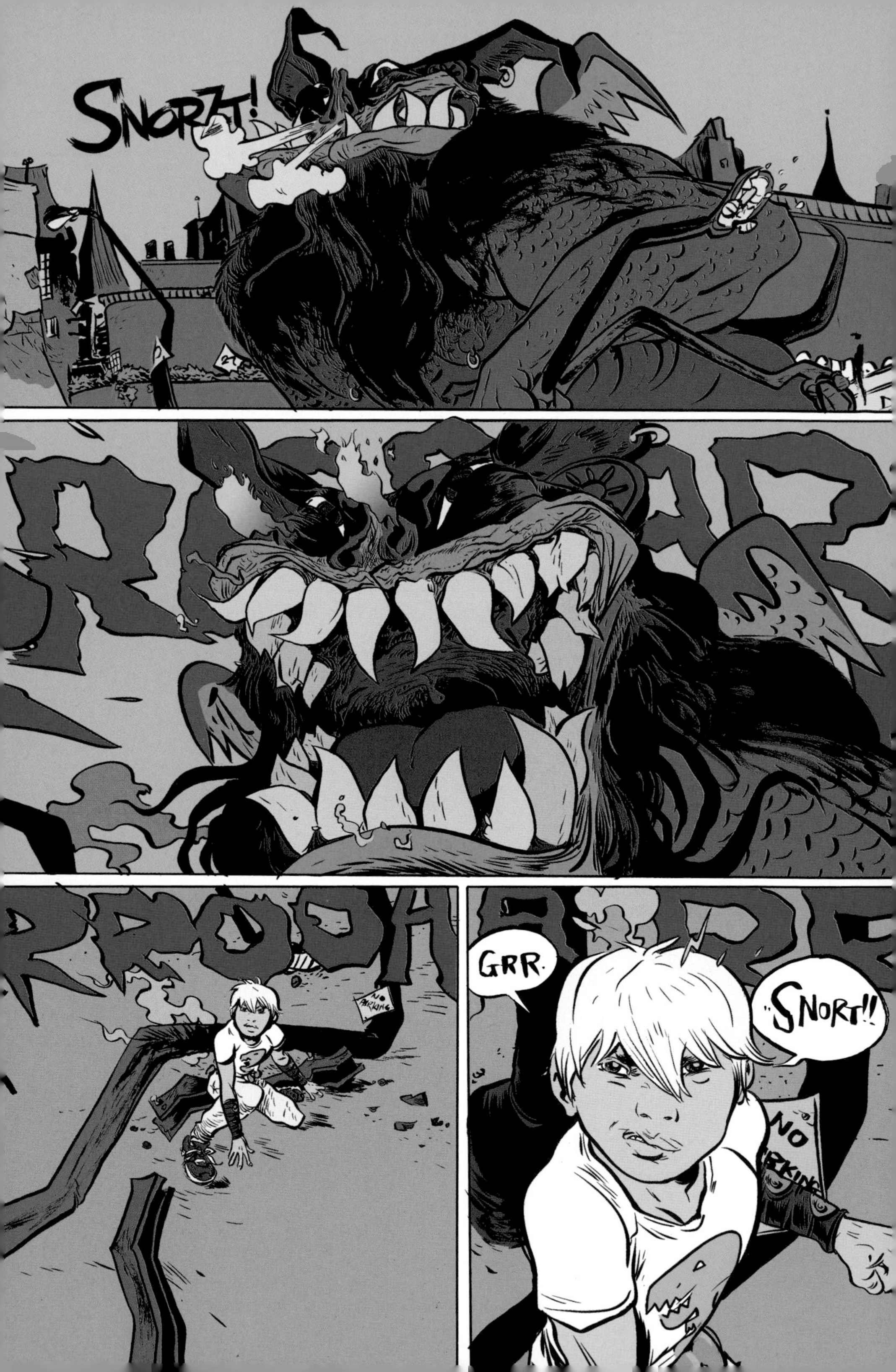
SNORZT!
NO PARKING
GRR.
SNORT!!

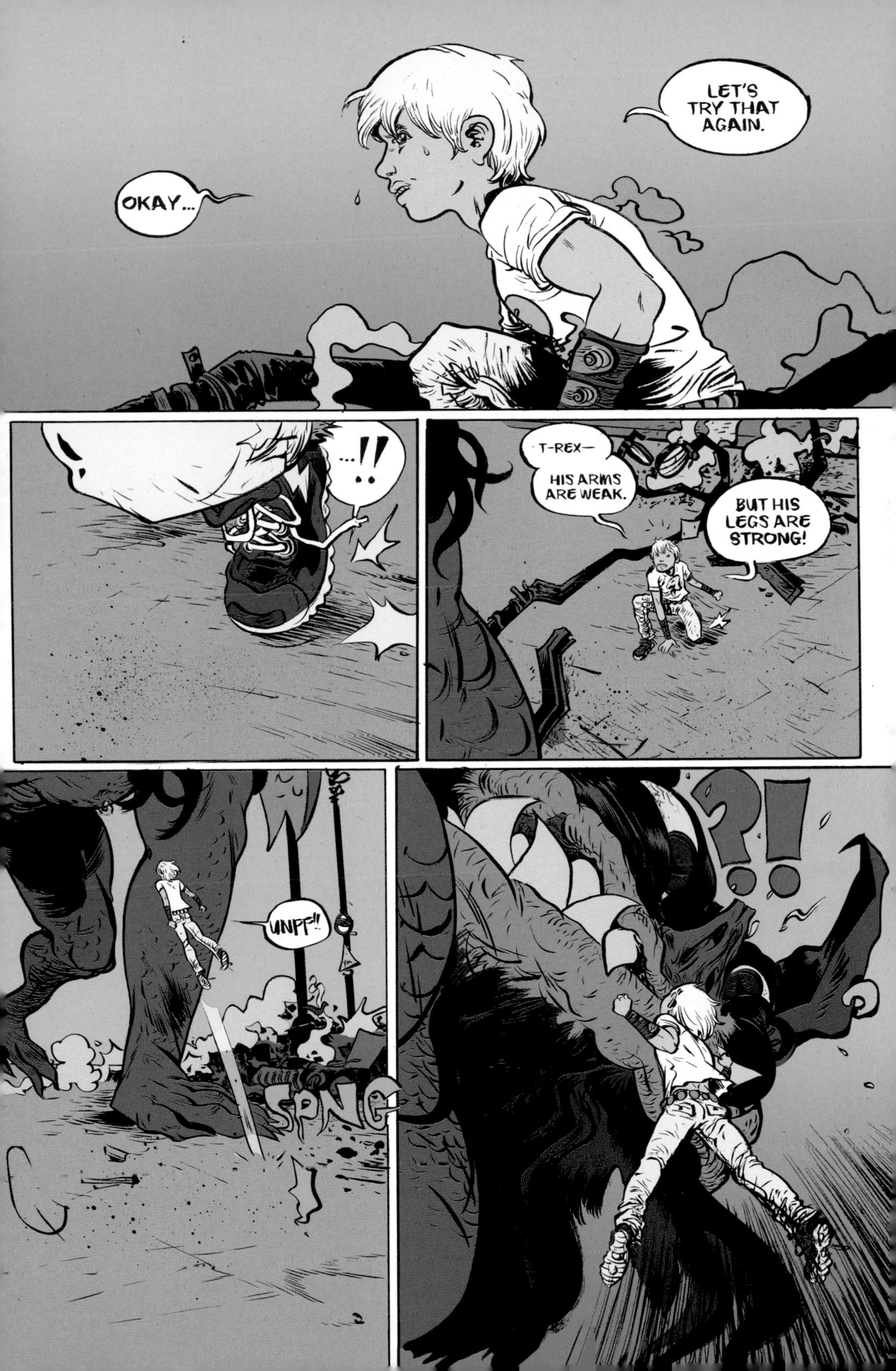
OKAY...
LET'S TRY THAT AGAIN.
...!!
T-REX—
HIS ARMS ARE WEAK.
BUT HIS LEGS ARE STRONG!
UNPF!!
SPNG
?!

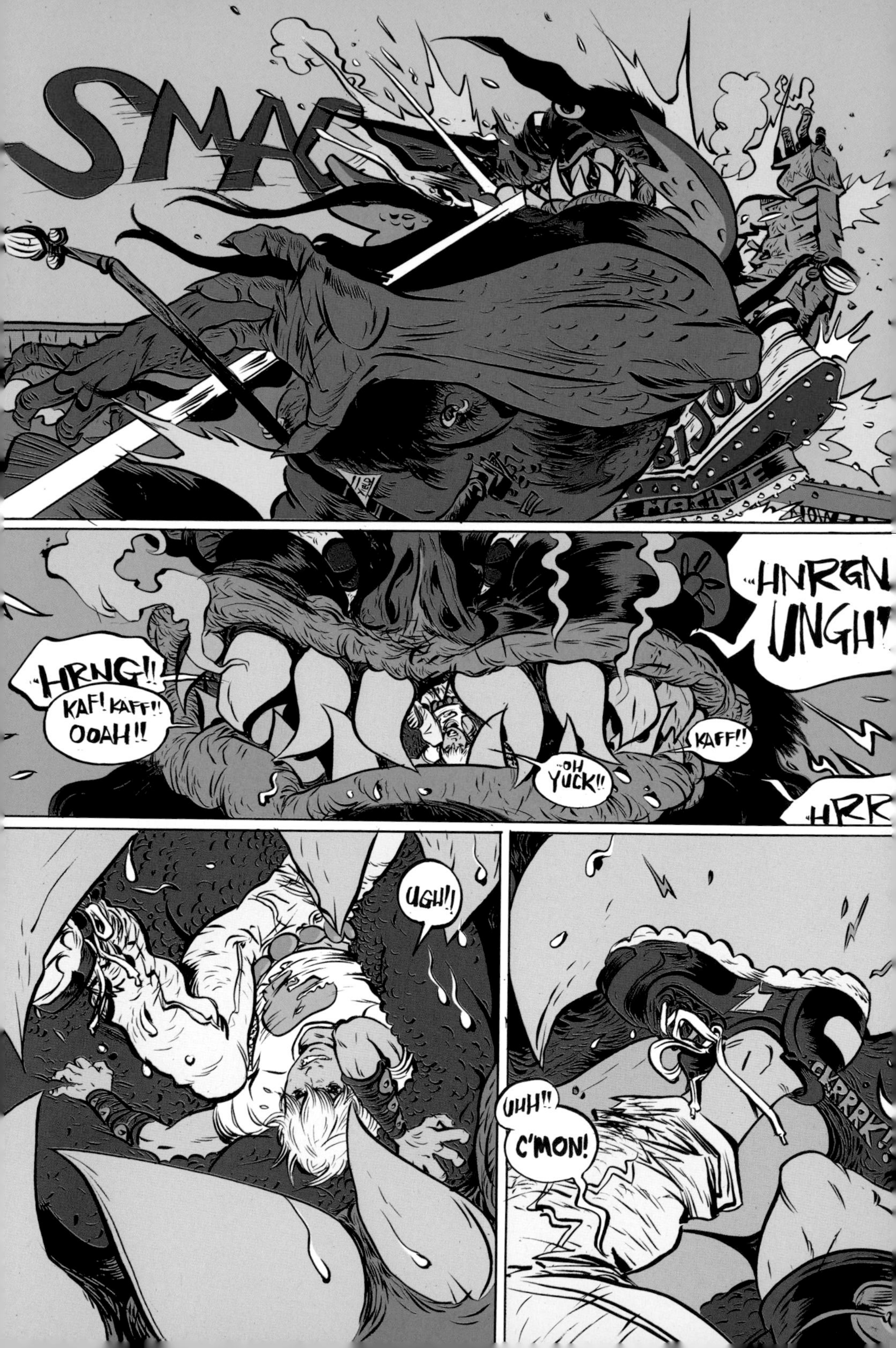
SMAK
BIJOU
..HNRGN UNGH'
..HRNG!! KAF! KAFF!! OOAH!!
KAFF!!
..OH YUCK!!
..HRR
UGH!!
UUH!! C'MON!

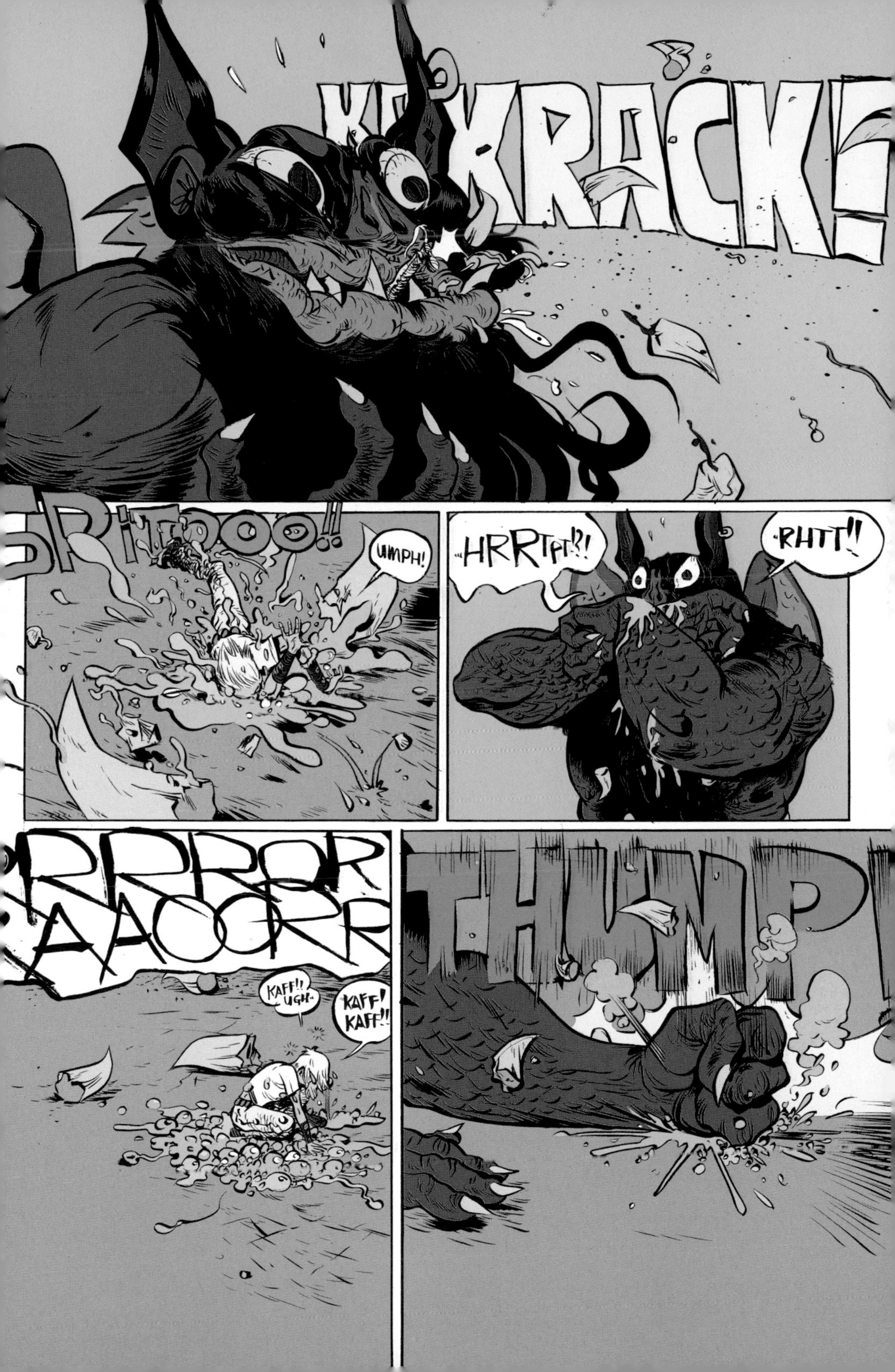
KRACK!
SPITOOO!!
UMPH!
HRRTPT!?!
RHTT!!
PRRROR
RAAOORR
KAFF!! UGH
KAFF! KAFF!!
THUMP!

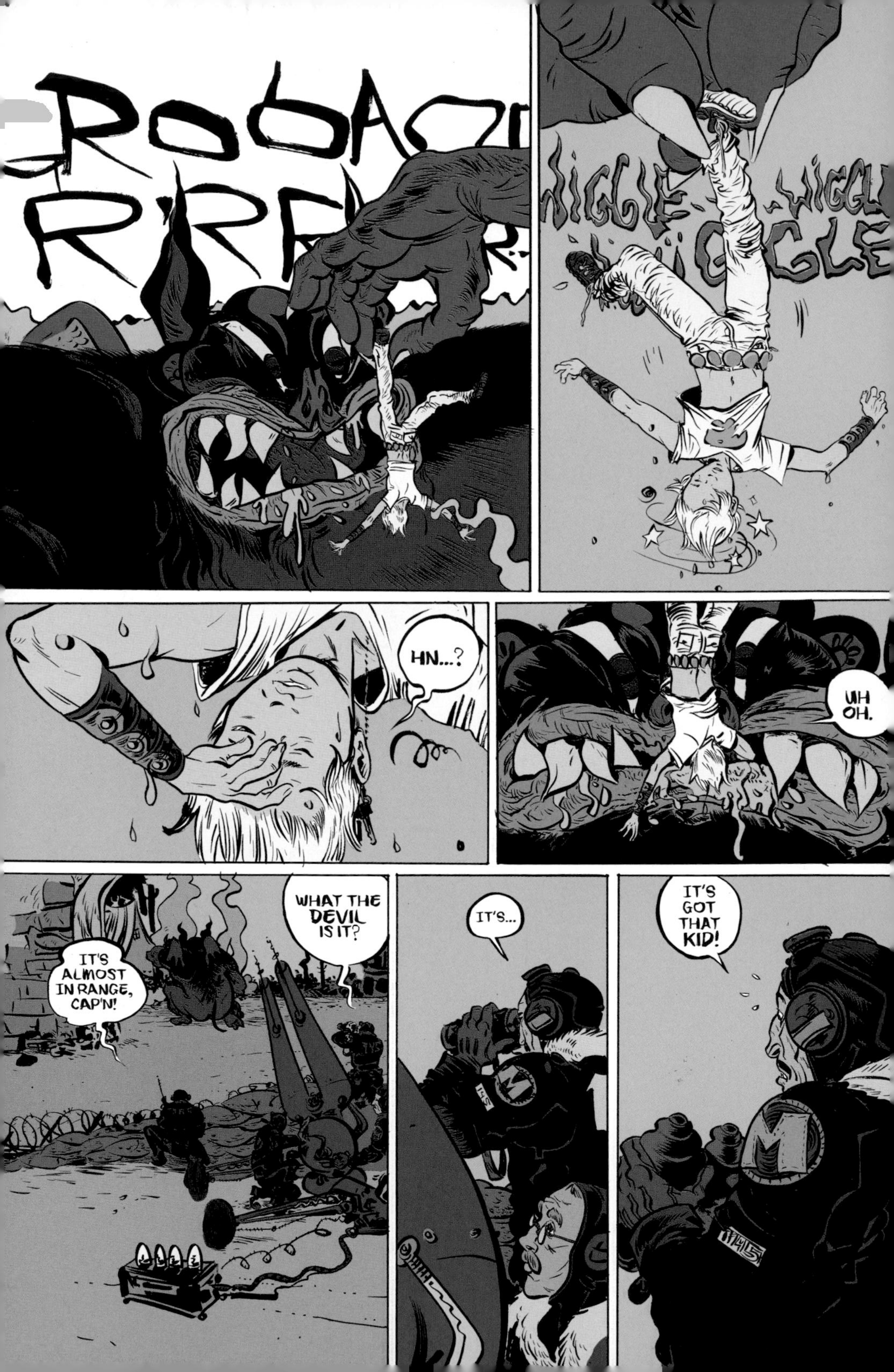
GROOAAR RRRR
WIGGLE WIGGLE WIGGLE
HN...?
UH OH.
WHAT THE DEVIL IS IT?
IT'S ALMOST IN RANGE, CAP'N!
IT'S...
IT'S GOT THAT KID!

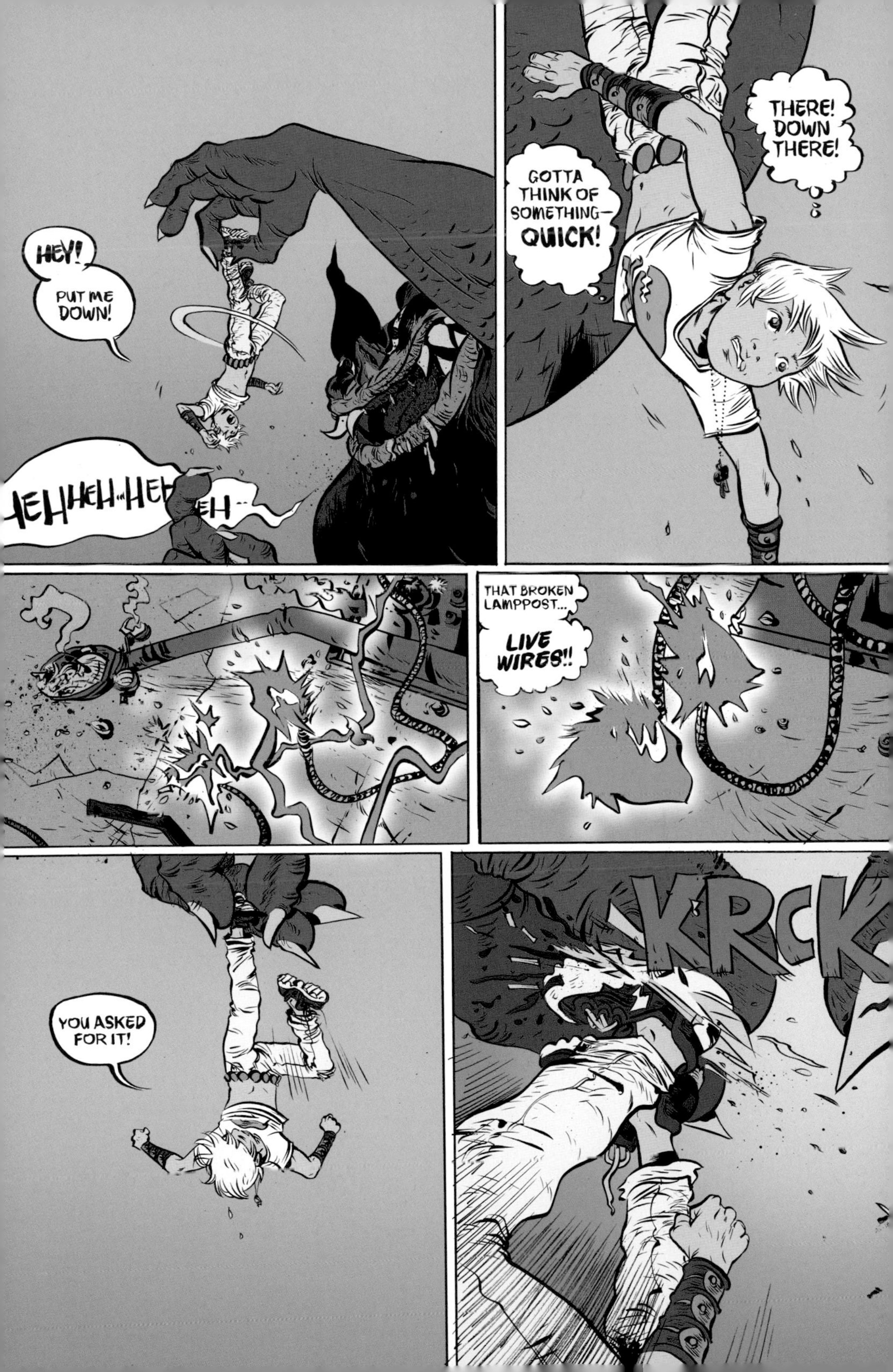
HEY!
PUT ME DOWN!
HEHHEH..HEH HEH..
GOTTA THINK OF SOMETHING— QUICK!
THERE! DOWN THERE!
THAT BROKEN LAMPPOST...
LIVE WIRES!!
YOU ASKED FOR IT!
KRCK

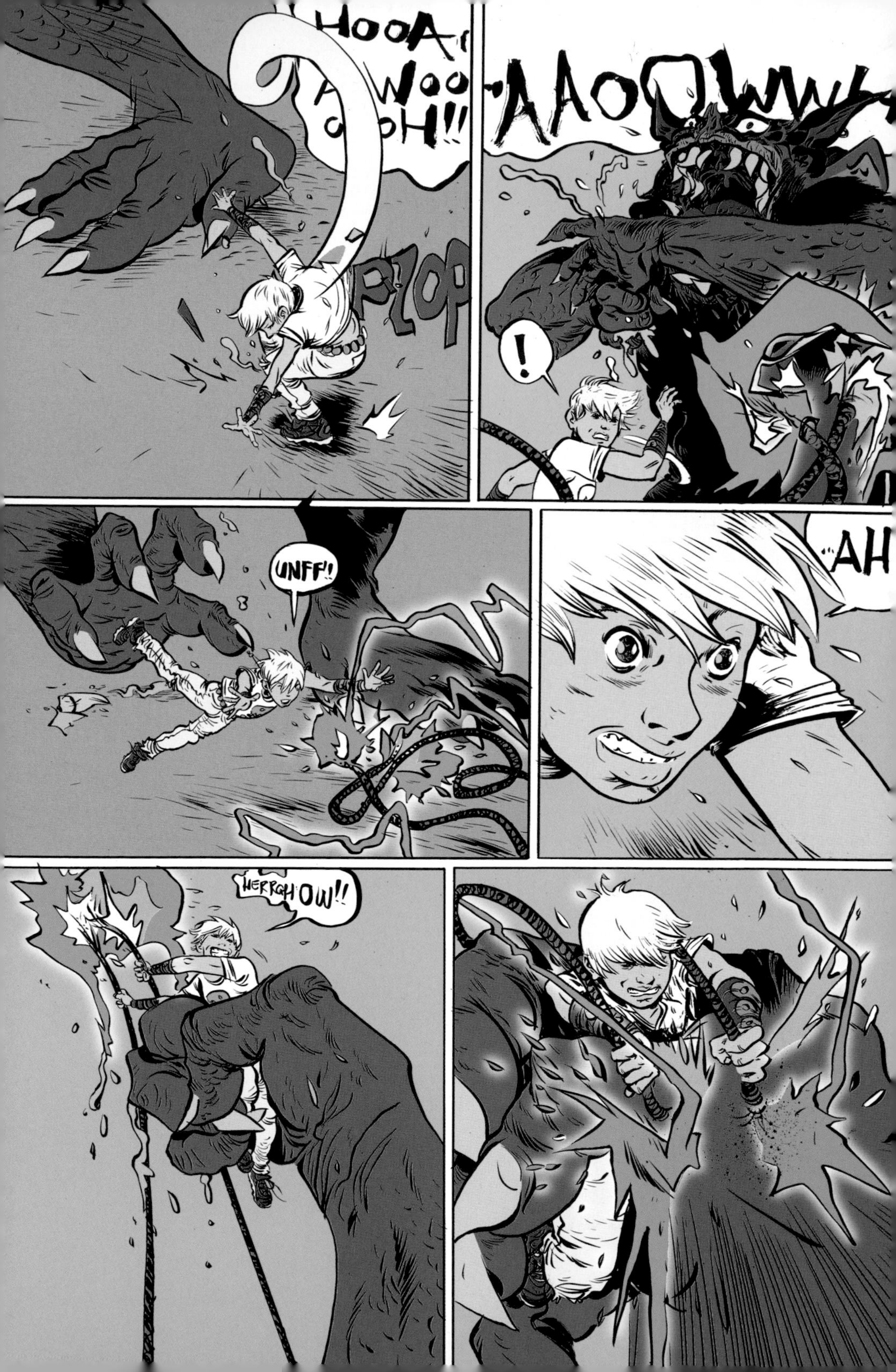
HOOA
WOO
OH!!
AAOOOWWW
!
UNFF!!
...AH
HERRGH OW!!

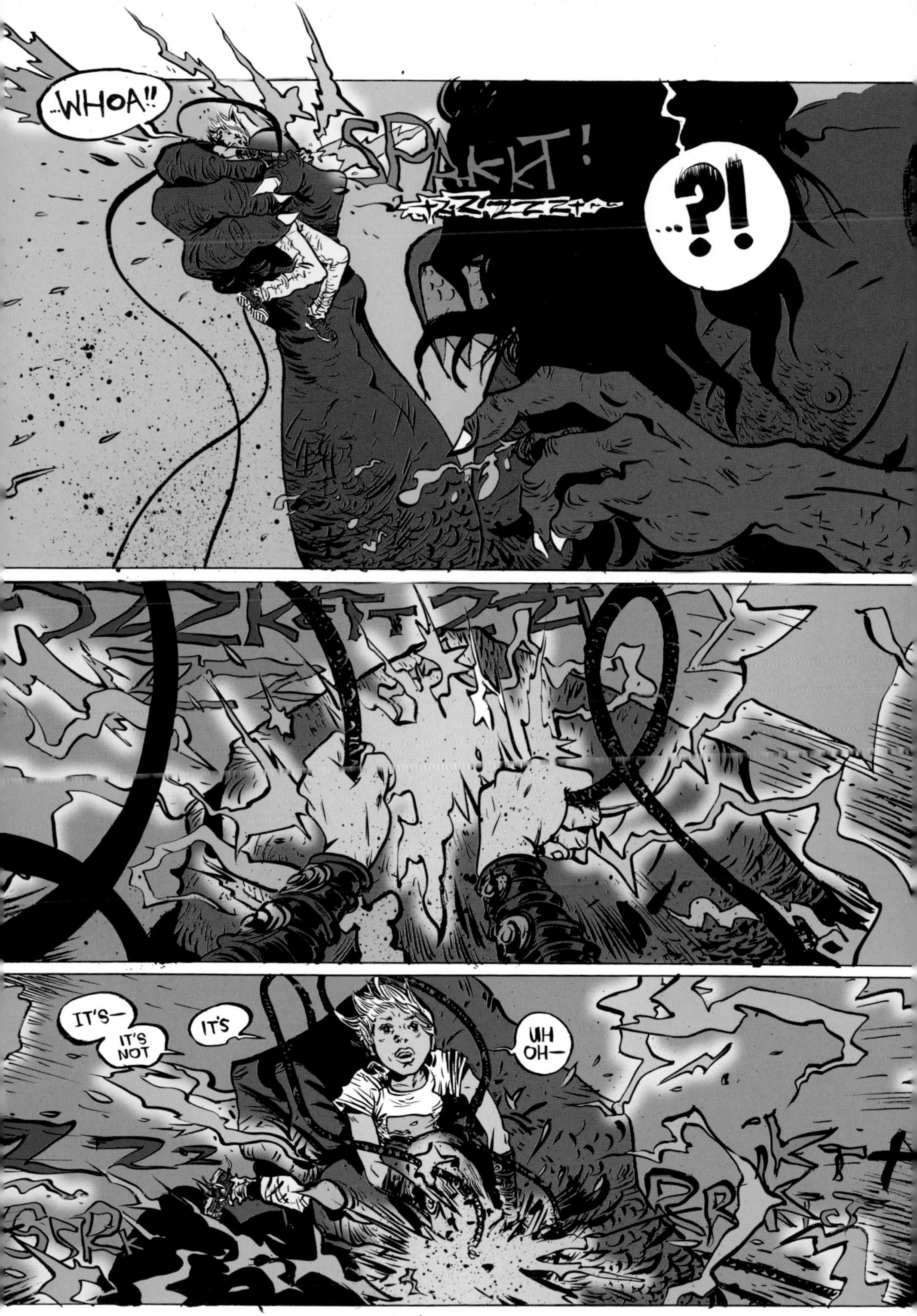
...WHOA!!
SPAKKT!
...?!
IT'S—
IT'S NOT
IT'S
UH OH—

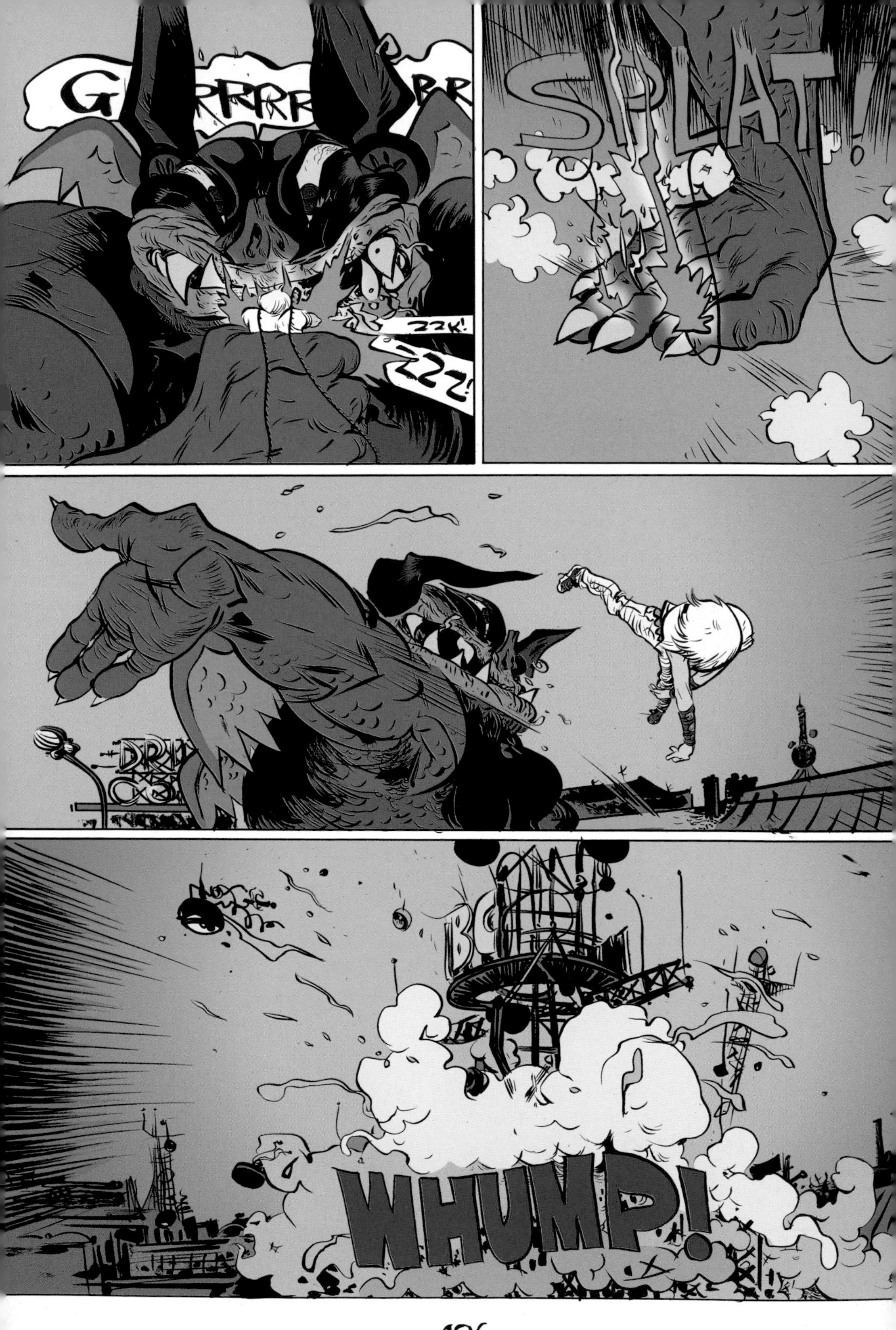
GRRRRRRRR
ZZK!
ZZZ!
SPLAT!
WHUMP!

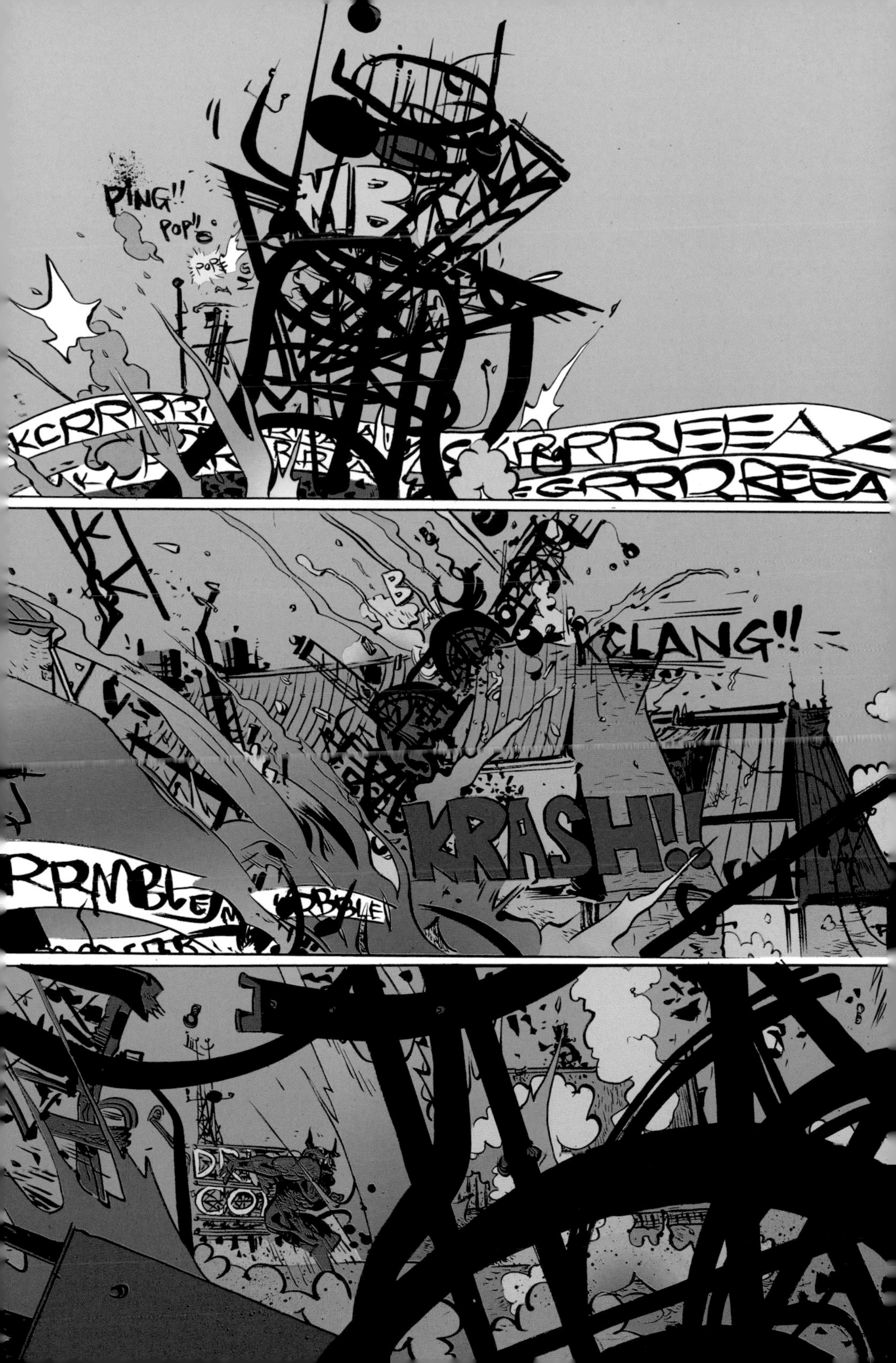
PING!!
POP!!
POP!
KCRRRRR!
GRRRREEAK
GRRRRREEA
KLANG!!
KRASH!!
RRMBLE

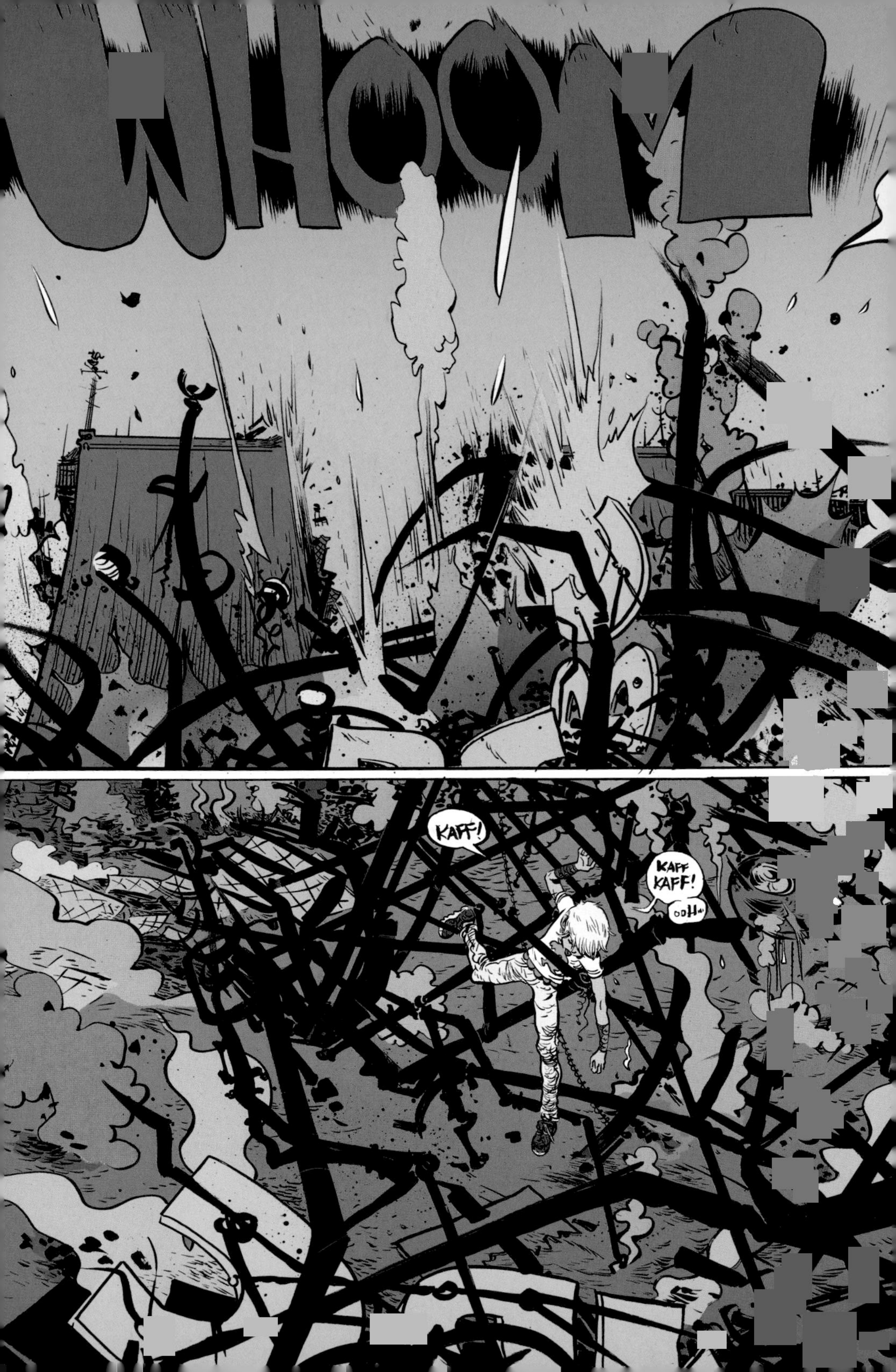
WHOOM
KAFF!
KAFF KAFF!
OOH...

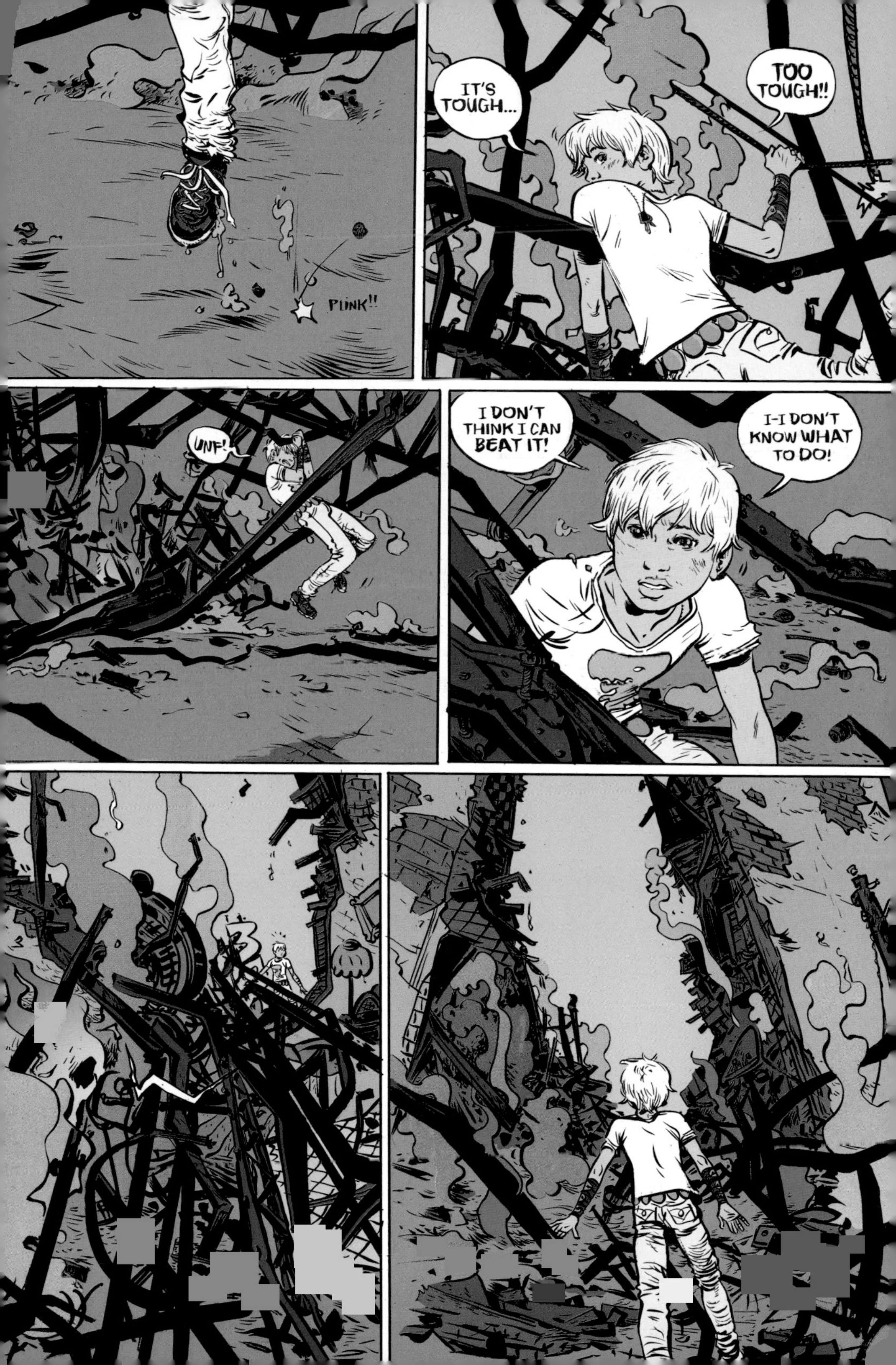
PLINK!!
IT'S TOUGH...
TOO TOUGH!!
UNF!
I DON'T THINK I CAN BEAT IT!
I-I DON'T KNOW WHAT TO DO!

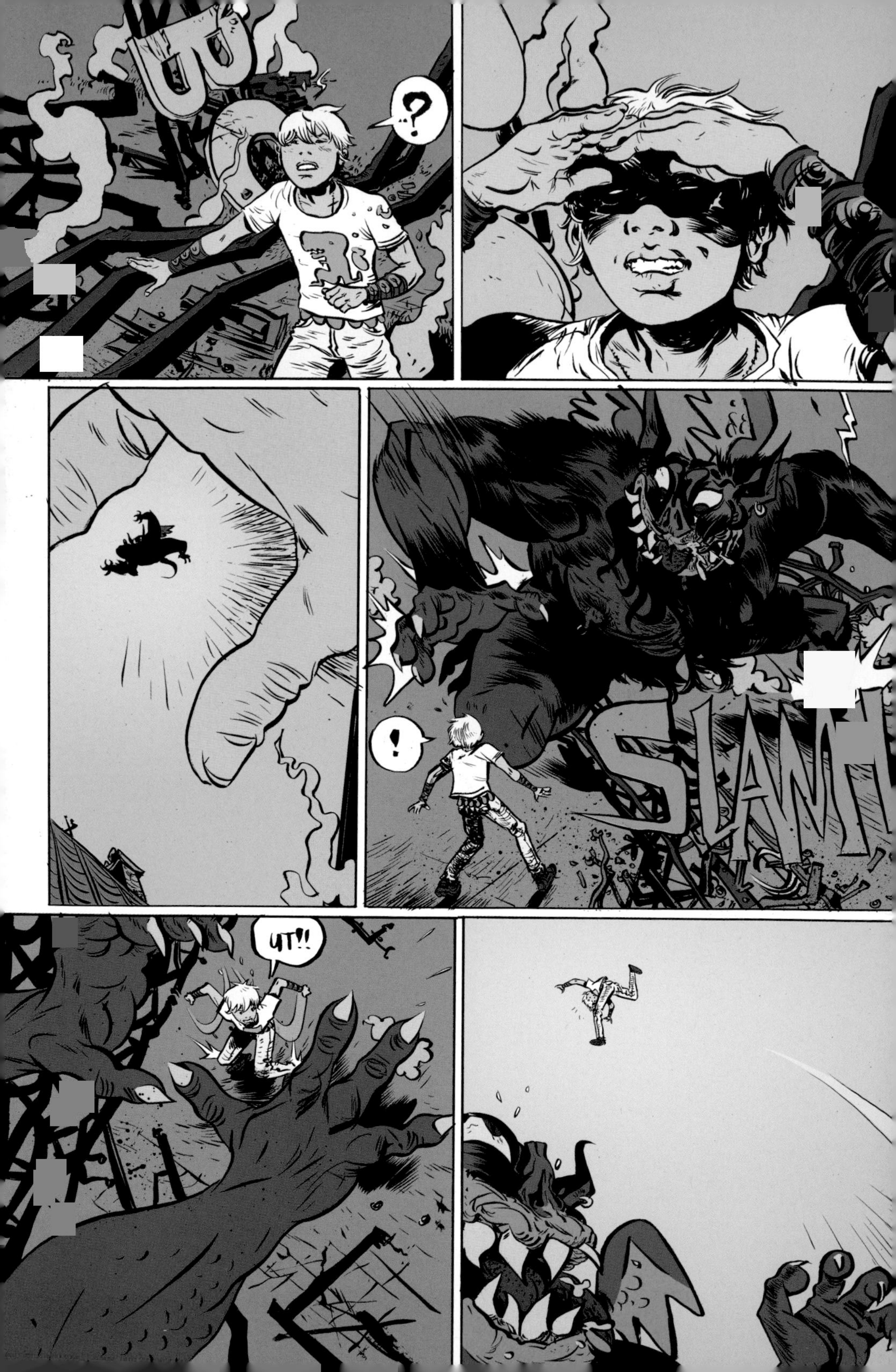
?
!
SLAM
UT!!

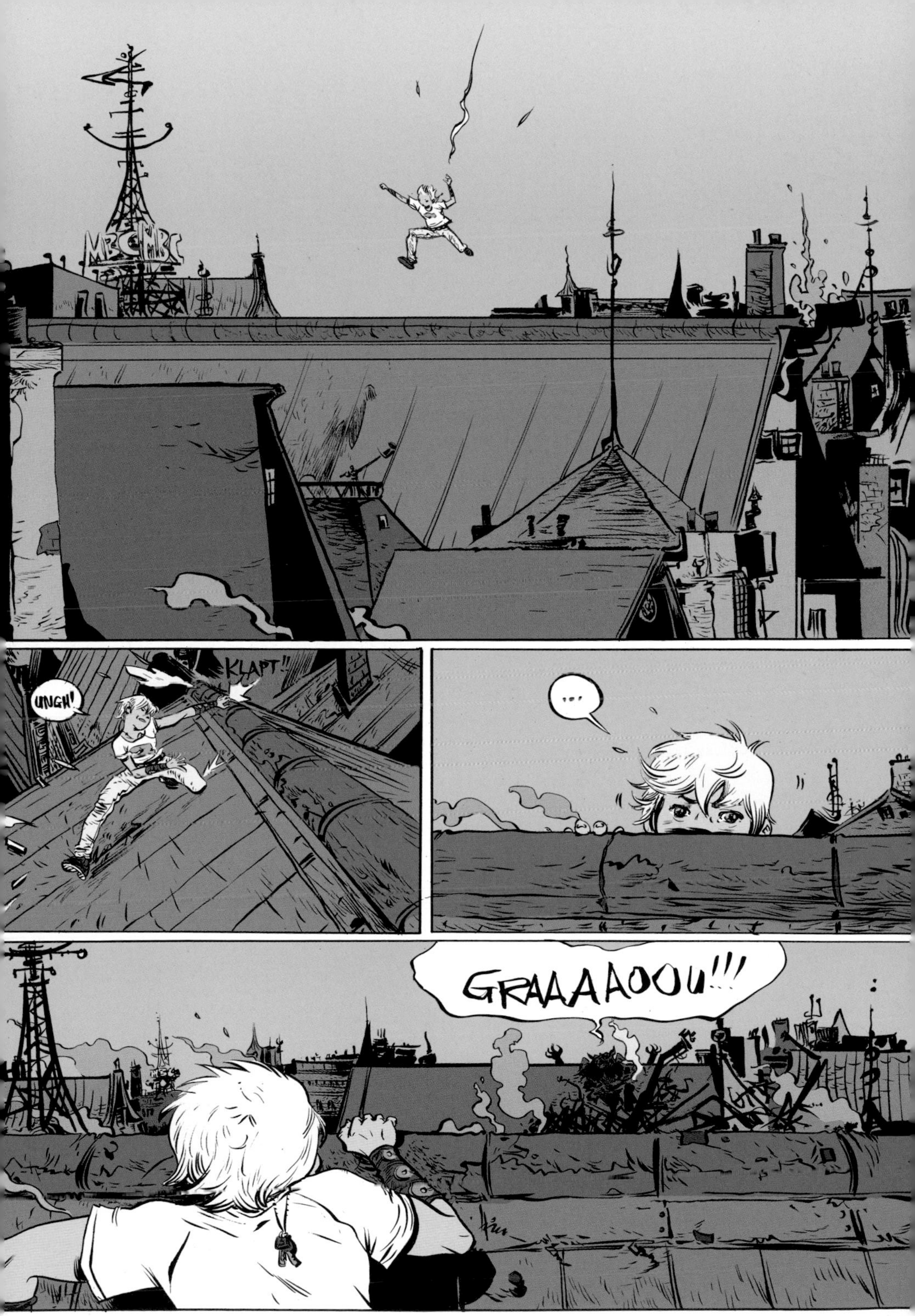
KLAPT!!
UNGH!
...
GRAAAAOOU!!!

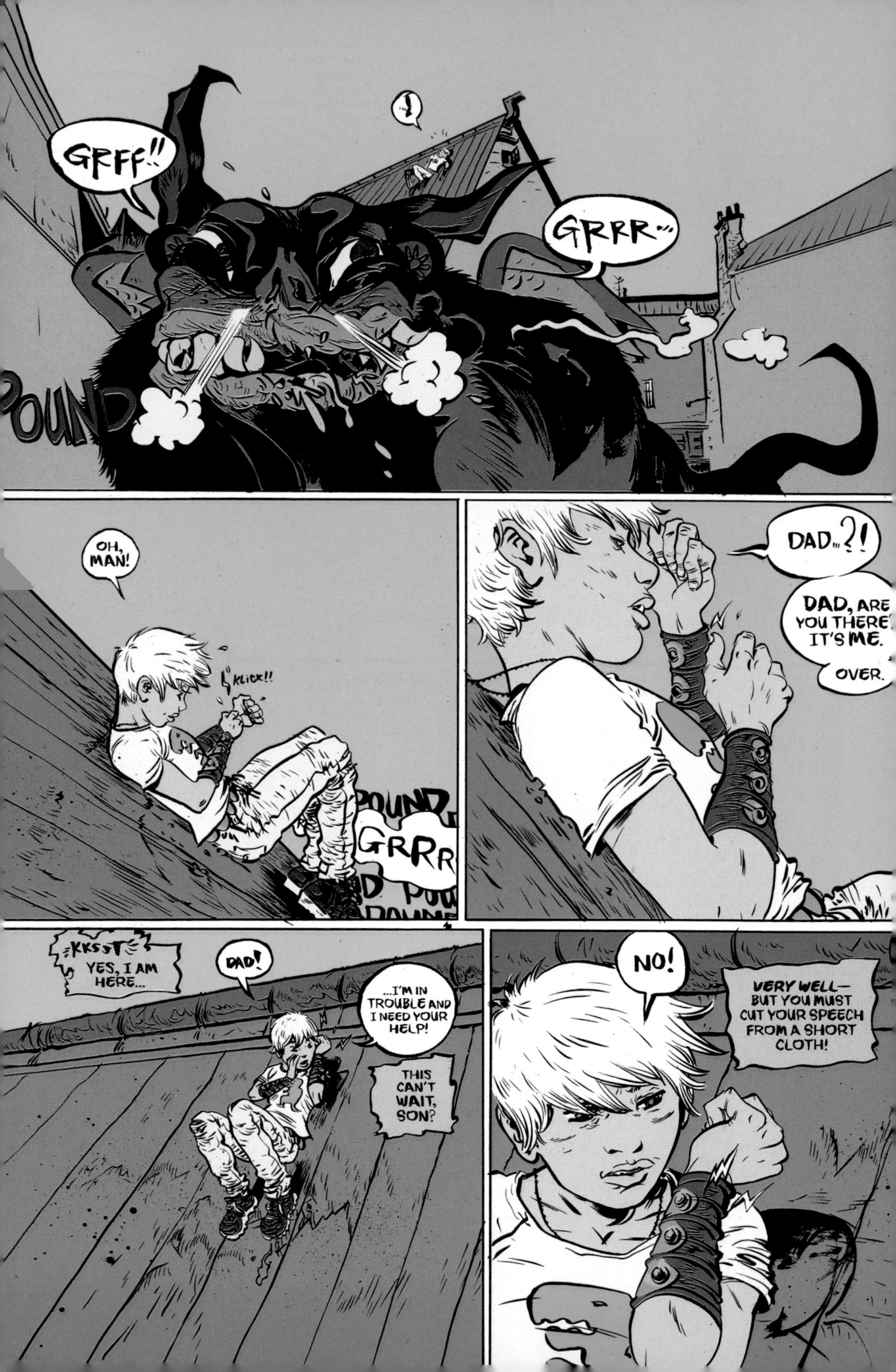

!
GRFF!!
GRRR...
POUND
OH, MAN!
KLICK!!
POUND
GRRR
POUND
DAD...?!
DAD, ARE YOU THERE? IT'S ME.
OVER.
KKSST
YES, I AM HERE...
DAD!
...I'M IN TROUBLE AND I NEED YOUR HELP!
THIS CAN'T WAIT, SON?
NO!
VERY WELL— BUT YOU MUST CUT YOUR SPEECH FROM A SHORT CLOTH!

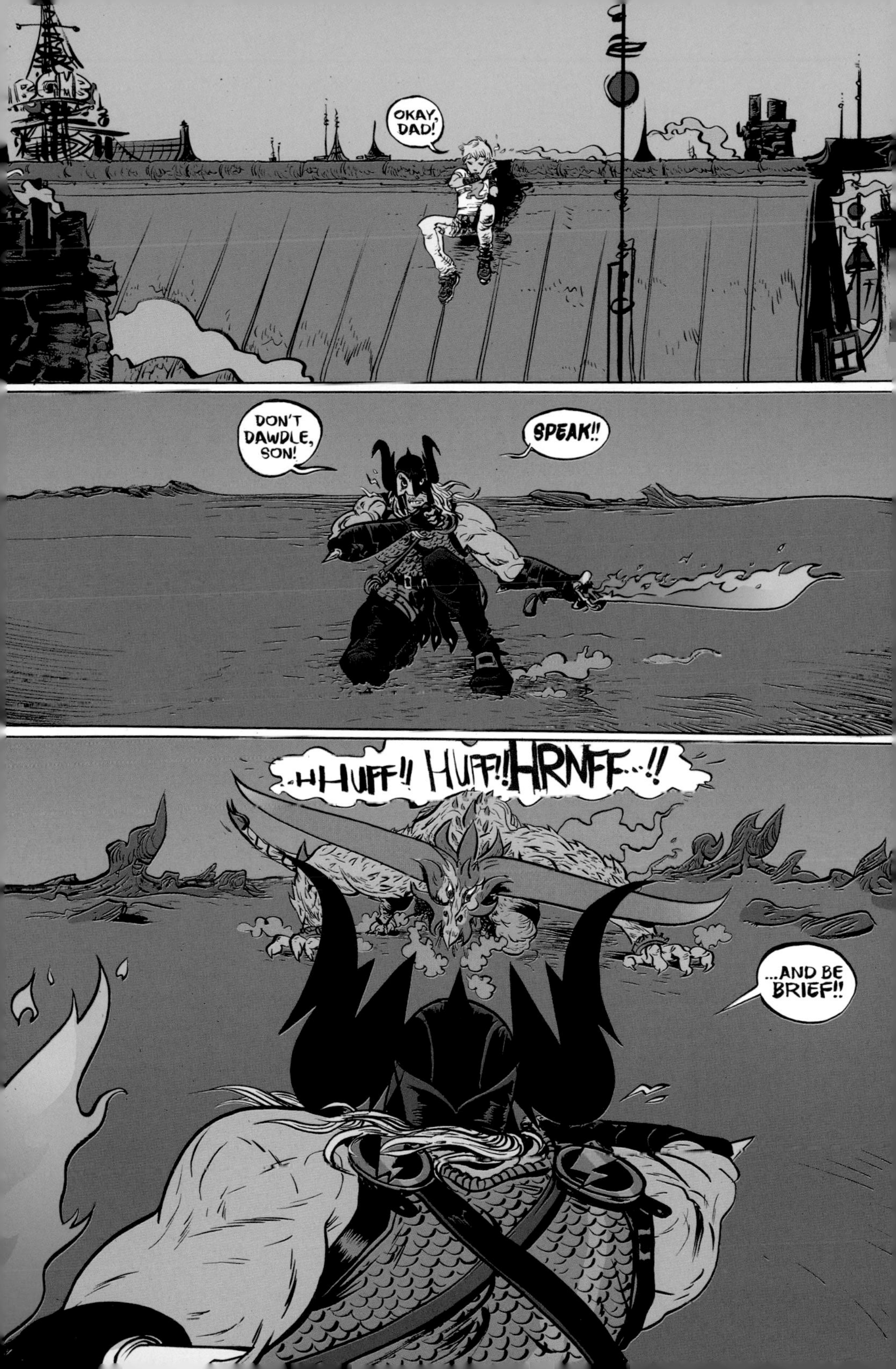
OKAY, DAD!
DON'T DAWDLE, SON!
SPEAK!!
..HHUFF!! HUFF!! HRNFF...!!
...AND BE BRIEF!!

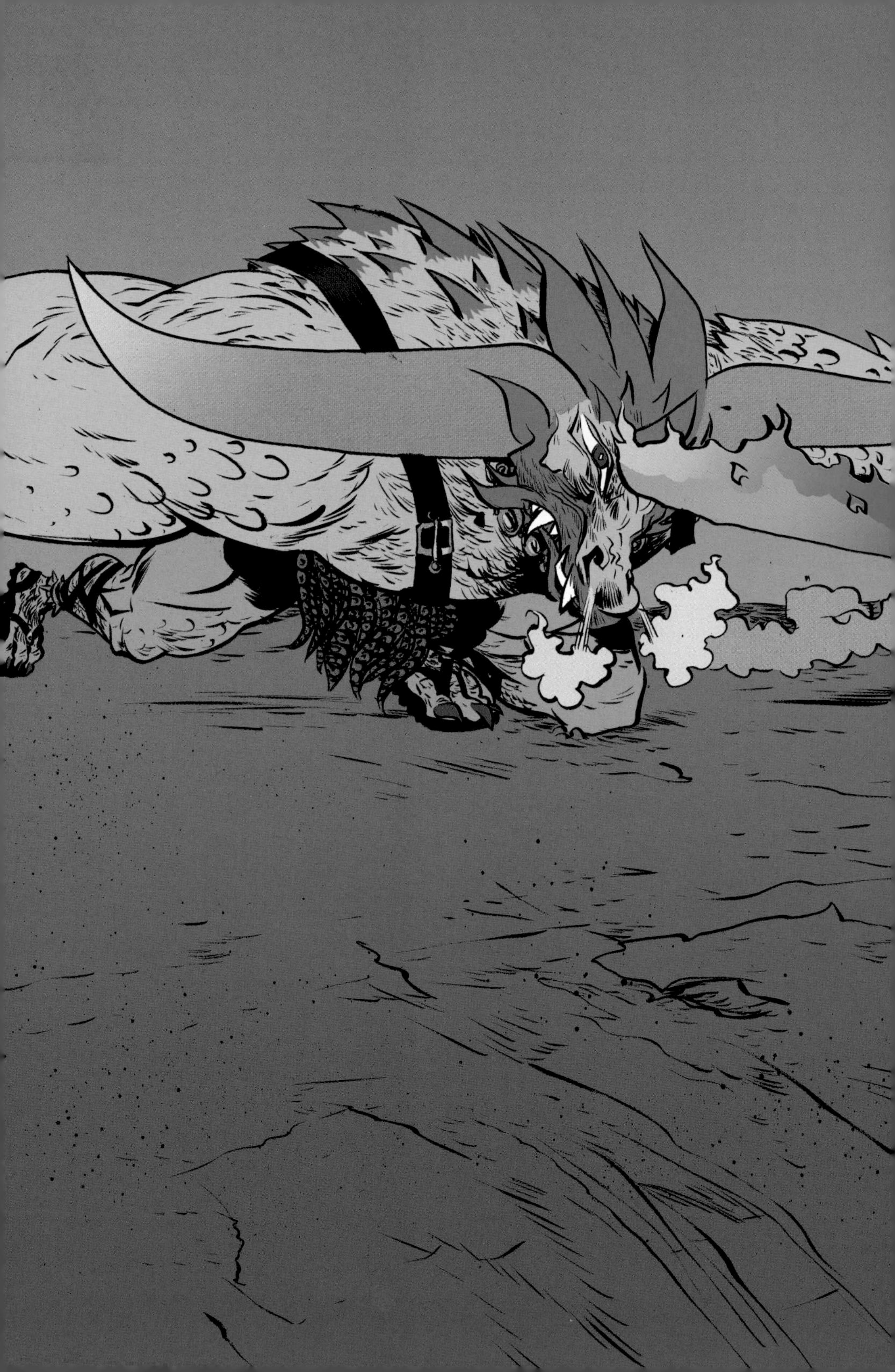

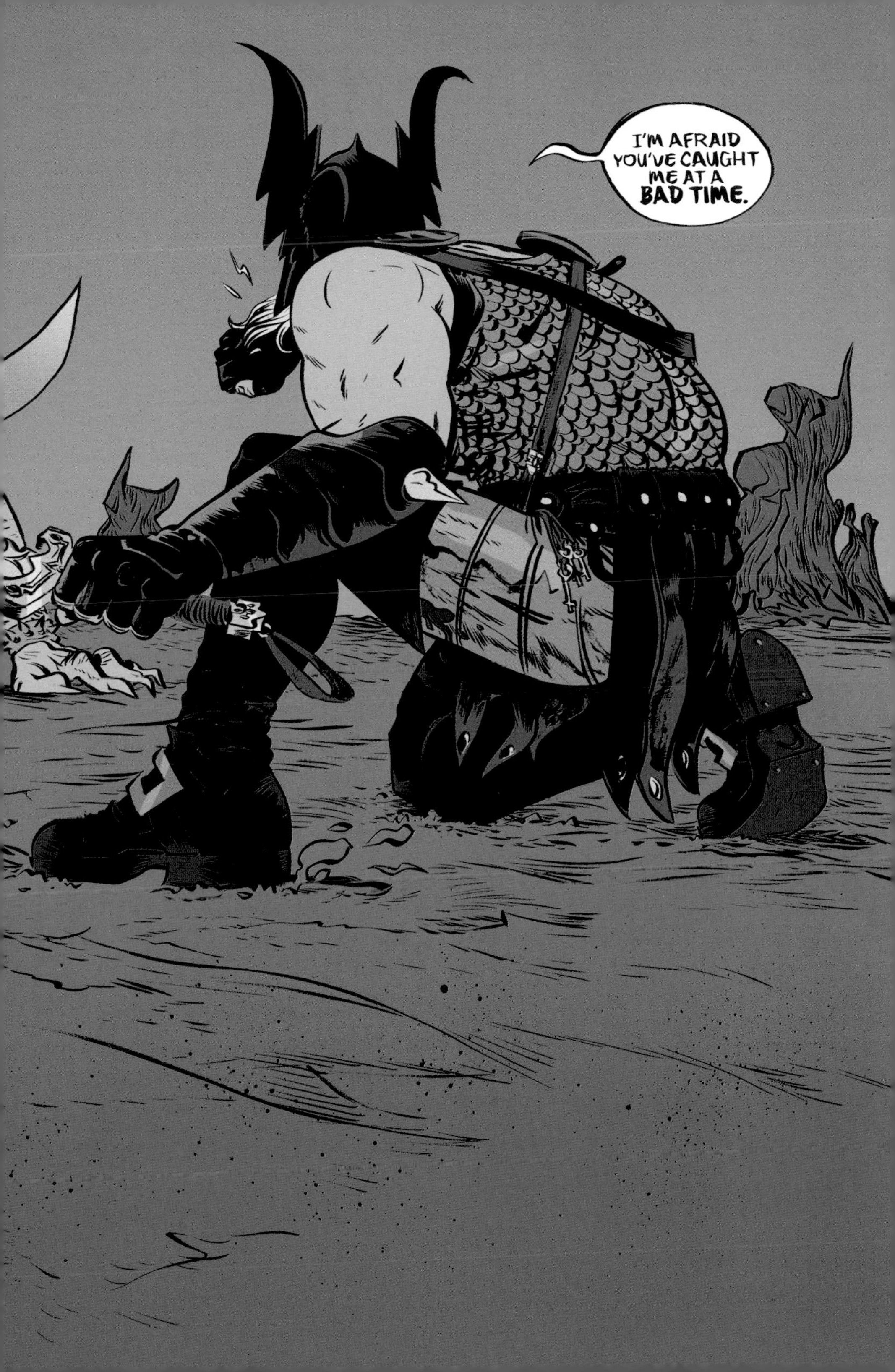
I'M AFRAID YOU'VE CAUGHT ME AT A BAD TIME.

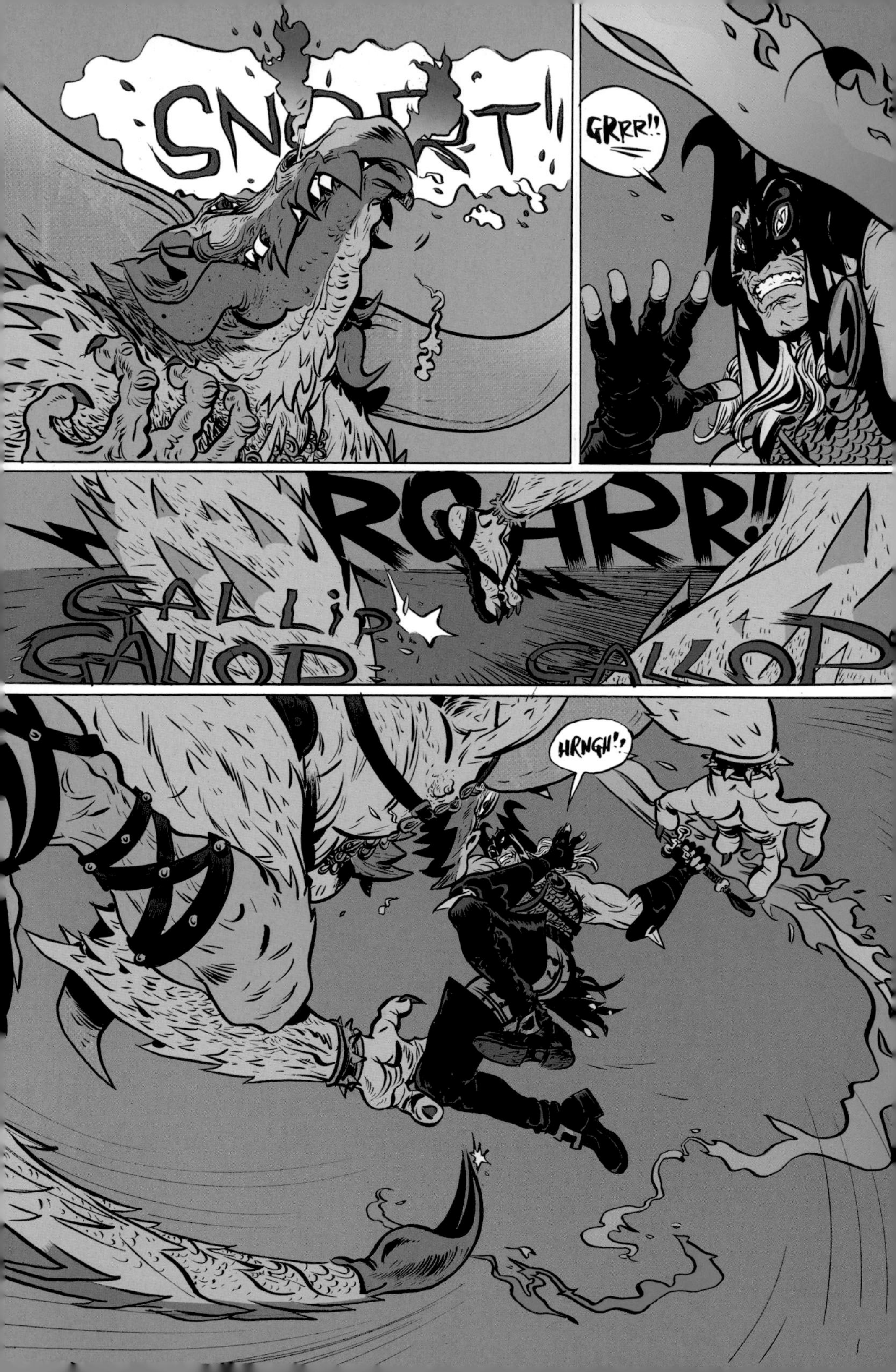
SNORT!!
GRRR!!
ROAHRR!!
GALLIP
GALLOP
GALLOP
HRNGH!?

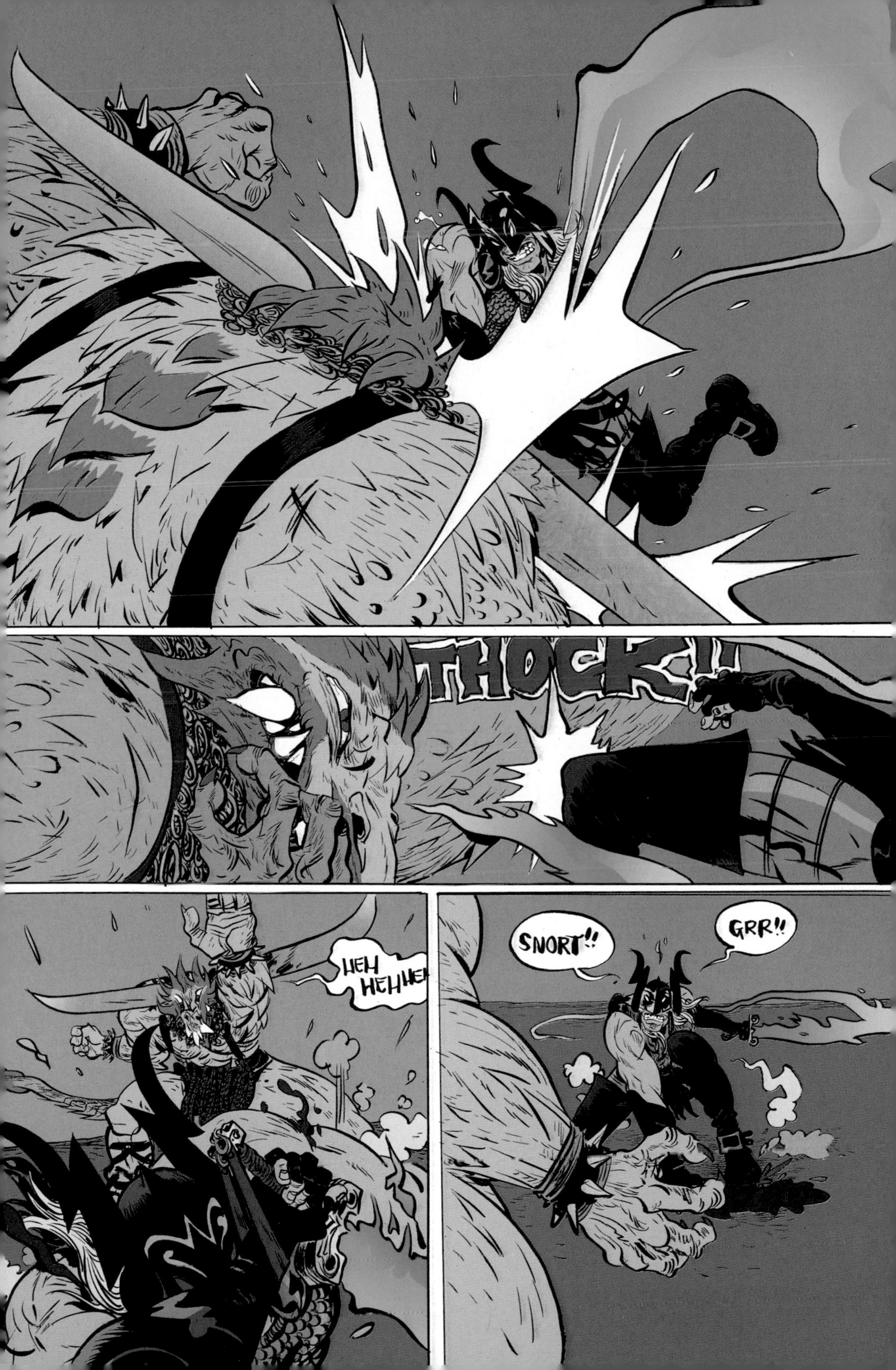
THOCK!!
HEH HEHHEH
SNORT!!
GRR!!

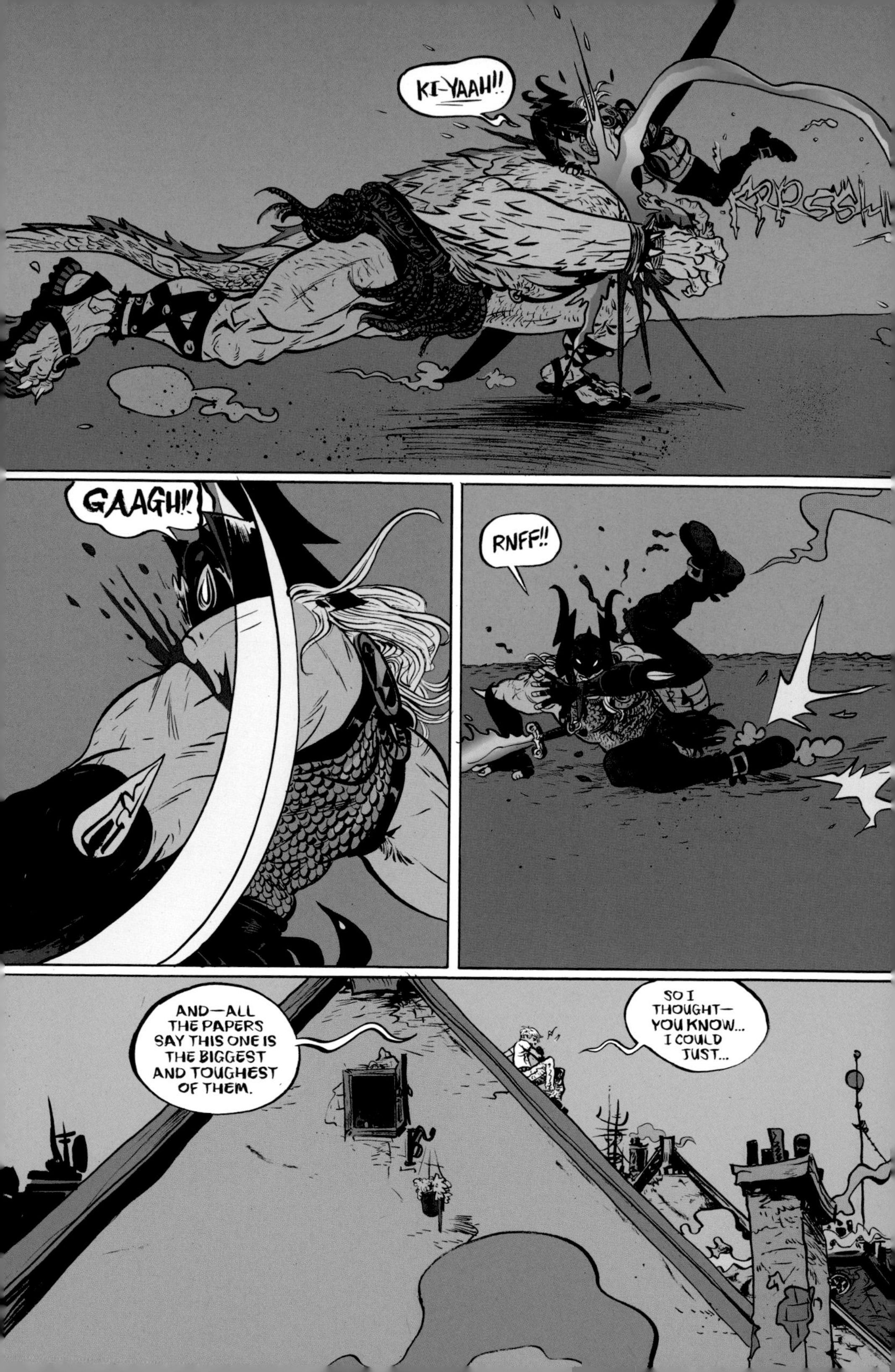
KI-YAAH!!
KRRSSH
GAAGH!!
RNFF!!
AND—ALL THE PAPERS SAY THIS ONE IS THE BIGGEST AND TOUGHEST OF THEM.
SO I THOUGHT— YOU KNOW... I COULD JUST...

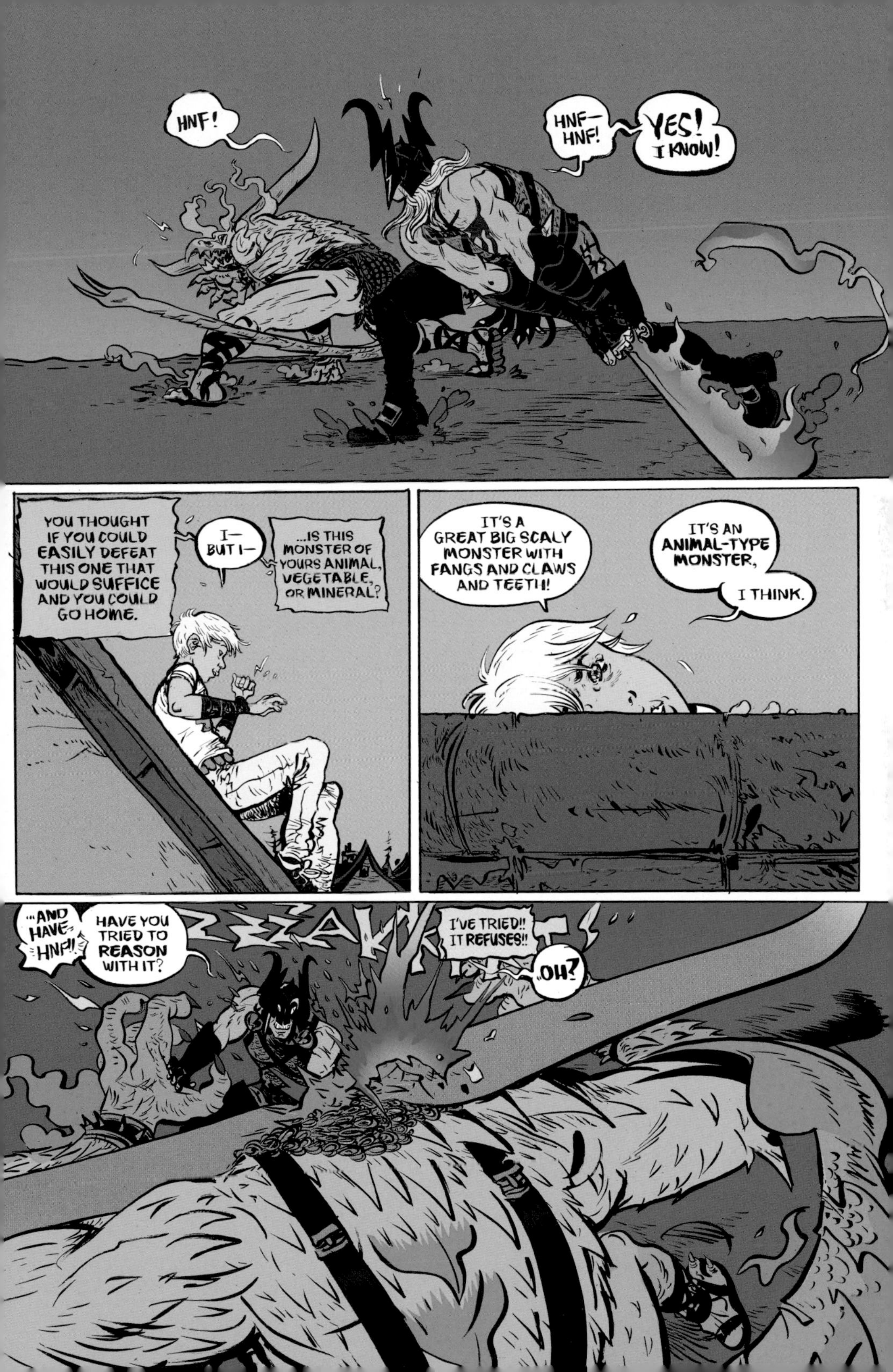
HNF!
HNF—HNF!
YES! I KNOW!
YOU THOUGHT IF YOU COULD EASILY DEFEAT THIS ONE THAT WOULD SUFFICE AND YOU COULD GO HOME.
I— BUT I—
...IS THIS MONSTER OF YOURS ANIMAL, VEGETABLE, OR MINERAL?
IT'S A GREAT BIG SCALY MONSTER WITH FANGS AND CLAWS AND TEETH!
IT'S AN ANIMAL-TYPE MONSTER,
I THINK.
...AND HAVE—HNF!!
HAVE YOU TRIED TO REASON WITH IT?
I'VE TRIED!! IT REFUSES!!
OH?

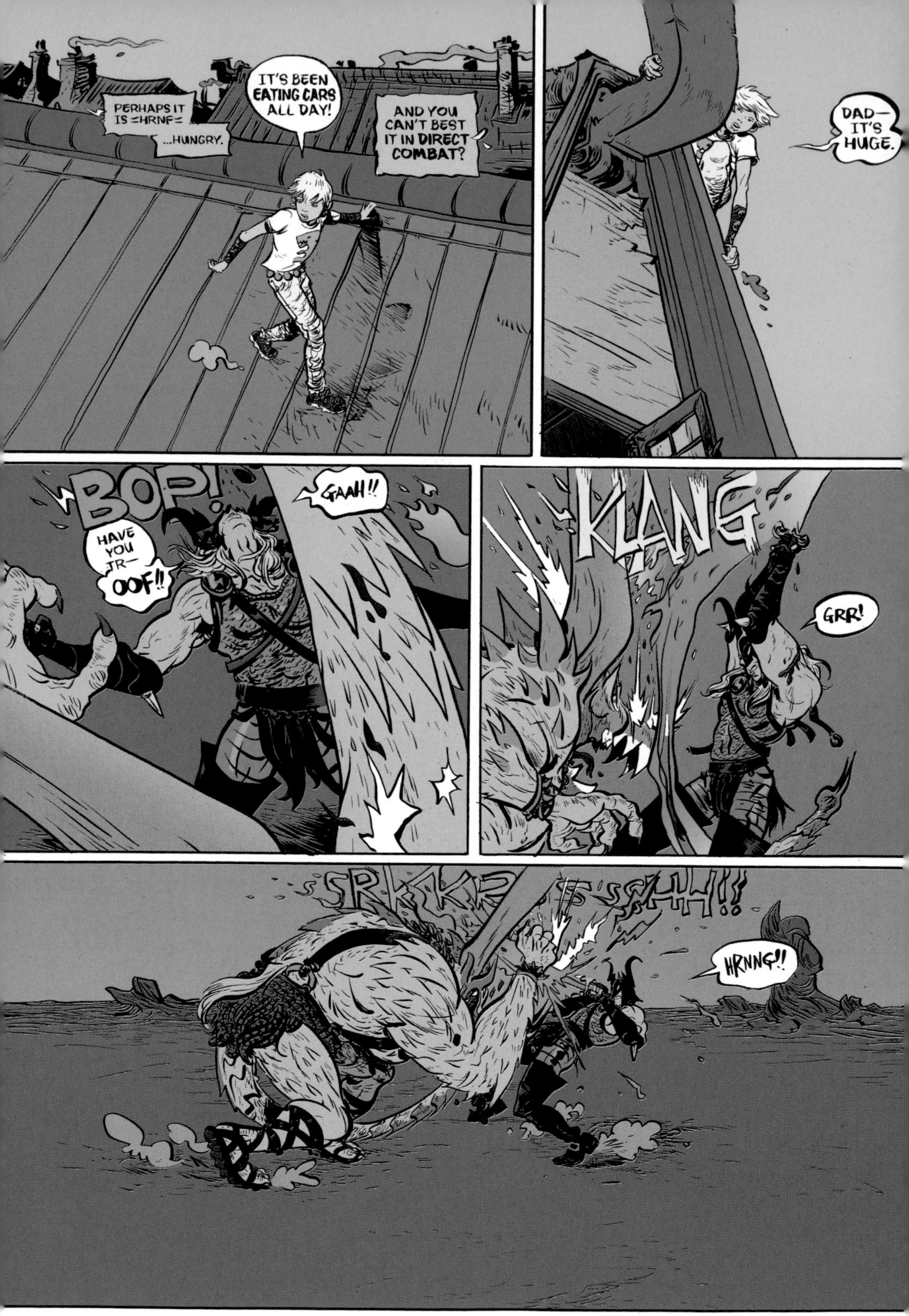
PERHAPS IT IS =HRNF=
...HUNGRY.
IT'S BEEN EATING CARS ALL DAY!
AND YOU CAN'T BEST IT IN DIRECT COMBAT?
DAD— IT'S HUGE.
BOP!
HAVE YOU TR—
OOF!!
GAAH!!
KLANG
GRR!
SRKKK SSSHH!!
HRNNG!!

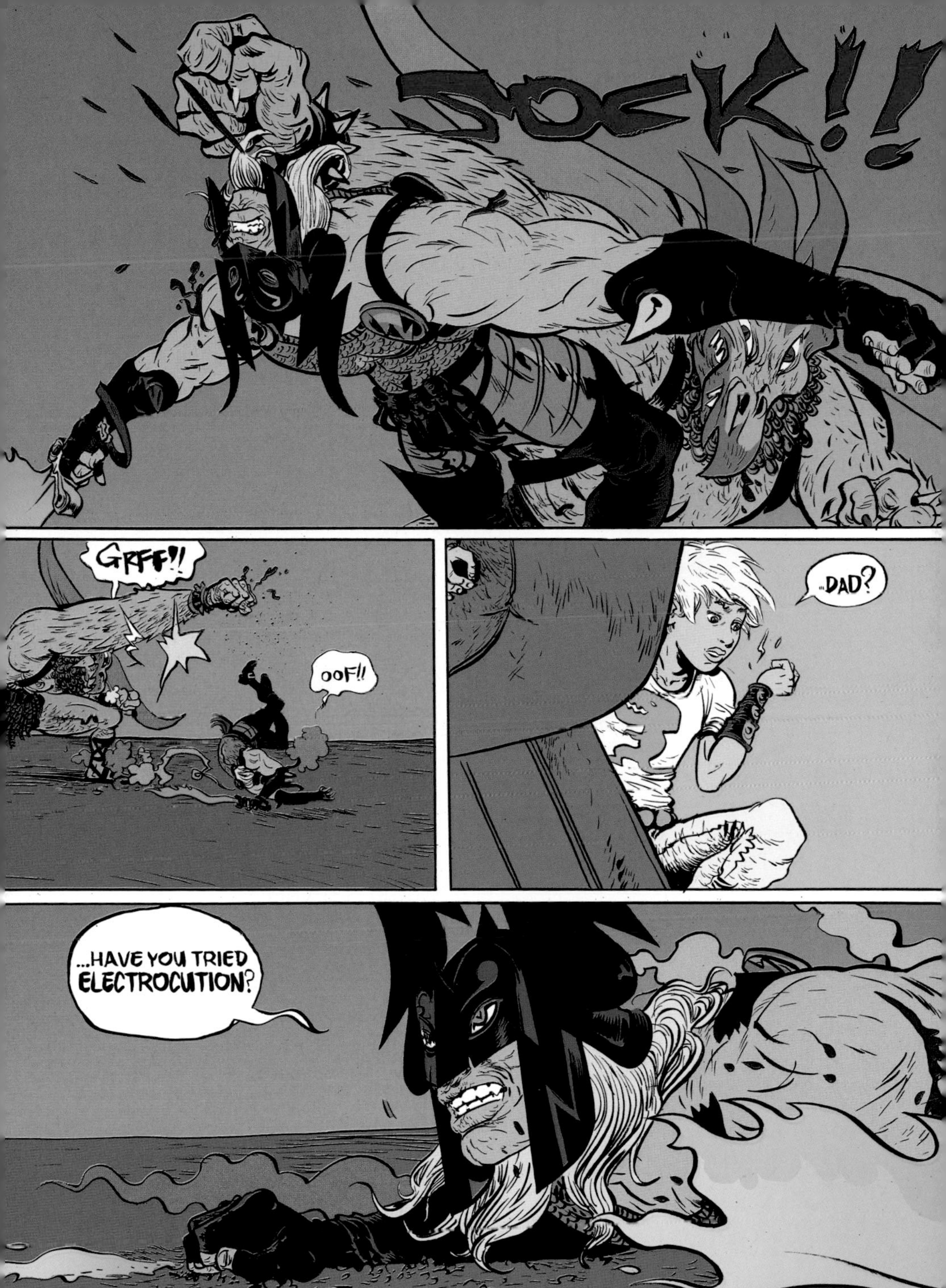
SOCK!!
GRFF!!
OOF!!
...DAD?
...HAVE YOU TRIED ELECTROCUTION?

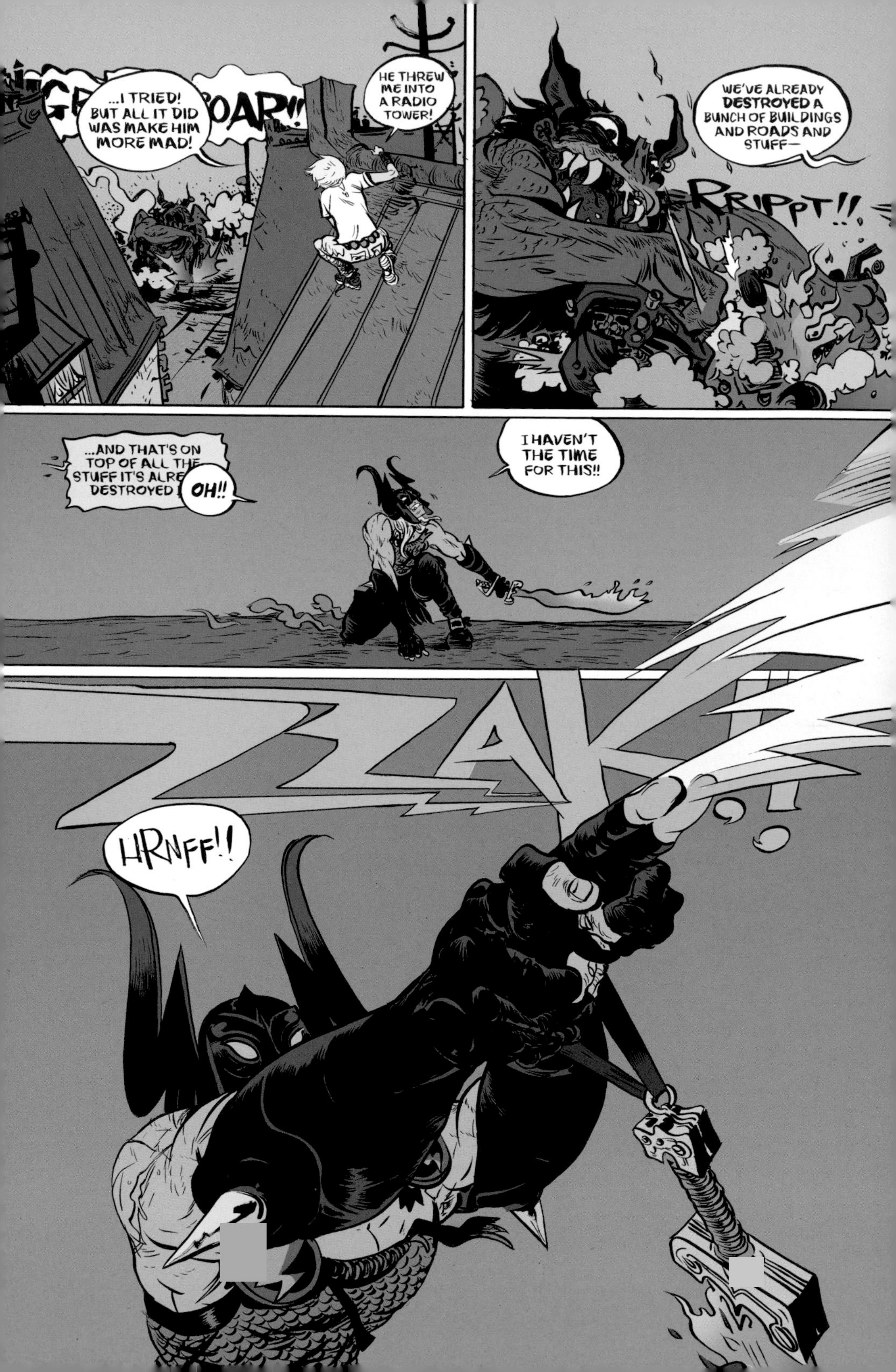

...I TRIED! BUT ALL IT DID WAS MAKE HIM MORE MAD!
HE THREW ME INTO A RADIO TOWER!
WE'VE ALREADY DESTROYED A BUNCH OF BUILDINGS AND ROADS AND STUFF—
RRIPPT!!
...AND THAT'S ON TOP OF ALL THE
OH!!
I HAVEN'T THE TIME FOR THIS!!
HRNFF!!

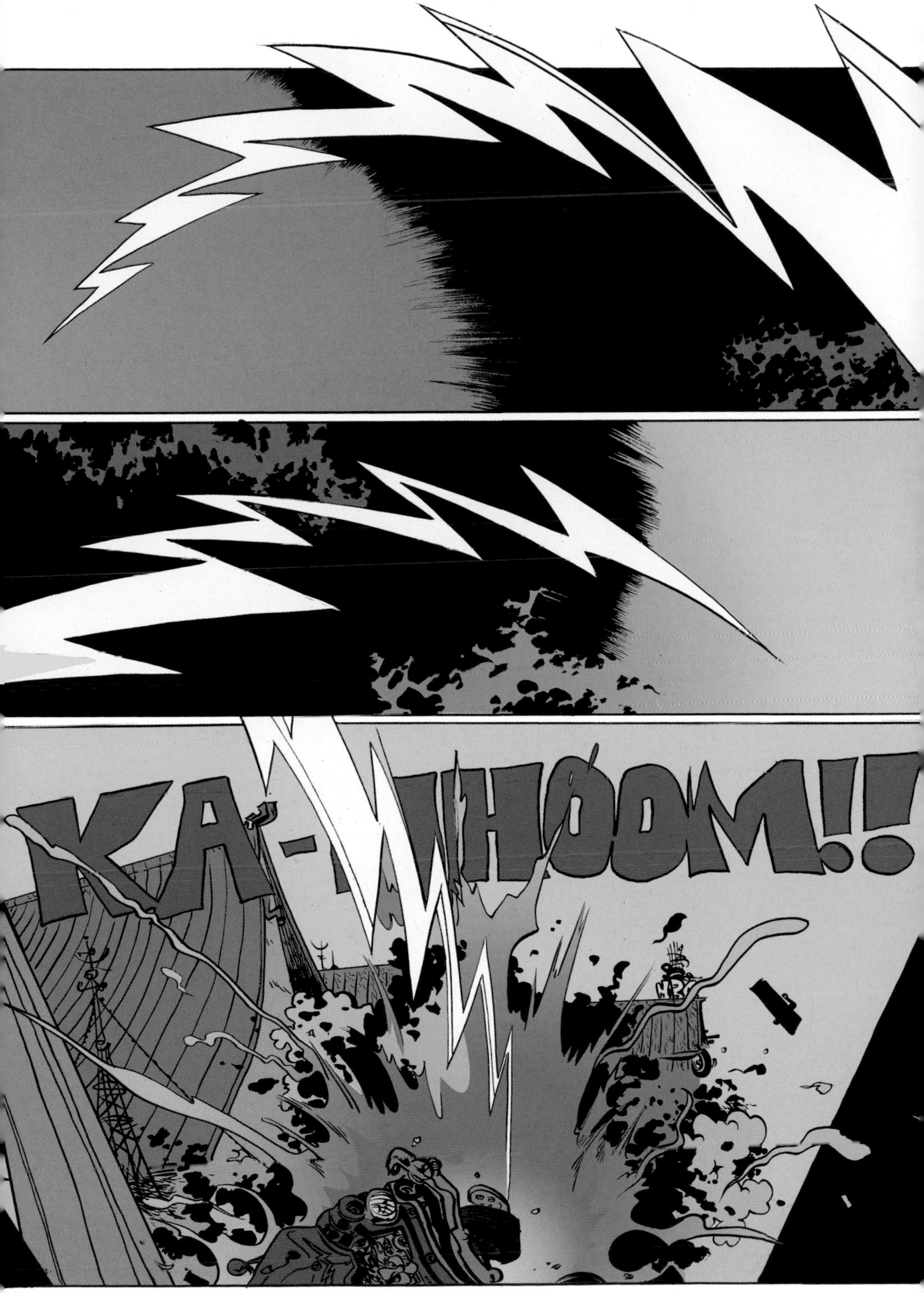
KA-WHOOM!!

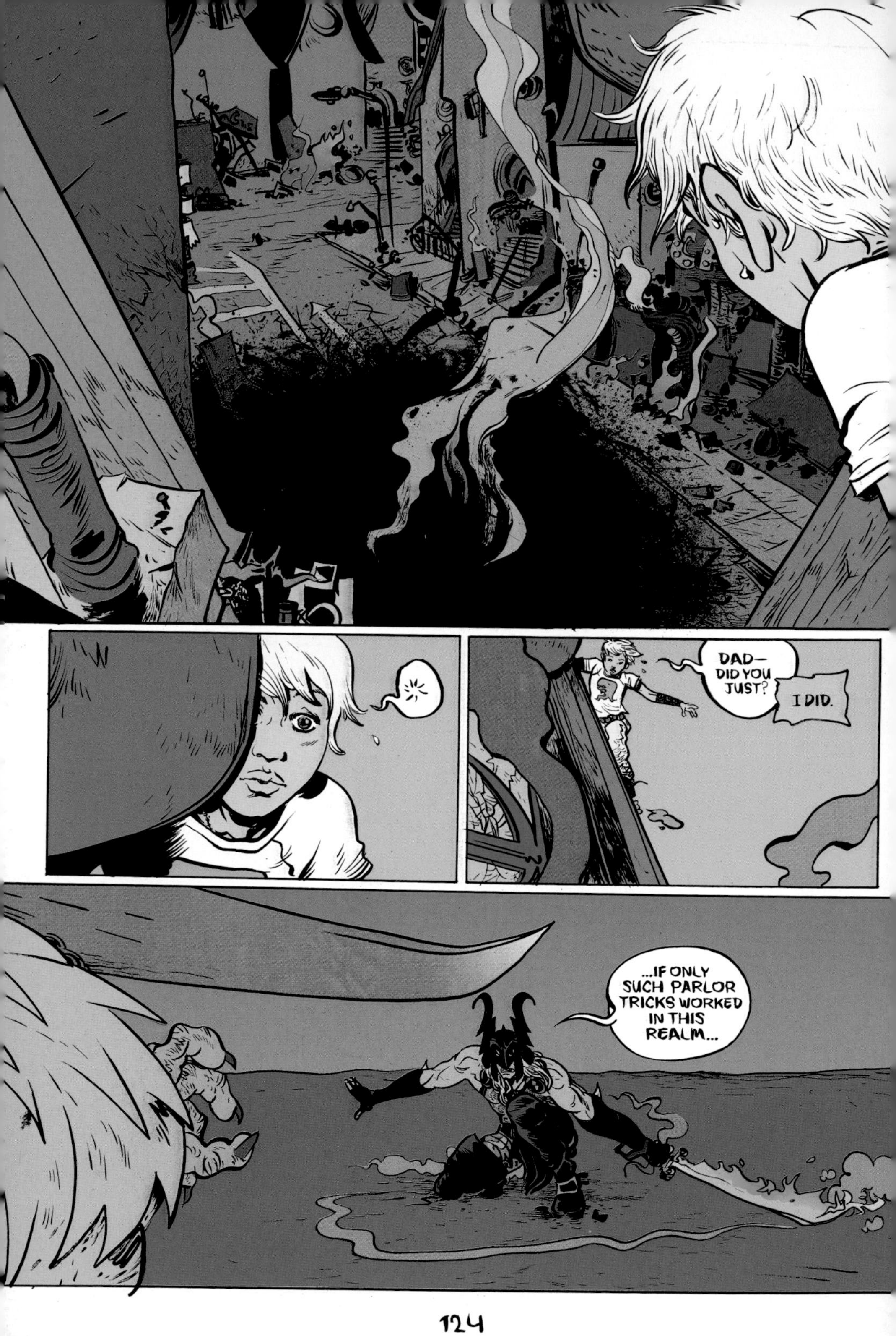
DAD—
DID YOU
JUST?
I DID.
...IF ONLY
SUCH PARLOR
TRICKS WORKED
IN THIS
REALM...

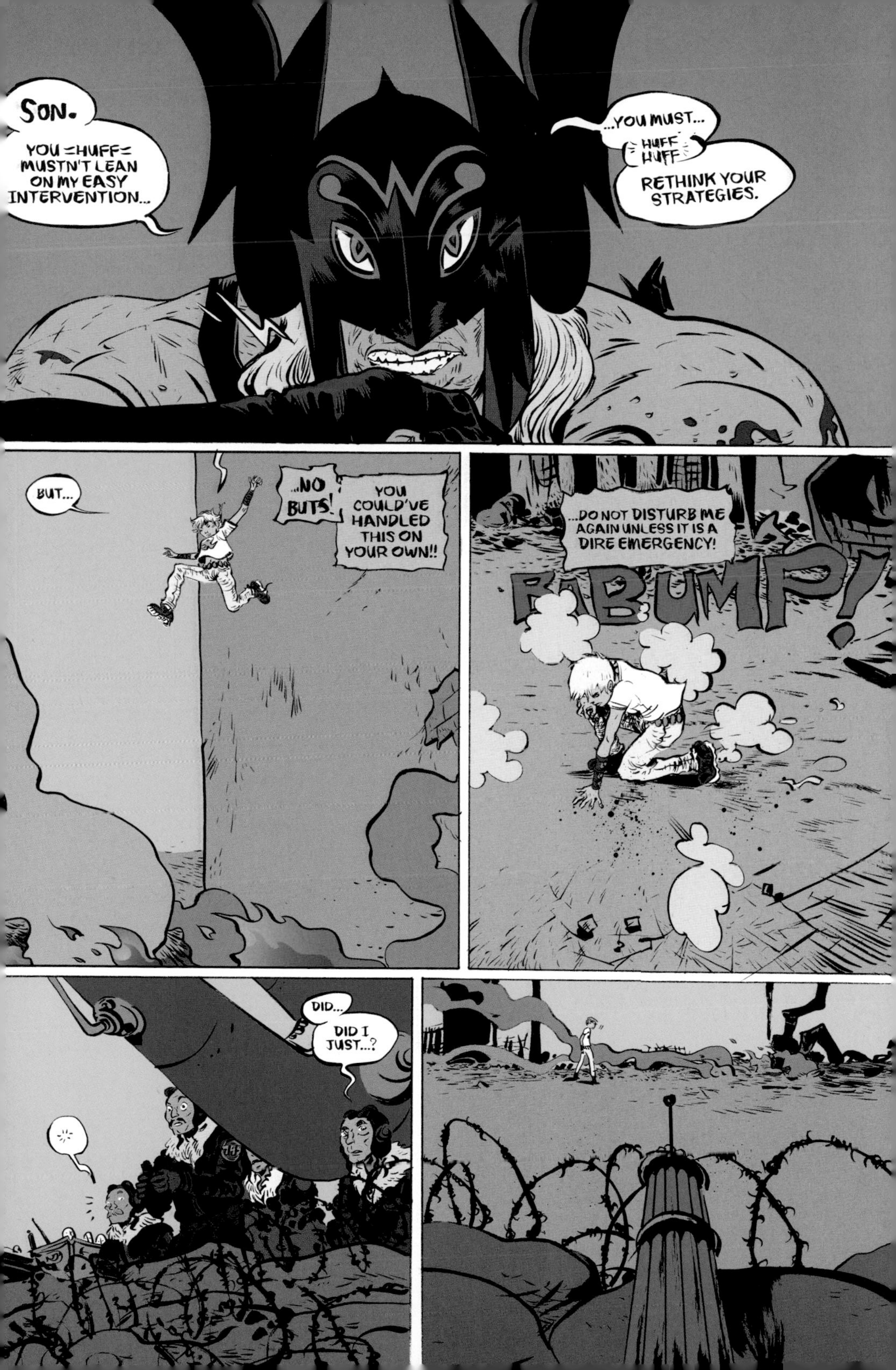
SON.
YOU =HUFF= MUSTN'T LEAN ON MY EASY INTERVENTION...
...YOU MUST...
HUFF HUFF
RETHINK YOUR STRATEGIES.
BUT...
...NO BUTS!
YOU COULD'VE HANDLED THIS ON YOUR OWN!!
...DO NOT DISTURB ME AGAIN UNLESS IT IS A DIRE EMERGENCY!
BABUMP!
DID...
DID I JUST...?

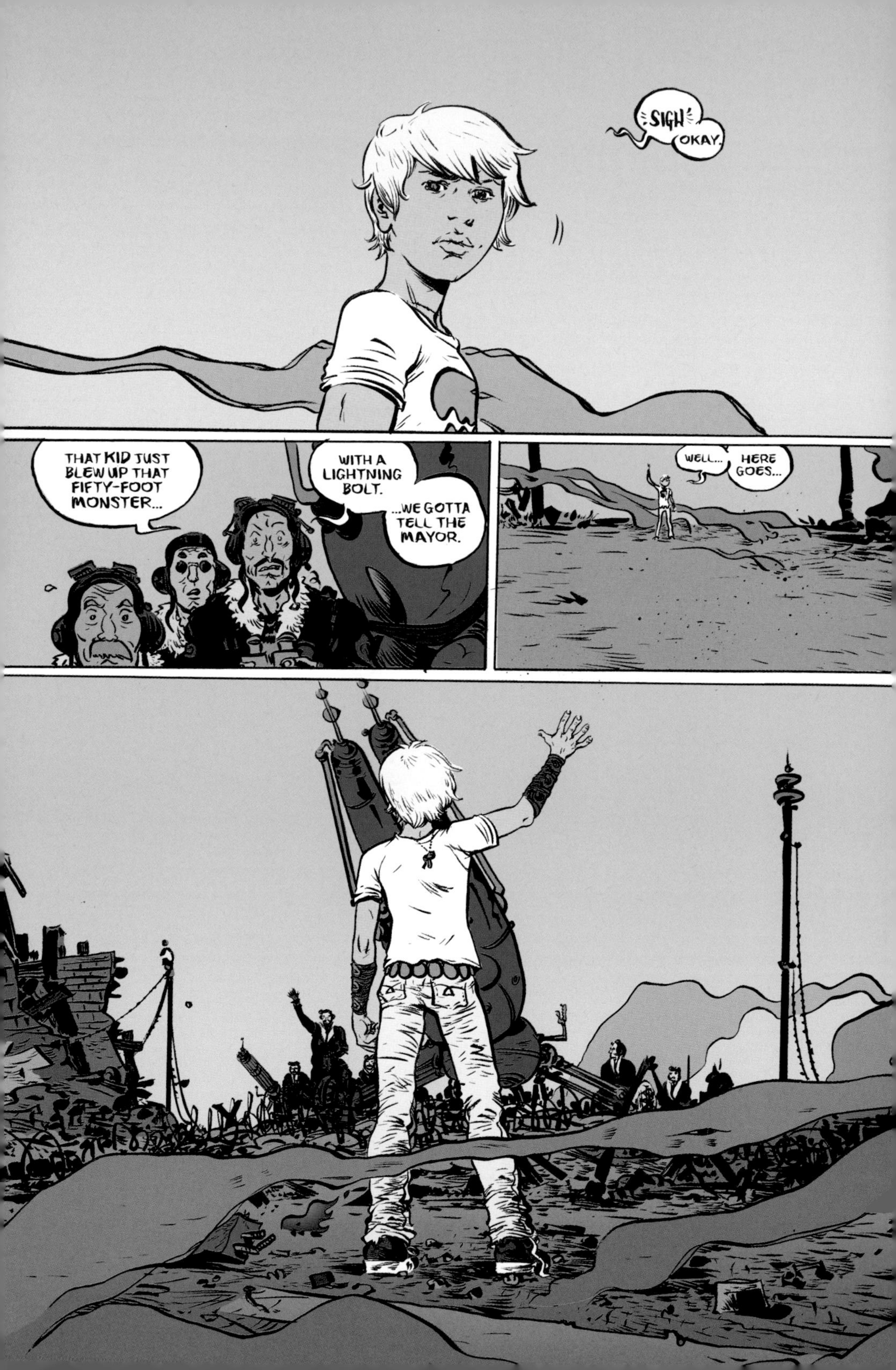
SIGH
OKAY.
THAT KID JUST BLEW UP THAT FIFTY-FOOT MONSTER...
WITH A LIGHTNING BOLT.
...WE GOTTA TELL THE MAYOR.
WELL...
HERE GOES...

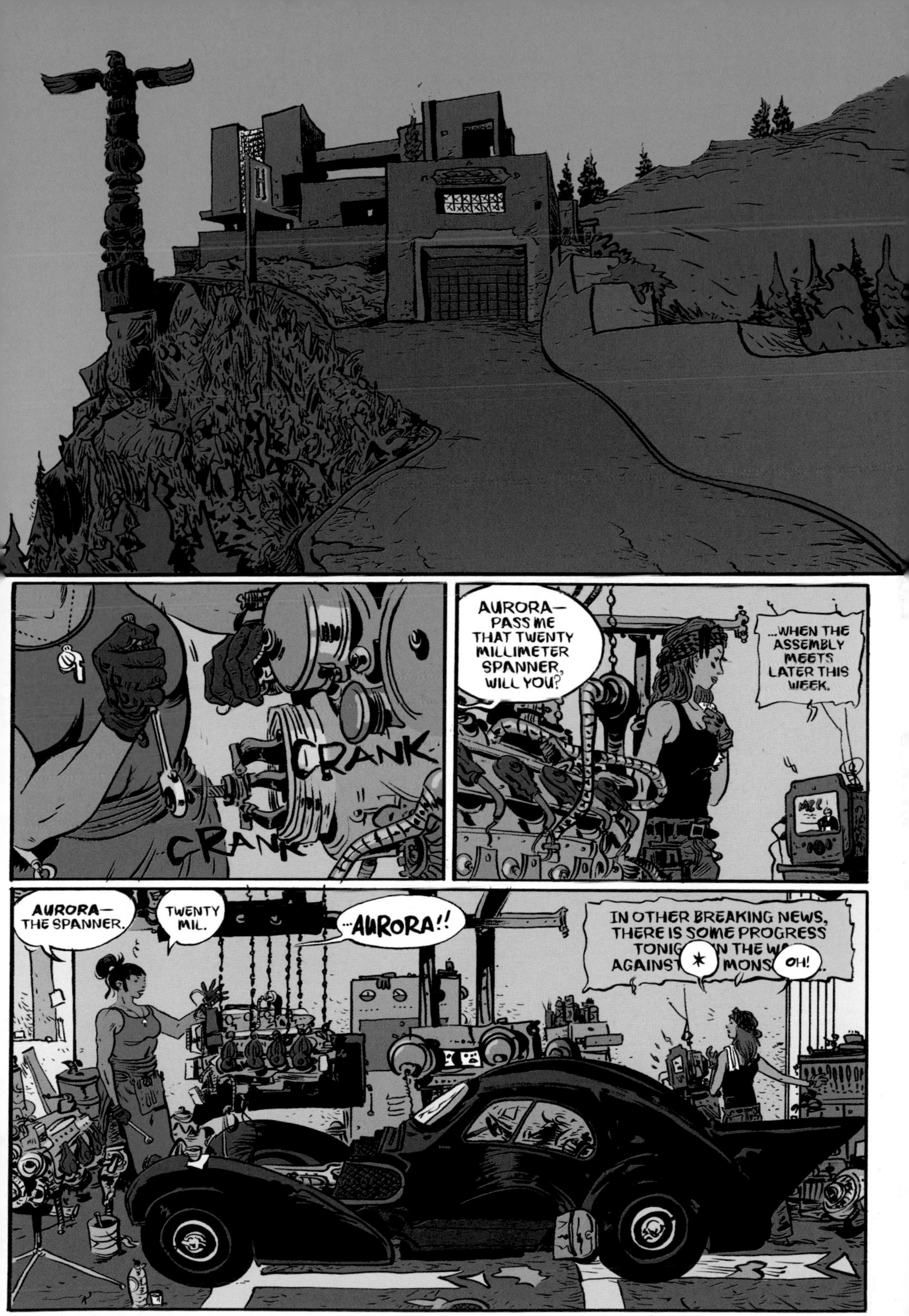
CRANK
CRANK
AURORA— PASS ME THAT TWENTY MILLIMETER SPANNER, WILL YOU?
...WHEN THE ASSEMBLY MEETS LATER THIS WEEK.
AURORA— THE SPANNER.
TWENTY MIL.
...AURORA!!
IN OTHER BREAKING NEWS, THERE IS SOME PROGRESS TONIG IN THE WA AGAINST MONS
*
OH!

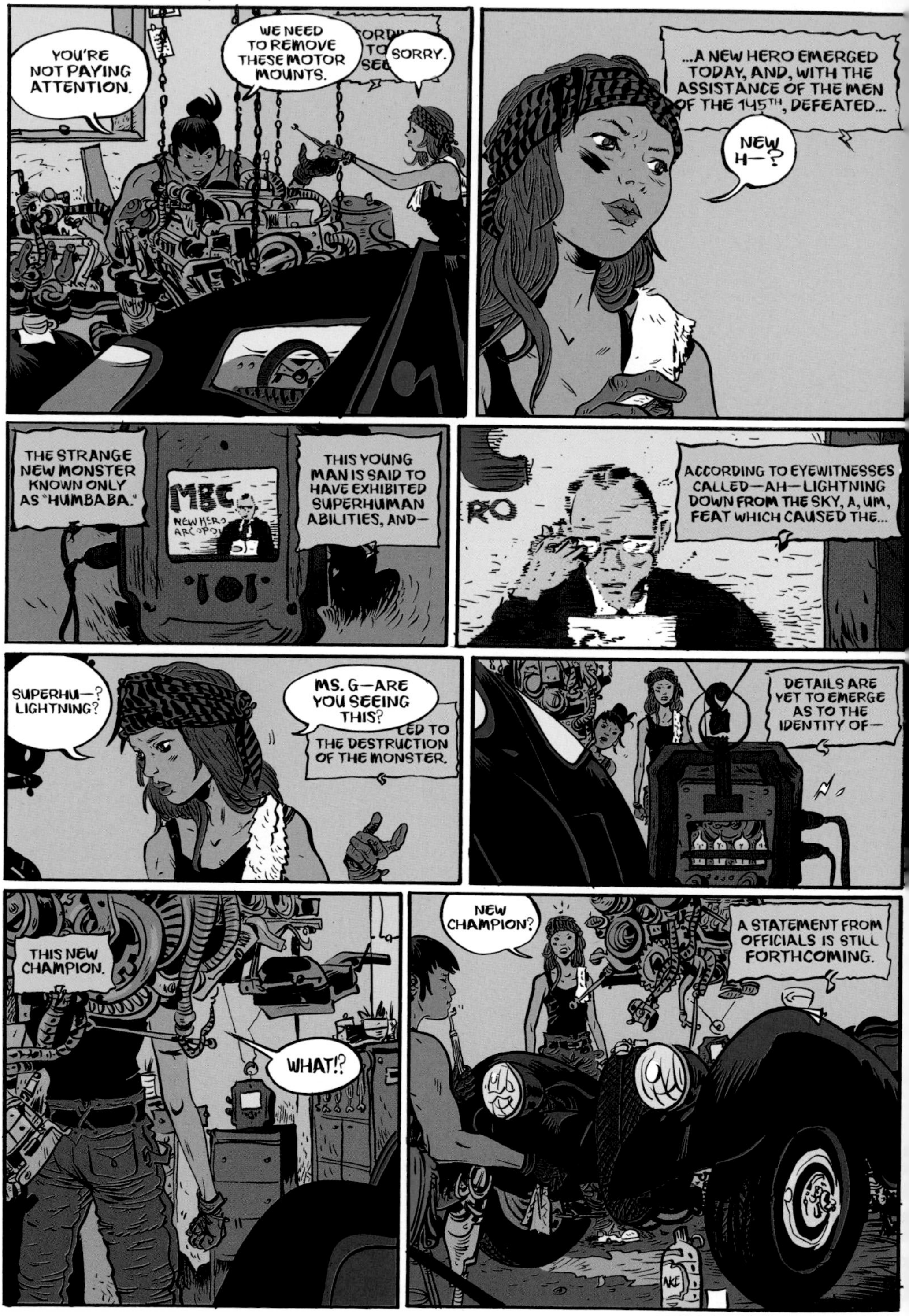
YOU'RE NOT PAYING ATTENTION.
WE NEED TO REMOVE THESE MOTOR MOUNTS.
SORRY.
...A NEW HERO EMERGED TODAY, AND, WITH THE ASSISTANCE OF THE MEN OF THE 145TH, DEFEATED...
NEW H—?
THE STRANGE NEW MONSTER KNOWN ONLY AS "HUMBABA."
MBC
THIS YOUNG MAN IS SAID TO HAVE EXHIBITED SUPERHUMAN ABILITIES, AND—
ACCORDING TO EYEWITNESSES CALLED—AH—LIGHTNING DOWN FROM THE SKY, A, UM, FEAT WHICH CAUSED THE...
SUPERHU—? LIGHTNING?
MS. G—ARE YOU SEEING THIS?
LED TO THE DESTRUCTION OF THE MONSTER.
DETAILS ARE YET TO EMERGE AS TO THE IDENTITY OF—
THIS NEW CHAMPION.
WHAT!?
NEW CHAMPION?
A STATEMENT FROM OFFICIALS IS STILL FORTHCOMING.

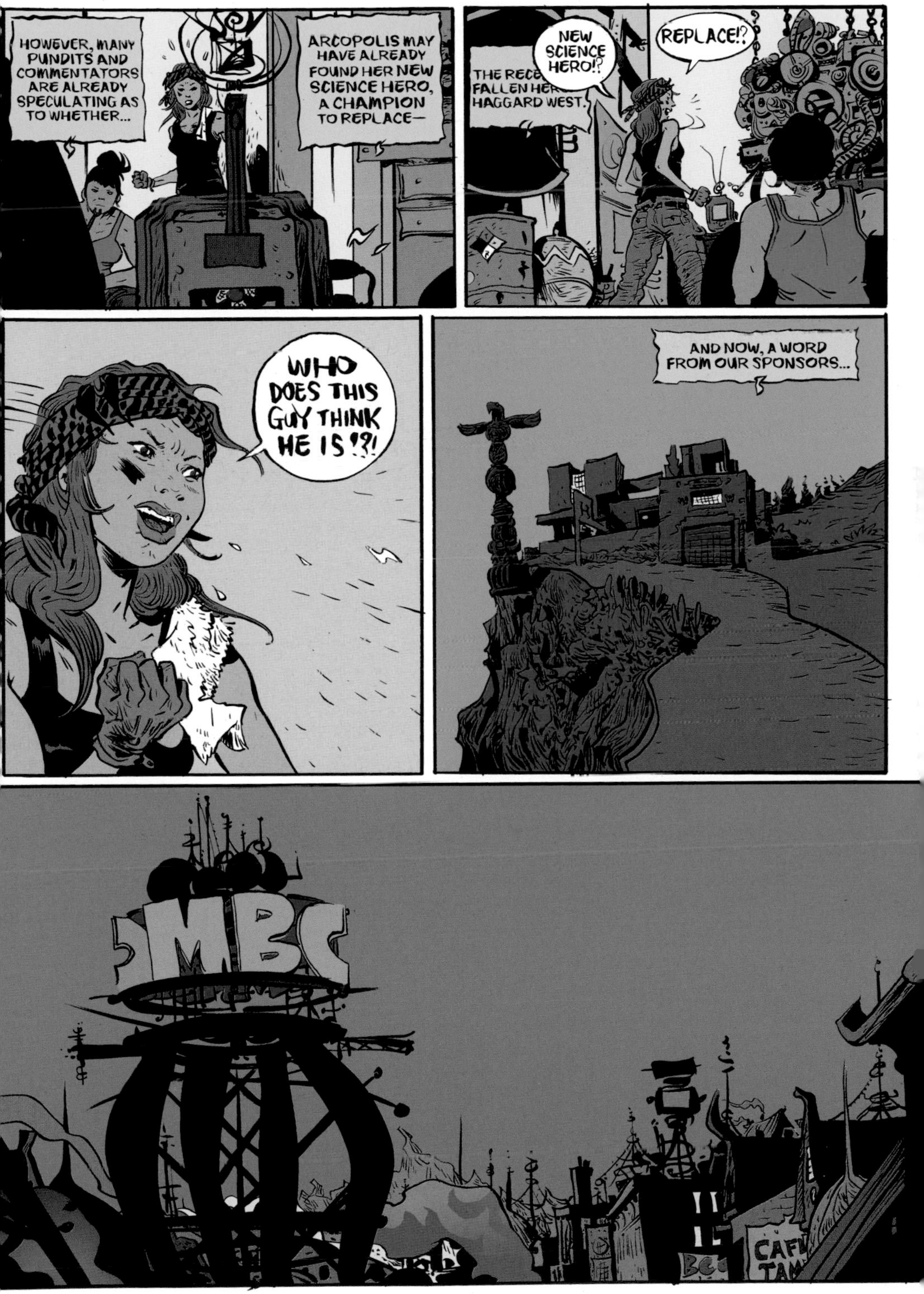
HOWEVER, MANY PUNDITS AND COMMENTATORS ARE ALREADY SPECULATING AS TO WHETHER...
ARCOPOLIS MAY HAVE ALREADY FOUND HER NEW SCIENCE HERO, A CHAMPION TO REPLACE—
THE RECE FALLEN HER HAGGARD WEST.
NEW SCIENCE HERO!?
REPLACE!?
WHO DOES THIS GUY THINK HE IS!?!
AND NOW, A WORD FROM OUR SPONSORS...
MBC

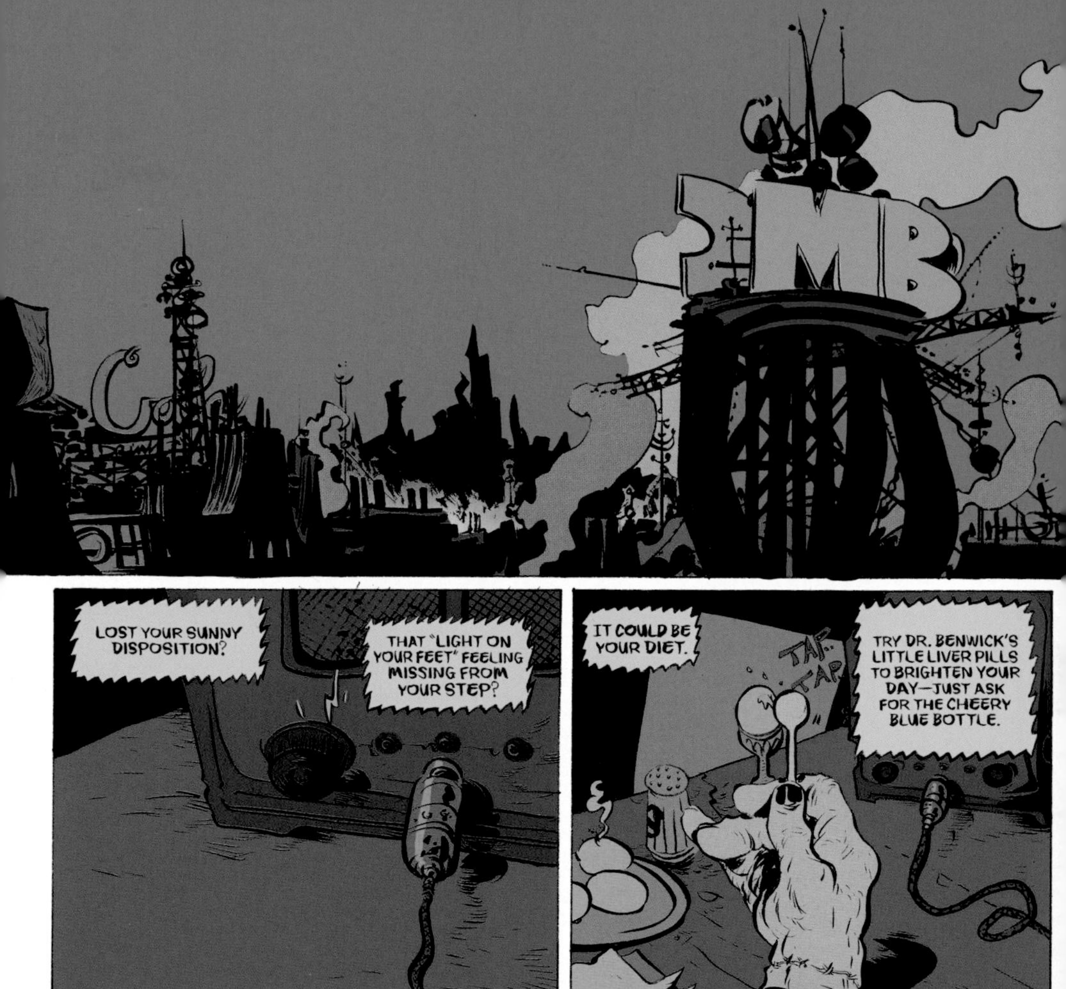
LOST YOUR SUNNY DISPOSITION?
THAT "LIGHT ON YOUR FEET" FEELING MISSING FROM YOUR STEP?
IT COULD BE YOUR DIET.
TAP TAP
TRY DR. BENWICK'S LITTLE LIVER PILLS TO BRIGHTEN YOUR DAY—JUST ASK FOR THE CHEERY BLUE BOTTLE.
AND NOW FOR THE NEWS, COMING TO YOU LIVE FROM THE M.B.C.
...A SIGNIFICANT STEP FORWARD IN THE CITY'S FIGHT AGAINST THE MONSTERS OCCURED TODAY WHEN AN UNKNOWN HERO APPEARED TO AID THE BRAVE FIGHTING MEN OF THE 145TH AGAINST THE HUMBABA.

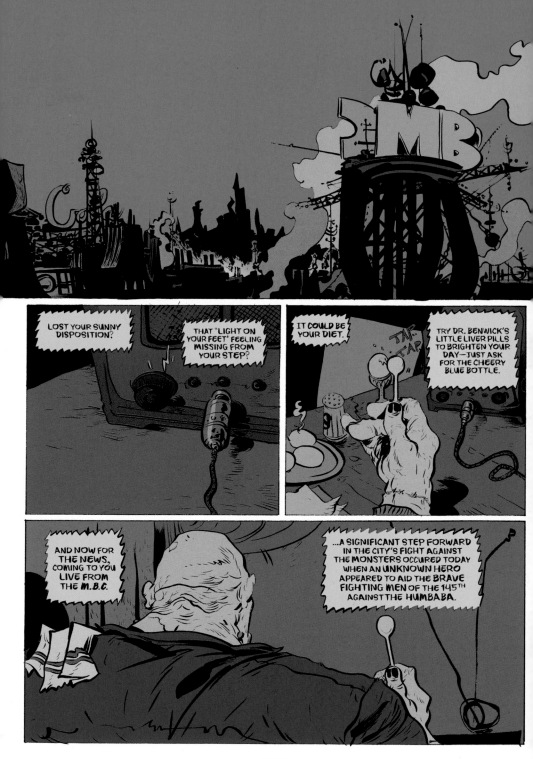

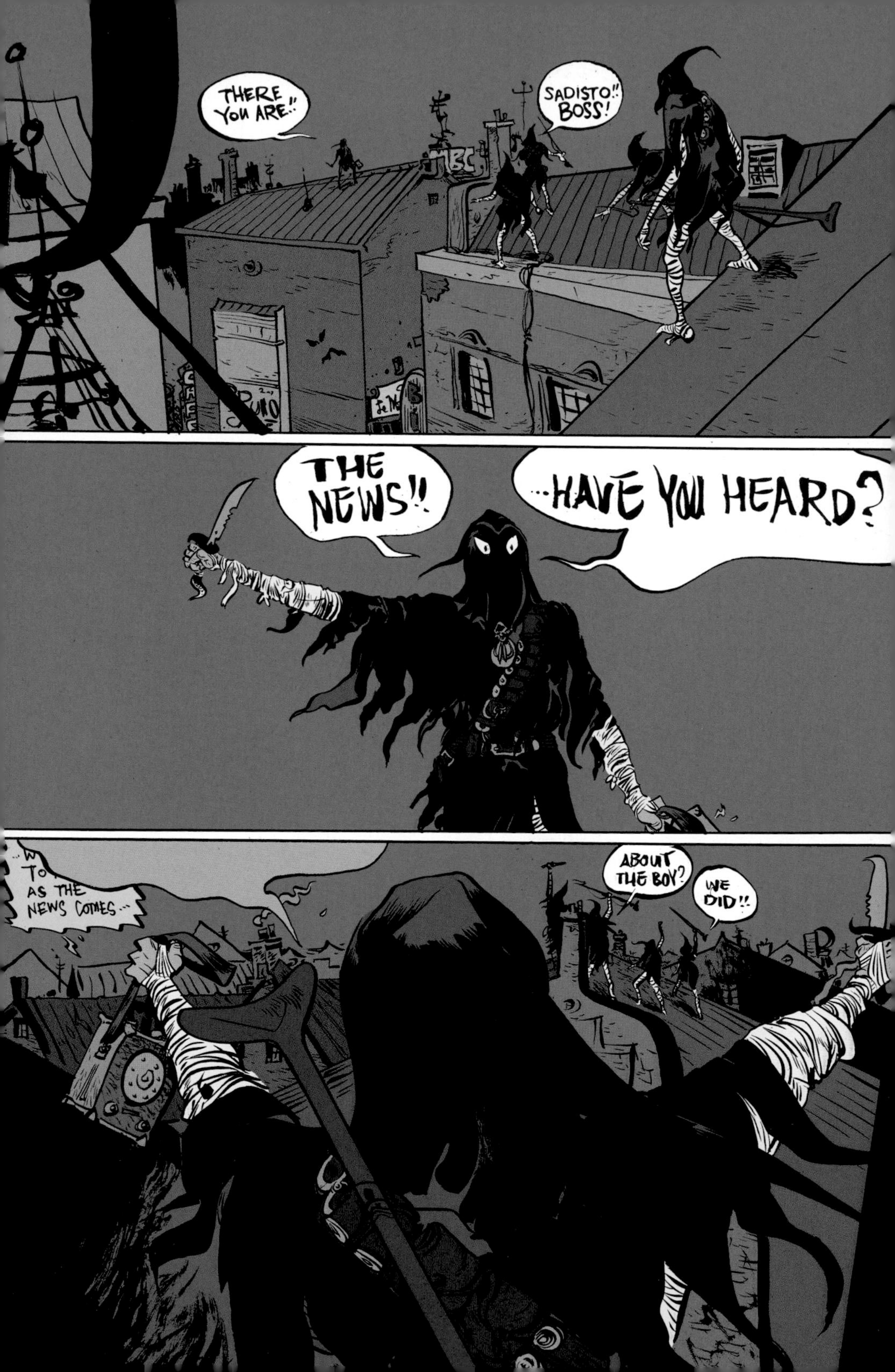
THERE YOU ARE!!
SADISTO!! BOSS!
THE NEWS!!
...HAVE YOU HEARD?
AS THE NEWS COMES...
ABOUT THE BOY?
WE DID!!

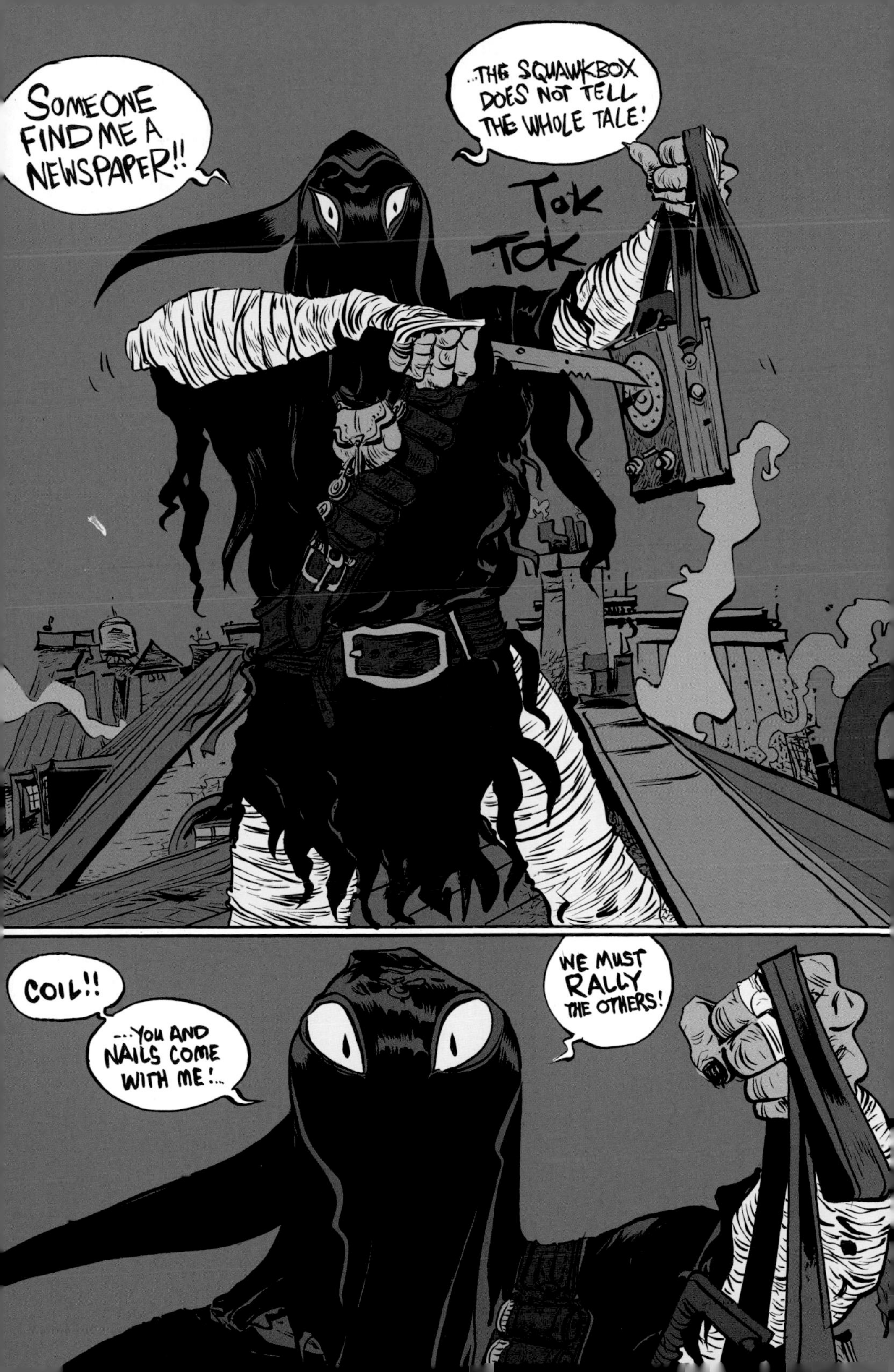
SOMEONE FIND ME A NEWSPAPER!!
...THE SQUAWKBOX DOES NOT TELL THE WHOLE TALE!
TOK TOK
COIL!!
...YOU AND NAILS COME WITH ME!...
WE MUST RALLY THE OTHERS!

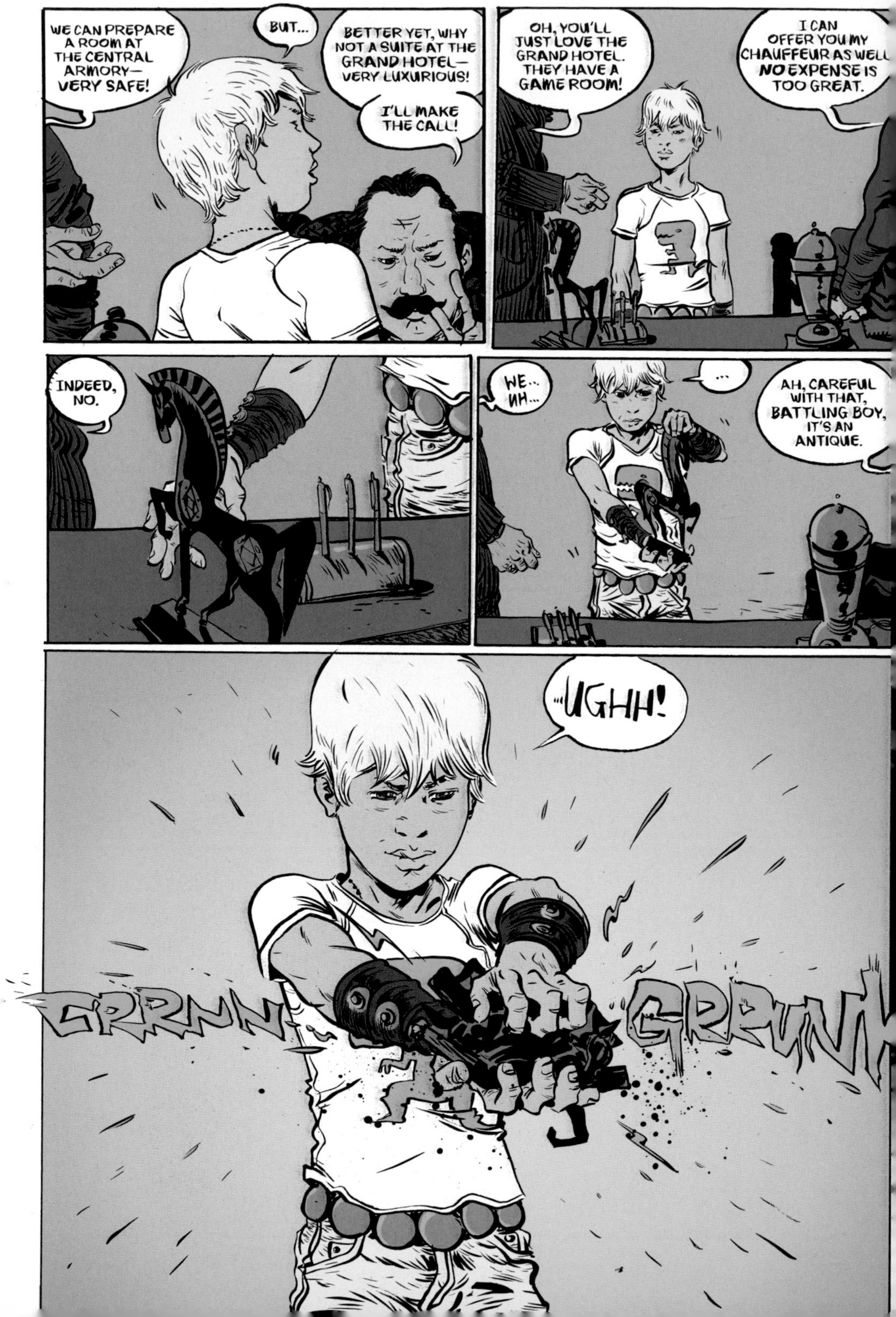
WE CAN PREPARE A ROOM AT THE CENTRAL ARMORY— VERY SAFE!
BUT...
BETTER YET, WHY NOT A SUITE AT THE GRAND HOTEL— VERY LUXURIOUS!
I'LL MAKE THE CALL!
OH, YOU'LL JUST LOVE THE GRAND HOTEL. THEY HAVE A GAME ROOM!
I CAN OFFER YOU MY CHAUFFEUR AS WELL. NO EXPENSE IS TOO GREAT.
INDEED, NO.
WE... UH...
...
AH, CAREFUL WITH THAT, BATTLING BOY, IT'S AN ANTIQUE.
..UGHH!
GRRNN
GRRNK

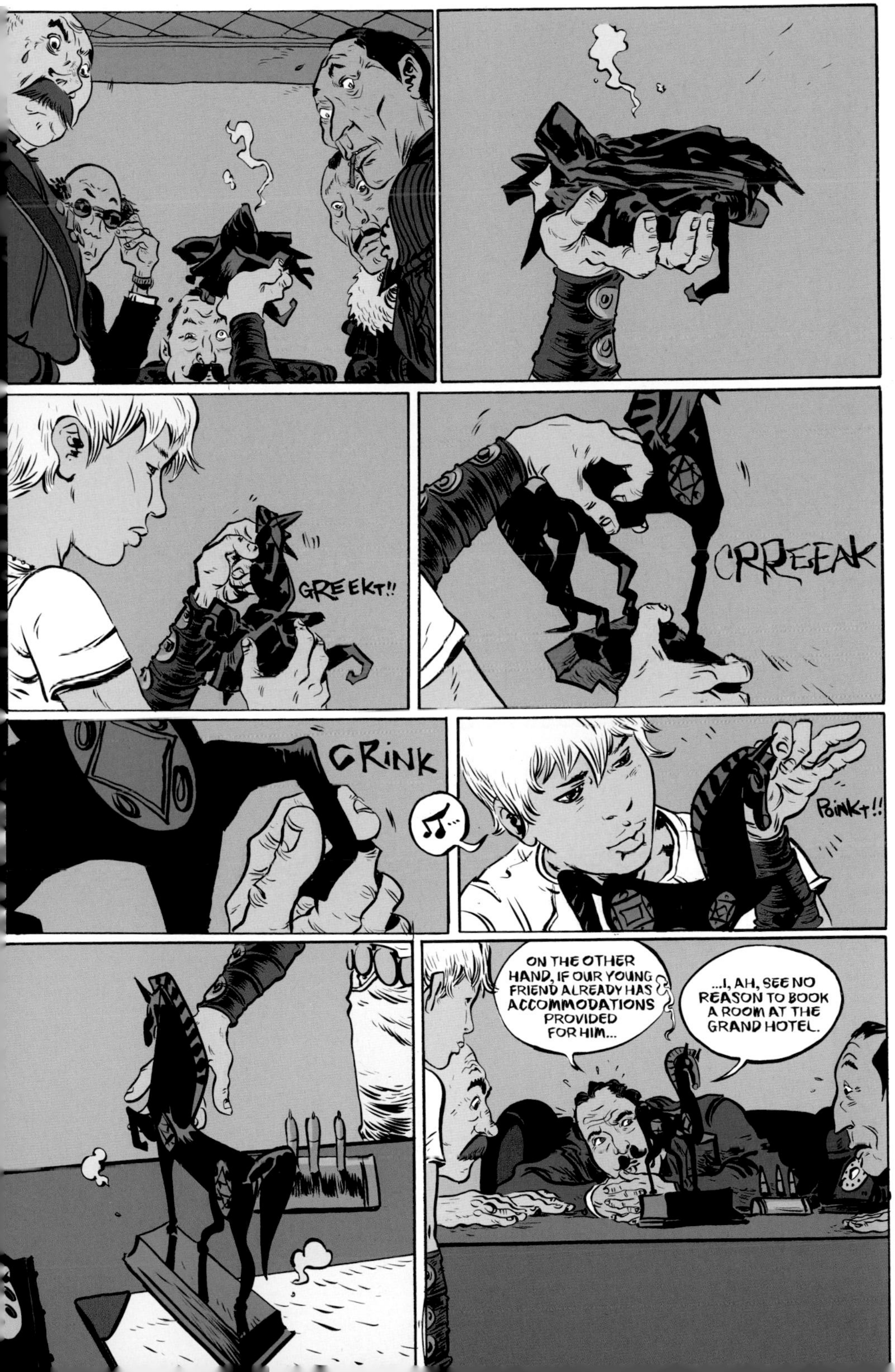
GREEKT!!
CRREEAK
GRINK
POINKT!!
ON THE OTHER HAND, IF OUR YOUNG FRIEND ALREADY HAS ACCOMMODATIONS PROVIDED FOR HIM...
...I, AH, SEE NO REASON TO BOOK A ROOM AT THE GRAND HOTEL.

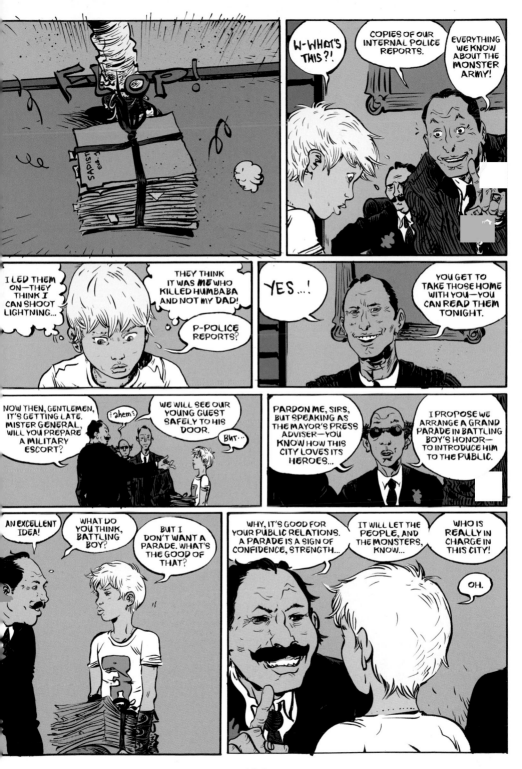

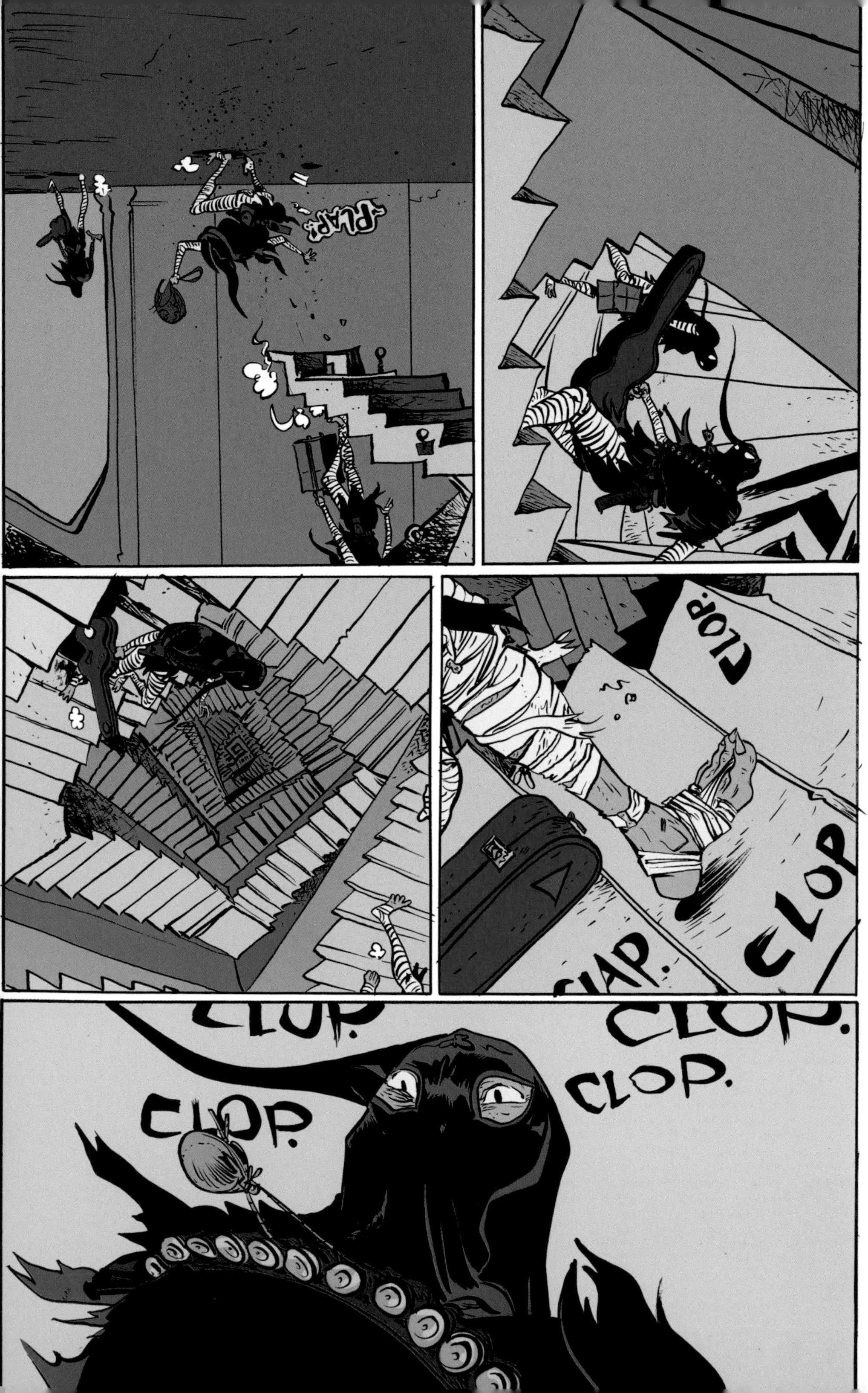
PLAP!
CLOP
SLAP.
CLOP
CLOP.
CLOP.
CLOP.
CLOP.

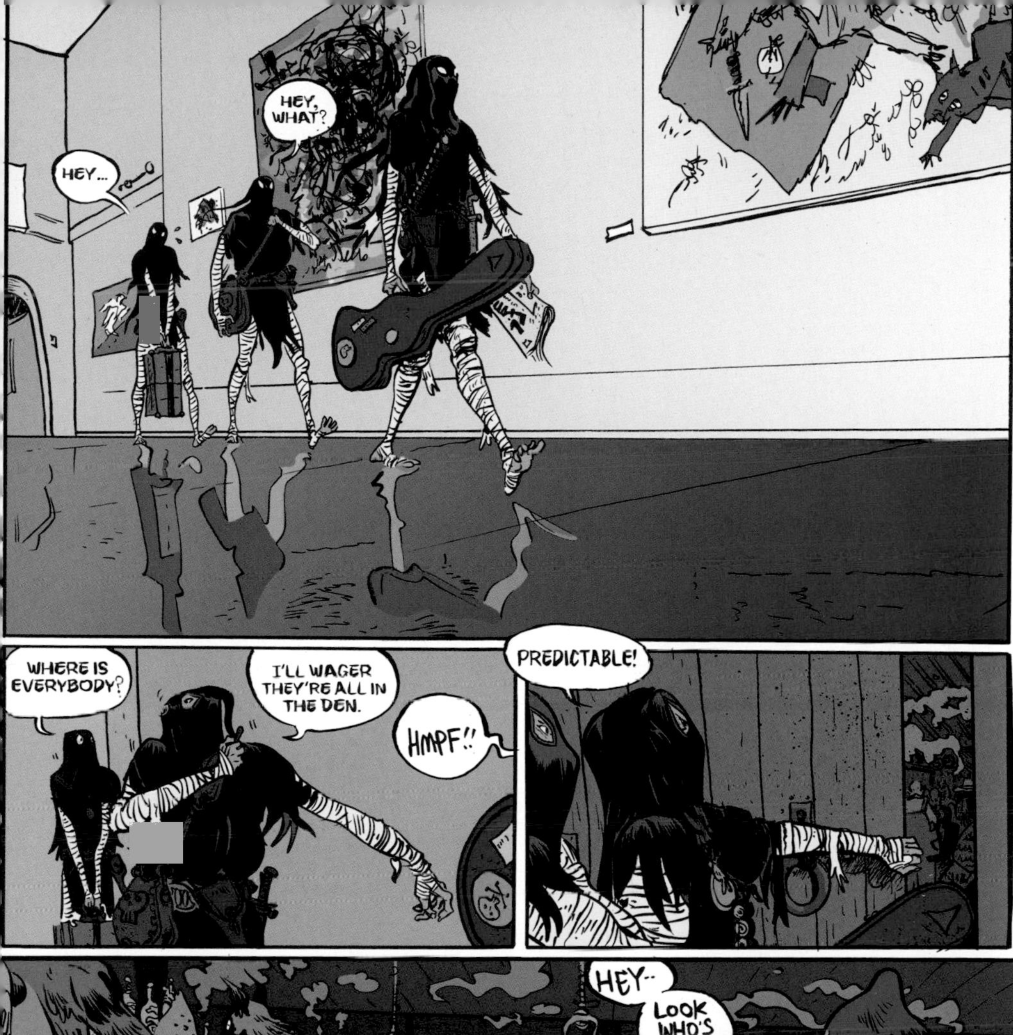
HEY...
HEY, WHAT?
WHERE IS EVERYBODY?
I'LL WAGER THEY'RE ALL IN THE DEN.
HMPF!!
PREDICTABLE!
HEY--
LOOK WHO'S HERE!

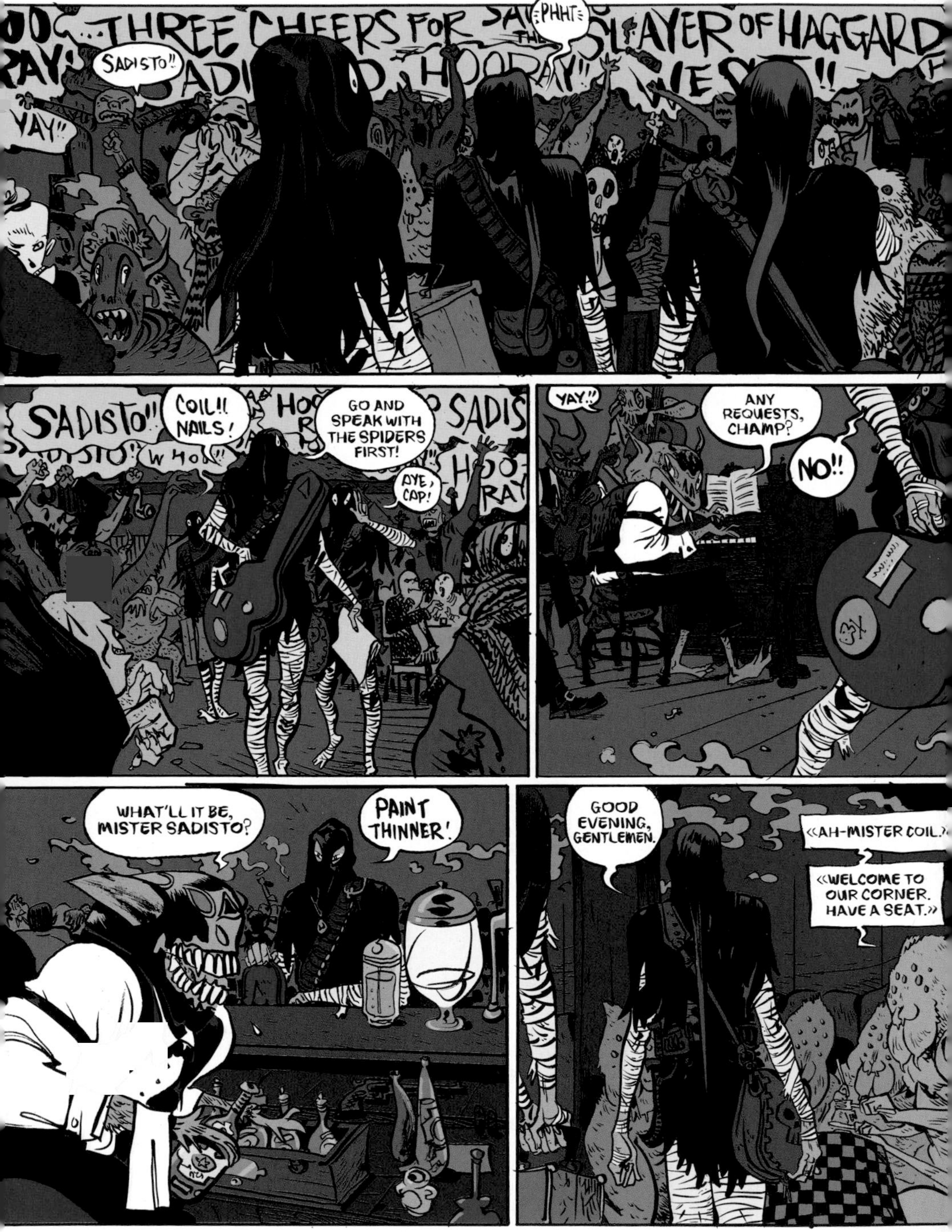
...THREE CHEERS FOR
PHHT
SLAYER OF HAGGARD
SADISTO!!
HOORAY!!
YAY!!
SADISTO!!
COIL!! NAILS!
GO AND SPEAK WITH THE SPIDERS FIRST!
AYE, CAP!
HOO-RAY
YAY!!
ANY REQUESTS, CHAMP?
NO!!
WHAT'LL IT BE, MISTER SADISTO?
PAINT THINNER!
GOOD EVENING, GENTLEMEN.
«AH—MISTER COIL.»
«WELCOME TO OUR CORNER. HAVE A SEAT.»

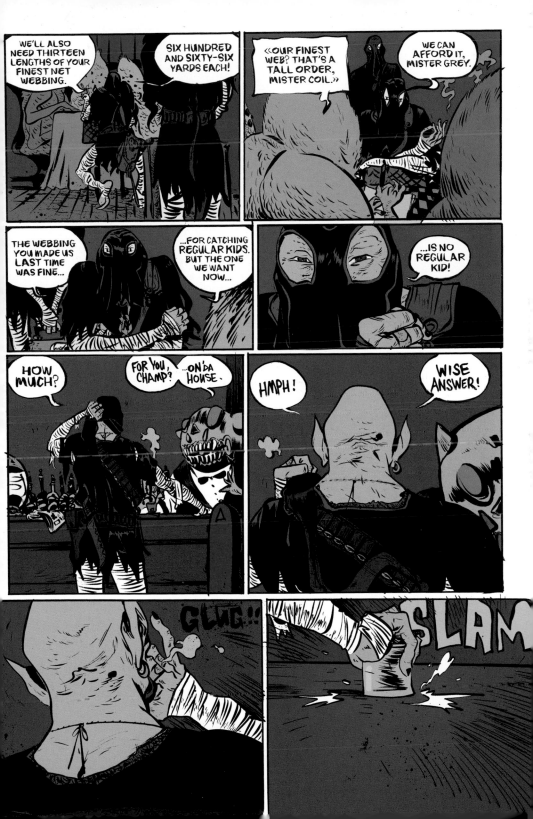

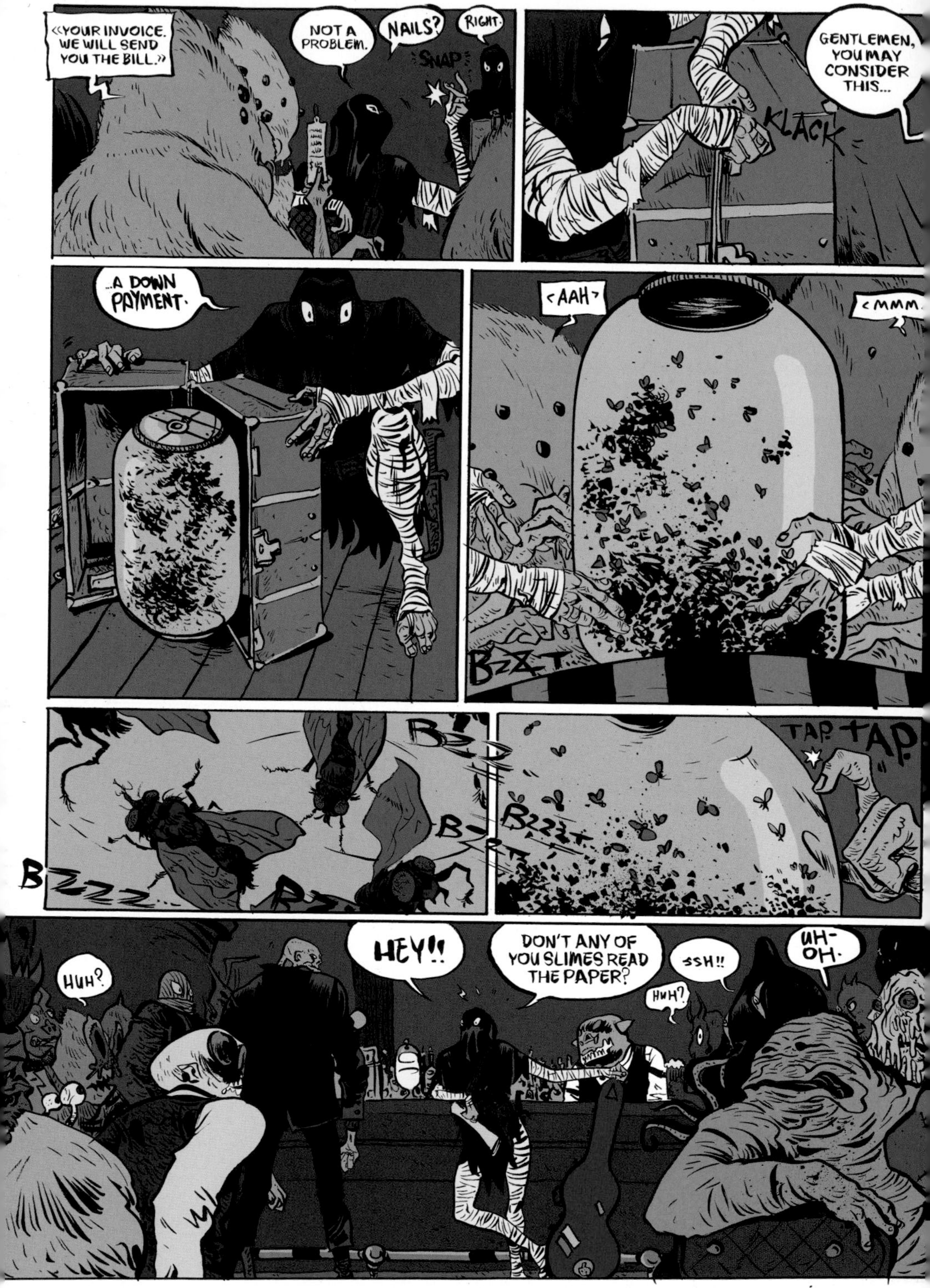

<<YOUR INVOICE. WE WILL SEND YOU THE BILL.>>
NOT A PROBLEM.
NAILS?
RIGHT.
SNAP
GENTLEMEN, YOU MAY CONSIDER THIS...
KLACK
...A DOWN PAYMENT.
<AAH>
<MMM.
BZZT
BZZ
B-ZZ
BZZZT
BZZZZ
TAP TAP
HUH?
HEY!!
DON'T ANY OF YOU SLIMES READ THE PAPER?
SSH!!
HUH?
UH-OH.

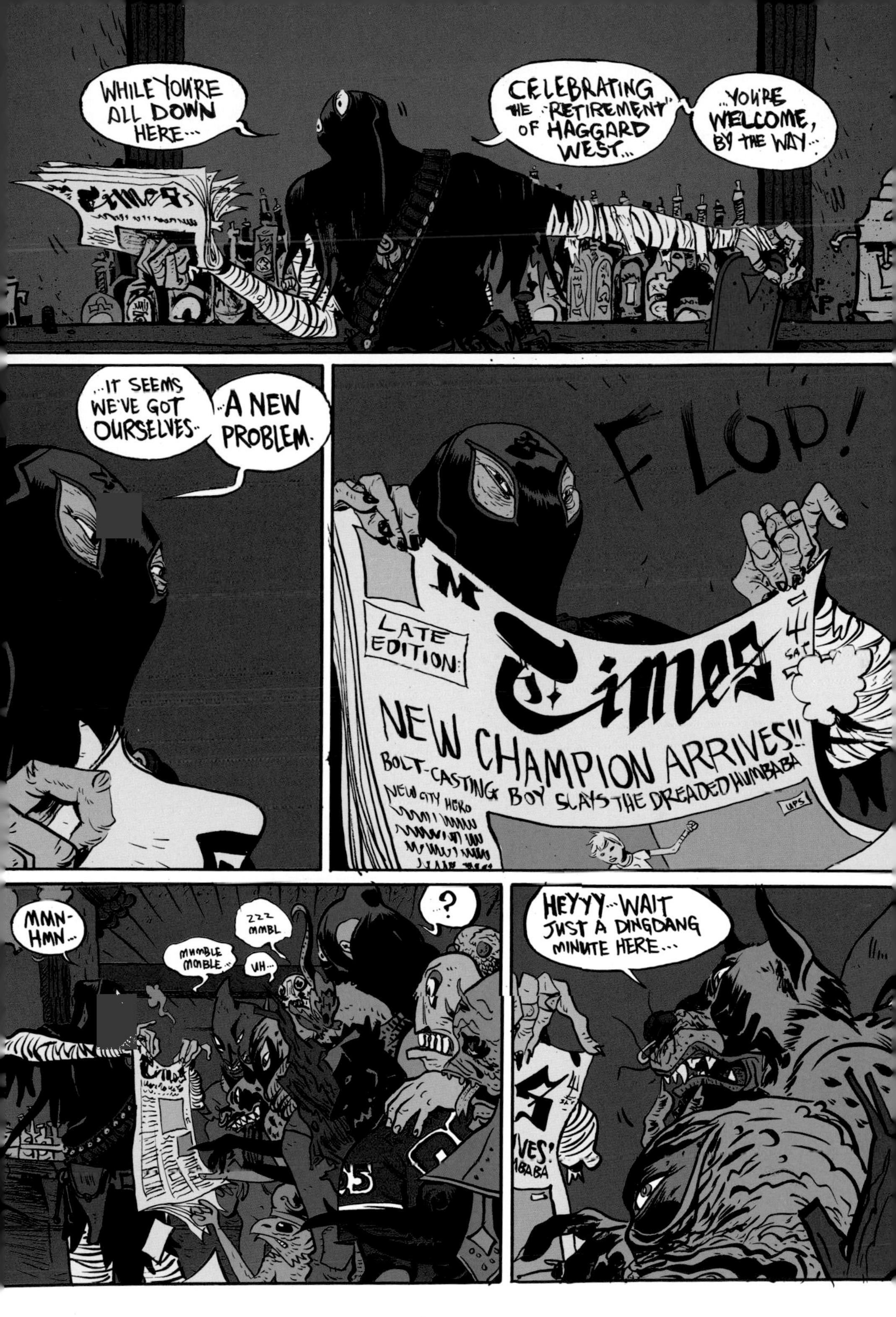
WHILE YOU'RE ALL DOWN HERE...
CELEBRATING THE "RETIREMENT" OF HAGGARD WEST...
...YOU'RE WELCOME, BY THE WAY...
...IT SEEMS WE'VE GOT OURSELVES...
...A NEW PROBLEM.
FLOP!
LATE EDITION:
Times
NEW CHAMPION ARRIVES!!
BOLT-CASTING BOY SLAYS THE DREADED HUMBABA
NEW CITY HERO
MMN-HMN...
MUMBLE MUMBLE...
ZZZ MMBL
UH...
...?
HEYYY...WAIT JUST A DINGDANG MINUTE HERE...

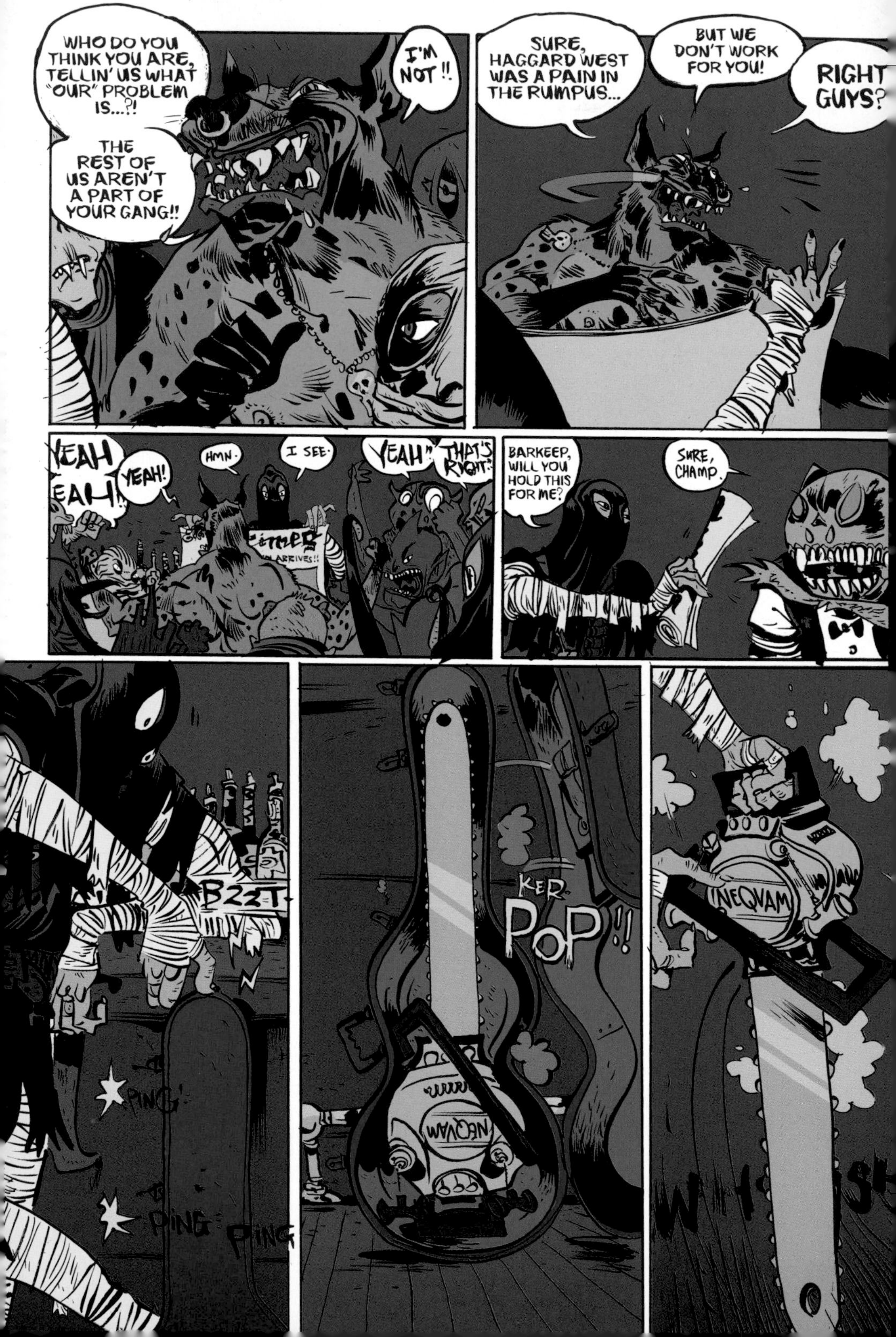
WHO DO YOU THINK YOU ARE, TELLIN' US WHAT "OUR" PROBLEM IS...?!
THE REST OF US AREN'T A PART OF YOUR GANG!!
I'M NOT!!
SURE, HAGGARD WEST WAS A PAIN IN THE RUMPUS...
BUT WE DON'T WORK FOR YOU!
RIGHT GUYS?
YEAH
YEAH!
YEAH!
HMN.
I SEE.
YEAH
THAT'S RIGHT!
BARKEEP, WILL YOU HOLD THIS FOR ME?
SURE, CHAMP.
BZZT
PING
PING
PING
KER POP!!
NEQVAM
NEQVAM

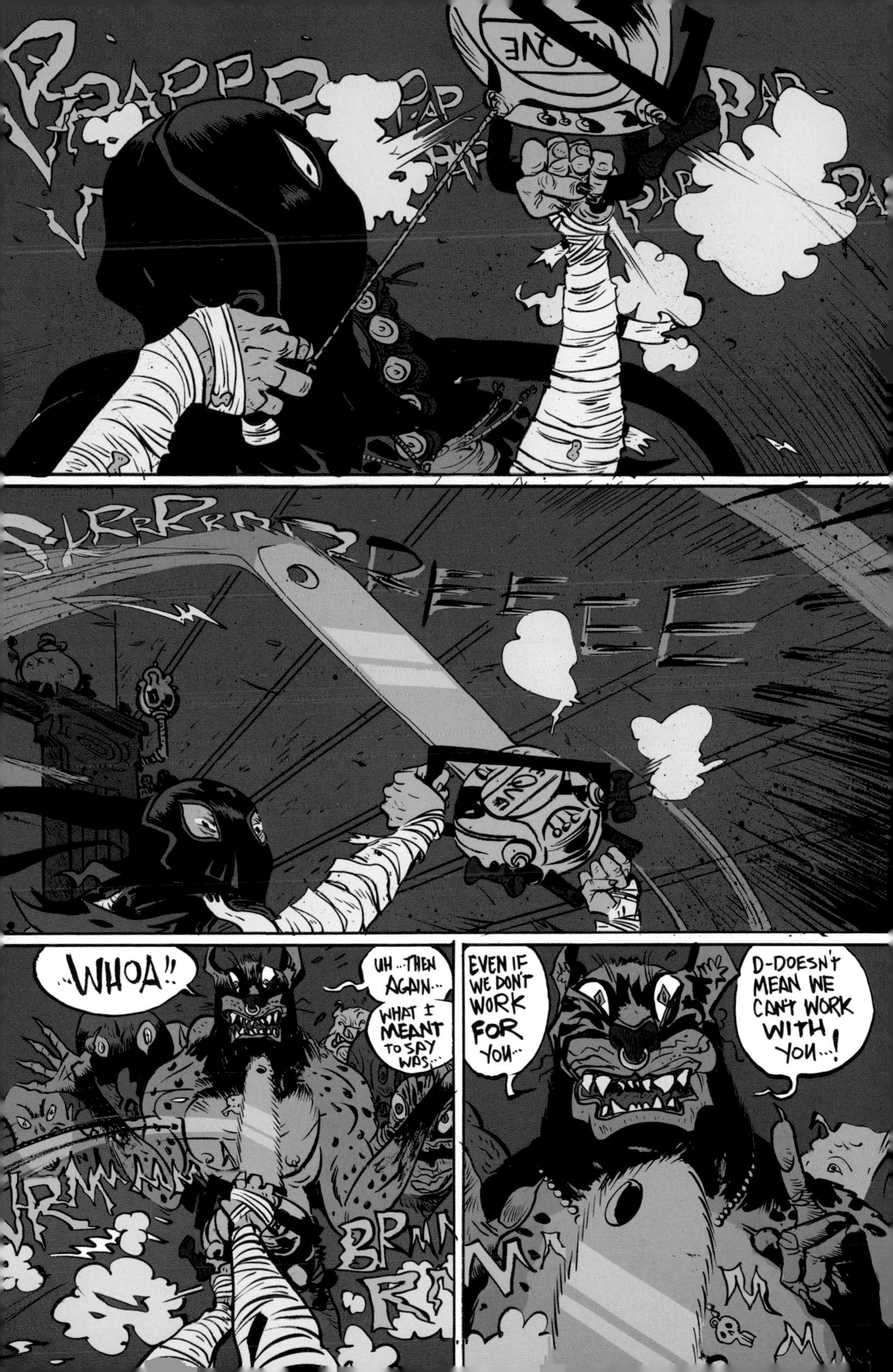
..WHOA!!
UH...THEN AGAIN...
WHAT I MEANT TO SAY WAS...
EVEN IF WE DON'T WORK FOR YOU...
D-DOESN'T MEAN WE CAN'T WORK WITH YOU...!

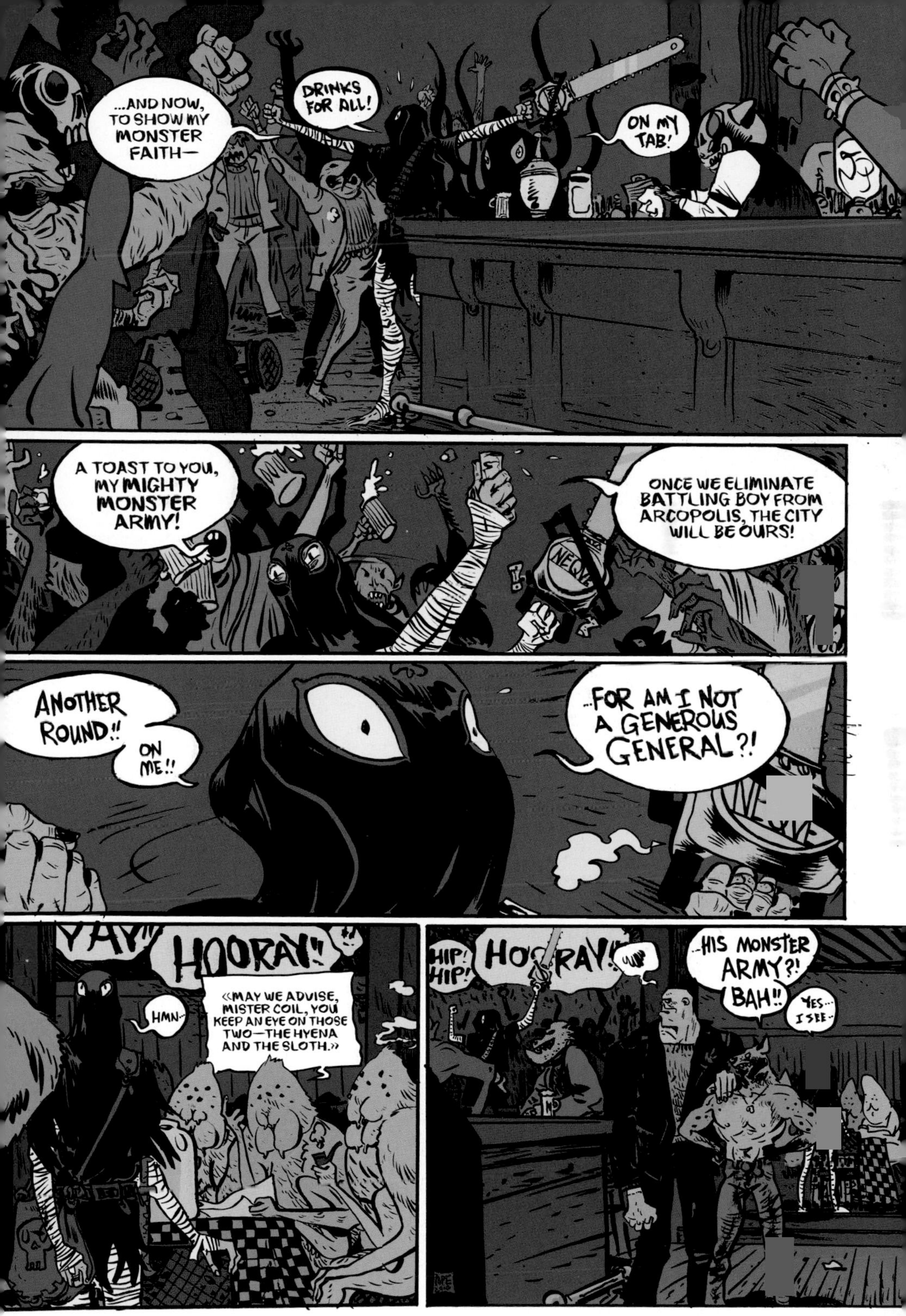
...AND NOW, TO SHOW MY MONSTER FAITH—
DRINKS FOR ALL!
ON MY TAB!
A TOAST TO YOU, MY MIGHTY MONSTER ARMY!
ONCE WE ELIMINATE BATTLING BOY FROM ARCOPOLIS, THE CITY WILL BE OURS!
ANOTHER ROUND!!
ON ME!!
...FOR AM I NOT A GENEROUS GENERAL?!
HOORAY!!
HMN...
«MAY WE ADVISE, MISTER COIL, YOU KEEP AN EYE ON THOSE TWO—THE HYENA AND THE SLOTH.»
HIP! HIP!
HOORAY!!
...HIS MONSTER ARMY?! BAH!!
YES... I SEE...

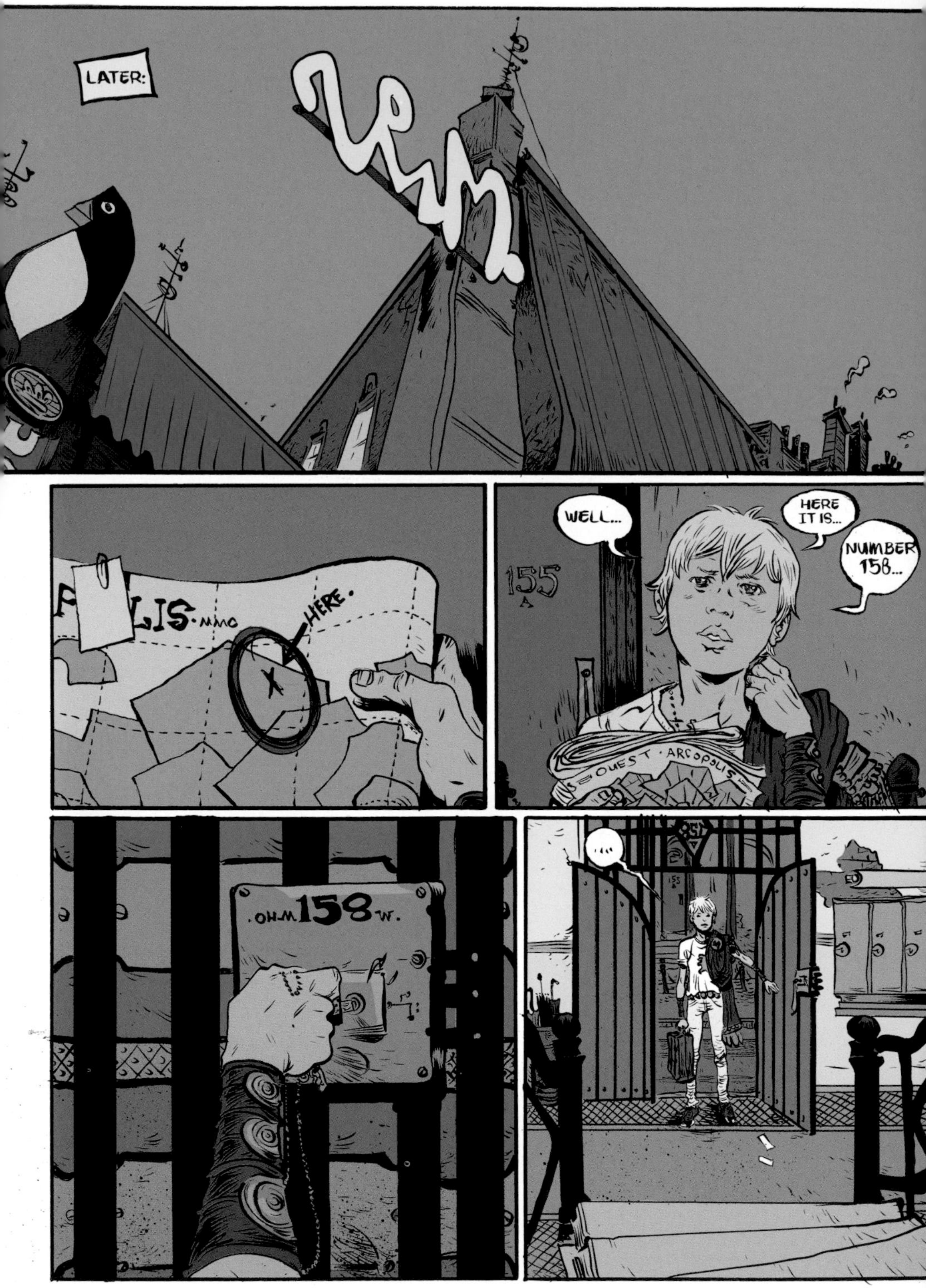
LATER:
LIS.
HERE.
155
WELL...
HERE IT IS...
NUMBER 158...
OUEST · ARCOPOLIS
.OHM 158 W.
...

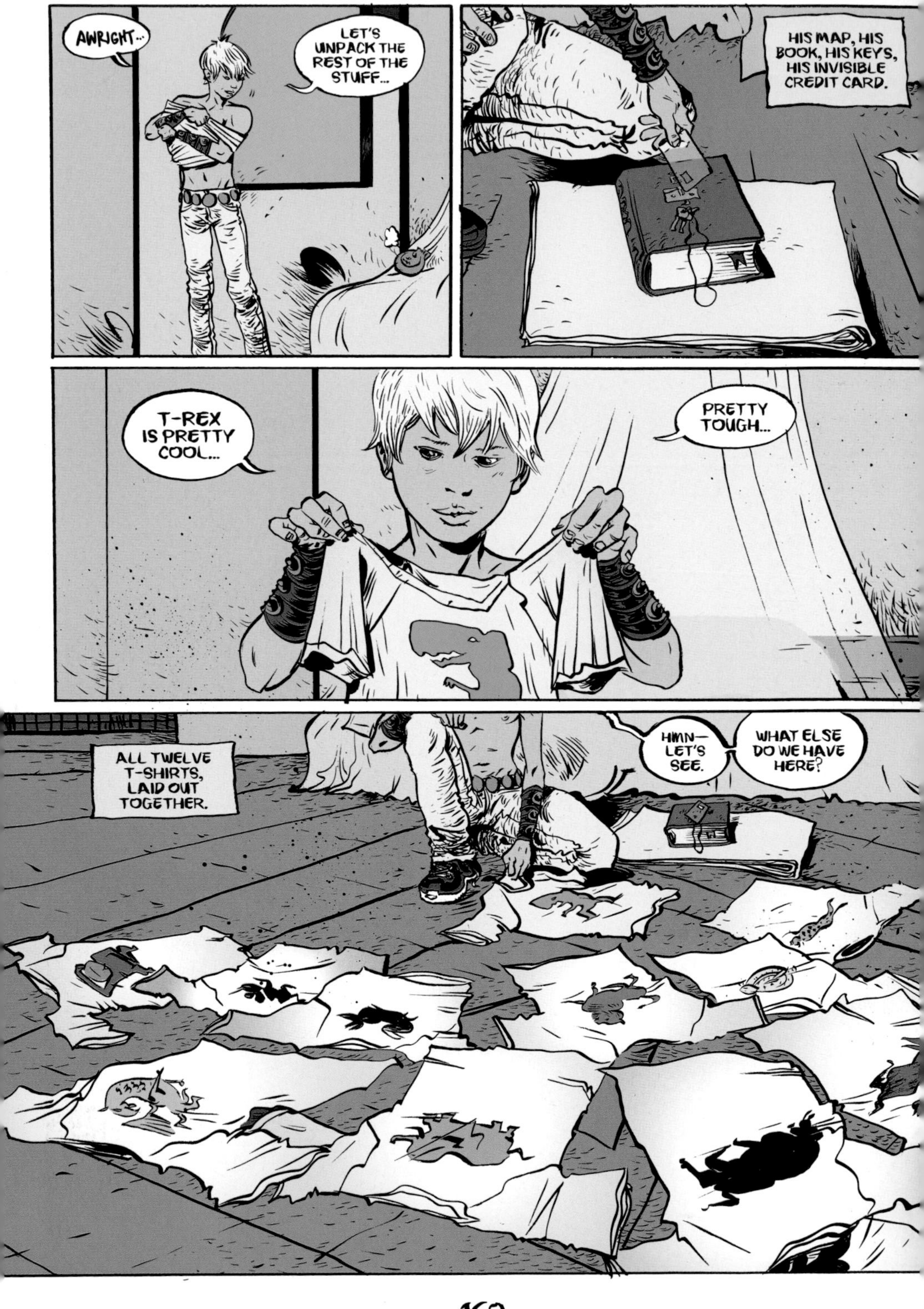
AWRIGHT...
LET'S UNPACK THE REST OF THE STUFF...
HIS MAP, HIS BOOK, HIS KEYS, HIS INVISIBLE CREDIT CARD.
T-REX IS PRETTY COOL...
PRETTY TOUGH...
ALL TWELVE T-SHIRTS, LAID OUT TOGETHER.
HMN— LET'S SEE.
WHAT ELSE DO WE HAVE HERE?

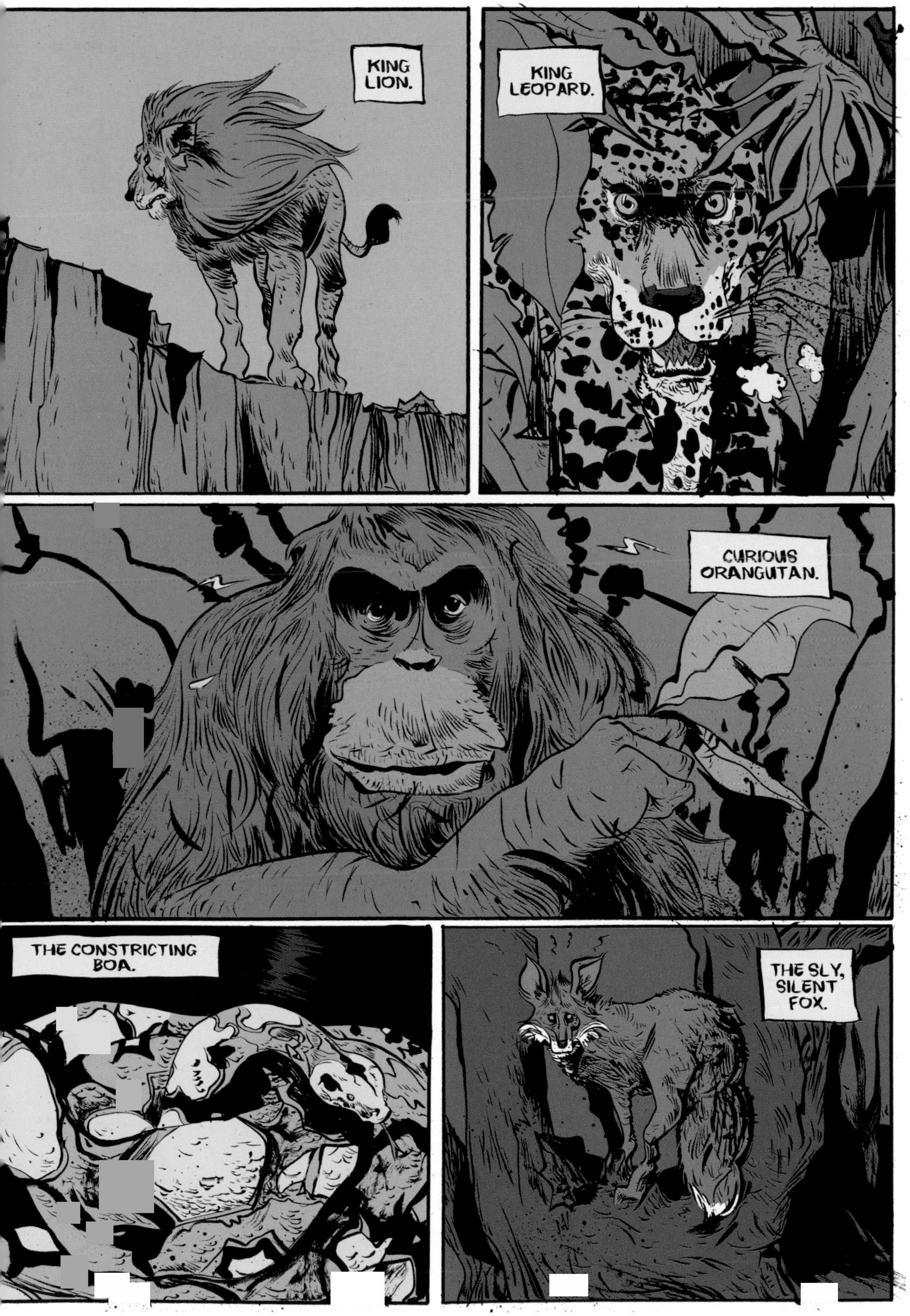
KING LION.
KING LEOPARD.
CURIOUS ORANGUTAN.
THE CONSTRICTING BOA.
THE SLY, SILENT FOX.

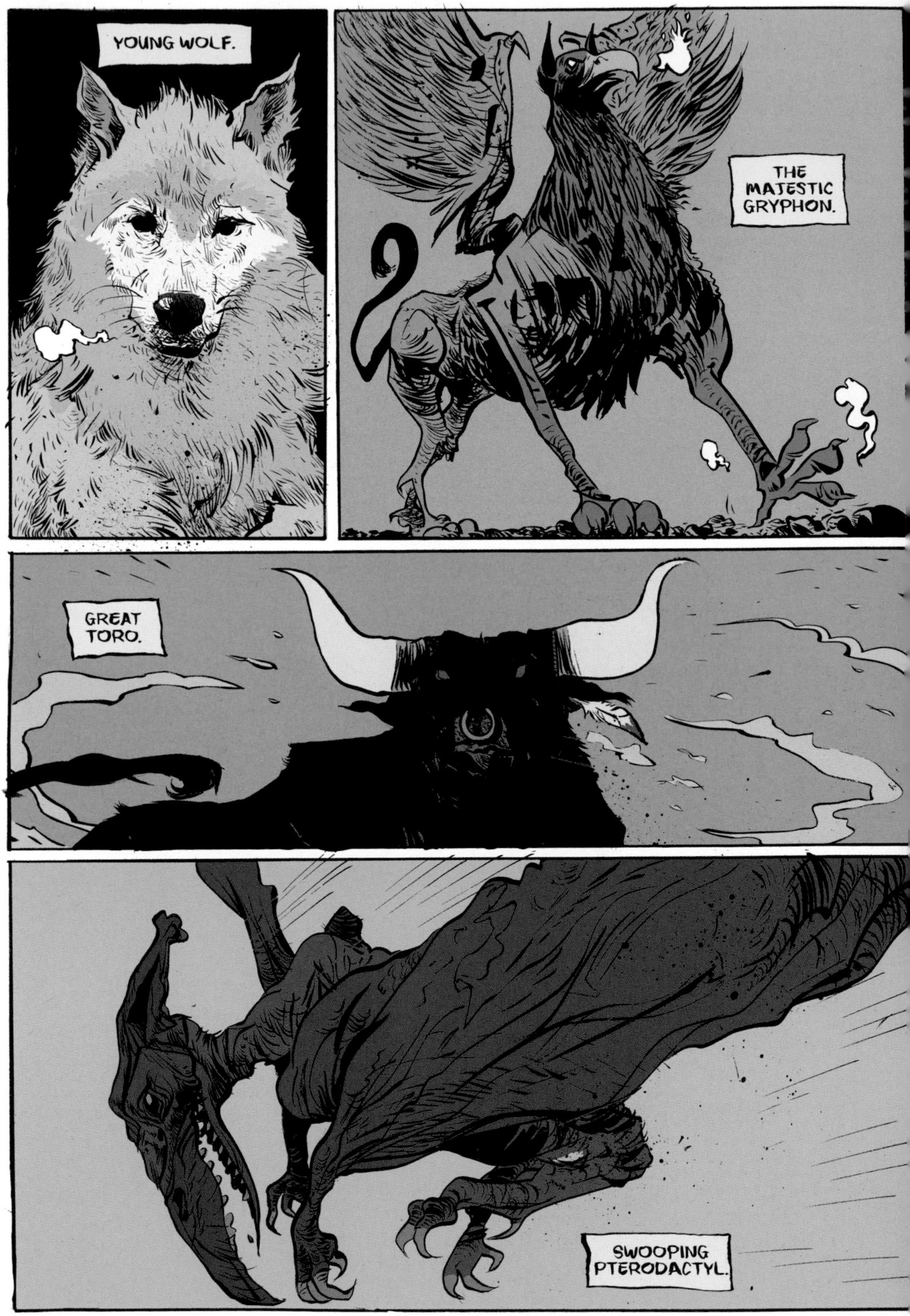
YOUNG WOLF.
THE MAJESTIC GRYPHON.
GREAT TORO.
SWOOPING PTERODACTYL.

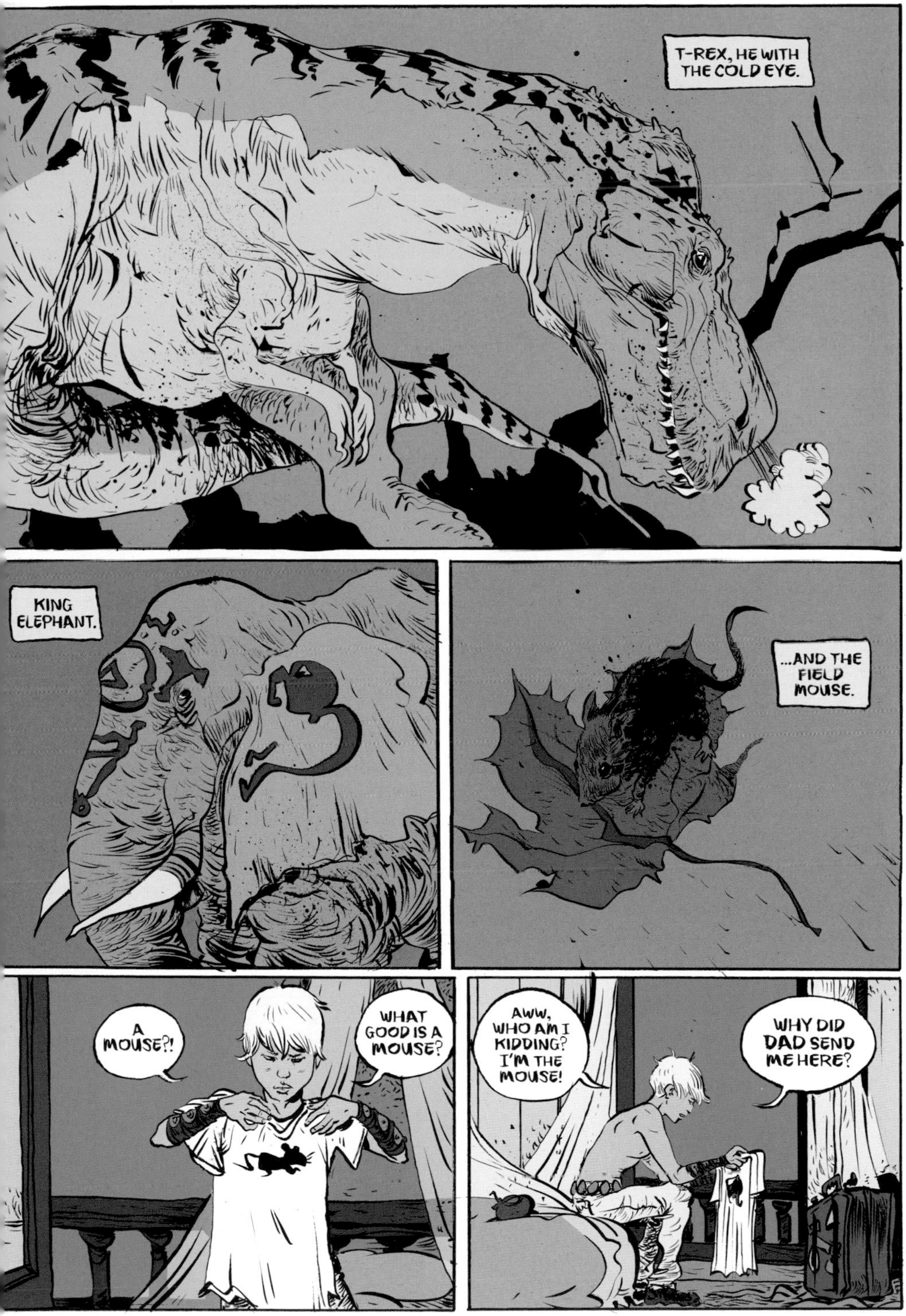

T-REX, HE WITH THE COLD EYE.
KING ELEPHANT.
...AND THE FIELD MOUSE.
A MOUSE?!
WHAT GOOD IS A MOUSE?
AWW, WHO AM I KIDDING? I'M THE MOUSE!
WHY DID DAD SEND ME HERE?

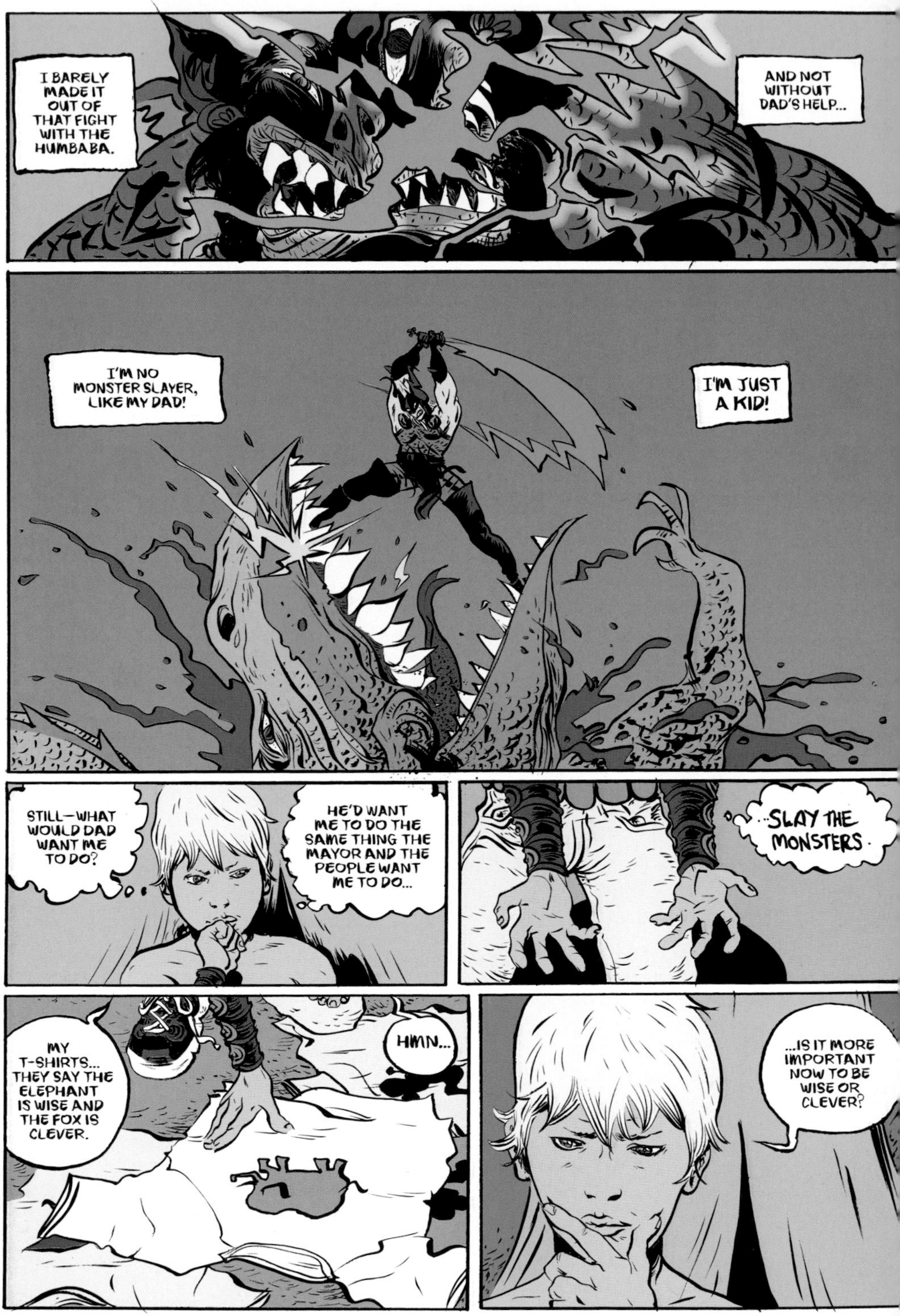

I BARELY MADE IT OUT OF THAT FIGHT WITH THE HUMBABA.
AND NOT WITHOUT DAD'S HELP...
I'M NO MONSTER SLAYER, LIKE MY DAD!
I'M JUST A KID!
STILL—WHAT WOULD DAD WANT ME TO DO?
HE'D WANT ME TO DO THE SAME THING THE MAYOR AND THE PEOPLE WANT ME TO DO...
...SLAY THE MONSTERS.
MY T-SHIRTS... THEY SAY THE ELEPHANT IS WISE AND THE FOX IS CLEVER.
HMN...
...IS IT MORE IMPORTANT NOW TO BE WISE OR CLEVER?

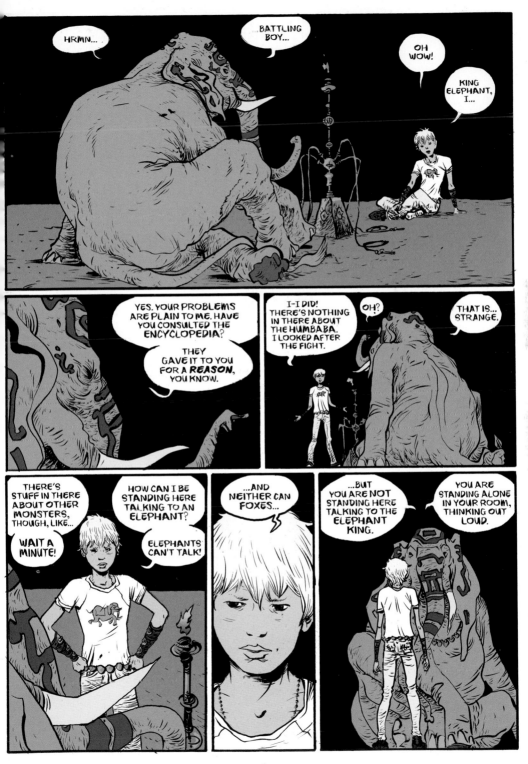

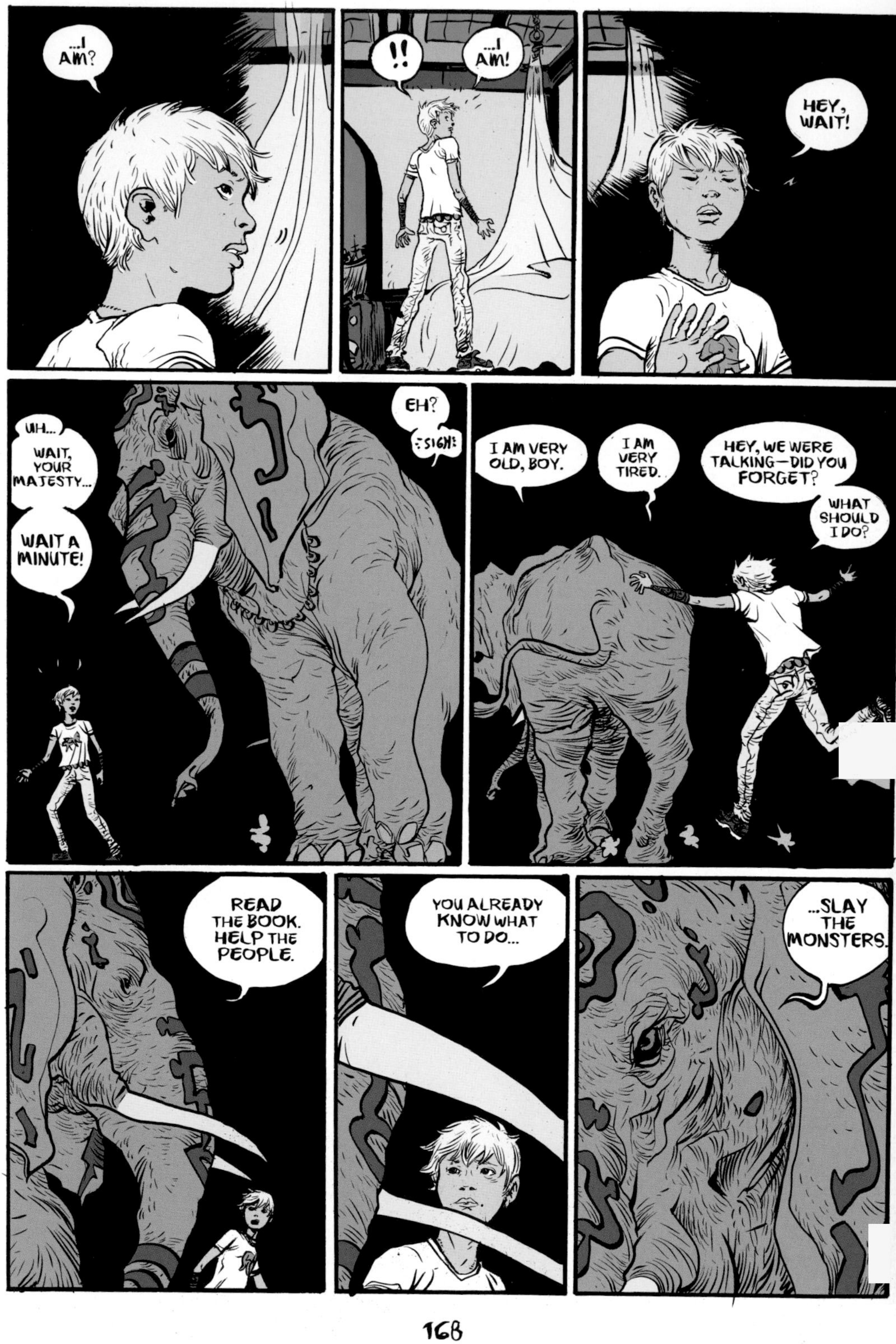
...I AM?
!!
...I AM!
HEY, WAIT!
UH...
WAIT, YOUR MAJESTY...
WAIT A MINUTE!
EH?
:SIGH:
I AM VERY OLD, BOY.
I AM VERY TIRED.
HEY, WE WERE TALKING—DID YOU FORGET?
WHAT SHOULD I DO?
READ THE BOOK. HELP THE PEOPLE.
YOU ALREADY KNOW WHAT TO DO...
...SLAY THE MONSTERS.

169

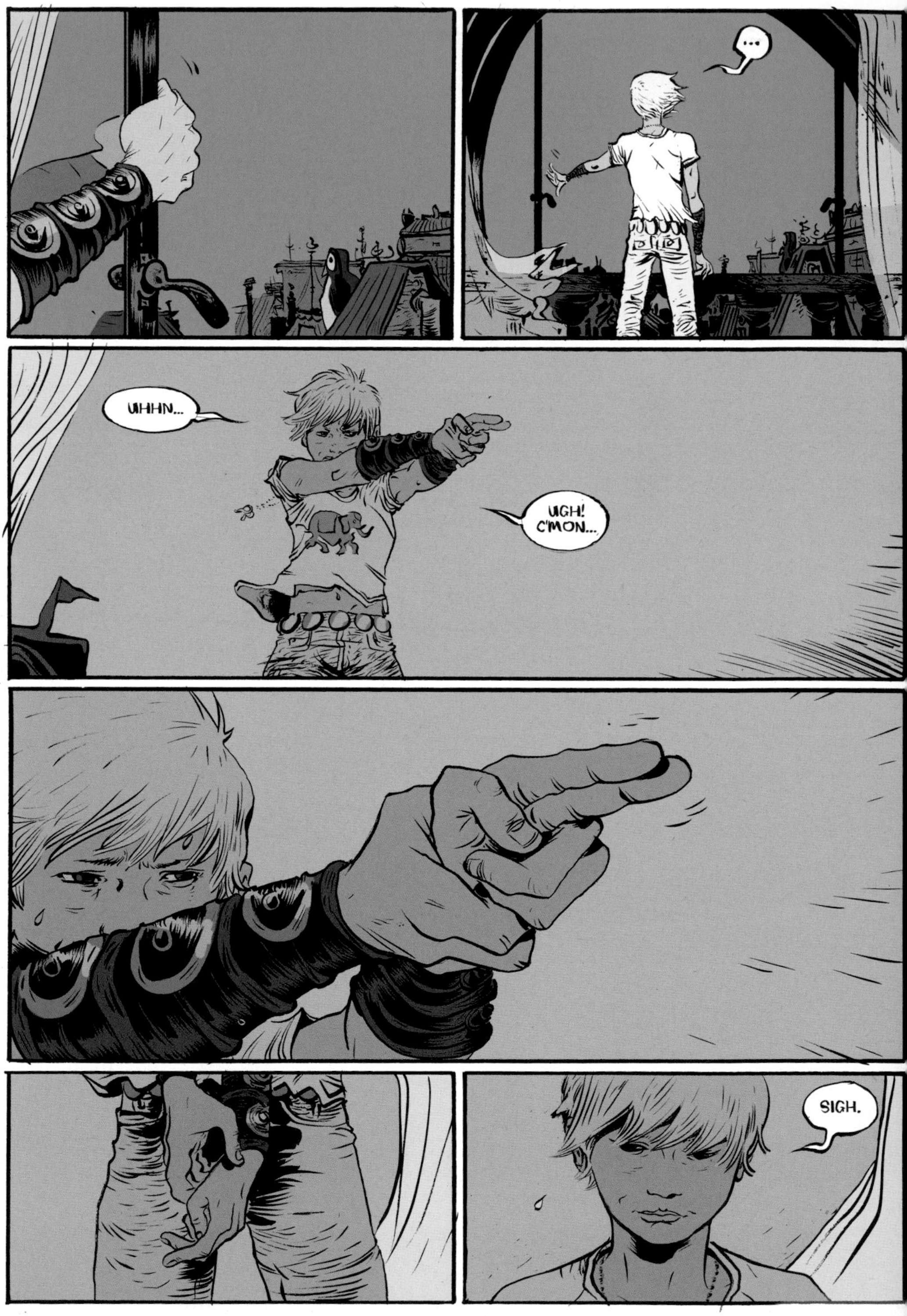

...
UHHN...
UGH! C'MON...
SIGH.

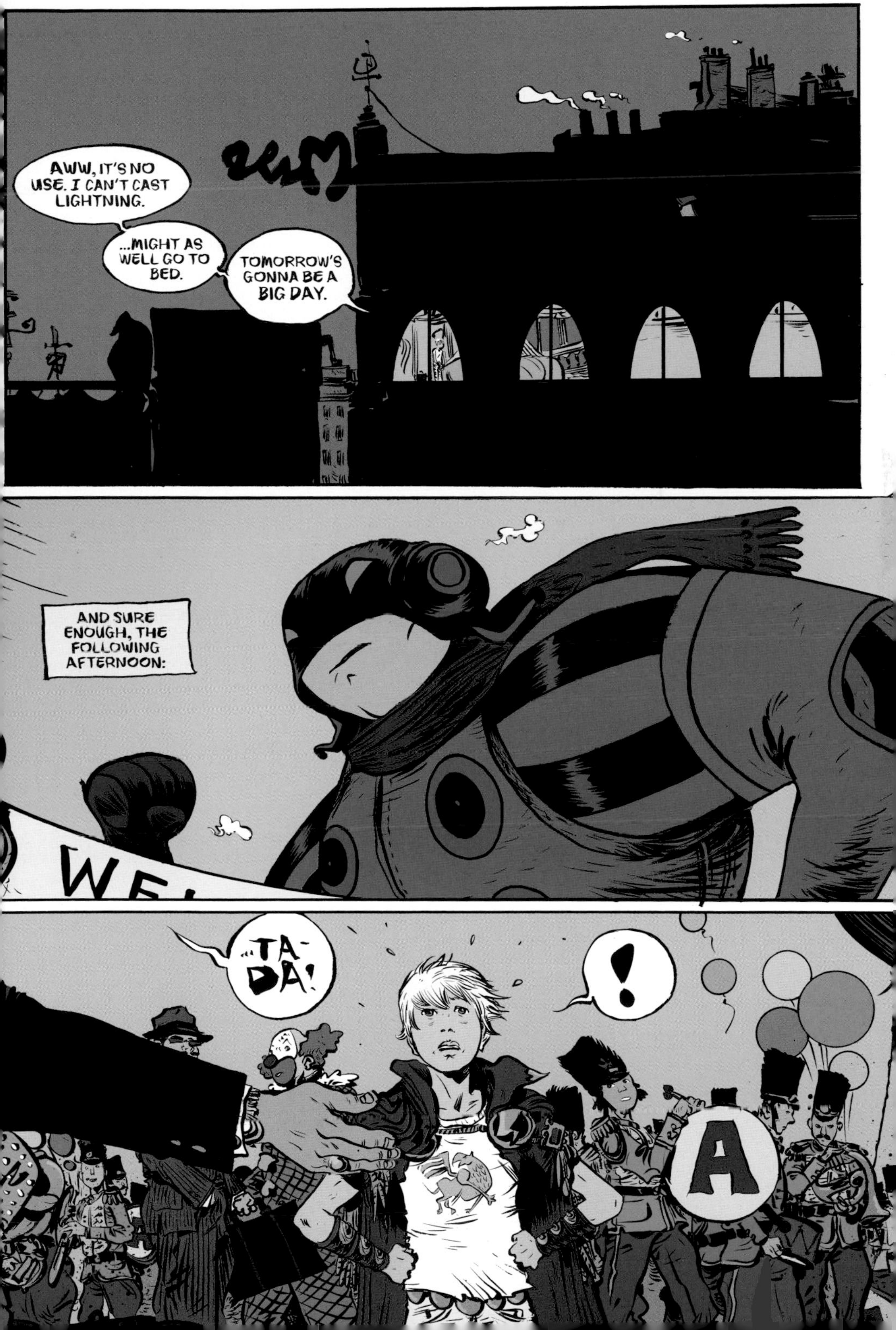
AWW, IT'S NO USE. I CAN'T CAST LIGHTNING.
...MIGHT AS WELL GO TO BED.
TOMORROW'S GONNA BE A BIG DAY.
AND SURE ENOUGH, THE FOLLOWING AFTERNOON:
...TA-DA!
!
A

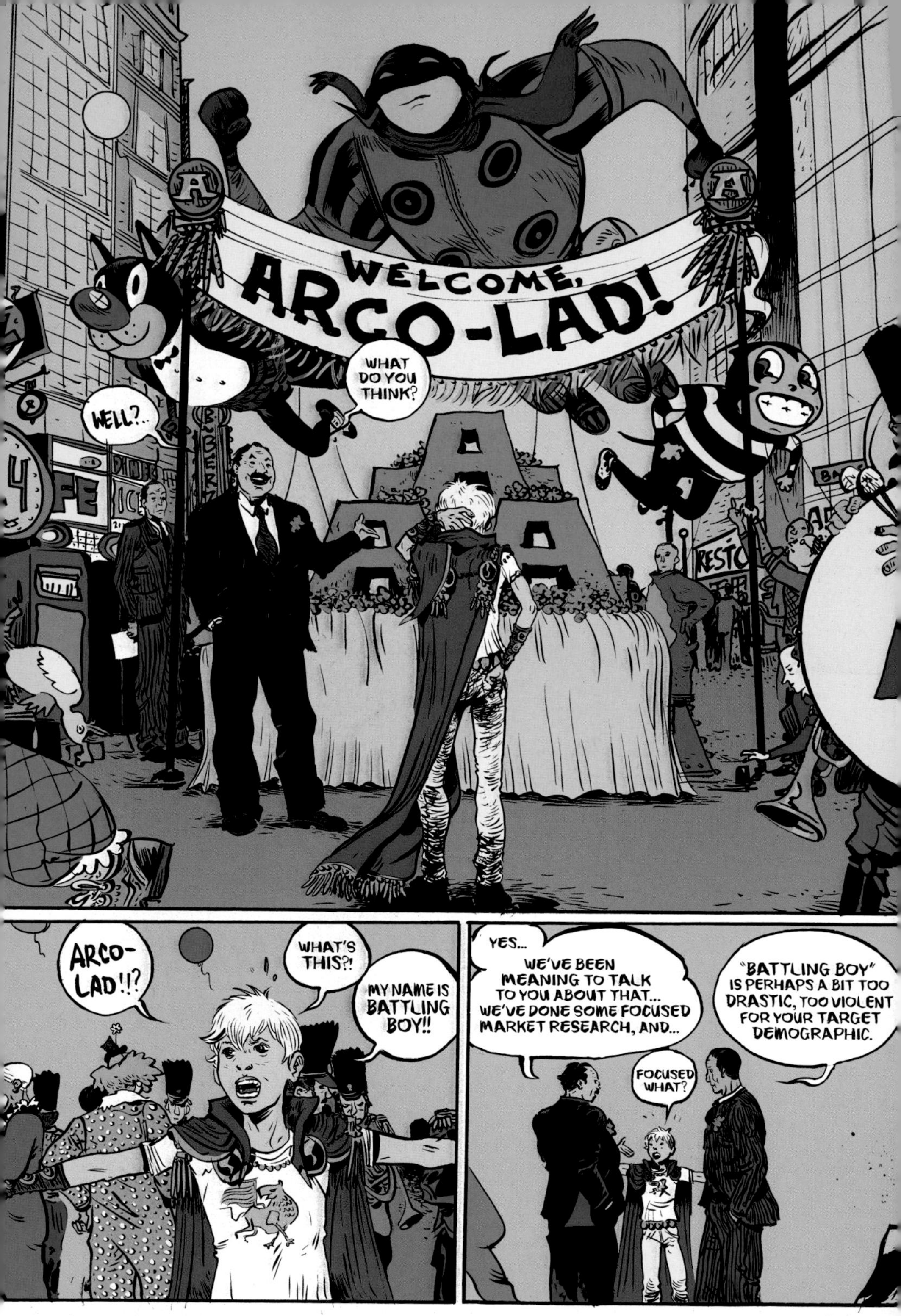
WELCOME, ARCO-LAD!
WELL?..
WHAT DO YOU THINK?
ARCO-LAD!!?
WHAT'S THIS?!
MY NAME IS BATTLING BOY!!
YES...
WE'VE BEEN MEANING TO TALK TO YOU ABOUT THAT... WE'VE DONE SOME FOCUSED MARKET RESEARCH, AND...
FOCUSED WHAT?
"BATTLING BOY" IS PERHAPS A BIT TOO DRASTIC, TOO VIOLENT FOR YOUR TARGET DEMOGRAPHIC.

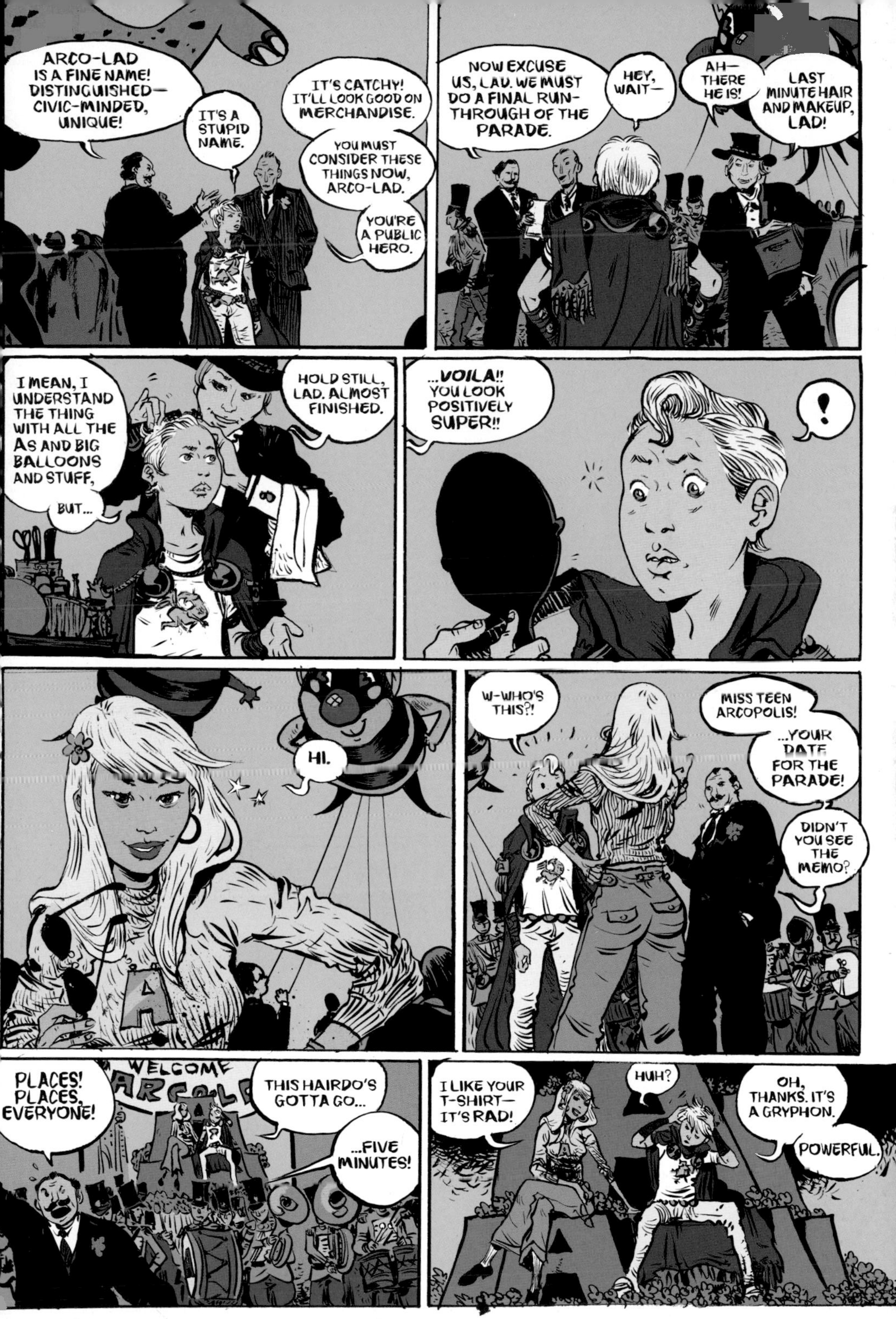
ARCO-LAD IS A FINE NAME! DISTINGUISHED— CIVIC-MINDED, UNIQUE!
IT'S A STUPID NAME.
IT'S CATCHY! IT'LL LOOK GOOD ON MERCHANDISE.
YOU MUST CONSIDER THESE THINGS NOW, ARCO-LAD.
YOU'RE A PUBLIC HERO.
NOW EXCUSE US, LAD. WE MUST DO A FINAL RUN-THROUGH OF THE PARADE.
HEY, WAIT—
AH— THERE HE IS!
LAST MINUTE HAIR AND MAKEUP, LAD!
I MEAN, I UNDERSTAND THE THING WITH ALL THE As AND BIG BALLOONS AND STUFF,
BUT...
HOLD STILL, LAD. ALMOST FINISHED.
...VOILA!! YOU LOOK POSITIVELY SUPER!!
!
HI.
W-WHO'S THIS?!
MISS TEEN ARCOPOLIS!
...YOUR DATE FOR THE PARADE!
DIDN'T YOU SEE THE MEMO?
WELCOME ARCO-L
PLACES! PLACES, EVERYONE!
THIS HAIRDO'S GOTTA GO...
...FIVE MINUTES!
I LIKE YOUR T-SHIRT— IT'S RAD!
HUH?
OH, THANKS. IT'S A GRYPHON.
POWERFUL.

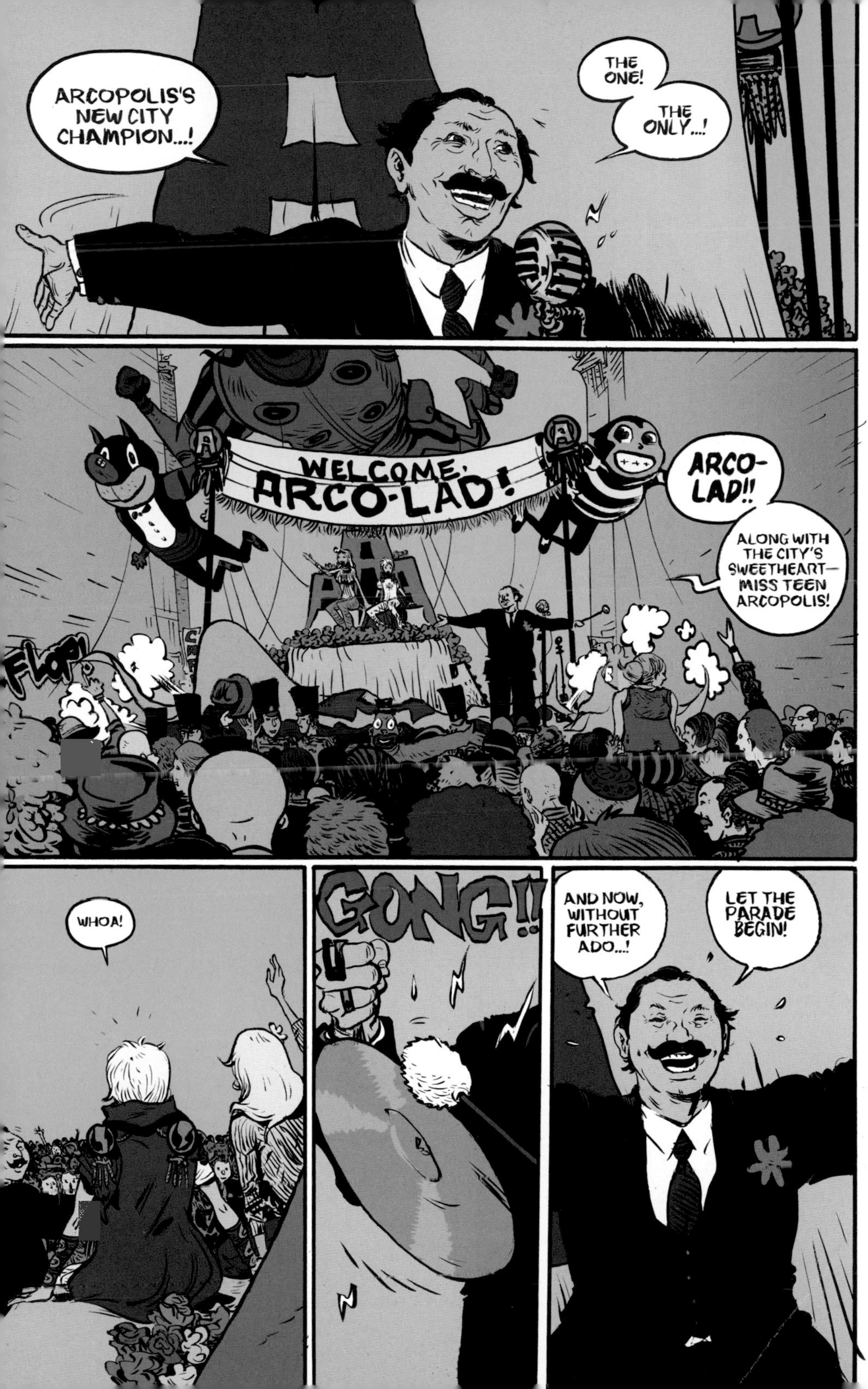
ARCOPOLIS'S NEW CITY CHAMPION...!
THE ONE!
THE ONLY...!
WELCOME, ARCO-LAD!
ARCO-LAD!!
ALONG WITH THE CITY'S SWEETHEART— MISS TEEN ARCOPOLIS!
FLOP!
WHOA!
GONG!!
AND NOW, WITHOUT FURTHER ADO...!
LET THE PARADE BEGIN!

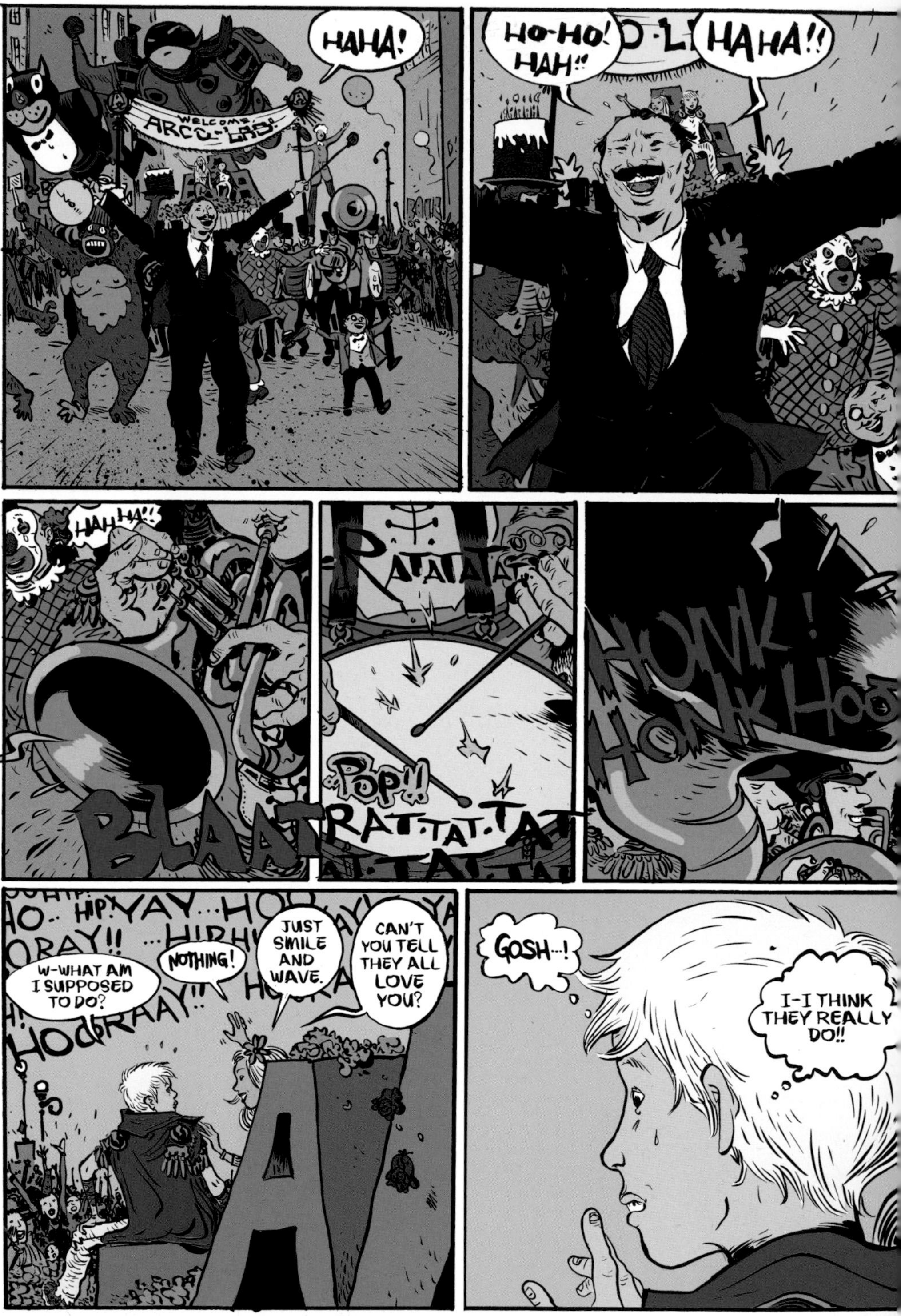

WELCOME ARCO-LAD!
HAHA!
HO-HO! HAH!!
HAHA!!
HAH HA!!
RATATATAT
HONK! HONK HOO
POP!!
BLAAT
RAT-TAT-TAT
HIP! YAY... HOO... HIP! HOORAY!! HOORAAY!!
W-WHAT AM I SUPPOSED TO DO?
NOTHING!
JUST SMILE AND WAVE.
CAN'T YOU TELL THEY ALL LOVE YOU?
GOSH...!
I-I THINK THEY REALLY DO!!

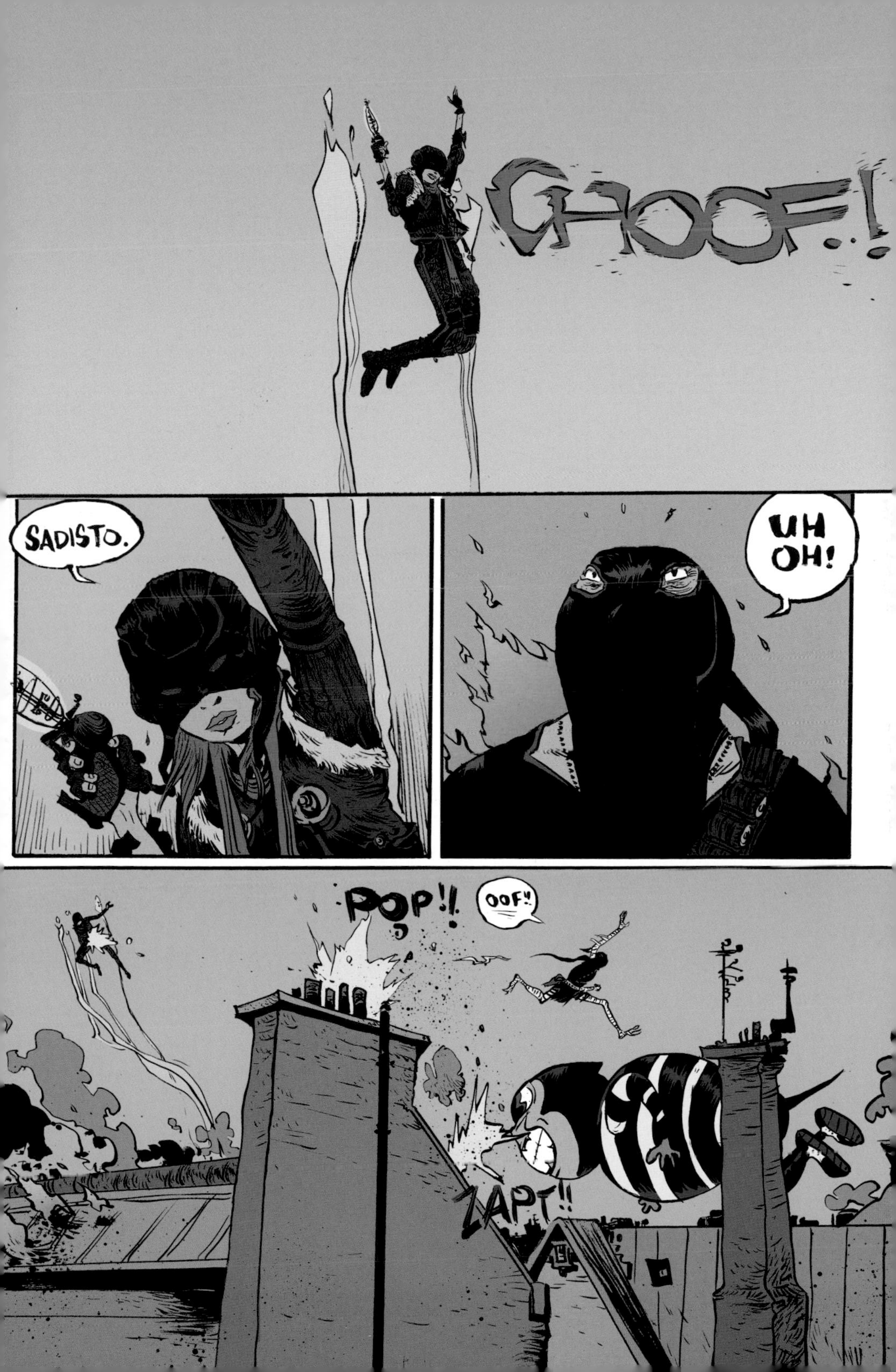
CHOOF!
SADISTO.
UH OH!
POP!!
OOF!
ZAPT!!

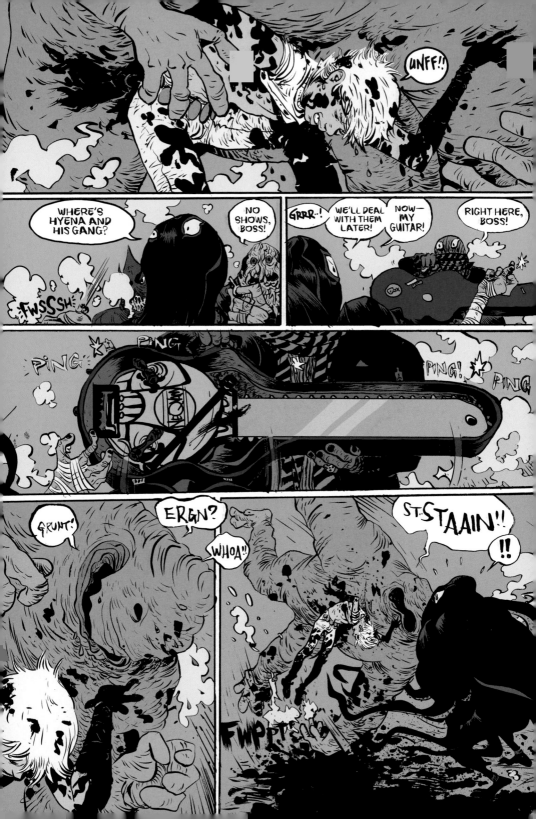

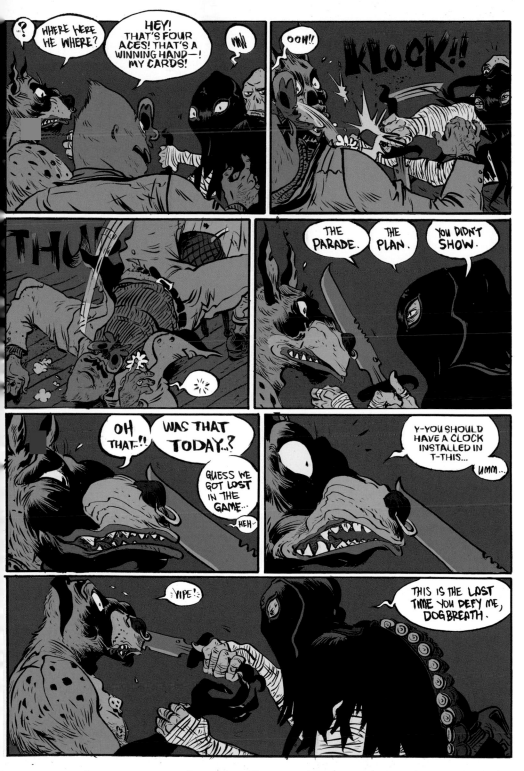

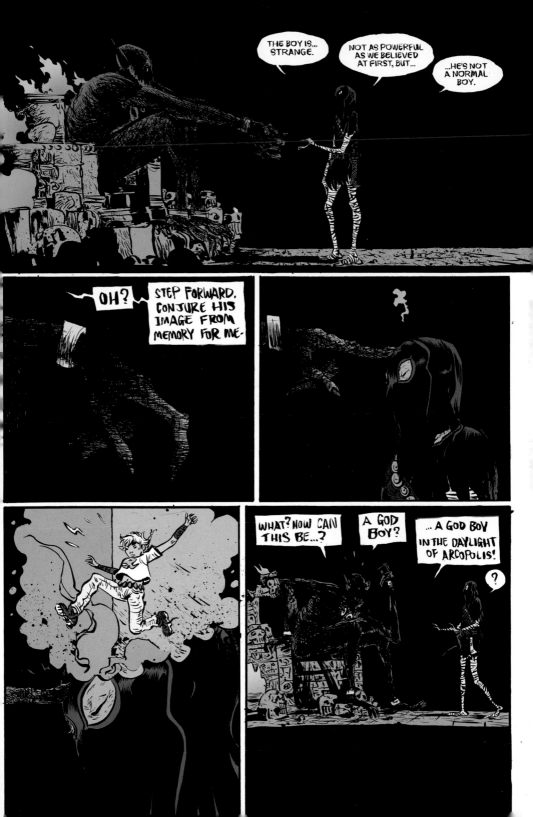

For Benjamin and Alexander

First Second
Copyright © 2013 by Paul Pope

Type set in "PPope," designed by John Martz
Assistance, scanning, and art cleanup by Casey Gonzalez
Colored by Hilary Sycamore and Sky Blue Ink.

Published by First Second
First Second is an imprint of Roaring Brook Press, a division of Holtzbrinck Publishing
Holdings Limited Partnership
175 Fifth Avenue, New York, New York 10010
All rights reserved

Cataloging-in-Publication Data is on file at the Library of Congress.

Paperback ISBN: 978-1-59643-145-4
Hardcover ISBN: 978-1-59643-805-7

First Second books may be purchased for business or personal use. For information on
bulk purchases please contact Macmillan Corporate and Premium Sales Department
at (800) 221-7945 x5442 or by email at specialmarkets@macmillan.com.

FIRST
EDITION

First edition 2013
Book design by Casey Gonzalez, with Colleen AF Venable and John Green
Printed in China by Toppan Leefung Printing Ltd., Kwun Tong, Kowloon, Hong Kong

Paperback: 10 9 8 7 6 5
Hardcover: 10 9 8 7 6 5 4 3